More Praise for *The Broom of the System*
and David Foster Wallace

"Wonderfully odd . . . Mr. Wallace possesses a wealth of talents—a finely tuned ear for contemporary idioms; an old-fashioned storytelling gift; a seemingly endless capacity for invention and an energetic refusal to compromise."
—*The New York Times*

"Gut splitting laughs . . . runs the gamut from sex to TV preachers, from *Gilligan's Island* to Wittgensteinian philosophy. . . . Beneath the poetry, beneath the bubbling humor, something sinister is cooking. Wallace has something to say about society, something heedful."
—*The Philadelphia Inquirer*

"Remarkable . . . hip but true . . . emerging from the tradition of Thomas Pynchon's *V* and John Irving's *The World According to Garp*."
—*The New York Times Book Review*

"Wonderful . . . outlandish . . . *The Broom of the System* stands apart from the pack. Offbeat and inventive, it's filled with some of the most deadly accurate contemporary dialogue ever captured in print. . . . You're in for a good time."
—*The Cleveland Plain Dealer*

"Wallace, like Nabokov, the writer whom he most resembles, has a seemingly inexhaustible bag of literary tricks."
—*Chicago Tribune*

"A prodigiously inventive, hugely funny writer whose best work challenges and reinvents the art of fiction."
—*The Atlanta Journal-Constitution*

"Wallace is the real thing. . . . Beneath the fun and the verbal high jinks, there is a passionate and deeply serious writer at work."
—*San Francisco Chronicle*

"Wallace can make you laugh out loud with his devilish wit."
—*The Kansas City Star*

PENGUIN BOOKS

THE BROOM OF THE SYSTEM

David Foster Wallace is the award-winning author of several short story and essay collections; two novels; including the bestselling *Infinite Jest*; as well as the biography *Everything and More: A Compact History of Infinity*. His most recent story collection is *Oblivion*. His essays and stories have appeared in *Harper's Magazine*, *The New Yorker*, *Playboy*, and *The Paris Review*. He lives in southern California.

THE BROOM

OF THE SYSTEM

DAVID FOSTER WALLACE

PENGUIN BOOKS

PENGUIN BOOKS

Published by the Penguin Group

Penguin Group (USA) Inc., 375 Hudson Street, New York, New York 10014, U.S.A.

Penguin Group (Canada), 90 Eglinton Avenue East, Suite 700, Toronto, Ontario,
    Canada M4P 2Y3 (a division of Pearson Penguin Canada Inc.)

Penguin Books Ltd, 80 Strand, London WC2R 0RL, England

Penguin Ireland, 25 St Stephen's Green, Dublin 2, Ireland (a division of Penguin Books Ltd)

Penguin Group (Australia), 250 Camberwell Road, Camberwell, Victoria 3124,
    Australia (a division of Pearson Australia Group Pty Ltd)

Penguin Books India Pvt Ltd, 11 Community Centre, Panchsheel Park,
    New Delhi – 110 017, India

Penguin Group (NZ), 67 Apollo Drive, Rosedale, North Shore 0632, New Zealand
    (a division of Pearson New Zealand Ltd)

Penguin Books (South Africa) (Pty) Ltd, 24 Sturdee Avenue, Rosebank,
    Johannesburg 2196, South Africa

Penguin Books Ltd, Registered Offices: 80 Strand, London WC2R 0RL, England

First published in the United States of America by Viking Penguin Inc. 1987
Published in Penguin Books 2004

10 9 8

THE LIBRARY OF CONGRESS HAS CATALOGED
THE HARDCOVER EDITION AS FOLLOWS:
Wallace, David Foster.
    The broom of the system.
    I. Title.
PS3573.A425635B7   1987   813'.54   86-40230
ISBN 0-670-81230-7 (hc.)
ISBN 978-0-14-200242-1 (pbk.)

Printed in the United States of America
Set in Goudy Old Style

This project is dedicated to:

Mark Andrew Costello
and *Susan Jane Perkins*
and *Amy Elizabeth Wallace*

ACKNOWLEDGMENTS

The author thanks the following for their help:

Robert Boswell
Gerald Howard
William Kennick
Bonnie Nadell
Andrew Parker
Dale Peterson
The Trustees of Amherst College

PART ONE

1 ▶ 1981

Most really pretty girls have pretty ugly feet, and so does Mindy Metalman, Lenore notices, all of a sudden. They're long and thin and splay-toed, with buttons of yellow callus on the little toes and a thick stair-step of it on the back of the heel, and a few long black hairs are curling out of the skin at the tops of the feet, and the red nail polish is cracking and peeling in curls and candy-striped with decay. Lenore only notices because Mindy's bent over in the chair by the fridge picking at some of the polish on her toes; her bathrobe's opening a little, so there's some cleavage visible and everything, a lot more than Lenore's got, and the thick white towel wrapped around Mindy's wet washed shampooed head is coming undone and a wisp of dark shiny hair has slithered out of a crack in the folds and curled down all demurely past the side of Mindy's face and under her chin. It smells like Flex shampoo in the room, and also pot, since Clarice and Sue Shaw are smoking a big thick j-bird Lenore got from Ed Creamer back at Shaker School and brought up with some other stuff for Clarice, here at school.

What's going on is that Lenore Beadsman, who's fifteen, has just come all the way from home in Shaker Heights, Ohio, right near Cleveland, to visit her big sister, Clarice Beadsman, who's a freshman at this women's college, called Mount Holyoke; and Lenore's staying with her sleeping bag in this room on the second floor of Rumpus Hall that Clarice shares with her roommates, Mindy Metalman and Sue Shaw. Lenore's also come to sort of check out this college, a little bit. This is because even though she's just fifteen she's supposedly quite intelligent and thus accelerated and already a junior at Shaker School and thus thinking about college, application-wise, for next year. So she's visiting. Right now it's a Friday night in March.

Sue Shaw, who's not nearly as pretty as Mindy or Clarice, is bringing the joint over here to Mindy and Lenore, and Mindy takes it and lets her toe alone for a second and sucks the bird really hard, so it glows bright and a seed snaps loudly and bits of paper ash go flying and floating, which Clarice and Sue find super funny and start laughing at really hard, whooping and clutching at each other, and Mindy breathes it in really deep and holds it in and passes the bird to Lenore, but Lenore says no thank you.

"No thank you," says Lenore.

"Go ahead, you brought it, why not . . . ," croaks Mindy Metalman, talking the way people talk without breathing, holding on to the smoke.

"I know, but it's track season at school and I'm on the team and I don't smoke during the season, I can't, it kills me," Lenore says.

So Mindy shrugs and finally lets out a big breath of pale used-up smoke and coughs a deep little cough and gets up with the bird and takes it over across the room to Clarice and Sue Shaw, who are by a big wooden stereo speaker listening to this song, again, by Cat Stevens, for like the tenth time tonight. Mindy's robe's more or less open, now, and Lenore can see some pretty amazing stuff, but Mindy just walks across the room. Lenore can at this point divide all the girls she's known neatly into girls who think deep down they're pretty and girls who deep down think they're really not. Girls who think they're pretty don't care much about their bathrobes being undone and are good at makeup and like to walk when people are watching, and they act different when there are boys around; and girls like Lenore, who don't think they're too pretty, tend not to wear makeup, and run track, and wear black Converse sneakers, and keep their bathrobes pretty well fastened at all times. Mindy sure is pretty, though, except for her feet.

The Cat Stevens song is over again, and the needle goes up by itself, and obviously none of these three feel like moving all the way to start it again, so they're just sitting back in their hard wood desk chairs, Mindy in her faded pink terry robe with one shiny smooth leg all bare and sticking out; Clarice in her Desert boots and her dark blue jeans that Lenore calls her shoe-horn jeans, and that white western shirt she'd worn at the state fair the time she'd had her purse stolen, and her blond hair flooding all over the shirt, and her eyes very blue right now; Sue Shaw with her red hair and a green sweater and green tartan skirt and fat white legs with a bright red pimple just over one knee, legs crossed with one foot jiggling one of those boat shoes, with the sick white soles—Lenore dislikes that kind of shoe a lot.

Clarice after a quiet bit lets out a long sigh and says, in whispers, "Cat . . . is . . . *God,*" giggling a little at the end. The other two giggle too.

"God? How can Cat be God? Cat *exists.*" Mindy's eyes are all red.

"That's offensive and completely blaphemous," says Sue Shaw, eyes wide and puffed and indignant.

"*Blaph*emous?" Clarice dies, looks at Lenore. "*Blas*phemous," she says. Her eyes aren't all that bad, really, just unusually cheerful, as if she's got a joke she's not telling.

"Blissphemous," says Mindy.

"Blossphemous."

"Blousephemous."

"Bluesphemous."

"Boisterous."

"Boisteronahalfshell."

"Bucephalus."

"Barney Rubble."

"Baba Yaga."

"Bolshevik."

"*Blaph*emous!"

They're dying, doubled over, and Lenore's laughing that weird sympathetic laugh you laugh when everybody else is laughing so hard they make you laugh too. The noise of the big party downstairs is coming through the floor and vibrating in Lenore's black sneakers and the arms of the chair. Now Mindy slides out of her desk chair all limp and shlomps down on Lenore's sleeping bag on the floor next to Clarice's pretend-Persian ruglet from Mooradian's in Cleveland, and Mindy modestly covers her crotch with a corner of her robe, but Lenore still can't help but see the way her breasts swell up into the worn pink towel cloth of the robe, all full and stuff,

even lying down on her back, there, on the floor. Lenore uncon-
siously looks down a little at her own chest, under her flannel shirt.

"Hunger," Sue Shaw says after a minute. "Massive, immense,
uncontrollable, consuming, uncontrollable, *hunger*."

"This is so," says Mindy.

"We will wait"—Clarice looks at her watch on the underside of
her wrist—"one, that is *one* hour, before eating anything what-
soentirelyever."

"No we can't possibly *possibly* do that."

"But do it we shall. As per room discussions of not one week ago,
when we explicitly agreed that we shall not gorge when utterly
flapped, lest we get fat and repulsive, like Mindy, over there, you
poor midge."

"Fart-blossom," Mindy says absently, she's not fat and she knows
it, Lenore knows it, they all know it.

"A lady at all times, that Metalman," Clarice says. Then, after
a minute, "Speaking of which, you might just maybe either fix your
robe or get dressed or get up off your back in Lenore's stuff, I'm not
really all up for giving you a gynecological exam, which is sort of
what you're making us do, here, O Lesbia of Thebes."

"Stuff and bother," says Mindy, or rather, "Stuth and bozzer";
and she gets up swaying and reaching for solid things, goes over to
the door that goes into her little single bedroom off the bathroom.
She got there first in September and took it, Clarice had said in a
letter, this Playboy-Playmatish JAP from Scarsdale, and she's shed-
ding what's left of her bathrobe, battered into submission, leaving
it all wet in Lenore's lap in the chair by the door, and going through
the door with her long legs, deliberate steps. Shuts the door.

Clarice looks after her when she's gone and shakes her head a
tiny bit and looks over at Lenore and smiles. There are sounds of
laughter downstairs, and cattle-herd sounds of lots of people dancing. Lenore just loves to dance.

Sue Shaw takes a big noisy drink of water out of a big plastic
Jetsons glass on her desk up by the front door. "Speaking of which,
you didn't by any chance happen to see Splittstoesser this morning?"
she says.

"Nuh-uh," says Clarice.

"She was with Proctor."

"So?"

"At seven o'clock? Both in nighties, all sleepy and googly, coming out of her room, together? Holding *hands*?"

"Hmmm."

"Now if anybody ever told me that *Splittstoesser* . . ."

"I thought she was engaged to some guy."

"She *is*."

They both laugh like hell.

"Awww."

"Who's Splittstoesser?" Lenore asks.

"Nancy Splittstoesser, at dinner? The girl in the red V-neck, with the earrings that were really little fists?"

"Oh. But what about her?"

Clarice and Sue look at each other and start to laugh again. Mindy Metalman comes back in, in gym shorts and an inside-out sweatshirt with the arms cut off. Lenore looks at her and smiles at the floor.

"What?" Mindy knows something's up right away.

"Splittstoesser and Proctor," Sue gets out.

"I meant to *ask* you." Mindy's eyes get all wide. "They're in the bathroom this morning? In the same *shower?*"

"Ahh, no!" Sue's going to die, Mindy starts to laugh too, that weird sympathetic laugh, looking around at them.

"They're, uh, together now? I thought Nancy was engaged."

"She . . . *is*," Clarice making Lenore laugh, too.

"Godfrey Jaysus."

It settles down after a while. Sue does the "Twilight Zone" theme in a low voice. "Who . . . will be struck next . . . ?"

"Not entirely sure I even understand what you guys are, uh . . ." Lenore is asking, looking around.

So Clarice tells Lenore all this business about how Pat Proctor's a bull and what bulls are and how quite a few of the girls get pretty friendly and all, here at this women's college.

"You're kidding."

"No."

"That's just incredibly gross." And this sets Mindy and Sue off again. Lenore looks at them. "Well doesn't that kind of thing sort of give you guys the creeps a little bit? I mean I—"

"Well it's just part of life and everything, what people want to do is more or less their own . . ." Clarice is putting the needle on that song again.

There's a silence for about half the song. Mindy's at her toes, again, over at the bunkbeds. "The thing is, I don't know if we should say," says Sue Shaw, looking over at Clarice, "but Nancy Splittstoesser sort of got assaulted right before Thanksgiving, on the path out by the Widget House, and I think she—"

"Assaulted?" Lenore says.

"Well, raped, I guess, really."

"I see." Lenore looks up behind Sue at a poster over Clarice's desk, which is of a really muscular guy, without a shirt on, making all his muscles from the back, his back all shiny and bulging every which way. The poster's old and ripped at the edges from tape; it had been in Clarice's room at home and their father had not been pleased, the light from the high ceiling makes a bright reflection at the back of the man's head and hides it in white.

"I think it kind of messed her up," says Sue.

"How hard to understand," Lenore says softly. "Raped. So she just doesn't like males now, because of that, or—?"

"Well I think it's hard to say, Lenore," Clarice with her eyes closed, playing with a button on her shirt pocket. She's in front of their air vent, with her chair leaning back, and her hair's all over, a yellow breeze around her cheeks. "Probably just safe to say she's pretty confused and messed up temporarily, 'ntcha think?"

"Sure, I guess."

"You a virgin Lenore?" Mindy's on the lower bunk, Sue's bed, with her picked and flakey feet up and toes hooked into the springs on the underside of Clarice's mattress.

"You bitch," Clarice says to Mindy.

"I'm just *asking*," says Mindy. "I doubt Lenore's too hung up about what—"

"Yes I'm a virgin, I mean I've never had, you know, sexual intercourse with anybody," Lenore says, smiling at Clarice that it's OK, really. "Are you a virgin Mindy?"

Mindy laughs. "Oh very much so."

Sue Shaw snorts into her water. "Mindy's saving herself for the right marine battalion." Clarice and Lenore laugh.

"Fuck you in the ear," Mindy Metalman says mildly, she's all relaxed, almost asleep. Her legs are all curved and faintly muscular and the skin's so smooth it almost glows because she'd recently gotten "waxed" at home, she'd told Lenore, whatever that meant.

"This happen a lot?"

"What happen?"

"Rapes and assaults and stuff?"

Clarice and Sue look away, all calm. "Sometimes, probably, who knows, it's hard to say, because it gets covered up or not reported or something a lot of the time, the College isn't exactly nuts about—"

"Well how many times that you know of?"

"Idle know. About maybe, I guess I know of about ten women—"

"Ten?"

". . . ."

"How many women do you even know total, here?"

"Lenore, I don't know," Clarice says. "It's just not . . . it's just common sense, is what it is, really. If you're careful, you know, and stay off the paths at night . . ."

"Security's really good here, really," says Sue Shaw. "They'll give you rides just about anywhere on campus at night if it's far, and there's a shuttle bus that goes from the library and the labs back here to the rear dorms every hour, with an armed guard, and they'll take you right up to the—"

"Armed guard?"

"Some of them are pretty cute, too." Clarice winks at Lenore.

"You never told me about any of this stuff at Christmas, Clarice. Armed guards and stuff. Doesn't it bother you? I mean back at home—"

"I don't think it's too different anywhere else, Lenore," says Clarice. "I don't think it is. You get used to it. It's really just common sense."

"Still, though."

"There is of course the issue of the party," says Mindy Metalman from the bunk, pretty obviously changing the subject. The noise is still loud from underneath their room.

What's going on is that the dorm is giving a really big party, here, tonight, downstairs, with a bitching band called Spiro Agnew and the Armpits and dancing and men and beer with ID's. It's all really cute and clever, and at dinner downstairs Lenore saw them putting up plastic palm trees and strings of flowers, and some of the girls had plastic grass skirts, because tonight's was a theme party, with the theme being Hawaiian: the name of the party on a big lipstick banner on a sheet out in front of Rumpus said it was the "Comonawannaleiya" party, which Lenore thought was really funny and clever, and they were going to give out leis, ha, to all the men who came from other schools and could get in with ID's. They had a whole room full of leis, Lenore had seen after dinner.

"There is that," says Clarice.

"Thus."

"So."

"Not me," says Sue Shaw. "Nawmeboy, never again, I said it and I meant it. *Pas moi.*"

Clarice laughs and reaches over for the Jetsons glass.

"The issue, however," says Mindy from the bed, her sweatshirt slipped all down at the shoulder and about ready to fall off, it looks like, "the issue is the fact that there is . . . food, *food* down in the dining room, spread under the laughing fingers of the plastic palms, that we all helped buy."

"This is true," Clarice sighs, hitting the repeat on the stereo. Her eyes are so blue they look hot, to Lenore.

"And all we've got is just those far too scrumptious mashed potatoes in the fridge," Mindy says, which is true, just a clear Tupperware dish full of salty Play-Doh Rumpus mashed potatoes, which was all they could steal at dinner, seeing as how the kitchen ran out of cookies, then the bread . . .

"But you guys said no way you'd go down," says Lenore. " 'Member you guys kept telling me how gross it was, these parties, mixers, and like a meat market, and how you could get sucked in, 'as it were,' you said, and how you just had to avoid going down at all costs, and how I shouldn't, you know . . ." She looks around, she wants to go down, she loves to dance, she has a killer new dress she got at Tempo in East Corinth for just such a—

"She wants to go, Clarice," Mindy says, throwing her legs over the side of the bunk and sitting up with a bounce, "and she *is* our guest, and there is the Dorito factor, and if we stayed for like six quick minutes . . ."

"So I see." Clarice looks all droopy-lidded at Lenore and sees her eagerness and has to smile. Sue Shaw is at her desk with her back turned, her butt is really pretty fat and wide in the chair, pooching over the sides, Lenore sees.

Clarice sighs. "The thing is Lenore you just don't know. These things are so unbelievably tiresome, unpleasant, we went all first semester and you just really literally get nauseated, physically ill after a while, ninety-nine point nine percent of the men who come are just *lizards*, *reptiles*, and it's clear awfully fast that the whole thing is really just nothing more than a depressing ritual, a rite that we're expected by God knows who to act out, over and over. You can't even have conversations. It's really repulsive." And she drinks water out of the Jetsons glass. Sue Shaw is nodding her head at her desk.

"*I* say what we do," Mindy Metalman hits the floor and claps her hands, "is Lenore goes and puts on that *fabulous* violet dress I saw you hang up, and we three stay and attend to the rest of this joint, for a second, and then we all just scamper down really quick, and Lenore gets a condensed liberal arts education and one or two dances while we steal about seven *tons* of food, then we come right back up, David Letterman's on in less than an hour."

"No," says Sue Shaw.

"Well then you can stay here, nipplehead, we'll get over it, if one semi-bad experience is going to make you hide away like a —"

"Fine, look, let's just do that." Clarice looks less than thrilled. They all look at each other. Lenore gets a nod from Clarice and jumps up and goes to Mindy's little annex bedroom to put on her dress as Clarice starts glaring in earnest at Mindy and Mindy gives little stuff-it signals to Sue Shaw, over in the corner.

Lenore brushes her teeth in a tiny bathroom redolent of Metalman and Shaw, washes her face, dries it with a towel off the floor, puts Visine in, finds some of that bright wet-looking lipstick Mindy owns in an old Tampax box on the toilet, gets the lipstick out, knocks the Tampax box over, a compact falls in the toilet and she has to fish it out, her shirt's wet, the arm's soaked, she takes the shirt off and goes into Mindy's bedroom. She has to get her bra, since the dress fabric is really thin, violet cotton, pretty as hell with her brown hair, which is luckily clean, and a bit of lipstick, she looks eighteen, very nearly, and her bra's in the bottom of her bag on Mindy's bed. Lenore rummages in her bag. Mindy's room is really a sty, clothes all over, an Exercycle, big James Dean poster on the inside of the door, Richard Gere too oh of course, pictures of some nonfamous guy on a sailboat, *Rolling Stone* magazine covers, Journey concert poster, super-high ceiling like the other rooms, here with a bright blanket tacked one side on the ceiling and one on the wall and sagging, a becalmed candy sail. There's a plastic thing on the dresser, and Lenore knows it's a Pill-holder, for the Pill, because Clarice has got one and so does Karen Daughenbaugh, who's more or less Lenore's best friend at Shaker School. There's the bra, Lenore puts it on. The dress. Combs her hair with a long red comb that has black hair in it and smells like Flex.

A scritch. The Cat Stevens goes off all of a sudden, in the main room. There's loud knocking on the front door, Lenore can hear. She comes back in with the others with her white dress pumps in her hand as Sue Shaw opens the door and Mindy tries to disperse smoke with an album cover. There's two guys outside, filling the doorway, grinning, in matching blue blazers and tartan ties and chinos and those shoes. There's nobody with them.

"Hey and howdy, ma'am," says one of them, a big, tall, tan-in-the-spring-type guy with thick blond hair and a sculptured part and a cleft chin and bright green eyes. "Does Melinda Sue Metalman live here, by any chance at all?"

"How did you get up here," says Sue Shaw. "No one gets upstairs here without an escort, see."

The one guy beams. "Please to meet you. Andy 'Wang-Dang' Lang; my colleague, Biff Diggerence." And he not very subtly pushes the door open with one big hand, and Sue goes back a little on her heels, and the two just walk right in, all of a sudden, Wang-Dang and Biff. Biff's shorter than Lang, and broader, a rectangular person. They've both got Comonawannaleiya cups, with beer, in their hands.

They're a bit tight, apparently. Biff especially: his jaw is slack and eyes are dull and his cheeks are all red in hot patches.

Wang-Dang Lang finally says to Sue, while he's looking at Clarice, "Well I'm just afraid your security personnel here are pretty trusting, 'cause when I told them I was Father Mustafa Metalman, Miss Metalman's second cousin and spiritchul advisor, and then gave them some spiritchul advice of their own, they just . . ." He stops and looks around and whistles. "Unbelievably nice room here. Biff you ever see ceilings so *hah* in a dorm?"

Lenore sits back down in her chair by the door to Mindy's room, barefoot, watching. Mindy pulls up her sweatshirt. Clarice and Sue face the two men, their arms crossed.

"I'm Mindy Metalman," says Mindy Metalman. The guys don't even look over at her for a second, they're still looking the room over, then the tall one looks at Mindy, and he starts nudging Biff, staring at her.

"Hi Mindy, I'm Wang-Dang Lang, Biff Diggerence on my right, here," gesturing, looking at Mindy all wide-eyed still. Comes over and shakes her hand, Mindy sort of shakes it back, looking around at the others.

"Do I know you?"

Wang-Dang smiles. "Well now quite regrettably I must say no, but you do, if I'm not entirely mistaken, know Doug Dangler, over at Amherst College? He's my roommate, or rather me and Biff's roommate? And when we said how we were comin' over here to the Comonolay party, the Dangle-man just said 'Wanger,' he said, he said 'Wanger, Melinda Metalman lives in Rumpus Hall, and I'd really be just ever so much more than obliged if you'd pay your respects, to her, for me,' and so I—"

"Doug Dangler?" Mindy's eyes are mad eyes, Lenore sees, sort of. "Listen I do *not* know any Doug Dangler at Amherst, I think you're mixed up, so maybe you just better go back downst—"

"Sure you know Doug, Doug's a kick-ass guy," the aforementioned Biff is heard from, short and broad with watery denim eyes dull and beady with party, and a little blond beardish thing sprouting from his chin, making it look a little like an armpit, Lenore thinks. His voice is low and rather engagingly grunty. Lang's is soft and smooth and nice, although he does seem to fall in and out of some sort of accent, at times. He says:

"Ma'am now I know for a fact you met Doug Dangler because he told me all about it, at length." His bottle-green eyes fall on Lenore. "It was at a party at Femur Hall, right after Christmas break and Winterterm and all? You were standing talking to this guy, and y'all were more than a little taken with each other, when the guy very unfortunately got taken slightly under the weather and vomited a tiny bit in your purse? *That* was Doug Dangler." Lang smiles triumphantly. Biff Diggerence laughs ogg-ogg, his shoulders go up and down together. Lang continues, "And he said how he was real sorry and could he pay to have your purse cleaned? And but you said no and were all . . . mind-bogglingly nice about it, and when you were rescuing items from your purse you on purpose dropped that piece of paper that had your name and box number and phone and all on it, that phone bill? Doug picked that sucker up, and that's how you met him," smiling, nodding.

"*That* was that guy?" Mindy says. "He said I gave him my name on purpose? That's just a lie. That was utterly disgusting. I had to throw that purse away. He, I remember he came up to me" (to Clarice and Sue) "and put his hand on the hem of my sweater, and said how he had this hangnail that had got caught on my sweater, and how he couldn't get away, it was stuck, ha ha, but he did it for like *two hours*, until finally he threw up on me." To Wang-Dang Lang she says, "He was bombed out of his mind. He was so drunk he was actually drooling. I remember drool was coming out of his mouth."

"Well now Melinda surely you know how we can all tend to get that way at certain times." Lang nudges Biff Diggerence, who almost falls on Sue Shaw, who squeals and backs toward the door with her arms crossed.

"Look, I think you better leave," Clarice says from now over by Lenore. "We're all really tired and you're really not supposed to be up here without—"

"But, now, we just got here, really," Wang-Dang Lang smiles. He looks around again. "I couldn't impose on you ladies for a small can of beer, could I, by any chance, if you maht possibly . . . ?" gesturing over at Sue's little fridgelette by the bunks. And then he sits down in Sue's wooden desk chair by the door, by a speaker. Biff still stands by Sue, facing Clarice and Lenore. Sue looks at Clarice, Mindy at Biff, who grins yellowly, Wang-Dang Lang over at Lenore in her chair at the back by Mindy's door, sitting watching. Lenore feels like a clot in her pretty violet dress and bit of lipstick and bare feet, wondering what to do with her shoes, if she should throw a shoe at Lang, it's got a sharp heel, are the police on their way?

"Look, we don't have any beer, and if we did it's just rude for you guys to come in here uninvited and ask us for beer, and I *don't* know Doug Dangler, and I think we'd really just appreciate it if you'd leave."

"I'm sure there's all the beer you could possibly want downstairs," Clarice says.

Biff Diggerence now belches a huge belch, one of almost unbelievable duration, clearly a specialty, then he has another swallow out of his Comonawannaleiya cup. Lenore involuntarily mutters something about how disgusting this burp was; all eyes go to her. Lang smiles broadly:

"Well hi there. What's *your* name?"

"Lenore Beadsman," says Lenore.

"Whey you from, Lenore?"

"Lenore's my sister," Clarice says, moving toward the door and looking at Biff Diggerence. "She's fifteen and she's visiting and she's invited, which I'm afraid you're really not, so if you'll just let me out for a quick second, here . . ."

Biff Diggerence steps over like a dancer, with a flourish, to block the door with his body.

"Hmmm," says Clarice. She looks at Mindy Metalman. Mindy goes over to Lenore, gets her damp robe off the back of the chair, puts it on over her armless sweatshirt. Lang smiles warmly. Biff watches Mindy for a second, then turns around abruptly at the door, starts banging his head on the door, over and over, really hard. Wang-Dang Lang laughs. The banging isn't all that loud compared with the noise of the party and all, though, suddenly, because the music's now a lot louder, they must have opened the dining room doors at eleven.

"Thing about Biff," Wang-Dang Lang shouts over the pounding

to Clarice and Mindy Metalman, "beer does not entirely agree with him because he is, we've found, for some reason physically incapable of . . . um . . . emptying his stomach in crisis. As they say. Just can't do it, 'matter how much he drinks, which is often more than can be explained by known physical laws. It's dangerous, right Digger?" Wang-Dang shouts over to the pounding Biff. "So instead of booting, the big fella here finds himself having recourse to . . ."

". . . Pounding his head against the wall," Clarice finishes for him with a little mouth-smile, she obviously remembers Creamer and Geralamo and company, Lenore can tell. Lang nods at Clarice with an engaging grin. Biff finally stops and turns back around, resting his back against the door, beaming, with a red forehead, a little cross-eyed. The muscles in his big neck are corded. He closes his eyes and leans back and breathes heavily.

"Well if we could just stay and rest up and catch our breaths for just a couple of seconds for the second half of the big luau, down there, we'll be more than obliged to you," says Lang. "And I'll be giving old Doug the bad and from what I can see most unfortchinit news about your not remembering him, Melinda-Sue. He'll be hurt, I'll just tell you right now, in advance. He is a shy and sinsitive person."

"Seems like a common problem over there at Amherst," says Clarice. Lenore smiles at her.

Meanwhile Mindy has gone over to the ashtray to see about the corpse of the joint. Lenore can tell Mindy's decided not to be intimidated, all of a sudden. Mindy's shiny legs through the robe are now right by Wang-Dang Lang's face, he's still sitting in the chair, his nose about even with her waist. Lang looks down at his shoes, with the white soles, he's shy, almost, Mindy makes even him shy, Lenore sees. Mindy resuscitates the joint with a big plastic lighter that says "When God Made Man She Was Only Joking." She pauses, watches it. It glows, she takes it back with her to the edge of Sue Shaw's bed, sits down, faces Lang off the end of the bunk. The room's all quiet, except for party noise, underneath. Mindy concentrates on the j-bird, then pauses again, then looks at Lang and holds the joint out to him.

"Well now aren't you kind," Lang says softly. He takes a bit of a polite puff, smiles at Mindy.

"Who *are* you guys, anyway?" Mindy asks. Clarice and Sue are glaring at her.

Lang stops and smiles broadly, taken aback. Holds out his hand. "I personally am Andrew Sealander 'Wang-Dang' Lang, class of '83, from Nugget Bluff, Texas, residing now at 666 Psi Phi fraternity, Amherst College, Massachusetts, U.S.A."

"A sophomore."

"Affirmative. As is Bernard Werner 'Biff' Diggerence, of Shillington, Pennsylvania." A pause, all pregnant. Lang looks up at Biff, who seems still to be sleeping at the door.

"We've actually, I'll tell you ladies in confidence, been sent out," Wang-Dang leans all conspiratorially toward Mindy and Lenore. "We've actually been sent out for what could be termed our 'nitiation."

"Oh, shit," Clarice says, her arms crossed, leaning against the wall. Biff Diggerence is now showing signs of life; he's to be seen stroking Sue Shaw's hair with a hot-dog finger, and winking down at her, making clicking noises with the corner of his mouth, as Sue whimpers and gets set to cry.

"Initiation?" Mindy says.

"Affirmative. The High Demiurge and Poobah of the Psi Phi fraternal order of brothers himself has sent us out on a . . .," a burp, here, ". . . a sort of quest, you might say. We find ourselves in search of personal decoration."

"Decoration."

"Auto . . . graphs," Biff laughs ogg and gives a little pound on the wall with the back of his head, for emphasis.

"Autographs?"

"We need you girls to sign our asses," says Biff, coming to the point, smiling down at Sue Shaw.

"Sign your asses?" says Mindy Metalman.

"That is unfortunately affirmative," Lang says, flashing a smile full of bright teeth over at Lenore. "We are required . . . ," fishing for a piece of paper in the pocket of his blazer, perusing, ". . . we are requahred to secure the signatures of no fewer than *fahv* of Mount Holyoke's loveliest before sunrise tomorrow. We figger of course we can sign each other, being friends and all, but that's just one each." He looks around significantly at each of the girls, gives

Lenore a bit of a wink. "Means we need, according to my figures, four more."

Lenore notices Sue Shaw sitting there all quiet, looking at her leather shoes with the white soles. Biff's hands are in Sue's bright red hair.

"So wait," says Clarice. "You mean you want us to sign your bottoms?"

"Please."

"*Bare?*"

"Well, clearly yes, that's the whole—"

"Sweet shrieking mother of Christ what nerve." Clarice says in amazement, staring at Lang. "And it just never occurred to you geniuses that we might say no? I'm saying no."

"Your prerogative entirely," says Wang-Dang Lang. " 'Course we very regrettably will find ourselves unable to leave until you do." He now has his hand lightly on Mindy's bare leg, Lenore notices. Lenore shivers a bit. Clarice makes a sudden move for the door, Biff moves in front of the knob, Clarice stops, Biff pounds the door with the back of his head again, a few times, emphasizing the general state of affairs.

Clarice stops, clearly now for a second just so mad she can't really say or do anything at all. "You shiny bastards," she finally gets out. "You Amherst guys, U-Mass too, all of you. Just because you're bigger, physically just take up more space, you think—*do* you think?— think you can rule everything, make women do whatever stupid rotten disgusting stuff you say you want just because you're drunk? Well up yours, sideways." She looks from Lang to Biff. "You come over to our parties, grinning like apes on the bus no doubt, you get smeared in about two minutes, trash us, act like we're meat, or furniture, think you can just . . . ," looking around, "*invade* us, our *room*, for no other reason than that you're just stronger, that you can block the door and pound your big greasy stupid heads on it? Screw you. Screw you."

Lang laughs. "Regrettably an invitation extended in anger, I'm afraid." He laughs again. Mindy smiles a bit, too. Lang's hand is still on her leg.

But Biff is miffed, here, suddenly. "Well screw you right back

Miss Rodeo Shirt," he says to Clarice, obviously now in one of those alcoholically articulate periods. "Just come off it. This place is just the biggest . . . ," looking around, "the biggest giant joke!" He looks to Lang for support; Lang is whispering something to Mindy Metalman.

But Biff is pissed. "You have these parties that you advertise out our ears, all this cute teasing bullshit, 'Come to the Comonawannaleiya party, get lei'd at the door,' ha. 'Win a trip to the hot tubs for two,' blah-blah-blah. You're just teases of the cockular sort, is what you are. So we come, like you ask and advertise for, and we put on ties, and we come over, and then we find you got security guards at the doors, with freaking *guns*, and we gotta have our hands stamped like fifth-graders for beer, and all the girls look at us like we're rapists, and plus, besides, all the girls down there look like Richard Nixon, while all the real babes lock themselves up up here—"

"Like you lovely ladies, you must admit," Wang-Dang Lang says with a smile.

Biff Diggerence whirls and whomps the door with his forehead a few times, really hard. He stays facing the door, his sails apparently windless, for a moment.

"I'm afraid he's quite inebriated," says Lang.

Lenore stands up, in her dress. "Please let me out."

Lang and Mindy stand. Sue stands. Everyone's standing with Lenore. Lang smiles and nods his head. "So if you'd just be kind enough to put your . . . Jocelyn Hancock on . . . my . . . ," struggling with the belt of his chinos. Mindy looks away. Biff, still breathing at the door, does his belt too. He even brought a pen; Lenore can see it sticking out of his pocket.

"No, I'm not going to touch you, much less sign you," says Lenore.

Wang-Dang Lang looks at her, vaguely puzzled. "Well then we're real unfortunately not going to be able to leave."

"That's fortunately of very little concern to me because I'm not going to be here because I'm leaving," Lenore says.

"I'll sign," Sue Shaw says quietly.

Clarice stares at Sue. "What?"

"I want them out. I'll sign." She doesn't look up. She looks at her shoes. Biff's pants drop with a heavy sound, he's still facing the door. His bottom is big, broad, white, largely hairless. A vulnerable bottom, really. Lenore evaluates it calmly.

"Whuboutchoo, Melinda-Sue?" Lang asks Mindy. Lang's in his underpants.

Mindy really looks at Lang, looks him in the eye. There's no expression on her. After a moment she says, "Sure, why not."

"*You* can sign the front if you want," laughs Wang-Dang.

"This is disgusting. I'm leaving, let me leave, please," says Lenore. She turns. "You're a coward," she says to Sue Shaw. "You have ugly feet," she says to Mindy Metalman. "Look at her feet, Andy, before you do anything rash." She turns to the door. "Get out of the way, Boof, or whatever your name is."

Biff turns, the first time Lenore's ever seen a man naked. "No."

Lenore throws one of her spiky white high-heeled dress shoes, the kind with the metal straps, at Biff Diggerence's head. It misses his head and hits the door above him and makes a loud sound and the heel sticks in the wood of the door. The white shoe hangs there. As if the noise of the shoe's hitting the door were just the last straw, Sue Shaw gives a yelp and begins to cry a little, although she's still a bit dry from being recently stoned. She has Biff's pen in her hand.

"Let me leave or I'll put out your eye with my shoe," Lenore says to Biff, hefting her other shoe. Wang-Dang Lang is holding Mindy Metalman's hand.

"Let her out, she doesn't even go here," says Clarice. "I'll sign too, you drips."

"Let me out," says Lenore.

Biff finally gets away from the door, still holding his empty Comonawannaleiya cup. He has to go over anyway, obviously, to present his bottom to Sue Shaw, there in the corner. He takes little comic steps because his pants are down around his ankles, and Lenore sees his genitals bob and waggle as he takes his tiny shuffles over to Sue. Lenore runs past in bare feet, gets her shoe out of the door. Pulls it out, the heel, looks back. Lang is kissing Mindy's creamy cheek, with a faraway, laughing expression, in his underwear. Sue is kneeling, signing Biff. Clarice has her arms crossed. Tapping her fingers on her arms.

Lenore runs out into the tiled hall, away. Outside there will be air, Lenore wants out of Rumpus Hall very much, and gets out, finally she does, but only after negotiating a hall door, a stair door, a hall door, and a front door, all locked tight from the inside. Out in the crusty March lawn, by the wash of the well-lit street, amid crowds of boys in blue blazers going up the walk, putting Certs in their mouths, she enjoys a brief nosebleed.

2 **1990**

"Is this cuddling? Is what we're doing cuddling?"

"I think this satisfies standard cuddling criteria, yes."

"I thought so."

". . . ."

"You have a really bony pelvis, you know. See how it protrudes?"

"I do have a bony pelvis. My wife used to comment on my pelvis, sometimes."

"I have a pretty bony pelvis, too, don't you think? Feel."

"It is bony. I think women are supposed to have bony pelvises."

"I think it's also in my case like a family thing. Both my brothers have bony pelvises. My younger brother has a really mammoth pelvis."

". . . ."

"Mmmm."

". . . ."

"A story, please."

"You want a story."

"Please."

"Did get a rather interesting one today."

"Go for it."

"Depressing, though."

"I want to hear it."

"Concerned a man who suffered from second-order vanity."

"Second-order vanity?"

"Yes."

"What's that?"

"You don't know what second-order vanity is?"

"No."

"How interesting."

"So what is it?"

"Well, a second-order vain person is first of all a vain person. He's vain about his intelligence, and wants people to think he's smart. Or his appearance, and wants people to think he's attractive. Or, say, his sense of humor, and wants people to think he's amusing and witty. Or his talent, and wants people to think he's talented. Et cetera. You know what a vain person is."

"Right."

"A vain person is concerned that people not perceive him as stupid, or dull, or ugly, et cetera et cetera."

"Gotcha."

"Now a second-order vain person is a vain person who's also vain about appearing to have an utter lack of vanity. Who's enormously afraid that other people will perceive him as vain. A second-order vain person will sit up late learning jokes in order to appear funny and charming, but will deny that he sits up late learning jokes. Or he'll perhaps even try to give the impression that he doesn't regard himself as funny at all."

". . . ."

"A second-order vain person will be washing his hands in a public restroom, and will be unable to resist the temptation to admire himself in the mirror, to scrutinize himself, but he'll pretend he's fixing a contact lens or getting something out of his eye while he does so, so that people won't perceive him as the sort of person who admires himself in mirrors, but rather as the sort of person who uses mirrors only to attend to reasonable, un-vain business."

"Oh."

"This story that came today concerned a man who was second-order vain about his appearance. Vain as hell about his appearance, obsessed with his body, but also obsessed with the desire that no one know of his obsession. He goes to simply enormous lengths to hide his vanity from his girlfriend. Did I mention he lives with a girl, an apparently ravingly beautiful and also very nice girl?"

"No."

"Well he does, who loves him like mad, and he loves her. And they're getting along fine, although the man is of course under quite a bit of strain, obsessed and also obsessed with hiding his obsession."

"Gee."

"Indeed. And one day in the bathtub the man notices something strange on his leg, a kind of a raised gray spot, and he goes to a doctor and is diagnosed as being in the first stages of a certain nonfatal but quite disfiguring disease, that will eventually leave this apparently very handsome man not a little disfigured."

". . . ."

"Unless, that is, he consents to undergo a tremendously complicated and expensive treatment procedure, for which he has to fly all the way to Switzerland, and spend just about his whole life savings, which savings are in a joint bank account and require his lovely girlfriend's cosignature to withdraw."

"Wow."

". . . ."

"Still, though, if he's all that vain and anxious not to be disfigured."

"Well, but you forget he's also extremely anxious not to be perceived as the sort of man who's anxious not to be disfigured. The thought of his girlfriend knowing that he is the sort of man who would spend his life savings and fly all the way to Switzerland just to keep from being disfigured horrifies him."

"What is this disease? Is this supposed to be leprosy?"

"Something like leprosy, was my impression. Maybe not as bad. I think leprosy can kill you. Anyway, that's not the point. The point is that the idea of his girlfriend finding out he is vain so horrifies the man that he delays and delays making the decision to fly to Switzerland for the treatment, and in the meantime the spot is growing and the skin on his leg is getting grayer, and flaking off in sheets, and the bones are swelling and getting gnarled, which condition he tries to hide by buying a novelty cast and putting it on his leg and telling his girlfriend his leg's mysteriously broken, but the condition is meanwhile spreading to his other leg, and up his stomach and back, and also by implication I think we're to assume his genitals; and so he takes to his bed and keeps himself covered with blankets and tells his girlfriend he's mysteriously sick, and he also by the way starts making an effort to be really cold and aloof to the girlfriend, to keep her at a distance, even though he really loves her to distraction. And he only gets out of bed when she's off at work, she sells women's clothes, and only when she's gone will he get out of bed and stand in front of the full-length mirror in their bathroom, for hours, gazing at himself in horror, and gently sponging the gray flakes off his increasingly twisted body."

"Lordy."

"Yes and days go by and the disease continues to progress, spreading to the man's upper body and arms and hands, which he tries to hide by claiming he's mysteriously horribly cold, and wearing heavy sweaters and ski mittens, and he's also being increasingly cruel and nasty and bitter toward his lovely roommate, and won't let her come near him, and gives her to understand that she's done something terrible, and made him angry, but won't tell her what it is, and the girlfriend begins to sit up at night in the bathroom crying, and the man can hear her, and his heart is breaking because he loves her so, but he's got this obsession about not being ugly, and of course now if he tells her the truth and shows her everything, not only will she see that he's all of a sudden ugly, but it will also become clear to her that he has the original obsession about not being ugly, see for instance the cast, sweaters and mittens, and of course he's doubly obsessed about not revealing that original obsession. So he gets meaner and meaner to this sweet beautiful girl who loves him, and eventually, even though she's a wonderful girl and deeply in love with him, she's also only human and eventually becomes pissed off, little by little, simply in self-defense, and starts being cold and distant back, and relations between the two get strained, which is breaking the man's heart, deep down. And meanwhile of course the disease is still spreading, it's on his neck, and almost to the height of his highest turtleneck sweater, and also one or two gray flaky gnarls are appearing on the man's nose, previews of coming attractions, the man sees. And so one morning, on about the last day the man figures he can keep it all hidden from the girlfriend, and also the morning after a really major and disastrous fight that clearly almost broke the girl's heart, the girl is sitting in the bathroom, crying, and the man quietly gets out of bed and bundles up and goes and takes a cab to see his doctor."

" . . . . "

"Well, and the doctor's quite upset, understandably, at the man's not having called him in so long, what was he to think? And the doctor's also of course more than a little concerned about the spread of the disease, and he looks the man over and clucks his tongue and says that this is just about the latest the expensive Switzerland-treatment can start and still be effective, and that if they delay any longer the disease will swallow the man completely and become irreversible and he'll be alive but gray and flaky and gnarled all over for all time. The doctor looks at the man and says he's going to go out of the office and let him think it over. The doctor clearly thinks the guy's out of his mind for not being in Switzerland already. And so the man sits in the office, alone, all bundled up, with his mittens on, and has a real crisis, and his heart is breaking, and he's incredibly horrified, because of the obsession-obsession, but finally he has a breakthrough, which is not too subtly symbolized by a ray of sunlight breaking through the heavy clouds that are in the sky that day and coming through the window of the doctor's office and hitting the man, but and anyway he sees in this breakthrough that the most important thing is really his wonderful, lovely girlfriend and their love, and that that's what really matters, and so he decides to call her and tell her everything and get her to come down and co-sign the withdrawal slip for his life savings so he can hop a flight to Switzerland that very day, and to hell with the horror of telling her, even though it will be unbelievably horrifying."

"Wow."

"And the way the story ends is with the man sitting at the doctor's desk, with the phone in his mitten, listening to the phone ring in the apartment, and it's ringing quite a few times, though not yet a ridiculous number of times, but enough so it's just becoming by implication unclear whether the girlfriend is even still there or not, whether she's taken off, maybe for good. And that's how it ends, with the man there and the phone ringing in his mitten and the patch of sun on him through the doctor's window."

"Good Lord. Are you going to use it?"

"No. Too long. It's a long story, over forty pages. Also poorly typed."

" . . . . "

"Stop that."

" . . . . "

"Lenore, stop it. Not even remotely funny."

". . . ."

". . . ."

"Except how did you know so much about it?"

"Know about what?"

"Second-order vanity. You were like really surprised I didn't know about second-order vanity."

"What shall I say? Shall I simply say I'm a man of the world?"

". . . ."

". . . ."

"Ginger ale?"

"Not right now, thank you though."

3 **1990**

/a/

A nurse's aide threw the contents of a patient's water glass out a window, the mass of water hitting the ground dislodging a pebble, which rolled across the angled pavement and fell with a click on a stone culvert in the ditch below, startling a squirrel having at some sort of nut right there on the concrete pipe, causing the squirrel to run up the nearest tree, in doing which it disturbed a slender brittle branch and surprised a few nervous morning birds, one of which, preparatory to flight, released a black-and-white glob of droppings, which glob fell neatly on the windshield of the tiny car of one Lenore Beadsman, just as she pulled into a parking space. Lenore got out of the car while the birds flew away, making sounds.

Flowerbeds of pretend marble, the plastic sagging and pouty-lipped in places from the heat of the last month, flanked the smooth concrete ramp that ran up from the edge of the parking lot to the Home's front doors, the late-summer flowers dry and grizzled in the deep beds of dry dirt and soft plastic, a few brown vines running weakly up the supports of the handrails that went along the ramp above the flowerbeds, the paint of the handrails bright yellow and looking soft and sticky even this early in the day. Dew glittered low in the crunchy August grass; light from the sun moved in the lawn as Lenore went up the ramp. Outside the doors an old black woman stood motionless with her walker, her mouth open to the sun. Above the doors, along a narrow tympanum of sun-punched plastic again pretending to be igneous marble, ran the letters SHAKER HEIGHTS NURSING HOME. On either side of the doors, impressed into stone walls that reached curving away out of sight to become the building's face, were entombed the likenesses of Tafts. Inside the doors, in the glass tank between outer and inner entries, languished three people in wheelchairs, blanket-lapped even in the greenhouse heat of the mid-morning glass, one with a neck drooping so badly to the side that her ear rested on her shoulder.

"Hi," Lenore Beadsman said as she hurried through an inner glass door frosted in the sunlight with old fingerprints. Lenore knew the prints were from the wheelchair patients, for whom the metal bar with the PUSH sign on it was too high and too hard. Lenore had been here before.

The Shaker Heights Home had just one story to it. This level was broken into many sections and covered a lot of territory. Lenore came out of the hot tank and down the somewhat cooler hall toward this particular section's receiving desk, with the tropical overhead fan rotating slowly over it. Inside the doughnut reception desk was a nurse Lenore hadn't seen before, a dark-blue sweater caped over her shoulders and held with a metal clasp on which was embossed a profile of Lawrence Welk. People in wheelchairs were everywhere, lining all the walls. The noise was loud and incomprehensible, rising and falling, notched by nodes of laughter at nothing and cries of rage over who knew what.

The nurse looked up as Lenore got close.

"Hi, I'm Lenore Beadsman," Lenore said, a little out of breath.

The nurse stared at her for a second. "Well that's not terribly amusing, is it," she said.

"Pardon me?" Lenore asked. The nurse gave her the fish-eye. "Oh," Lenore said, "I think the thing is we've never met. Madge is usually here, where you are. I'm Lenore Beadsman, but I guess I'm here to see Lenore Beadsman, too. She's my great-grandmother, and I—"

"Well, you just," the nurse looked at something on the big desk, "you just let me ring Mr. Bloemker, hold on."

"Is Gramma all right?" Lenore asked. "See I was just in—"

"Well I'll just let you speak to Mr. Bloemker, hello Mr. Bloemker? A Lenore Beadsman here to see you in B? He'll be right out to see you. Please hang on."

"I guess I'd rather just go ahead and see Lenore. Is she OK?"

The nurse looked at her. "Your hair is wet."

"I know."

"And uncombed."

"Yes, thank you, I know. See I was just in the shower when my landlady called up the stairs that I had a phone call from Mr. Bloemker."

"How did your landlady know?"

"Pardon?"

"That you had a phone call from Mr. Bloemker."

"Well it's a neighbor's phone, that I use, but she didn't—"

"You don't have a phone?"

"What *is* this? No I don't have a phone. Listen, I'm very sorry to keep asking, but is my Gramma all right or not? I mean Mr. Bloemker said to come right over. Should I call my family? Where's Lenore?"

The nurse was staring at a point over Lenore's left shoulder; her face had resolved into some kind of hard material. "I'm afraid I'm in no position to say anything about . . . ," looking down, ". . . Lenore Beadsman, area F. But now, if you'll just be so kind as to wait a moment, we can—"

"Where's the morning nurse who's supposed to be here? Where's Madge? Where's Mr. Bloemker?"

Mr. Bloemker appeared in the dim recesses of a corridor, beyond the reach of light from the reception area.

"Ms. Beadsman!"

"Mr. Bloemker!"

"Shush," said the nurse; Lenore's shout had produced a groundswell of sighs and moans and objectless shouts from the wheelchaired forms lining the perimeter of the circular reception station. A television went on in a lounge off the hall, and Lenore caught a glimpse of a brightly colored game show as she hurried down toward Mr. Bloemker.

"Mr. Bloemker."

"Hello Ms. Beadsman, thank you so much for coming so quickly and so early. Were you to be at work soon?"

"Is my great-grandmother all right? Why did you call?"

"Why don't we just nip over to my office."

"Well but I don't understand why I can't just . . ." Lenore stopped. "Oh my Lord. She didn't . . . ?"

"Oh dear me no, please come with me. I—careful, watch the . . . good morning, Mrs. Feltner." A woman careened past in a wheelchair.

"Who's that nurse at the desk?"

"Just through this door, here."

"This isn't the way to Gramma's room."

"This way."

/b/

Well, now, just imagine how you'd feel if your great-grandmother—great it could really probably be argued in more than one sense of the word, which is to say the supplier of your name, the person under whose aegis you'd first experienced chocolate, books, swing sets, antinomies, pencil games, contract bridge, the Desert, the person in whose presence you'd first bled into your underwear (at sixteen, now, late sixteen, grotesquely late as we seem to remember, in the east wing, during the closing theme of "My Three Sons," when the animated loafers were tapping, with you and Lenore watching, the slipping, sick relief, laughter and scolding at once, Gramma used her left arm and there was her old hand in Lenore's new oldness), the person through whose personal generosity and persuasiveness vis à vis certain fathers you'd been overseas, twice, albeit briefly, but still, your great-grandmother, who lived right near you—were just all of a sudden missing, altogether, and was for all you knew lying flat as a wet Saltine on some highway with a tire track in her forehead and her walker now a sort of large trivet, and you'll have an idea of how Lenore Beadsman felt when she was informed that *her* great-grandmother, with whom all the above clauses did take place, was missing from the Shaker Heights Nursing Home, in Shaker Heights, right near Cleveland, Ohio, near which Lenore lived, in East Corinth.

/c/

Combination Embryonic Journal and Draft Space for Fieldbinder
Collection
Richard Vigorous
62 Bombardini Building
Erieview Plaza
Cleveland, Ohio
Reasonable reward for proper and discreet return.

25 August

Lenore, come to work, where I am, remove yourself from the
shower immediately and come to work now, I'll not come down for
my paper until you are here, Mandible is getting suspicious when I
call.

/d/

The outside of a door, which like all the doors here looked like
solid wood but was really hollow and light and rattled in its latch
when the office window was open and the wind blew, said DAVID
BLOEMKER, ADMINISTRATOR OF FACILITY. The office, like the rest of
the Home, smelled faintly of urine.

"I'm sorry, but I don't think I understand what you're saying,"
Lenore said.

Mr. Bloemker had sad wet brown eyes and blinked behind round
glasses as he pulled and scratched at his beard, in the heat. "What
I am saying, Ms. Beadsman, is that with all possible apologies and
every assurance that we are doing everything within our power to
resolve the situation, I must report to you that area F's Lenore
Beadsman is at this point in time missing."

"I don't think I understand what 'missing' means."

"I am afraid that it means that we are unable to determine her
present whereabouts."

"You don't know where she is."

"That is unfortunately right."

"What," said Lenore, "you mean you don't know where she is in the Home?"

"Oh my no, if she were on the grounds, there would be no situation of any significance. No, we have—those of us on hand at the moment have covered the entire facility."

"So, what, she's somewhere off the grounds?"

"That would seem to be so, to our extreme distress." Mr. Bloemker's fingers, with their long nails, sank into his beard.

"Well how may I ask did that happen?" said Lenore.

"This is not entirely clear to anyone," looking off, out the window, at the sun through the trees on a car right by the window. It was Lenore's car, with the spot on the windshield.

"Well was she here last night?"

"We are at this time unable to determine that."

"There must have been a nurse who looked in on her last night—what does she say?"

Mr. Bloemker looked at her sadly. "I'm afraid we are at present unable to contact the relevant nurse."

"And why is that."

"I am afraid we don't know where she is."

"Either?"

A sad smile. "Either."

"Gee."

Mr. Bloemker's telephone buzzed. Lenore eyed it as he went to answer it. Not a Centrex, no crossbar. Something primitive, single-line unretrievable transfers, no hunters. "Yes," Mr. Bloemker was saying. "Yes. Please."

He hung up gently and went back to blinking moistly at Lenore. Lenore had a thought. "All right, but what about Mrs. Yingst, in the next room?" she said. "She and Lenore are like this. Mrs. Yingst is sure to know when she was last around. Have you talked to Mrs. Yingst?"

Mr. Bloemker looked at this thumb.

"Mrs. Yingst is . . . around, isn't she?"

"Not at this time, unfortunately, no."

"Meaning she's missing too."

"I am afraid I must say yes." Mr. Bloemker's eyes shone with regret. Lenore thought she saw a bit of egg in his beard.

"Well, listen, what exactly's going on here, then? Is everybody gone and you have no idea where they are? I think I just don't understand the situation, yet, completely."

"Oh Ms. Beadsman, nor in truth do I, to my profound grief," a movement in one side of his face. "What I have been able to determine is that at some point in the last, shall we say, sixteen hours some number of residents and staff here at the facility have become . . . unavailable to access."

"Meaning missing."

"Yes."

"Well how many is 'some number'?"

"At this time it looks to be twenty-four."

"Twenty-four."

"Yes."

"How many of them are patients?"

"Twenty residents are at this time unavailable."

"Meaning twenty patients."

"We prefer to call them residents, Ms. Beadsman, since as you know we try to offer an environment in which—"

"Fine, well, but don't a lot of the missing 'residents' need IV's to get fed and stuff? And little things like insulin, and antibiotics, and heart medicine, and help dressing and taking showers? Lenore can hardly even move her left arm this summer, and plus it's pretty cold for her, outside, for very long, so I just don't see how they could —"

"Ms. Beadsman, please rest assured that you and I are in more than complete agreement on this. That I am as confused and distraught as are you. As disoriented." Mr. Bloemker's cheeks yielded to the force of his beard-abuse, began to move around, so it looked like he was making faces at Lenore. "I find myself facing a situation I, believe me, never dreamt of possibly encountering, monstrous and disorienting." He licked his lips. "As well, just allow me to say, one for which my training as facility administrator prepared me not at all, not at all."

Lenore looked at her shoe. Mr. Bloemker's phone buzzed and flashed again. He reached and listened. "Please," he said into the phone. "Thank you."

He hung up and then for some reason came around the desk, as if to take Lenore's hand, to comfort. Lenore stared at him, and he stopped. "So have you called my father over at Stonecipheco?" she asked. "Should I call him? Clarice is just over in the city, my sister. Is she in on this news?"

Mr. Bloemker shook his head, his hand trailing. "We've contacted no one else at this time. Since you are Lenore's only really regular visitor from among her family, I thought of you first."

"What about the other patients' families? If there's like twenty gone, this place should be a madhouse."

"There are very few visitors here as a rule, you would be surprised. In any event we have contacted no one else as yet."

"And why haven't you."

Mr. Bloemker looked at the ceiling for a second. There was a really unattractive brown stain soaked into the soft white tile. Light from the sun was coming through the east windows and falling across the room, a good bit of it on Bloemker, making one of his eyes glow gold. He leveled it at Lenore. "The fact is that I have been instructed not to."

"Instructed? By whom?"

"By the owners of the facility."

Lenore looked up at him sharply. "Last I knew, the owner of the facility was Stonecipheco."

"Correct."

"Meaning basically my father."

"Yes."

"But I thought you said my father didn't know anything about this."

"No, I said I had not contacted anyone else as of yet, is what I said. As a matter of fact, it was *I* who was contacted early this morning at home and informed of the state of affairs by a . . . ," sifting through papers on his desk, ". . . a Mr. Rummage, who apparently serves Stonecipheco in some legal capacity. How he knew of the . . . situation is utterly beyond me."

"Karl Rummage. He's with the law firm my father uses for personal business."

"Yes." He twisted some beard around a finger. "Well apparently it is . . . not wished to have the situation of cognizance to those other than the owners at this moment by the owners."

"You want to run that by me again?"

"They don't want anyone to know just yet."

"Ah."

". . . ."

"So then why did you call me? I mean thank you very much for doing so, obviously, but . . ."

Another sad smile. "Your thanks are without warrant, I'm afraid. I was instructed to do what I did."

"Oh."

"The obvious inference to draw here is that the fact that you are after all a Beadsman . . . and enjoy some connection to the ownership of the facility through Stonecipheco . . ."

"That's just not true."

"Oh really? In any event it's clear that you can be relied on for a measure of discretion beyond that of the average relative-on-the-street."

"I see."

Bloemker took a deep breath and rubbed a gold eye with a white finger. In the air around him a whirlpool of dust motes was created. It whirled. "There is in addition the fact that the resident whose temporary unavailability is relevant to you, that is to say Lenore, enjoyed a status here—with the facility administration, the staff, and, through the force of her personality and her evident gifts, especially with the other residents—that leads one to believe that, were the mislocation a result of anything other than outright coercion on the part of some outside person or persons, which seems unlikely, it would not be improper to posit the location and retrieval of Lenore as near assurance of retrieving the other misplaced parties."

"I didn't understand any of that."

"Your great-grandmother was more or less the ringleader around here."

"Oh."

"Surely you knew that."

"Not really, no."

"But you were here," looking at a sheet on his desk, "often several times a week, sometimes for long periods. Of time."

"We talked about other stuff. We sure never talked about any rings being led. And usually there wasn't anybody else around, what with the heat of the room." Lenore looked at her sneaker. "And also you know my just plain grandmother's a . . . resident here, too, in area J. Lenore's daughter-in-law."

"Concarnadine."

"Yes. She . . . uh, she is here, isn't she?"

"Oh yes," said Bloemker. He looked at a sheet, then at Lenore. "As . . . far as I am aware. Perhaps you'll excuse me for a moment." He went to his phone. Lenore watched him dial in-house. A three-digit relay means no crossbar. Bloemker was asking someone something in an administrative undertone Lenore couldn't hear. "Thank you," she heard him say. "Yes."

He smiled. "We'll simply check to be sure."

Lenore had had a thought. "Maybe it would be good if I had a look at Lenore's room, took a look around, maybe see if I could notice something."

"That's just what I was going to suggest."

"Is your beard OK?"

"I'm sorry? Oh, yes, nervous habit, I'm afraid, the state of affairs at the . . ." Mr. Bloemker pulled both hands out of his beard.

"So shall we go?"

"Certainly."

"Or should I call my father from here?"

"I cannot get an outside line on this phone, I'm sorry."

"I didn't think so."

"After you."

"Thank you."

/e/

The Home was broken into ten sections, areas they were called, each roughly pentagonal in shape, housing who knows how many patients, the ten areas arranged in a circle, each area accessible by two and only two others, or via the center of the circle, a courtyard filled with chalky white gravel and heavy dark plants and a pool of concentric circles of colored water distributed and separated and kept unadulterated by a system of plastic sheeting and tubing, the tubing leading in toward the pool in the center from a perimeter of ten smooth, heavy wooden sculptures of jungle animals and Tafts and Stonecipher Beadsmans I, II, and III, with a translucent plastic roof high overhead that let in light for the plants but kept rain or falling dew from diluting the colors of the pool, the interior planes of each of the ten sections walled in glass and accessing into the courtyard, the yard itself off-limits to residents because the gravel was treacherous to walk in, swallowed canes and the legs of walkers, mired wheelchairs, and made people fall over—people with hips like spun glass, Lenore had once told Lenore.

Down a corridor, through a door, around the perimeter of one area, past a gauntlet of reaching wheelchaired figures, out a glass panel, through the steamy crunch of the courtyard gravel, through another panel and halfway around the perimeter of area F, Mr. Bloemker led Lenore to her great-grandmother's room, put his key in the lock of another light, pretend-wood door. The room was round, looked with big windows into the east parking lots with a view at the corner of which glittered, spangled with light through the trees in the wind, Lenore's little red car again. The room was unbelievably hot.

"You didn't turn the heat down?" Lenore said.

Mr. Bloemker stayed in the doorway. "The owners had installed an automatic duct complex to this room that is as difficult to dismantle as it is resistant to malfunction. We are also of course expecting that Lenore will be back with us very soon."

Steam hung in the air of the room, you could feel each breath on your lips, the windows sweated broadly, the movement of the sun through the trees made a dark green flutter on the white walls.

Lenore Beadsman, who was ninety-two, suffered no real physical disability save a certain lack of capacity on her left side, and the complete absence of any kind of body thermometer. She now depended for her body's temperature on the temperature of the air around her. She had in effect become sort of cold-blooded. This had come to the attention of her family in 1986, after the death of her husband, Stonecipher Beadsman, when she began to take on a noticeable blue hue. The temperature in Lenore's room here at the Home was 98.6 degrees. This simultaneously kept Gramma alive and comfortable and kept her visitors down to Lenore and a brief bare minimum of other patients and staff and very occasionally Lenore's sister, Clarice.

The room contained a bed that was made, a desk and bedside table sheened with humidity, a water glass on the bedside table whose contents had almost evaporated, a bureau on which were ranged some jars of Stonecipheco baby food, some vaguely malevolent black cords snaking out from a wall, the remnants of a cable hookup to a television Gramma had caused to be removed, a chair, a closet door, a clotted shaker of salt, and on a black metal TV tray a little clay horse Lenore had gotten Gramma in Spain a long time ago. The walls were bare.

"OK," Lenore said, looking around, "she pretty obviously took her walker." She opened the closet door. "She couldn't have taken very many clothes . . . here's her suitcase . . . or taken much underwear," looking in the bureau drawers. Lenore picked up one of the jars of Stonecipheco baby food, one with a red-ink drawing of a laughing baby on the label. Strained beef flavor. "She eats this stuff?" she asked, looking over at Mr. Bloemker, who stood with a sweat-shiny face in the doorway, massaging his chin.

"Not to my knowledge."

"I'd bet money she doesn't." Lenore went to the desk. There were three light, empty drawers. One locked drawer.

"Did you open this drawer, here?"

"We were unable to locate the key."

"Ah." Lenore went to the TV table, took the little clay horse and popped its head off, and out fell a key and fluttered a tiny picture of Lenore, out of a locket. The picture was old and dull. The key made a sound on the metal table. Mr. Bloemker wiped at his forehead with the sleeve of his sportcoat.

Lenore opened the drawer. In it were Gramma's notebooks, yellow and crispy, old, and her copy of the *Investigations*, and a small piece of fuzzy white paper, which actually turned out to be a torn-off label from another jar of Stonecipheco food. Creamed peach. On the white back of the label something was doodled. There was nothing else in the drawer. Which is to say there was no green book in the drawer.

"This is just weird," Lenore was saying. She looked at Mr. Bloemker. "She didn't take the *Investigations,* which is like her prize possession because it's autographed, or her notebooks either. Except I guess she did take a book. She kept a book in here. Have you ever maybe seen a green book, pretty heavy, bound with a sort of greenish leather, with like a little decorative lock and clasp?"

Mr. Bloemker nodded at her. There was a drop of sweat hanging from his nose. "I do think I recall seeing Lenore with such a book. I had rather assumed it was her diary, or a record of her days at Cambridge, which I knew were immensely important to her."

Lenore shook her head. "No, that's more or less what these are," indicating the yellowed notebooks in the open drawer. "No, I don't know what this thing was, but she had it and the *Investigations* with her all the time. Remember how when she'd go out of her room here her nightgown would be all sagging down in front? She couldn't carry the books and use her walker, so she had this big pocket on the front of her nightgown, and she'd put them in there, and it'd sag." Lenore felt herself beginning to get upset, remembering. "Did she, had she gone out of the room much the last few days?"

There were wet sounds as Mr. Bloemker worked at his face. "I know for a fact that as a matter of established routine Lenore was out in the area F lounge for some period every afternoon. Holding forth. When were you last here, may I ask?"

"I think a week ago today."

Mr. Bloemker's eyebrows went up. Drops stopped and started on his forehead.

"The thing is that my brother was getting set to go back to college," said Lenore. "I've been helping him buy stuff and arrange things and work out some things with my father, when I haven't been working. There was a lot of stuff to arrange."

"His college must begin terribly early. It's not yet even September."

"No, the place he goes—which is this place called Amherst

College? In Massachusetts?—it doesn't start for a couple weeks yet, but he wanted to go visit our mother before the year started and everything."

"Visit your mother?"

"She's sort of resting, in Wisconsin."

"Ah."

"Listen, should I call her and tell her what's going on? She's Lenore's relative too. I really think we better call the police."

Mr. Bloemker's glasses had slipped almost all the way down his nose. He pushed them up, and they immediately slid down again. "What I can do at this point is pass along to you the information and requests relayed to me very early by Mr. Rummage." He tugged at his cuffs. "The police are not going to be contacted at this point in time. The owners are of the opinion, for reasons which I must in all honesty confess remain at this moment hazy to me, that this is an internal nursing-care-facility matter which can be brought to some quick resolution without resort to outside aid. If of course it be so, the advantages accruing in terms of minimal embarrassment and impediment to the facility are obvious. You are requested to inform no one of any details of the situation until you have spoken to your father. You are requested to contact your father at your very earliest opportunity."

"Dad is really hard to contact, usually."

"Nevertheless."

Lenore looked back at the open desk drawer. "This is making very little sense to me. And what about the relatives of the staff who are . . . unavailable right now? Won't their families find their unavailability a little out of the ordinary? They're going to be apt to want to call the police, don't you think? I don't blame them. I'd like to call the police, too."

Mr. Bloemker's glasses suddenly fell off his nose and he caught them, barely, and wiped the bridge of his nose with his fingers. "It is at this point unclear whether the families of the unavailable staff are themselves unavailable because of normal extra-Home commitments, or whether they too have become unavailable in a manner similar to that of the staff, but the in a way fortuitous though of course also quite disquieting fact remains . . ."

"What was all that?" Lenore said from back at Gramma's drawer.

"The families aren't around, either."

"Gosh."

"What are you doing?" Bloemker asked. Lenore was looking at the ink drawing on the back of the Stoneciphco label that lay on top of the notebooks in the desk drawer. It featured a person, apparently in a smock. In one hand was a razor, in the other a can of shaving cream. Lenore could even see the word "Noxzema" on the can. The person's head was an explosion of squiggles of ink.

"Looking at this thing," she said.

Mr. Bloemker moved closer. He smelled like a wet diaper. "What is it," he asked, looking over Lenore's shoulder.

"If it's what I think it is," said Lenore, "it's a sort of joke. A what do you call it. An antinomy."

"An antinomy?"

Lenore nodded. "Gramma really likes antinomies. I think this guy here," looking down at the drawing on the back of the label, "is the barber who shaves all and only those who do not shave themselves."

Mr. Bloemker looked at her. "A barber?"

"The big killer question," Lenore said to the sheet of paper, "is supposed to be whether the barber shaves himself. I think that's why his head's exploded, here."

"Beg pardon?"

"If he does, he doesn't, and if he doesn't, he does."

Mr. Bloemker stared down at the drawing. Smoothed his beard.

"Look, can we leave?" Lenore asked. "It's really hot. I want to leave."

"By all means."

Lenore put the Stoneciphco label in her purse and shut the drawer. "I'll put the key here on the desk, but I don't think anybody other than the police ought to go looking through Gramma's stuff, assuming the police get called, which I really think they ought to."

"I quite agree. You are taking the . . . ?"

"Antinomy."

"Yes."

"Is that OK?"

"The person on the telephone said nothing indicating otherwise."

"Thanks."

There was a knock at the door. A staff member handed a note to Mr. Bloemker. Bloemker read the note. The staff member looked at Lenore's dress and shoes for a moment and left.

"Well of course as I fully expected Concarnadine Beadsman is still with us, over in J," Mr. Bloemker said. "Would you perhaps care to see her before you—?"

"No thanks, really," Lenore cut him off. "I really have to get to work. What time is it, by the way?"

"Almost noon."

"God, I'm going to be really late. I'm going to get killed. I hope Candy isn't mad about covering. Look, is there a phone where I can dial out to call and say I'll be late? I really need to call."

"There are dial-out phones at every reception station. I'll show you."

"I remember, come to think of it."

"Of course."

"Look, I'm going to be in touch, soon, obviously. I'm going to get hold of my father from work, and I'll tell him he should call you."

"That would be enormously helpful, thank you." Mr. Bloemker's shirt had soaked the outline of a thin V through his sportcoat.

"And of course please call me if anything happens, if you find anything out. Either at work or over at the Tissaws' house."

"Rest assured that I will. You are still employed at Frequent and Vigorous?"

"Yes. Have you got the number?"

"Somewhere, I'm sure."

"Really, let me give it to you to be sure. We get an incredible amount of wrong numbers." Lenore wrote the number on a card from her purse and handed it to Mr. Bloemker. Mr. Bloemker looked at the front of the card.

" 'Rick Vigorous: Editor, Reader, Administrator, All-Around Literary Presence, Frequent and Vigorous Publishing, Inc.'?"

"Never mind, just there's the number. Can we please go to the dial-out phone? I'm hideously late, and being here longer isn't going to help get Lenore back, I can see."

"Of course. Let me get the door."

"Thank you."

"Not at all."

/f/

25 August

I have a truly horrible dream which invariably occurs on the nights I am Lenoreless in my bed. I am attempting to stimulate the clitoris of Queen Victoria with the back of a tortoise-shell hairbrush. Her voluminous skirts swirl around her waist and my head. Her enormous cottage-cheese thighs rest heavy on my shoulders, spill out in front of my sweating face. The clanking of pounds of jewelry is heard as she shifts to offer herself at best advantage. There are odors. The Queen's impatient breathing is thunder above me as I kneel at the throne. Time passes. Finally her voice is heard, overhead, metalled with disgust and frustration: "We are not aroused." I am punched in the arm by a guard and flung into a pit at the bottom of which boil the figures of countless mice. I awake with a mouth full of fur. Begging for more time. A ribbed brush.

/g/

One big problem with owning one of those new Mattel ultra-compact cars, which was what Lenore owned, was that the plastic car had a plastic choke which had to be engaged while the car warmed up for not fewer than five minutes, which was particularly irritating in the summer, because Lenore had to sit in the small oven that was the car for these five minutes, while the engine raced like mad and made a lot of unpleasant noise, before she could get going and have some cooler air blow on her. While she made the choke-wait in the Home's parking lot, Lenore watched an ant nibble at something in the wad of bird droppings that lay near the top of her windshield.

The ant was torn off the windshield by the wind when Lenore hit the Inner Belt of I-271 and started going seriously fast. The offices of the publishing firm of Frequent and Vigorous were in that part of downtown Cleveland called Erieview Plaza, right near Lake Erie. Lenore took the Inner Belt south and west from Shaker Heights, preparatory to her being flung by I-271 northward into the city itself, which meant that she was for a while with her car tracing the outline of the city of East Corinth, Ohio, which was where she had her apartment, and which determined the luxuriant and not unpopular shape of the Inner Belt Section of I-271.

East Corinth had been founded and built in the 1960's by Stonecipher Beadsman II, son of Lenore Beadsman, Lenore Beadsman's grandfather, who was unfortunately killed at age sixty-five in 1975 in a vat accident during a brief and disastrous attempt on the part of Stonecipheco Baby Food Products to develop and market something that would compete with Jell-O. Stonecipher Beadsman II had been a man of many talents and even more interests. He had been a really fanatical moviegoer, as well as an amateur urban planner, and he had been particularly rabid in his attachment to a film star named Jayne Mansfield. East Corinth lay in the shape of a profile of Jayne Mansfield: leading down from Shaker Heights in a nimbus of winding road-networks, through delicate features of homes and small businesses, a button nose of a park and a full half-smiling section of rotary, through a sinuous swan-like curve of a highway extension and tract housing, before jutting precipitously westward in a huge, swollen development of factories and industrial parks, mammoth and bustling, the Belt curving back no less immoderately a couple miles south into a trim lower border of homes and stores and apartment buildings and some boarding houses, including that in which Lenore Beadsman herself lived and from which she had driven up over Jayne Mansfield to the Shaker Heights Home this morning. Families and firms owning property along the critical western boundary of the suburb were required by zoning code to paint their facilities in the most realistic colors possible, a condition to which property owners in the far westward section near Garfield Heights (where the industrial swelling was most pronounced) particularly objected, and as one can imagine the whole East Corinth area was immensely popular with airline pilots, who all tended to demand landing patterns into Cleveland-Hopkins Airport over East Corinth, and who made a constant racket, flying low and blinking their lights on and off and waggling their wings. The people of East Corinth, many of them unaware of the shape their town really lay in, a knowledge not exactly public, crawled and drove and walked over the form of Jayne Mansfield, shaking their fists at the bellies of planes. Lenore had lived in East Corinth only two years, ever since she had gotten out of college and decided she did not want to live at home or enter Stonecipheco, all at once. To the south, 271 gave way to 77, and 77 led down through Bedford, Tallmadge, Akron, and Canton before stretching into the Great Ohio Desert, with its miles of ash-fine black sand, and cacti and scorpions, and crowds of fishermen, and concession stands at the rim.

There were two reliable ways to identify the Bombardini Building, which was where the firm of Frequent and Vigorous made its home. A look from the south at Erieview Tower, high and rectangular not far from the Terminal section of Cleveland's downtown, reveals that the sun, always at either a right or a left tangent to the placement of the Tower, casts a huge, dark shadow of the Building over the surrounding area—a deep, severely angled shadow that joins the bottom of the Tower in black union but then bends precipitously off to the side, as if the Erieview Plaza section of Cleveland were a still pool of water, into which the Tower had been dipped, the shadow its refracted submergence. In the morning, when the shadow casts from east to west, the Bombardini Building stands sliced by light, white and black, on the Tower's northern side. As the day swells and the shadow compacts and moves ponderously in and east, and as clouds begin to complicate the shapes of darknesses, the Bombardini Building is slowly eaten by black, the steady suck of the dark broken only by epileptic flashes of light caused by clouds with pollutant bases bending rays of sun as the Bombardini Building flirts ever more seriously with the border of the shadow. By mid-afternoon the Bombardini Building is in complete darkness, the windows glow yellow, cars go by with headlights. The Bombardini Building, then, is easy to find, occurring nowhere other than on the perimeter of the sweeping scythe of the Midwest's very most spectacular shadow.

The other aforementioned identifying feature was the white skeleton of General Moses Cleaveland, which found itself in shallow repose in the cement of the sidewalk in front of the Bombardini

Building, its outline clearly visible, of no little interest to passing pedestrians and the occasional foraging dog, the latter's advances discouraged by a thin bit of electrified grillwork, the General's rest thus largely untroubled save by the pole of a sign which jutted disrespectfully out of Cleaveland's left eye socket, the sign itself referring to a hugely outlined parking space in front of the Building and reading: THIS SPACE RESERVED FOR NORMAN BOMBARDINI, WITH WHOM YOU DO NOT WANT TO MESS.

Frequent and Vigorous Publishing shared the Bombardini Building with the administrative facilities of the Bombardini Company, a firm involved in some vague genetic engineering enterprises about which Lenore in all honesty cared to know as little as possible. The Bombardini Company occupied most of the lower three floors and a single vertical line of offices up the six-story height of the Bombardini Building's east side. Frequent and Vigorous took a vertical line of narrow space on the western side of the Building for three floors, then swelled out to take almost all the top three. The Frequent and Vigorous telephone switchboard, where Lenore worked, was in the western corner of the cavernous Bombardini Building lobby, across the huge back wall of which, cast through the giant windows in the front wall of the lobby, the Erieview shadow steadily and even measurably moved, eating the wall. Time could with reasonable accuracy be measured by the position of the shadow against the back wall, except when the black-and-white window-light flickered like a silent movie during the fickle shadow-period of mid-day.

Which it now was. Lenore was hideously late. She hadn't been able to get through to Candy Mandible on the phone, either. The Shaker Heights Home's phones were apparently on the fritz: F and V's number had put Lenore in touch with Cleveland Towing.

"Frequent and Vigorous," Candy Mandible was saying into the switchboard console phone. "Frequent and Vigorous," she said. "No this is not Enrique's House of Cheese. Shall I give you that number, even though it might not work? You're welcome."

"Candy God I'm so sorry, it was unavoidable, I couldn't get through." Lenore came back behind the counter and into the switchboard cubicle. The window high overhead flashed a cathedral spear of sun, then was dark.

"Lenore, you're like three hours late. That's just a little much."

"My supervisor wouldn't take it. I'd get fired if I pulled anything like what you guys pull," Judith Prietht shot off between calls beeping at the Bombardini Company switchboard console a few feet away in the tiny cubicle.

Lenore put her purse by the Security phones. She came close to Candy Mandible. "I tried to call you. Mrs. Tissaw called me out of the shower at like nine-thirty because Schwartz had answered this call for me. I had to go to the nursing home right away."

"Something's wrong."

"Yes." Lenore saw that Judith Prietht's ears were aprick. "Can I just talk to you later? Will you be home later on?"

"I'll be off over at Allied at six," Candy said. "I was supposed to be over there at freaking twelve—but it's OK," seeing Lenore's expression. "Clint said he'd get somebody to cover for me as long as I wanted. Are you all right? Which one is it?"

"Lenore."

"She didn't . . . ?"

"It's *unclear*."

"Unclear?"

"My supervisor, you gotta have reasons for being late, and submit 'em in advance, and they have to get signed by Mr. Bombardini," Judith said amid beepings and rings. "But then we have a real business, we get real calls. Bombardini Company. Bombardini Company. One moment."

"She's being particularly pleasant today," said Lenore. Candy made a strangle-motion at Judith, then started to get her stuff together.

Their console sounded. Lenore got it. "Frequent and Vigorous," she said. She listened and looked up at Candy. "Bambi's Den of Discipline?" she said. "No, this is most definitely not Bambi's Den of Discipline . . . Candy, do you have the number of a Bambi's Den of Discipline?" Candy gave her the number but said it probably wouldn't make any difference. Lenore recited the number and released.

"Bambi's Den of Discipline?" she said. "That's a new one. What do you mean there's probably no difference?"

"I can't figure it out, I don't see nothing wrong," a voice came from under the console counter, under Lenore's chair, by her legs. Lenore looked down. There were big boots protruding from under the counter. They began to jiggle; a figure struggled to emerge. Lenore shot her chair back.

"Lenore, there's line trouble that I guess started last night, Vern said," Candy said. "This is Peter Abbott. He's with Interactive Cable. They're trying to fix the problem."

"Interactive Cable?"

"Like the phone company, but not the phone company."

"Oh." Lenore looked listlessly at Peter Abbott. "Hi."

"Well hello hello," said Peter, winking furiously at Lenore and pulling up his collar. Lenore looked up at Candy as Peter played with something hanging from his tool belt.

"Peter is very friendly, it seems," said Candy Mandible.

"Hmm."

"Well I can't see nothing wrong in there, I'm stumped," Peter said.

"What's the problem?" Lenore asked.

"It's not good," said Candy. "We I guess more or less don't have a number anymore. Is that right?" She looked at Peter Abbott.

"Well, you got line trouble," said Peter.

"Right, which apparently in this case means we don't have a number anymore, or rather we do, but so does like the whole rest of Cleveland, in that we now all of a sudden *share* a single number with all these other places. All these places that share our line tunnel. You know all those numbers we were just one off of, and we'd just get the wrong numbers all the time—Steve's Sub, Cleveland Towing, Big B.M. Cafe, Fuss 'n' Feathers Pets, Dial-a-Darling? Well now they're like all the same number. You dial their numbers, and the F and V number rings. Plus a whole lot of new ones: a cheese shop, some Goodyear service office, that Bambi's Den of Discipline, which by the way gets a disturbing number of calls. We've all got the same number now. It's nuts. Is that right what I said?" she asked Peter Abbott. She got her stuff and got ready to leave, looking at her watch.

"Yeah, line trouble," Peter Abbott said.

"At least now you'll have calls. At least now you'll have something to do for a change," said Judith Prietht. "Bombardini Company. Bombardini Company."

"How come she's not messed up?" Lenore gestured at Judith.

"Different line tunnels," Peter Abbott said. "Bombardini Inc.'s lines are actually it turns out in this tunnel pretty far away, a few blocks west of Erieview. The calls just get into here via a matrix sharing-thread transfer, which is a real complicated plus ancient thing. Your lines are in a tunnel right under this building, under the lobby, out under that guy's skeleton." Peter Abbott pointed at the floor.

"So then why are you up here instead of down with the lines?" Candy Mandible wanted to know.

"I'm not a tunnel man. I'm a console man. I don't do tunnels. They sent some guy from Tunnels down there early this morning. It's gotta be his problem. I can't find nothing up here with what you girls got. This's a twenty-eight, right? I haven't lost my mind?"

"Right, Centrex twenty-eight."

"I know it's a Centrex, that's all I do, I'm bored as shit with Centrexes, excuse my French."

"Well what did the guy from the tunnel say?" Lenore asked. Candy was answering a phone.

"Dunno, 'cause I haven't talked to him. I sure can't call him, am I right?"

"What, we can't dial out on this, either?"

"I was just makin' a joke. You can call out OK. Just try again if you get an automatic loop into one of the other in-tunnel points. No, I just hafta talk to the tunnel guy in person, back at the office. We hafta write up reports." Peter looked at Lenore. "You married?"

"Oh, brother."

"This one's not married either, right?" Peter Abbott asked Candy, nodding over at Lenore. His hair wasn't blond so much as just yellow, like a crayon. His face had the color of a kind of dark nut. Not the sort of tan that comes from the sun. Lenore sensed CabanaTan. The guy looked like a photographic negative, she decided.

He sighed. "Two unmarried girls, in distress, working in this tiny little office . . ."

"Women," Candy Mandible corrected.

"I'm not married either," Judith Prietht called over. Judith Prietht was about fifty.

"Groovy," said Peter Abbott.

"So can Bambi and Big Bob and all the others even get any calls, now?" Lenore asked. "Do their phones ring at all?"

"Sometimes, sometimes not," Peter Abbott said, jingling his belt. "The point is they can't be sure where it'll ring, and neither can you, which is obviously subpar service. Your number's not picking you out of the network like it should, it's as we say picking out a target set and not a target."

"Lovely."

"At least now you'll have some calls to answer," said Judith Prietht. "All you ever get is wrong numbers anyway. You guys are going to go bankrupt. Who ever heard of a publishing house in Cleveland?"

"I like your shoes," Peter Abbott said to Lenore. "I got some shoes just like that."

"Does Rick know about all this?" Lenore asked Candy.

Candy stopped. "Rick. Lenore, call him right away."

"What's the matter?"

"Who knows what's ever the matter. All I know is first he just had a complete *spasm* about your not being here. This was at like ten-o-one. And then now he keeps calling down all the time, to see if you're here yet. He keeps pretending it's different people asking for you, holding his nose, putting a hankie over the phone, trying this totally pitiful English accent, pretending it's outside calls for you, which he should know I can tell it isn't because he knows the way the console light flashes all fast when they're in-house calls. God knows he spends enough time down here. And now he hasn't come down for his paper, even, he's just sitting up there brooding, playing with his hat."

"What else does he have to do?" said Judith Prietht, who was unwrapping wax paper from a sandwich and blinking coquettishly at Peter Abbott, who was in turn trying to stare down over the counter into Lenore's cleavage.

"God, well I really need to talk to him, too," said Lenore.

"Sweetie, I *forgot* for a second. How just totally horrible. You must be out of your head. Are you sure you're all right?"

THE BROOM OF THE SYSTEM 52

"I think so. Vern'll be in at six. I'll call Rick as soon as I can. I have to call my father, too. And his lawyer."

"I sense something in the wind," said Peter Abbott.

"You hush," said Candy Mandible. She squeezed Lenore's arm as she passed. "I'm late. I have to go. You come home tonight, hear?"

"I'll call and let you know," Lenore said.

"What, you guys are roommates?" Peter Abbott asked.

"Partners in crime," Judith Prietht snorted.

"Lucky room, is all I can say."

"Let's just have a universal dropping dead, except for Lenore," said Candy. She walked off across the marble lobby floor into the moving blackness.

"She's got another job?" Peter Abbott asked.

"Yes." The console beeped. "Frequent and Vigorous."

"Where at?"

Lenore held up a finger for him to wait while she dealt with somebody wanting to price a set of radials. "Over at Allied Sausage Casings, in East Corinth?" she said when she'd released.

"What a gnarly place to work. What does she do?"

"Product testing. Tasting Department."

"What a disgusting job."

"Somebody has to do it."

"Glad it's not me, boy."

"But I do assume you have some kind of job to do? Like fixing our lines?"

"I'm off. I'll be in touch—if possible." Peter Abbott laughed and left, jingling. He walked into a moving patch of light in the middle of the lobby and the light disappeared, taking him with it.

The console began to beep.

"Frequent and Vigorous," Lenore said. "Frequent and Vigorous."

4 1972

TRANSCRIPT OF MEETING BETWEEN THE HONORABLE
RAYMOND ZUSATZ, GOVERNOR OF THE STATE OF OHIO;
MR. JOSEPH LUNGBERG, GUBERNATORIAL AIDE; MR. NEIL
OBSTAT, GUBERNATORIAL AIDE; AND MR. ED ROY
YANCEY, VICE PRESIDENT, INDUSTRIAL DESERT DESIGN,
INCORPORATED, DALLAS, TEXAS; 21 JUNE 1972.

GOVERNOR: Gentlemen, something is not right.

MR. OBSTAT: What do you mean, Chief?

GOVERNOR: With the state, Neil. Something is not right with our state.

MR. LUNGBERG: But Chief, unemployment is low, inflation is low, taxes
haven't been raised in two years, pollution is way down except for
Cleveland and who the hell cares about Cleveland—just kidding, Neil—
but Chief, the people love you, you're unprecedentedly ahead in the
polls, industrial investment and development in the state are at an all-
time high. . . .

GOVERNOR: Stop right there. There you go.

MR. OBSTAT: Can you expand on that, Chief?

GOVERNOR: Things are just too good, somehow. I suspect a trap.

MR. LUNGBERG: A trap?

GOVERNOR: Guys, the state is getting soft. I can feel softness out there.
It's getting to be one big suburb and industrial park and mall. Too
much development. People are getting complacent. They're forgetting
the way this state was historically hewn out of the wilderness. There's
no more hewing.

MR. OBSTAT: You've got a point there, Chief.

GOVERNOR: We need a wasteland.

MR. LUNGBERG and MR. OBSTAT: A wasteland?

GOVERNOR: Gentlemen, we need a desert.

MR. LUNGBERG and MR. OBSTAT: A desert?

GOVERNOR: Gentlemen, a desert. A point of savage reference for the good people of Ohio. A place to fear and love. A blasted region. Something to remind us of what we hewed out of. A place without malls. An Other for Ohio's Self. Cacti and scorpions and the sun beating down. Desolation. A place for people to wander alone. To reflect. Away from everything. Gentlemen, a desert.

MR. OBSTAT: Just a super idea, Chief.

GOVERNOR: Thanks, Neil. Gentlemen may I present Mr. Ed Roy Yancey, of Industrial Desert Design, Dallas. They did Kuwait.

MR. LUNGBERG: Hey, there's apparently a lot of desert in Kuwait.

MR. YANCEY: You bet, Joe, and we believe we can provide you folks with a really first-rate desert right here in Ohio.

MR. OBSTAT: What about the cost?

GOVERNOR: Manageable.

MR. LUNGBERG: Where would it be?

MR. YANCEY: Well gentlemen, the Governor and I have conferred, and if I could just direct your attention to this map, here . . .

MR. OBSTAT: That's Ohio, all right.

MR. YANCEY: The spot we have in mind is in the south of your great state. Right about . . . here. Actually here to here. Hundred square miles.

MR. OBSTAT: Around Caldwell?

MR. YANCEY: Yup.

MR. LUNGBERG: Don't quite a few people live around there?

GOVERNOR: Relocation. Eminent domain. A desert respects no man. Fits with the whole concept.

MR. LUNGBERG: Isn't that also pretty near Wayne National Forest?

GOVERNOR: Not anymore.

(Mr. Lungberg whistles.)

MR. OBSTAT: Hey, my mother lives right near Caldwell.

GOVERNOR: Hits home, eh Neil? Part of the whole concept. Concept has to hit home. Hewing is violence, Neil. We're going to hew a wilderness out of the soft underbelly of this state. It's going to hit home.

MR. LUNGBERG: You're really sold on this, aren't you, Chief?

GOVERNOR: Joe, I've never been more sold on anything. It's what this state needs. I can feel it.

MR. OBSTAT: You'll go down in history, Chief. You'll be immortal.

GOVERNOR: Thanks, Neil. I just feel it's right, and after conferring with Mr. Yancey, I'm just sold. A hundred miles of blinding white sandy nothingness. 'Course there'll be some fishing lakes, at the edges, for people to fish in . . .

MR. LUNGBERG: Why white sand, Chief? Why not, say, black sand?

GOVERNOR: Go with that, Joe.

MR. LUNGBERG: Well, really, if the whole idea is supposed to be contrast, otherness, blastedness, should I say sinisterness? Sinisterness is the sense I get.

GOVERNOR: Sinisterness fits, that's good.

MR. LUNGBERG: Well, Ohio is a pretty white state: the roads are white, the people tend to be on the whole white, the sun's pretty bright here. . . . What better contrast than a hundred miles of black sand? Talk about sinister. And the black would soak up the heat a lot better, too. Be really hot, enhance the blastedness aspect.

GOVERNOR: I like it. Ed Roy, what do you think? Can cacti and scorpions live in black sand?

MR. YANCEY: No problem I can see.

MR. OBSTAT: What about the cost of black sand?

MR. YANCEY: A little more expensive, probably. I'd have to talk to the boys in Sand. But I feel I can commit now to saying it'd be manageable in the context of the whole project.

GOVERNOR: Done.

MR. LUNGBERG: When do we start?

GOVERNOR: Immediately, Joe. Hewing is by nature a fast, violent thing.

MR. OBSTAT: Chief, just let me say I'm excited. You have my congratulations, man to man and citizen to Governor.

GOVERNOR: Thanks, Neil. You better go call your Mom, big fella.

MR. OBSTAT: Right.

MR. LUNGBERG: What about a name, Chief?

GOVERNOR: A name? That's a typically excellent point, Joe. I never thought of the name issue.

MR. LUNGBERG: May I make a suggestion?

GOVERNOR: Go.

MR. LUNGBERG: The Great Ohio Desert.

GOVERNOR: The Great Ohio Desert.

MR. LUNGBERG: Yes.

GOVERNOR: Joe, a super name. I take my hat off to you. You've done it again. Great. It spells size, desolation, grandeur, and it says it's in Ohio.

MR. LUNGBERG: Not too presumptuous?

GOVERNOR: Not at all. Fits the concept to a T.

MR. OBSTAT: I take my hat off to you too, Joe.

MR. YANCEY: Damn fine name, Joe.

GOVERNOR: So we're all set. Concept. Desert. Color. Name. All that's left is the hewing.

MR. YANCEY: Well let's get down to it, then.

5   1990

/a/

Suppose someone had said to me, ten years ago, in Scarsdale, or on the commuter train, suppose the person had been my next-door neighbor, Rex Metalman, the corporate accountant with the unbelievable undulating daughter, suppose this was back in the days before his lawn mania took truly serious hold and his nightly paramilitary sentry-duty with the illuminated riding mower and the weekly planeloads of DDT dropping from the sky in search of perhaps one sod webworm nest and his complete intransigence in the face of the reasonable and in the beginning polite requests of one or even all of the neighbors that hostilities against the range of potential lawn enemies that obsessed him be toned down, at least in scale, before all this drove a wedge the size of a bag of Scott's into our tennis friendship, suppose Rex Metalman had speculated in my presence, then, that ten years later, which is to say now, I, Rick Vigorous, would be living in Cleveland, Ohio, between a biologically dead and completely offensive-smelling lake and a billion-dollar man-made desert, that I would be divorced from my wife and physically distanced from the growth of my son, that I would be operating a firm in partnership with an invisible person, little more, it seems clear now, than a corporate entity interested in failure for tax purposes, the firm publishing things perhaps even slightly more laughable than nothing at all, and that perched high atop this mountain of the unthinkable would be the fact that I was in love, grossly and pathetically and fiercely and completely in love with a person eighteen count them eighteen years younger than I, a woman from one of Cleveland's first families, who lives in a city owned by her father but who works answering telephones for something like four dollars an hour, a woman whose uniform of white cotton dress and black Converse hightop sneakers is an unanalyzable and troubling constant, who takes somewhere, I suspect, between five and eight showers a day, who works in neurosis like a whaler in scrimshaw, who lives with a schizophrenically narcissistic bird and an almost certainly nymphomaniacal bitch of a roommate, and who finds in me, somewhere, who knows where, the complete lover . . . suppose all this were said to me by Rex Metalman, leaning conversationally with his flamethrower over the fence between our properties as I stood with a rake in my hand, suppose Rex had said all this to me, then I almost certainly would have replied that the likelihood of all *that* was roughly equal to the probability of young Vance Vigorous, then eight and at eight in certain respects already more of a man than I, that young Vance, even as we stood there to be seen kicking a football up into the cold autumn sky and down through a window, his laughter echoing forever off the closed colored suburban trees, of strapping Vance's eventually turning out to be a . . . a *homosexual*, or something equally unlikely or preposterous or totally out of the question.

Now the heavens resound with unkind giggles. Now that it's become undeniably apparent even to me that I have a son who lends to the expression "fruit of my loins" whole new vistas of meaning, that I am here and do do what I do when there is anything to do, when I feel an empty draft and look down and find a hole in my chest and spy, in the open polyurethane purse of Lenore Beadsman, among the aspirins and bars of hotel soap and lottery tickets and the ridiculous books that mean nothing at all, the clenched purple fist of my own particular heart, what am I to say to Rex Metalman and Scarsdale and the sod webworms and the past, except that it does not exist, that it has been obliterated, that footballs never climbed into crisp skies, that my support checks disappear into a black void, that a man can be and is and must be reborn, at some point, perhaps points? Rex would be confused and would, as whenever confused, hide his discomfort by dynamiting an area of his lawn. I would stand, cold rake in white hand, knowing what I know, in a rain of dirt and grass and worms, and shake my head at all around me.

Then who is this girl who owns me, whom I love? I refuse to ask or answer who she is. *What* is she? This is a thin-shouldered, thin-armed, big-breasted girl, a long-legged girl with feet larger than average, feet that tend to point out a bit when she walks . . . in her black basketball sneakers. Did I say troubling? These are shoes that I love. I will confess that I once in a moment of admittedly irresponsible degeneracy tried to make love to one of the shoes, a 1989 All-Star hightop, when Lenore was in the shower, but failed to be able to bring the thing off, for familiar reasons.

But what of Lenore, of Lenore's hair? Here is hair that is clearly within and of itself every color—blond and red and jet-black-blue and honeynut—but which effects an outward optical compromise with possibility that consists of appearing simply dull brown, save for brief teasing glimpses out of the corner of one's eye. The hair hangs in bangs, and the sides curve down past Lenore's cheeks and nearly meet in points below her chin, like the brittle jaws of an insect of prey. Oh, the hair can bite. I've been bitten by the hair.

And her eyes. I cannot say what color Lenore Beadsman's eyes are; I cannot look at them; they are the sun to me.

They are blue. Her lips are full and red and tend to wetness and do not ask but rather demand, in a pout of liquid silk, to be kissed. I kiss them often, I admit it, it is what I do, I am a kisser, and a kiss with Lenore is, if I may indulge a bit for a moment here, not so much a kiss as it is a dislocation, a removal and rude transportation of essence from self to lip, so that it is not so much two human bodies coming together and doing the usual things with their lips as it is two sets of lips spawned together and joined in kind from the beginning of post-Scarsdale time, achieving full ontological status only in subsequent union and trailing behind and below them, as they join and become whole, two now utterly superfluous fleshly bodies, drooping outward and downward from the kiss like the tired stems of overblossomed flora, trailing shoes on the ground, husks. A kiss with Lenore is a scenario in which I skate with buttered soles over the moist rink of lower lip, sheltered from weathers by the wet warm overhang of upper, finally to crawl between lip and gum and pull the lip to me like a child's blanket and stare over it with beady, unfriendly eyes out at the world external to Lenore, of which I no longer wish to be part.

That I must in the final analysis remain part of the world that is external to and other from Lenore Beadsman is to me a source of profound grief. That others may dwell deep, deep within the ones they love, drink from the soft cup at the creamy lake at the center of the Object of Passion, while I am fated forever only to intuit the presence of deep recesses while I poke my nose, as it were, merely into the foyer of the Great House of Love, agitate briefly, and make a small mess on the doormat, pisses me off to no small degree. But that Lenore finds such tiny frenzies, such conversations just inside the Screen Door of Union, to be not only pleasant and briefly diverting but somehow apparently right, fulfilling, significant, in some sense wonderful, quite simply and not at all surprisingly makes me feel the same way, enlarges my sense of it and me, sends me hurrying up the walk to that Screen Door in my best sportjacket and flower in lapel as excited as any schoolboy, time after time, brings me charging to the cave entrance in leopardskin shirt, *avec* club, bellowing for admittance and promising general kickings of ass if I am impeded in any way.

We met, oddly enough, not at the Bombardini Building, but at the office of the counselor whose ear it turned out we shared, Dr. Curtis Jay, a good man but a strange and in general I'm coming to believe thoroughly poor psychologist, about whom I don't wish to speak at the moment because I am more than a little incensed at his latest and completely preposterous interpretation of a certain dream that has recently been recurring and troubling me not a little, a dream having to do with Queen Victoria, manipulative prowess, and mice—obviously to any reasonable sensitivity a profoundly sexual dream, which Dr. Jay tiresomely insists is not sexually fixated but has rather to do with what he terms "hygiene anxiety," which I simply and flatly reject, along with Jay's whole Blentnerian hygiene-bent, which I believe he has at some level both pirated from and added to Lenore's own private well of neurotic cathex; rather I know that that's the case, because one of Dr. Jay's redeeming qualities, and certainly the chief reason why I continue to see him in the face of mounting evidence of major incompetence, is the fact that he is also completely unethical and an incorrigible gossip who tells me all of what Lenore tells him. All of it.

Lenore and I met in Dr. Jay's reception room, I clankily leaving his office, she waiting in the other fabric track-chair in flowing white gown and worn black Converses, reading, her legs crossed ankle on knee. I knew I had seen her at the firm's switchboard, had in fact gotten my paper from her that very day, and what with the setting I was a little embarrassed, but Lenore, oh so very Lenorishly I know now, was not. She said hello, and called me Mr. Vigorous, and said she hoped we would have things to publish soon, she felt in her marrow we would. She said "marrow." She said she was seeing Dr. Jay chiefly for help with feelings of disorientation and identity-confusion and lack of control, which I could to an extent understand, because I knew her to be the daughter of the proprietor of Stonecipheco Baby Food Products, one of Cleveland's very leading and if I may say so in my perception evil industries, at any rate certain to be an oppressive and unignorable influence in the life of anyone in any way connected with its helm. I recall that at this point her mechanical chair on its track was caused to move toward the door of the inner office of Dr. Jay—whose fondness for useless gadgets would, I'm convinced, be of significant interest to his colleagues—and we called goodbye. I looked at the back of her neck as she disappeared into Jay's lair, undid the seat belt of my own ridiculous carnival appliance, and went out into the brown lake breezes with a lighter heart, somehow.

How did things progress, after that? I see for the most part not isolated events, not history, but a montage, to some sort of music, not any sort of brisk or invigorating The Fighter Gets Ready For The Big Fight montage, but rather a gauzy, tinkly thing, Rick Vigorous Fashions An Infatuation With Someone About The Same Age As His Own Child And Prepares To Make A Complete Ass Of Himself Over And Over, moving in watercolor, over which is imposed in even more liquid hues the ghostly scene of Lenore and me running toward each other in slow motion through the pale gelatin of our respective inhibitions and various troubles.

I see me getting my *Plain Dealer* every morning from Lenore over the switchboard counter, blushing and enduring the snorts of Candy Mandible or of Ms. Prietht, both of whom I loathe. I see me looking for Lenore in Dr. Jay's waiting room, her time never again coinciding with mine, me slumped in my chair as it moves slowly, noisily, toward Jay's inner office. I see me, at night, in my bed, in my apartment, performing my two-fingered Ritual of Solace, while over my head swim filmy visions in which a certain flowing, predatory-haired, black-shoed figure begins to predominate. I see me squirming in my chair in Dr. Jay's office, wanting to ask him about Lenore Beadsman, to spill the emotional beans, but too embarrassed to do so yet, feeling like an idiot while Jay strokes his walrus mustache with his perfumed hankie and sagely interprets my discomfort and distraction as signs of an impending "breakthrough," and urges me to double the number of my weekly visits.

Finally I see me, fed up with the whole business, unable to concentrate on my lack of work at the firm, unable to do any useful work on the *Review*, which really did, thank God, require real work. So I see me lurking one day like a ridiculous furtive spying child behind a marble pillar, within snapping reach of the jaws of the Erieview shadow, in the lobby of the Bombardini Building, waiting for Judith Prietht to hearken to one of the many daily calls of her impossibly small bladder. I see me accosting Lenore Beadsman in the claustrophobic cubicle after Prietht leaves. I see Lenore looking up to smile at my approach. I see me exhausting the subject of the weather, then asking Lenore if she might perhaps care to have a drink, with me, after work. I see one of the rare occasions I've encountered in which the word "nonplussed" might profitably be used in description. I see Lenore momentarily nonplussed.

"I don't really drink," she said, after a moment, looking back down at her book.

I felt a sinking. "You don't drink liquid of any sort?" I asked her.

Lenore looked back up at me and gave a slow smile. Her moist lips curved up softly. They really did. I resisted the urge to lunge into disaster right there in the lobby. "I drink liquid," she admitted, after a moment.

"Splendid. What sort of liquid do you prefer to drink?"

"Ginger ale's an especially good liquid, I've always thought," she said, laughing. We were both laughing. I had a fierce and painful erection, one which, thanks to one of the few advantages of my physical character, was not even a potential source of embarrassment.

"I know a wonderful place where they serve ginger ale in thin glasses, with tiny straws," I said. I was referring to a bar.

"Sounds super."

"Good."

I see us in a bar, I hear a piano I did not hear, I feel me getting thinly intoxicated on perhaps half a weak Canadian Club and distilled water, having to urinate almost at once and coming back and having to urinate again right away. I see Lenore's lips close around the tiny short straw of her ginger ale with a natural delicate ease that sent shivers through the large muscles of my legs. We were made for each other. I see me learning all about Lenore, Lenore in one of her pricelessly rare unself-conscious moments telling me of a life she would, I can say now, come to believe was in some sense not hers.

Lenore had a sister and two brothers. Her sister was married to a rising executive at Stonecipheco and was in some vague way connected with the tanning-parlor industry. One brother was an academic in Chicago who was not well. One brother was on the last leg of his first year at Amherst College, in Amherst, Massachusetts. [I, Rick Vigorous, I insert here, had gone to Amherst.] What a coincidence, I said, I went to Amherst too. Gosh, said Lenore. I remember how the jaws of her hair caressed the straw as she drew the ginger ale out of the tall frosted glass. Yes, she said, her brother was at Amherst, her father had gone to Amherst, her sister had gone to Mount Holyoke, a few miles away [how well I knew], her grandfather had gone to Amherst, her great-grandfather had gone to Amherst, her grandmother and great-grandmother to Mount Holyoke, her great-grandmother on to Cambridge in the twenties, where she had been a student of Wittgenstein, she still had notes from his classes.

Which brother was at Amherst now?

Her brother LaVache.

Where had her other brother gone to school? What was her other brother's name? Would she like another ginger ale, with a tiny straw?

Yes that would be fine, his name was John, her other brother's name was really Stonecipher but he used LaVache which was his middle name and had been their mother's maiden name. John, the oldest, hadn't gone to college as such, he had a Ph.D. from U. Chicago, he had in junior high school proved certainly hitherto unprovable things, with a crayon from Lenore's own crayon box, on a Batman writing tablet, and had shocked hell out of everyone, and had gotten a Ph.D. a few years later without really going to any classes.

This was the one who was now not well.

Yes.

It was hoped that it was nothing serious.

It was unfortunately very serious. He was in his room, in Chicago, unable to receive any but a very few visitors, having problems eating food. Lenore did not wish to talk about it, at that point, obviously.

So then, where had Lenore gone to school, had Lenore gone to Mount Holyoke?

No, Lenore had not liked Mount Holyoke very much, she had gone to Oberlin, a small coed college south of Cleveland. Her sister's husband had gone there, too. Lenore had graduated two years ago next month. And I had gone to Amherst?

Yes, I had gone to Amherst, class of '69, had taken a quick Masters in English at Columbia, had gone to work at the publishing firm of Hunt and Peck, on Madison Avenue, in New York City.

That was a huge firm.

Yes. And for reasons that remain unclear, I was very successful there. I made obscene amounts of money for the House, rose to such dizzying editorial heights that my salary became almost enough to live on. I married Veronica Peck. I moved to Scarsdale, New York, a short distance from the City. I had a son. He was now eighteen.

Eighteen?

Yes. I was forty-two, after all. I was divorced, too, by the way.

I sure didn't look forty-two.

How sweet. I was squirming like this in my seat because I remembered a phone call I just had to make, for the firm.

I am back. I sure made a lot of really quick calls. Who was the Frequent in Frequent and Vigorous, anyway, could she ask.

This was to an extent unclear. Monroe Frequent, I knew, was a fabulously wealthy clothier and inventor. He had invented the beige leisure suit. He had invented the thing that buzzes when a car is started without the seat belts being fastened. He was now, understandably, a recluse. I had been approached by a representative in wrap-around sunglasses. Interest in publishing. Outside New York and environs. Bold, new. Huge amounts of capital to invest. Full partnership for me. A salary out of all proportion to industry norm. If it's assumed, as is reasonable, that our Frequent is Monroe Frequent, then it's becoming clear that Frequent and Vigorous is really just a crude tax dodge.

Golly.

Yes. The only real benefit for me was having the opportunity to start my own quarterly. A literary thing. Enthusiastic agreement to the condition. An air of legitimacy lent to the whole enterprise right off the bat, on Frequent's view.

The *Frequent Review?*

Yes. Last year's issues sold well.

It was a good quarterly.

How kind.

There was also the Norslan account, of course.

Yes, if publishing monosyllabic propaganda praising the virtues of a clearly ineffective and carcinogenic pesticide to be disseminated among the graft-softened bureaucracies of Third World countries could be considered an account, there was the Norslan account. Why on earth did she work as a telephone operator?

Well, she obviously needed money to buy food. Her best friend, Mandible, who had gone to Oberlin too for a while, worked as an operator. Et cetera.

Why didn't she work at Stonecipheco for undoubtedly more money and thus more food?

Food was not the issue. She felt little enough control over her life as it was. A job at Stonecipheco, or a home with her father and her old governess in Shaker Heights, would only localize and intensify feelings of helplessness, loss of individual efficacy of will. I hear me hearing the voice of Dr. Jay. I see me pounding the drum of my courage with a swizzle stick and trying to press my knee against Lenore's under the tiny plastic-wood table, and finding that her legs were not there. Me sweeping the area under the table with my leg, her not being there at all. Me being insanely curious about where her legs were.

I articulated my inability to understand this feeling of lack of control. Surely we all dealt with and reconciled ourselves to a life many of whose features were out of our control. It was part of living in a world full of other people with other interests. I was close to wetting my pants again.

No, that wasn't it. Such a general feeling of dislocation would not be a problem. The problem was a localized feeling. An intuition that her own personal perceptions and actions and volitions were not under her control.

What did "control" mean?

Who knew.

Was this a religious thing? A deterministic crisis? I had had a friend . . .

No. Determinism would be fine if she were able to feel that what determined her was something objective, impersonal, that she were just a tiny part of a large mechanism. If she didn't feel as though she were being used.

Used.

Yes. As if what she did and said and perceived and thought were having some sort of . . . function beyond herself.

Function. Alarm bells. Dr. Jay, after all. A plot thing?

No, not a plot thing, definitely not a plot thing, she wasn't making herself understood. The points of her hair swung like pendula below her chin as she shook her head. My napkin had unfortunately fallen under the table. How clumsy of me. Her legs were there, but curled back, underneath her chair, ankles crossed. Alarm bells or no, I wanted first to reach for an ankle, then to pee.

No, she simply felt—at times, mind you, not all the time, but at sharp and distinct intuitive moments—as if she had no real existence, except for what she said and did and perceived and et cetera, and that these were, it seemed at such times, not really under her control. There was nothing pure.

Hmmm.

Could we talk about something else? Why for instance did I see Dr. Jay?

Oh, just some dream-orientation, general rapping. I had a sort of detached interest in the whole analysis scene, really. My problems were without exception very tiny. Hardly worth discussing at that point. I saw Jay in particular because I liked him least of any of the [very many] Cleveland clinicians with whom I'd rapped. I found an atmosphere of antagonism vital to the whole process, somehow. Lenore too? No, Lenore had been referred to Jay by a physician, friend of the family, old old crony of her great-grandmother, a physician to whom Lenore had gone with a persistent nosebleed problem. She'd stayed ever since. She found Jay irritating but fascinating. Did I find him fascinating? Actually, I went simply to ride the chairs; I found the chairs fun things. A release.

The chairs. She loved the heavy clanking pull as the chain drew her down the track to the Sanctum. She had gone to a fair once with her brother and her governess, and had ridden a rollercoaster that at the start had pulled and clanked like that. Sometimes she really almost expected a drastic rollercoaster plunge when she entered Jay's inner office. [Give it time.] She had gone to the state fair in Columbus once with her sister Clarice and they had gotten lost in the House of Mirrors and Clarice's purse had been stolen by a man who had pretended to be a reflection until the very last moment. It had been scary as hell.

What did her mother do?

She was hanging out, more or less, in Wisconsin.

Were her parents divorced?

Not exactly. Could we go. She had to be at work to give me my paper in the morning, after all. Very late all of a sudden. Had she eaten, would she like something to eat? Ginger ale was surprisingly filling. Her car was in the shop, choke trouble. She had taken the bus to work that day. Well then. She had one of those new cars made by Mattel, also the maker of Hot Wheels. Only slightly larger than same. Really more toy than car. And so on.

I see us driving down the insanely shaped Inner Belt of I-271 South, toward lower East Corinth. I see Lenore in the car keeping her knees together and swinging both legs over to the side, toward me, so that I touch her knee with the back of my hand as I shift.

With my stomach I see disaster. I see me dropping Lenore off at her place, us on the porch of a huge gray house that looked black in the soft darkness of the April night, the house Lenore in a small voice said belonged to an oral surgeon who lent out two rooms to her and Mandible and one to a girl who worked for her sister at CabanaTan. Lenore lived with Mandible. I see her thanking me for the ginger ale and the ride. I see me leaning, lunging over the rustle of the white collar of her dress and kissing her before she has finished saying thank you. I see her kicking me, in the knee, where the knee nerve is, with a sneaker that is revealed to be surprisingly heavy and hard. I see me squealing and holding my knee and sitting down heavily on a step of the porch bristling with nails. I see me howling and holding my knee with one hand and my ass with the other and pitching headlong into an empty flowerbed of soft spring earth. I see Lenore kneeling beside me—how sorry, she didn't know what made her do that, I had surprised her, she had been taken by surprise, oh shit what had she done. I see me with dirt in my nose, I see lights going on in the gray house, in other houses. I am horribly sensitive to pain and almost begin to cry. I see Lenore run through the door of the oral surgeon's house. I see my car tilting ever closer as I hop madly toward it on one leg. I am convinced that I heard the voice of Candy Mandible high overhead.

I knew that I loved Lenore Beadsman when she failed to appear for work the next day. Mandible informed me with wide eyes that Lenore had assumed she was fired. I called Lenore's landlady, the surgeon's wife, a two-hundred-pound Bible-thumping born-again fanatic. I asked her to inform Lenore that she was in fact not fired. I apologized to Lenore. She was incredibly embarrassed. I was embarrassed. Her supervisor, the switchboard supervisor, Walinda Peahen, really did want to fire Lenore, ostensibly for not showing up for work. Walinda dislikes Lenore for her privileged background. I am Walinda's supervisor. I soothed her. Lenore began to hand me my paper as before.

Where are you now?
For there was the magic night later, a magic night, untalkaboutable, when my heart was full of heat and my bottom had healed and I left the office in a trance before six, descended, on wire, saw across the dark empty stone lobby Lenore in her cubicle, alone, for the moment Priethtless, reading, the switchboard mute as usual. I

slipped across the blackly shadowed floor and melted into the white desk-lamp light of the tiny office, behind Lenore at her console. She looked up at me and smiled and looked back down at her book. She was not reading. Through the giant window high over the cubicle a thin spear of the orange-brown light of a Cleveland sunset, saved and bent for a moment by some kindly chemical cloud around the Erieview blackness, fell like a beacon on the soft patch of cream just below Lenore's right ear, on her throat. I bent in my trance and pressed my lips gently to the spot. The sudden beeping of the switchboard mechanism was the beating of my heart, transported into Lenore's purse.

And Lenore Beadsman slowly took her right hand and slid it back up my own neck, cradling with soft hesitant warmth the right side of my jaw and cheek, her long fingers with their dull bitten nails holding me in position against her throat, comforting, her head now tilted left so I could feel the tiny thunder of an artery against my lips. I lived, truly and completely and for the first time in a very long time, in that moment. Lenore said, "Frequent and Vigorous" into the phone she held with her left hand, looking out into the approaching black. The magic of the night was that the magic has lasted. Come to work.

/b/

—Frequent and Vigorous. Frequent and Vigorous.

—Ms. Beadsman?

—Yes?

—David Bloemker.

—Mr. Bloemker!

—Ms. Beadsman, you are at . . . Frequent and Vigorous *Publishing,* are you not?

—Yes, why do—?

—I'm afraid I just dialed your number and spoke to a young lady who proposed to have me pay her for hurting me.

—We're having horrible mix-ups with our phone lines, is all. Have you—?

—No, unfortunately no. There are in addition, we find, one unfindable resident and one staff member.

—Pardon?

—Twenty-six missing, now.

—Sheesh.

—Have you been able to contact your father yet, Ms. Beadsman?

—His line's been busy. He talks on the phone at the office a lot. I was just about to try again. I'll have him call you, I promise.

—Thanks ever so. Again, please allow me to say just how sorry I am.

—OK, go ahead.

—Pardon me?

—Look, I've got a call waiting, I can see. I have to go. I'll be in touch.

—Thank you.

—Frequent and Vigorous.

—What are you . . . wearing?

—Excuse me?

—Are you . . . warmer than average, shall we say?

—Sir, this is the publishing firm of Frequent and Vigorous. Are you trying to reach Cleveland Dial-a-Darling?

—Oh. Well, yes. How embarrassing.

—Not at all. Shall I give you that number, though it may not work?

—Wait a minute. What are your own thoughts on pudding?

—Goodbye.

—Click.

—What a day. . . .

—Stonecipheco Baby Food Products.

—President's office, please, Lenore Beadsman calling.

—One moment.

—. . . At least it's not busy.

—President's office, Foamwhistle.

—Sigurd. Lenore.

—Lenore. What's goopin'?

—May I please speak to my father?

—Impossible.

—Emergency.

—Not here.

—Shit on a *twig*.

—Sorry.

—Listen, big emergency. He had someone ask me to call him right away. Family emergency.

—He's really unreachable right now, Lenore.

—Where is he?

—Annual summit with Gerber's. It's August, after all.

—Rats.

—Trying to mess with the old creamed-fruit demand curve.

—Sigurd, it could literally be life or death.

—Phoneless, sweet thing. You know the rules. You know how Gerber is.

—How long?

—Not sure. Not more than a couple, three days.

—Where are they?

—Not allowed to say.

—*Sigurd.*

—Corfu. Some dark and secluded spot on Corfu. All I know. I'll be murdered if he knows I told. I'll end up in a thousand jars of the whipped lamb, while the little Foamwhistles ironically starve.

—When did he leave?

—Yesterday, right after tennis with Spaniard, about eleven.

—How come you're not with him, secretarying? Who'll make his Manhattans?

—Roughing it. Didn't want me. Just him and Gerber, he said. Man to man. They may arm-wrestle, who knows? Alternately poking each other in the ribs, singing Amherst songs, trying to sink knives in each other's backs. A market-share struggle is not a pretty sight.

—Damn it, he told me to call him, and this was like this morning. He's got to . . . hey, you haven't heard from Dad's grandmother, have you?

—Lenore? No, thank God. Is she OK?

—Yes. Listen, I'm desperate, here. When exactly do you think he'll be back?

—There's an enormous skull on my tentative calendar in the square marked three days from now. That can only mean one thing.

—Hot spit in a hole.

—Listen, seriously, if there's anything I can do . . .

—Sweet Sigurd. My thing's lighting. I have another call. I have to go.

—Stay in touch.

—Bye . . . wait!

—What?

—What about Rummage? Did he take Rummage?

—Hey now, I don't know. That's definitely a thought. Try over at Rummage and Naw. You have the number?

—Are you kidding? Numbers I've got.

—So long.

—Frequent and Vigorous.

/c/

Which is of course not and never to say that things have been unceasingly rosy. My inability to be truly inside of and surrounded by Lenore Beadsman arouses in me the purely natural reactive desire to have her inside of and contained by me. I am possessive. I want to own her, sometimes. And this of course does not sit well with a girl thoroughly frightened of the possibility that she does not own herself.

I am madly jealous. Lenore has a quality that attracts men. It is not a normal quality, or a quality that can be articulated. ". . . ," he said, about to try to articulate it. "Vulnerability" is of course a bad word. "Playfulness" will not do. These both denote, and so fail. Lenore has the quality of a sort of game about her. There. Since that makes very little sense it may be right. Lenore soundlessly invites one to play a game consisting of involved attempts to find out the game's own rules. How about that. The rules of the game are Lenore, and to play is to be played. Find out the rules of my game, she laughs, with or at. Over the board fall shadows like the teeth of fences: the Erieview Tower, Lenore's father, Dr. Jay, Lenore's great-grandmother.

Lenore sometimes sings in the shower, loudly and well, Lord knows she gets enough practice, and I will hunch on the toilet or

lean against the sink and read submissions and smoke clove cigarettes, a habit I appropriated from Lenore herself.

Lenore's relationship with her great-grandmother is not a whole-
some thing. I've met the woman once or twice, mercifully short
appointments in a room so hot it was literally hard to breathe. She
is a small, birdish, sharp-featured thing, desperately old. She is not
spry. One is not even vaguely tempted ever to say "Bless her heart."
She is a hard woman, a cold woman, a querulous and thoroughly
selfish woman, one with vast intellectual pretensions and, I suppose,
probably commensurate gifts. She indoctrinates Lenore. She and
Lenore "talk for hours." Rather Lenore listens. There is something
sour and unsavory about it. Lenore Beadsman will not tell me anything important about her relationship with Lenore Beadsman. She
says nothing to Dr. Jay either, unless the little bastard is holding
back one last card on me.

It's clear, though, that this is a great-grandmother with Views. I
believe she is harming Lenore, and I believe she knows that she is,
and I believe she does not really care. She has, from what little I
can gather, convinced Lenore that she is in possession of some words
of tremendous power. No, really. Not things, or concepts. Words.
The woman is apparently obsessed with words. I neither am nor
wish to be entirely clear on the matter, but apparently she was some
sort of phenomenon in college and won a place in graduate study
at Cambridge, no small feat for a woman, in the twenties; but in
any event, there she studied classics and philosophy and who knows
what else under a mad crackpot genius named Wittgenstein, who
believed that everything was words. Really. If your car would not
start, it was apparently to be understood as a language problem. If
you were unable to love, you were lost in language. Being consti-
pated equalled being clogged with linguistic sediment. To me the
whole thing smacks strongly of bullshit, but old Lenore Beadsman
quite definitely bought it, and has had seventy years to simmer and
distill the brew she pours in Lenore's heat-softened porches every
week. She teases Lenore with a certain strange book, the way an
exceptionally cruel child might tease an animal with a bit of food,
intimating that the book has some special significance for Lenore,
but refusing to tell her what it is, "yet," or to show her the book,
"yet." Words and a book and a belief that the world is words and

Lenore's conviction that her own intimate personal world is only of, neither by nor for, her. Something is not right. She is in pain. I would like the old lady to die in her sleep.

Her daughter is in the same Home, over twenty years younger, a beautiful old woman, I've seen her, clear brown eyes and soft cheeks the color of a gently blooming rose and hair like liquid silver. An absolute idiot with Alzheimer's, unaware of who or where she is, a drooler out of moist, beautiful, perfectly preserved lips. Lenore hates her; both Lenores hate her. I do not know why this is so.

Lenore's great-grandmother's hair is white as cotton and hangs in bangs and curls down on either side of her head nearly to meet in points below her chin, like the mandibles of an insect.

Often we'll lie together and Lenore will ask me to tell her a story. "A story, please," she'll say. I will tell her what people tell to me, what people ask me to like and allow others to like, what they send me in their brown manilas and scrawled stamped return envelopes and cover-letters signed "Aspiringly Yours," at the *Frequent Review*. Telling stories that are not my own is at this point what I do, after all. With Lenore I am completely and entirely myself.

But I get sad. I miss my son. I do not miss Veronica. Veronica was beautiful. Lenore is pretty, and she has a quality we've decided is game-related. Veronica was beautiful. But a beauty like a frozen dawn, dazzling and achingly remote. She was cool and firm and smooth to the touch, decorated with soft, chilly blond hair wherever appropriate, graceful but not delicate, pleasant but not kind. Veronica was a seamless and flawless joy to behold and hold . . . exactly up to the point where one's interests conflicted with hers. Between Veronica and all others there lay the echoing chasm of Interest, a chasm impossible to bridge because it turned out to have only one side. The Veronica side. Which is, I have come to see, simply another way of saying that Veronica was incapable of love. At least of loving me.

Physically the marriage went from being a horror to being nothing at all. I cannot think, much less tell, of our wedding night, when all manner of shams were exposed. Finally Veronica came to accept and even appreciate the situation; it saved her effort and the tangy embarrassment of being embarrassed for me. To my knowledge she did not go elsewhere. Her existence, like her beauty and real worth, was intrinsically aesthetic, not physical or emotional. Veronica would be most comfortable, I remain convinced, as a human exhibit, motionless in the cool bright corner of a public hall, surrounded by a square of red velvet no-touch ropes, hearing only whispered voices and heels on tile. Veronica is now living on my support checks and preparing, I am told, to marry a quite old and thoroughly likeable man who owns a New York company involved in the manufacture of power-plant instrumentation. Go with God.

I miss my son, though. Which is not to say that I miss an eighteen-year-old Fordham aesthete whose long nails glitter with transparent polish and who wears pants without pockets. I miss my *son*. My child. He was a magical child, I'm thoroughly convinced. Special, special qualities. A special and hilarious infant. Veronica drew the first of many lines at changing diapers, so I would usually change our baby. I would change his diapers, and often as not, as he lay on his back, with little legs of dough kicking, as I removed soggy old hot or ominously heavy diaper and manipulated crinkly new plastic Pamper, he would urinate up onto my hanging necktie, a pale, sweetly thin jet, and there would be smells of powder, and my tie would be heavy at my throat, and would drip, and we would laugh together, toothless he and sad, sleepy I, at my urine-soaked tie. I still own some of these ties, stiff and hard and dull; they hang on little toothed racks and clunk against my closet door when the winds of memory blow through the dark places in my apartment.

This was a boy with an intimate but strange relation to the world around him, a dark-eyed silent boy who from the age of independent decision and movement reflected the world in his own special, wobbled mirror. Vance was for me a reflection. Vance would act out History and Event inside his own child's world.

At a very young age, very young, Vance would choose dark clothes, tie string around his head, put candy cigarettes in his mouth, and launch sudden, stealthy raids into rooms of the house, breathing hard and whirling, beating the air with his fists, finally diving behind furniture, crawling on his belly, clawing the air with a hooked finger. A lightning raid on the kitchen—the cat's food would disappear. A silent assault on my den—in the leg of my desk would appear the vertical scratch of a pin. A careless squad of patio ants would walk into ambush and be efficiently obliterated via tennis-ball bombardment as Veronica and I looked on and at each other over gin-and-tonics. We were puzzled and frightened, and Veronica suspected motor dysfunction, until we noticed Vance's eyes one night during dinner as on the evening news, correspondents brought us another installment of the death throes of the war in Indochina. Vance's unblinking eyes and soundless breathing. And as Kissinger left Paris triumphant, a home in Scarsdale demilitarized.

Sometimes in those days too we would find Vance alone in a room, facing the blank corner in which he stood, both arms stiffly upraised and two fingers of each hand out in Peace-signs. It began to become clear that, through the miracle of televsion, Vance Vigorous enjoyed a special relationship with Richard Nixon. As Watergate wore on in brilliant color, Vance took to furtive looks, pinched whiteness around the bridge of his nose, refusals to explain his whereabouts or give reasons for what he did. My tape recorder—admittedly tapeless and not even plugged in but nevertheless my tape recorder—began to appear places: under the dining room table at dinner, in the back seat of the car, under our bed, in the drawer of the mail table. Vance would, when confronted, look blankly at the tape recorder and at us. Then he would pretend to look at his watch. After the resignation, Vance was sick in bed for a week, with very real symptoms. We were frightened. There followed years in which he silently but with formal expression forgave every apparent wrong done him by us and the world; would fall and cover his chest with his hands at the slightest criticism; would flip backwards off the couch in the living room and land nicely on both feet, putting cracks in the ceiling each time; would wear his tiny suit to school and enlist a follower to carry the tiny briefcase he insisted we give him for Christmas; would walk blindfolded through rooms littered with torn drawings of the flag. Who knew what most of this was. This was the world the monadic Vance Vigorous received and mirrored through himself. I preferred him to the world, really.

He was a great athlete as a child, a maker of solid clanks with aluminum Little League baseball bats, heavy whumps with hard autumn footballs, gentle tissued whispers with the nets of basketball hoops. He could run sweeps in children's football, could run so fast and with such liquidly curving, teasing grace that he could make other boys fall down just trying to touch him. Feel what I felt in my chest, the little man in the beret, long coat whipped by the wind, watching the fruit of my loins. Vance was a boy who could make touchdowns from far away, make PeeWee mothers yell shrilly and release plastic-wrapped hair to clap into my ear, small-sounding outdoor claps, away on the wind like tattered things, as were the thuds of my leather gloves. The one little boy in those games on whom the helmet did not seem huge and hilariously out of place. A gracious blond black-eyed boy who never bragged and always helped others to their feet and gave credit where credit was due, before returning home, silent in the car beside me, to play Iranian hostage in his bedroom.

His last great historical act came when he was eleven, as school was beginning. A jumbo jet was brought down over a sea by a Russian fighter, killing congressmen and nuns and children, sending shoes and shirtsleeves and paperbacks and eyeglass frames floating onto the northern shores of Japan. Vance would stare for hours at magazine pictures of the plane's passengers, photos served up in large and vivid detail, family snapshots against green backyard colors, stiff yearbook photos, three-for-a-quarter shots of cheerleaders in Groucho noses; he looked at the eyes of the people in the pictures. One day soon after, he climbed onto the roof of the house and jumped off. All without a sound. Our house had only a basement and one story. The fall was twelve feet and sprained his ankle very thoroughly. Vance apologized. The next day he jumped off the roof again and broke a foot. He was taken to the hospital and moved from floor to floor, and was finally taken to a doctor off Central Park who somehow in one visit "cured" Vance of whatever ailed him. Vance never jumped or raided or fell or mimicked again. Veronica was very pleased. I had never thought there was anything particularly wrong with Vance at all, though of course jumping from high places was unacceptable. I was sad.

We entered a sad, sad time. As Vance grew older, I grew younger and sadder. Veronica retreated ever farther into her crystal case of polite indifference. Vance began, at her urging, listlessly to date girls, never went anywhere with one more than once, as far as I could tell. Vance waited silently for puberty and puberty waited until Vance was fifteen; he lost his size and strength advantage, and there were no more cold windy afternoons on crunchy sidelines. Only sounds of music from under Vance's door, and colored chalk on his fingers, and black circles under his black eyes, and the beautiful, beautiful drawings—flat and clear and sad as our cement drive, smooth and clean and as devoid of interstices as his mother—and the softly persistent sweet smell of marijuana from my son's basement room. Vance is now at Fordham, studying art. I have not talked to Vance in almost a year. I do not know why this is so.

I miss Vance with a fierceness we reserve for the absent who cannot return. Vance no longer exists. He was pithed in a Park Avenue office in 1983 by a man who charged us a hundred dollars for the procedure. Vance is, I happen to know for a fact, a homosexual, and probably a drug addict, washed and turning slowly in the odorless breezes of his mother's cold Scarsdale breath, producing his flat and soulless perfect chalk drawings with greater and greater precision. I have received one: a startled me in the lawn with my rake, Veronica appearing incongruously over my shoulder, carrying something to drink on a black tray. The picture was sent me in a brown envelope, in care of the *Frequent Review*, and so not even opened for weeks.

I miss Lenore, sometimes. I miss everyone. I can remember being young and feeling a thing and identifying it as homesickness, and then thinking well now that's odd, isn't it, because I *was* home, all the time. What on earth are we to make of that?

I miss and love with all my purple fist a strange girl from a flamboyant and frightening family, in many ways a flamboyant and frightening girl, perched high in the crow's nest of the Frequent and Vigorous vessel, scanning gray electrical expanses for the lonely spout of a legitimate telephone call. I am lately informed by Ms. Peahen that the possibility of such a call is, now, thanks to some malfunction in the phone system of which we are a part, even more remote than before. As I sit here, the block of the Erieview shadow slowly dips my office in liquid darkness. Halfway, now. It is one o'clock. My lights turn the shadow half of the office to licorice, and make the half still under the influence of the sun a glinting yellow-white horror at which I may not look. Lenore, I shall try once more, and if you are not here I will assume the worst, and will succumb finally to the charms of Moses Cleaveland, who even now grins and beckons whitely from the pavement six floors below. This is our last chance.

/d/

As Lenore sifted through a tidal wave of misdirected calls and got ready to try to call Karl Rummage over at Rummage and Naw, Walinda Peahen appeared in the cubicle behind the switchboard counter.

"Hi Walinda," Lenore said. Walinda ignored her and began to look through the Legitimate Call Log, a desperately thin notebook with one or two pages filled. Judith Prietht had hit her Position Busy button and was talking to a girlfriend on the private line.

"What these messages for you in the Log in Candy's writing?" Walinda turned and looked down at Lenore from under green eye shadow.

"I guess if they're legitimate then they're messages for me," said Lenore.

"Girl I ain't playin' with you, so I wish you'd learn not to play. You supposed to be here at ten. There's messages for you here at eleven and eleven-thirty."

"I was unavoidably detained. Candy said she'd cover."

"That flakey Frequent and Vigorous girl is getting chewed out by her supervisor," Judith Prietht was saying into her phone, watching.

"Girl detained where? How do I look if I think somebody workin' and they not?"

"I had to go to the nursing home."

"What time she get here?" Walinda asked Judith Prietht.

"Look, I don't want to say anything, I don't want to get her in trouble," Judith said to Walinda. Into the phone she said, "The supervisor wanted me to say when she got here, but I said I wouldn't, I didn't want to get her in trouble."

"I got here at like a little after twelve."

"Like a little after twelve. Girl that's over two hours late."

"It was an emergency."

"What kind of goddamn emergency?"

Judith Prietht had stopped talking into the phone and was watching intently.

"I can't tell you right at the moment, Walinda," Lenore said.

"Girl, you gone, you done, I don't care who you doin' up, you can't play. You done played the last time."

The console began to beep, the light with a quick, in-house flash.

"Don't even get it, you gone," Walinda said to Lenore. She reached for the phone and Accessed. "Operator . . ." Her eyebrows plunged. "Yes she is, Mr. Vigorous. Hold on one moment please." She held her hand over the phone as she passed it to Lenore. "I don't care what you get the little pecker to say, you gone," she hissed.

"She's really in trouble, it looks like, for a change," said Judith into her phone.

"Hi Rick."

6 1990

/a/

"How are your steaks, tonight?"

"Our steaks, sir, are if I may say so quite simply superb. Only the choicest cuts of beef, carefully selected and even more carefully aged, cooked to perfection as perfection is defined by your instructions, served with your choice of potato and vegetable and richly delicious dessert."

"Sounds scrumptious."

"Yes."

"I'll have nine."

"Pardon me?"

"Bring me nine steaks, please."

"You want *nine* steak dinners?"

"Please."

"And who, sir, may I ask is going to eat them?"

"You see anybody else sitting here? I'm going to eat them."

"And how on earth are you going to do that, sir?"

"Well, gee, let's see, I think I'll use my right hand to cut, tonight. I'll put pieces into my mouth, I'll masticate, acidic elements in my saliva will begin breaking down the muscle fiber. I'll swallow. Et cetera. Bring 'em on!"

"Sir, nine steaks would make anyone sick."

"Look at me. Look at this stomach. Do you think I'll get sick? No way. Come here—no, really, come around and look at this stomach. Let me lift up my shirt . . . here. See how much I can grab with my hand? I can't even sit close to the table. Have you ever seen anything so hugely disgusting in your whole life?"

"I've seen bigger stomachs."

"You're just being polite, you just want a tip. You'll get your tip, after you've brought me nine steak dinners, with perfection being defined as medium-rare, which is to say pink yet firm. And don't forget the rolls."

"Sir, this is simply beyond my range of experience. I've never served any one individual nine simultaneous orders on my own authority. I could get in horrible trouble. What if, for example, you have an embolism, God forbid? You could rupture organs."

"Didn't I say to look at me? Can't you tell what I am? Listen to me very carefully. I am an obese, grotesque, prodigal, greedy, gourmandizing, gluttonous *pig*. Is this not clear? I am more hog than human. There is room, physical room, for *you* in my stomach. Do you hear? You see before you a swine. An eating fiend of unlimited capacity. Bring me meat."

"Have you not eaten in a very long time? Is that it?"

"Look, you're beginning to bother me. I could bludgeon you with my belly. I am also, allow me to tell you, more than a little well-to-do. Do you see that Building over there, the one with the lit windows, in the shadow? I own that Building. I could buy this restaurant and have you terminated. I could and perhaps will buy this entire block, including that symbolically tiny Weight Watchers establishment across the street. See it? With the door and windows so positioned as to form a grinning, leering, hollow-cheeked face? It is within my financial power to buy that place, and to fill it with steaks, fill it with red steak, all of which I would and will eat. The door would under this scenario be jammed with a gnawed bone; not a single little smug psalm-singing baggy-skinned apostate from the cause of adiposity would be able to enter. They would pound on the door, pound. But the bone would hold. They'd lack the bulk to burst through. Their mouths and eyes would be wide as they pressed against the glass. I would demolish, physically crush the huge scale at the end of the brightly lit nave at the back of the place under a weight of food. The springs would jut out. Jut. What a delicious series of thoughts. May I see a wine list?"

"Weight Watchers?"

"*Garçon*, what you have before you is a dangerous thing, I warn you. Human beings act in their own interest. Huge, crazed swine do not. My wife informed me a certain time-interval ago that if I did not lose weight, she would leave me. I have not lost weight, as a matter of fact I have gained weight, and thus she is leaving. Q.E.D. And A-1, don't forget the A-1."

"But sir, surely with more time . . ."

"There is no more time. Time does not exist. I ate it. It's in here, see? See the jiggle? That's time, jiggling. Run, run away, fetch me my platter of fat, my nine cattle, or I'll envelop you in a chin and fling you at the wall!"

"Shall I fetch the *maître d'*, sir? To confer?"

"By all means, fetch him. But warn him against getting too close. He will be encompassed instantly, before he has time to squeak. Tonight I will eat. Hugely, and alone. For I am now hugely alone. I will eat, and juice might very well spurt into the air around me, and if anyone comes too near, I will snarl and jab at them with my fork—like *this*, see?"

"Sir, really!"

"Run for your very life. Fetch something to placate me. I'm going to grow and grow, and fill the absence that surrounds me with the horror of my own gelatinous presence. Yin and Yang. Ever growing, waiter. Run!"

"Right away, sir!"

"Some breadsticks might have been nice, too, do you hear? What kind of place is this, anyway?"

/b/

"I insist that you tell me."

"Could you just possibly wait, for about nine tenths of a second, while I decide *how* to tell you?"

"What does deciding have to do with it? There's a thing, and here am I, tell me the thing, *voilà*. Clearly there's something bothering you."

"Look, I'm obviously going to tell you, OK? Don't have a spasm.

It's just that the thing I have to tell is, *a*, unbelievably weird, and I don't even really understand it . . ."

"So let's have both our powers of understanding leveled at the thing, together. Whose power of understanding and persuasion soothed a potentially disastrously pissed-off Walinda for you, after all?"

". . . and *b*, is something I was told not to tell, so I have to figure out a way to tell you in a way that's going to least compromise my promise not to tell, and least make anything bad happen to the person whom the thing concerns."

"Clear as a bell. As clear as this water glass, Lenore."

"Don't flick your water glass. Look, you said this place had really great steaks, and you said you were starving, so why don't you just concentrate on the impending arrival of your steak, which I sort of think is coming right now?"

". . . ."

"Looks super, thank you. Rick, would we care for wine?"

"Yes."

"What kind?"

". . . ."

"What *kind*?"

". . . ."

"We'll maybe just have a bottle of your house red, if that's OK. . . . You are a baby. You have the understanding and compassion of a very very small child, sometimes."

"Lenore, it's simply that I love you. You know that. Every fiber of your being is loved by every fiber of my being. The thought of things about you, concerning you, troubling you, that I don't know about, makes blood run from my eyes, on the inside."

"Interesting image. Look, try your steak. You said you were in a position to eat a horse."

". . . ."

"Does that hit the spot?"

"My spot is reeling under the force of the blow. Now I insist that you tell me."

". . . ."

"Does this have to do with your trying to call that Rummage person while I was busy keeping Walinda from forcing me to choose between her services and yours, even though she was hired by Frequent himself? Shall I simply get up and go call Rummage right now?"

"He's not there. He's not here."

". . . ."

"He's apparently out of the country, with my father."

"Doing what?"

"I can't tell you."

"Is this the same 'I can't tell you,' or a different one?"

"Different."

"Deeply hurt and pissed off, now."

"Look, can I just assure you that I'll tell you later, and not tell you now, and think, and eat my salad? Would that be OK? I'll stay at your place tonight, which I actually really want to do, even though I told Candy I'd be back home tonight, and we'll talk. I really do need your advice. Yours especially, Rick. I just have to figure out what's going on myself, first, for a second, OK?"

"It's really quite bad, and it has to do with the nursing home, and no one has passed away."

"Eat your steak."

"I only—"

"Rick, who's that?"

"Where?"

"Over there, by himself, at that table?"

"You don't know who that is?"

"No."

"That's Norman Bombardini. Our landlord and Building-mate, of Bombardini Company and skeleton eye-socket fame."

"He's a large person."

"He is large."

"Gigantic, is more like it. Why's he snarling and gnawing on the edge of the table?"

"Good Lord. My understanding, which I get mostly from Warshaver over at the club, is that these are just not good times for Norman. Problems with his wife. Problems with his health."

"He looks like he really needs to lose some weight."

"I guess he's tried, off and on, for years. An interesting man. Warshaver hints around that his company is on the verge of a real—"

"Oh my God."

"What?"

"Look at what the waiter's bringing."

"Good Lord."

"There is just no way someone can eat all that."

"Poor Norman."

"Oh, that's sick. He could at least wait till the waiter put it on
the *table*."

"Must be really hungry."

"Nobody's that hungry. And did he just try to bite the waiter?
Was that an attempted bite?"

"Must be the light in here."

"He's really making a mess."

"I've never seen him like this."

"He's getting juice on the people at the other tables. That lady
just put her napkin on her head!"

"Is that a napkin? It's really quite fetching."

"You're horrible. Look, they're having to leave."

"Well, it looked like they were almost done, anyway."

"Well I'm not. I'm not going to look anymore."

"Probably wise."

" . . . ."

" . . . ."

"But I can't really help hearing, now, can I?"

"Unfortunately not."

"God, look at that, he's almost done with all that. He has eaten
a literal mountain of food in about two minutes."

"Well, a lot of it's on the floor, too, after all."

"I think I'm going to be physically ill."

"I'm frankly worried. This has almost taken my mind off your
present lack of trust in me. Norman is not right."

"How come I've never seen him? I see his car all the time, in
that space."

"I think there are size problems with the front door. He has a
special entrance on the east side. Elevator. Reinforced cables."

"Wow."

"...."

"Did he finish all that? Is he finished?"

"He's certainly slowing down. I sense something missing, though. See the way he's looking around?"

"Dear God, Rick, look at the floor."

"Dessert. That's what's missing. And here comes the waiter."

"Laws of nature will be violated if he eats all that and doesn't die."

"Lenore, listen, I think we should go over and see if there's anything we can do."

"Are you joking? I think that's an insane person, over there. I don't think it was the light, I think he really tried to bite the waiter. See the way the waiter's just sort of tossing the desserts onto the table from a safe distance?"

"Norman's sated, though, you can tell. The desserts are going at a normal rate, more or less."

"You've still got a lot of your own steak left, you know."

"The steak will keep. I feel vicariously gorged, anyway."

"What are you doing? Are you kidding? You've got to be kidding."

"Come on."

"Big mistake, Rick. Not something I wish to do."

"Be a sport."

"How are we going to get over there?"

"Serpentine. Follow me. Watch the—"

"I see it."

"Norman?"

"Who's that?"

"Rick Vigorous, Norman."

"Not a good time, Vigorous. The beast is at trough, as you can see."

"Norman, we were just at the other table, there, just beyond the vegetables, see?"

"...."

"... And thought we'd come over to see if anything in particular might be the tiniest bit wrong, and to introduce this young lady I'm with, who works in the Building, and whom you may or may not know."

"I don't think I know you, no."

"Norman Bombardini may I present Ms. Lenore Beadsman, Lenore, Mr. Bombardini."

"Pleased to meet you."

"Beadsman. Not related to Stonecipher Beadsman, by any chance?"

"Lenore is Mr. Beadsman's daughter."

"Daughter. Interesting. Stonecipheco Baby Foods. Not a bad line of products, really. A bit soft and runny for my taste, of course. . . ."

"Well, it's infant food, really, Norman."

". . . but any port in the proverbial storm. Please feel free to sit down."

"Shall we?"

"Ummm . . ."

"Let's."

"Just put the plates anywhere at all. You probably don't want to sit in that chair, at all, Ms. Beadsman, I predict."

"Not really."

"Here's another one."

". . . ."

"So, Norman."

"I don't suppose either of you would care for a bit of eclair?"

"No thank you."

"No thanks, Norman, really."

"Well, it's just as well, because you can't have any. They're mine. I paid for them and they're mine."

"No one disputes that."

"Staked your claim pretty thoroughly, I'd say."

"Ms. Beadsman, you're not one of those spunky girls, are you? One of those girls with spunk? My wife has spunk. Or rather she had spunk. Or rather she was my wife. Spunk is apt to make me uncontrollably ravenous, thus representing not an insignificant hazard to the possessor thereof."

"Lenore is comparatively devoid of spunk, really."

"Thanks, Rick."

"So, Norman. How are things?"

"Things are huge and grotesque and disgusting, Vigorous; surely you can see that."

"Pretty keen analysis, really."

"Careful, Ms. Beadsman. That was spunky, in my opinion."

"Norman, I couldn't help noticing that you're having rather more for dinner than seems completely natural. Or healthy."

"I'd go along with that, Vigorous."

"So I presume something is the matter."

"Astute as always."

". . . ."

"You want to know the story? I'd be happy to tell you. I think I have just enough caloric energy stored up to make it through the telling of the tale. It's short. I am monstrously fat. I am a glutton. My wife was disgusted and repulsed. She gave me six months to lose one hundred pounds. I joined Weight Watchers . . . see it there, right across the street, that gaunt storefront? This afternoon was the big six-month weigh-in. So to speak. I had gained almost seventy pounds in the six months. An errant Snickers bar fell out of the cuff of my pants and rolled against my wife's foot as I stepped on the scale. The scale over there across the street is truly an ingenious device. One preprograms the desired new weight into it, and if one has achieved or gone below that new low weight, the scale bursts into recorded whistles and cheers and some lively marching-band tune. Apparently, tiny flags protrude from the top and wave mechanically back and forth. A failure—see for instance mine—results in a flatulent dirge of disappointed and contemptuous tuba. To the strains of the latter my wife left, the establishment, me, on the arm of a svelte yogurt distributor whom I am even now planning to crush, financially speaking, first thing tomorrow morning. Ms. Beadsman, you will find an eclair on the floor to the left of your chair. Could you perhaps manipulate it onto this plate with minimal chocolate loss and pass it to me."

". . . ."

"Marvelous."

"Still, though, Norman, I know you to be a highly intelligent man. Surely turbulence with the wife is no reason to eat like this. To self-destruct. A purported failure at Weight Watchers . . . to hell with Weight Watchers!"

"No, Vigorous; as usual, no. I have come to see this afternoon that Weight Watchers—and diet enterprises, diet books, diet personalities, and diet cults in general—that they are almost inconceivably deep and profound things. They have tapped into a universe-view with which I find myself in complete agreement."

"A universe-view? Norman, I—"

"I see you're interested, Ms. Beadsman. Have I interested you?"

"Sort of."

"No small feat, I imagine, to interest a spunky, sharp-haired girl."

". . . ."

"Yin and Yang, Vigorous. Yin and Yang. Self and Other."

". . . ."

"Weight Watchers holds as a descriptive axiom the transparently true fact that for each of us the universe is deeply and sharply and completely divided into for example in my case, me, on one side, and everything else, on the other. This for each of us exhaustively defines the whole universe, Vigorous. The whole universe. Self and Other."

"Sounds uncontroversial to me, Norman."

"Yes and also not only that each of our universes has this feature, but that we are by nature without exception *aware* of the fact that the universe is so divided, into Self, on one hand, and Other, on the other. Exhaustively divided. It's part of our consciousness."

"Okey dokey."

"And then they hold as a *prescriptive* axiom the undoubtedly equally true and inarguable fact that we each ought to desire our own universe to be as *full* as possible, that the Great Horror consists in an empty, rattling personal universe, one where one finds oneself with Self, on one hand, and vast empty lonely spaces before Others begin to enter the picture at all, on the other. A non-full universe. Loneliness, Vigorous. Weight Watchers sees itself as a warrior in the great war against loneliness. Is that not noble? One moment. You, waiter! I wouldn't say no to a mint, you know! Feel free to bring some mints! Excuse me. Loneliness. Balance. The emptier one's universe is, the worse it is. This we all surely accept. Do either of you not accept this?"

". . . ."

". . . ."

"Now, Weight Watchers perceives the problem as one involving the need to have as much Other around as possible, so that the relation is one of minimum Self to maximum Other. This is a valid though, as I've seen this afternoon, by no means exclusive way to attack the problem. Are you getting my drift, Vigorous?"

"Well, a drift is such a—"

"It occurs to me that I couldn't care less. A full universe, Vigorous, Ms. Beadsman. We each need a full universe. Weight Watchers and their allies would have us systematically decrease the Self-component of the universe, so that the great Other-set will be physically attracted to the now more physically attractive Self, and rush in to fill the void caused by that diminution of Self. Certainly not incorrect, but just as certainly only *half* of the range of valid solutions to the full-universe problem. Is my drift getting palpable? Just as in genetic engineering, Vigorous. There is always more than one solution."

"I think I—"

"An autonomously full universe, Vigorous. An autonomously full universe, Ms. Beadsman."

"What should I do with these mints, here?"

"I'll just take the bowl, thank you. Rather than diminishing Self to entice Other to fill our universe, we may also of course obviously choose to fill the universe with *Self*."

"You mean . . . ?"

"Yes. I plan to grow to infinite size."

"Do I recall saying big mistake? Did I mention decks not being completely full?"

"Lenore, please. Norman, friend, really. A universe-view is one thing. No one can grow to infinite size."

"Has anyone ever tried?"

"Not to my knowledge, no, but . . ."

"Then do me the kindness not to shrilly monger finite failure until I've tried. No one had ever been able to give butter life, either, but . . ."

"What was that?"

"Nothing. To be ignored. A slip of the tongue."

" . . ."

"Yes and tonight Project Total Yang begins. I am going to grow and grow and grow. There will of course eventually cease to be room for anyone else in the universe at all, which I'm afraid will also mean the two of you, for which I apologize, but say also tough titty."

"Really, enjoyed it a lot, we'll have to do it again. We better go, my salad is attracting a fly, over there, I can see."

"Looks yummy."

"Unfortunately it's mine and not yet part of your universe, at least temporarily. Rick, should we just wade on back over . . . ?"

"Norman, I simply would not be honest if I didn't say right up front that I'm worried about you, about your emotional outlook, given what you've told me of your day today, with its attendant strains."

"Won't be an outlook, eventually. Only an inlook. I just hope I can financially crush that yogurt distributor before there ceases to be any meaningful difference between him and me. The light green mints are particularly good here, I think. You may if you wish each have one."

" . . . ."

" . . . ."

"Really quite good. Of course one other advantage of my approach to the Yin/Yang problem is that dieting becomes the worst possible thing to do. I find dieting makes me insanely angry at everything. Dieting makes me want to murder everyone around me."

"Instead of merely appropriating their space."

"You are not un-sharp, are you? Rather like your father. Your father whips a mean carrot. I could, of course, leave selected small corners of the universe unfilled for those who might arouse in me feelings of affection and attachment."

"I'll get back to you, probably, if things begin to crowd."

"Norman, friend, simply know that I am around and available should you ever wish to talk, I'll not say chew the fat, or perhaps should you simply wish to pal around. I am around for you, Norman."

"Your crowning virtue, Vigorous. Your best feature. You are always around."

"At least temporarily."

"Lenore, please."

"Ms. Beadsman, I am coming to like you, unless it's simply the inevitably favorable comparison of anyone with Vigorous here. Have you ever had intercourse with someone soon to be of infinite size?"

"On that note, I think, I'll just be going. . . . Rick?"

"Right. Norman?"

"Goodbye, Vigorous. Enjoy that Self while you can."

"I think the same route back would be . . ."

"No problem."

"Should we finish? Are you hungry?"

"Are you kidding? Let's just go. Drop me off, and I'll take a quick shower and grab some things and try to get Candy to drop me, and you can drive me back in the morning. I don't feel like squeezing into my car tonight."

"Right. There is of course still the issue of your not telling me an important thing."

"Tell tell tell."

"I could call Vern Raring at the switchboard and see if he knows."

"Good luck getting him instead of like Enrique the cheesemaker."

"Lines. I forgot. Walinda was livid. I'm sure all that made for quite a day, what with you being worried about untellable matters, et cetera."

"The badness of this day has been enormous."

"As it were."

"Not funny at all. That man has waddled around the bend."

"Well, look, he's trying to leave."

"Don't envy that busboy one bit."

"Hell of a check, I'll bet."

"I'll sure never park in his space."

"Here, allow me."

". . . ."

/a/

Lenore Beadsman was in possession of the following items. One of two square bedrooms with polished wood floors and inoperative fireplaces on the third floor of an enormous gray house belonging to a Cleveland oral surgeon, in East Corinth. Three large windows, two facing west, all so clean they squeaked, only one open, because only one had a screen. From the windows a view of the outside at the right-hand edge of which the tight seam of geometric suburban ground and dim sky was punctured by the far thin teeth of Cleveland. Windows through which late in the day came a sustained blast of pumpkin-colored Cleveland sunset. Windowsills that were really window shelves, and jutted out so far from the low window-bottoms they could be sat on, and were, although there were nails and sharp perpendicular paint chips, which problem was solved by the placement of black corduroy cushions, which Lenore also owned, on the sills.

A chest of drawers from Mooradian's in which were clothes and on top of which, leaning on a triangular cardboard support that folded out of its back, was a photo of Lenore, her sister, her two brothers, her great-grandmother, Lenore Beadsman, and her great-grandfather, Stonecipher Beadsman, grouped around a deep wooden globe of the earth in a pretend den in a photographer's concrete studio. Taken in 1977, when Lenore was eleven and temporarily minus front teeth. There was also, leaning back against that picture, an unframed picture of Lenore's mother, in her frilly white wedding dress, linen, next to a large window filled with filmy spring light, looking down and arranging some wedding-related items in her hands. The picture resting on a spread-out cotton handkerchief with "Midwestern Contract Bridge Championships, Des Moines, Iowa, 1971" embroidered onto one corner.

Three drawers of socks and panties and so on, and one drawer of soap. A bed, unfortunately at the moment unmade, with a shiny old heavy maple frame and a pillow with a pillowcase with a lion on it that Lenore had had for a very long time. A shelf in the refrigerator in the kitchen downstairs on which were crowded bottles of seltzer water and ginger ale, some dark old carrots with limp tops, some limes. An area of the freezer crammed full of plastic bags of frozen vegetables, frozen mixed vegetables, on which Lenore largely lived.

A soft easy chair, old, covered in thick brown pretend velvet, that could recline so far back one's head almost touched the floor. A footstool with a woven straw top. A small black table that served poorly as a desk and was at the moment bare anyway. A black wooden chair that went with the table and was irritating because one of its legs was shorter than the others. An even more irritating, blindingly white-bright overhead light fixture. Two ceramic low-wattage soft-light lamps with painted nut-and-flower scenes on the bases, purchased as alternatives to the overhead light, lamps that threw huge praying-mantis-ish shadows of Lenore and Candy Mandible on the room's cream walls after sunset.

Eleven boxes of books from college, most of them Stonecipheco boxes, with red-ink drawings of laughing babies on the cardboard sides. All the boxes unopened, the athletic tape wheedled from the college trainer on the pretext of a mysterious pre-graduation sore ankle not even cut off, yet, and turning yellow. The boxes piled on either side of the west windows and supporting a tape player and a case of tapes and a fuchsia depressed and budless from lack of water in the August heat. A popcorn popper that popped popcorn with hot air. A box of Kleenex. A pretend tortoise-shell hairbrush. An old walker in the east corner, with two aluminum parabolas joined by twin mahogany support bars with soft cloth handgrips and the name YINGST carved in the wood of a bar above a hanging Scotch-taped publicity photo of Gary, the especially smiley Lawrence Welk dancer. Half-access to a bathroom down the hall, meaning half-access to a sink, a commode, a medicine cabinet, a tub with a shower fixture, and a soap-crusted shower curtain covered with profiles of yellow parrots.

A bird cage on an iron post in the northern corner of the room. A mat of spread newspapers, beaded with fallen seed, on the floor below it. A huge bag of birdseed to the right of the newspaper, leaning against the wall. A bird, in the cage, a cockatiel, the color of a pale fluorescent lemon, with a mohawk crown of spiked pink feathers of adjustable height, two enormous hooked and scaly feet, and eyes so black they shone. A bird named Vlad the Impaler, who spent the bulk of his life hissing and looking at himself in a little mirror hanging by a string of Frequent and Vigorous paperclips in the iron cage, a mirror so dull and cloudy with Vlad the Impaler's own bird-spit that Vlad the Impaler could not possibly have seen anything more than a vague yellowish blob behind a pane of mist. Nevertheless. A bird that very occasionally and for a dispropor-tionate ration of seed could be induced to stop hissing and emit a weird, extraterrestrial "Pretty boy." A bird that not infrequently literally bit the hand that fed it, before returning to dance in front of its own shapeless reflection, straining and contorting always for a better view of itself. Lenore refused to clean the mirror anymore, because as soon as she did so it was, in about half an hour, covered with dried spit again. A Black and Decker hand vacuum to vacuum seeds and the odd fallen feather or guano bit lay on the floor to the right of the bag of seed, having fallen out of its wall mount a few nights before.

Some personal items in the bathroom. A closet full of white dresses. A shoe stand bulging like a raspberry with black canvas. A bookshelf over the desk table half full of books in Spanish. Also on the shelf an annoying clock that clicked and buzzed every minute on the minute, and a little clay Spanish horse with a removable head in which was Lenore's spare key. Above the west windows, broken venetian blinds that fell on the head of whoever tried to let them down. A tiny frosting of cracks in the glass of the tops of the windows, from airplane noise.

A manual called *Care for Your Exotic Bird.* A patch of chewed wall behind Vlad the Impaler's cage from where Vlad the Impaler had gnawed on the wall in the dark when the mirror-show had closed, a patch from which plaster protruded, and about which Mrs. Tissaw was not pleased, and in regard to which a bill was promised.

Rick dropped Lenore off and she ran upstairs and came into her room and took off her dress. There was music and clove smell from under Candy's door. Lenore's room was filled with sad hot orange sunset. Vlad the Impaler had his feet hooked into the bars at the top of his cage and was hanging upside down, trying to find some reflective purchase at the very bottom of his smeared mirror.

"Hi, Vlad the Impaler," said Lenore in her bra and panties and shoes.

"Hello," said Vlad the Impaler.

Lenore looked at the bird. "Pardon me?"

"I have to do what's right for me as a person," Vlad the Impaler said, righting himself and looking at Lenore.

"Holy cow."

"Women need space, too."

"Candy!" Lenore went and opened Candy Mandible's door. Candy was stretching, on the floor, doing near-splits, in a silver leotard, with a clove cigarette in her mouth.

"Christ, sweetie, I've been waiting, how are you?" Candy got up and moved to turn off her stereo.

"Come here quick, listen to Vlad the Impaler," Lenore said, pulling Candy by the hand.

"Nice outfit," said Candy. "What about the unclear emergency? How's Lenore and Concarnadine?"

"You're sweet, but that kind of talk can lead exactly nowhere," said Vlad the Impaler, staring dumbly at himself in his cloudy mirror. "My feelings for you *are* deep. I've never claimed they're not."

"What the hell is going on with him?" Lenore asked Candy.

"Hey, that's what I was just saying," Candy said, looking at Vlad the Impaler.

"Pardon me?" said Vlad the Impaler.

"I was rehearsing what to say to Clint tonight, tonight I'm going to break up with him, I decided. I was in here practicing while I waited for you."

"Hi, Vlad the Impaler," said Vlad the Impaler. "Here's some extra special-wecial food."

"How can he talk like that all of a sudden?" asked Lenore. "He only used to say 'Pretty boy,' and I had to like pour tons of seed down him every time, to get him to."

"There are lots of pretty girls in the world, Clinty, you're just so incredibly *serious*," Vlad the Impaler said.

"Clinty?" said Lenore.

"Clint Roxbee-Cox, the V.P. at Allied who drives the Mercedes? With the glasses and the sort of English accent?"

"Clint, Clint, Clint," twittered Vlad the Impaler.

"Shut up," said Candy Mandible.

"Anger is natural," said Vlad the Impaler. "Anger is a natural release, let it out."

"He could never talk like this before," Lenore said.

The orange light on the shiny wood floor began to have slender black columns in it as the sun started to dip behind downtown Cleveland.

"Weird as hell. I was in here at like six-thirty, and he just hissed and writhed. And I went for a run, and I came back, and I rehearsed what to say to Clint, and then I went to stretch out, and then you came," Candy said, tapping her cigarette ashes into Vlad the Impaler's cage.

"Of course you satisfy me, Clinty. Don't think you don't," said Vlad the Impaler.

"Did you feed him?" Lenore asked Candy.

"No way. I've still got that scar on my thumb," Candy said. "You said you'd do it all the time."

"Then how come his dish is full, here?"

"Women need space, too."

"He must not have eaten from it this morning," said Candy. "Is that a new bra?"

Vlad the Impaler began to peck at his seed; his pink mohawk rose spikily and fell.

"This is just like the bizarrest day of all time," Lenore said, untying her shoes. "Rick and I had dinner with Mr. Bombardini? Of Bombardini Company and skeleton eye-socket fame?"

"You met Norman Bombardini?" Candy said.

"I just don't know what you mean by love. Tell me what you mean by that word," Vlad the Impaler said.

"You're going to have to buy a very small gag," said Candy.

"Candy, the guy is trying to eat himself to death because his wife left him. He already weighs about a thousand pounds. He was eating eclairs off the floor." Lenore took her bathrobe from the bedpost and undid her bra in the sun and headed for the bathroom. Candy followed her down the hall.

"You can't hold me to promises I didn't make!" Vlad the Impaler called after them.

/b/

Lenore took her shower while Candy Mandible leaned against the sink and smoked a clove cigarette in the steam.

"I don't get it," Candy said. "How can they just let twenty patients walk out and not see them or stop them?"

"Hobble out, is more like it," Lenore said from the shower.

"Right."

"I'm just going to assume, I guess, that if my father knows about it, Lenore's OK. I'm going to assume that he took her to Corfu with him for this summit meeting with the president of this other baby food company. Except Gramma's always had about zero interest in the Company. Except Dad and Gramma more or less hate each other. Except Gramma really has to have things ninety-eight point six or she gets blue. Except there's like twenty-five other people gone too. Corfu would have to be pretty crowded. But I'm going to assume Dad took them somewhere. Except God I didn't even think he knew where the Home was, anymore. Even though he owns it. He always handles it through Rummage and Naw." The shower hissed on the curtain for a moment. "I don't know if I should wait till Dad comes back or not. I can't just fly to Corfu. I don't have any money. And plus who knows where they are in Corfu."

"Rick could lend you money. God knows Rick's got money."

"I haven't even told Rick about it yet. He's hurt." Lenore turned off the shower and stepped out.

"I think Rick sort of flipped out, a little bit, up there, today." Candy threw her cigarette in the toilet. It hissed for a second. She began to brush her teeth.

"He seemed OK at dinner. He just wants to know where I am

all the time. The one who's flipped and landed heavily is that
Norman Bombardini. He was talking about infinity, and living butter?"

"What?"

"My robe smells like the bottom of a rug," Lenore said, sniffing
at her brown robe. "It's all mildewy."

"You could see if Lenore's maybe staying with anybody else in
your family," said Candy.

"And what the hell is with Vlad the Impaler?"

"You could see if Lenore's with anybody else in your family."

"What? Yes. That's a good idea. Except no way she's with John,
he can't even be reached, and neither can LaVache, because Dad
told me he doesn't even have a phone. And why would Gramma
go all the way to Amherst? Maybe Clarice, I guess. Except if Gramma
was still around here, which Clarice obviously is, she'd have called
to at least let me know she was OK."

"Maybe she tried and could only get Steve's Sub."

"God, that's another thing, what a rotten day at work. That Peter
guy who looks like a negative never came back, and we sure didn't
hear from any tunnel guy." Lenore tried to get steam off the mirror.
Candy dried Lenore's back with a towel and took off her silver
leotard and stepped into the shower. Lenore stuck her arm in behind
the plastic curtain and Candy handed her the soap and Lenore gently
soaped Candy's back, the way Candy liked. "And we get call after
call at the board, almost all wrong, and Prietht was laughing."

"I'm really going to kill her. I'm going to murder her, soon. A
negative?"

"And Walinda was just unbelievably mad that I was late. She
was really going to fire me. She kept saying, 'Don't play.' "

"When she says 'Don't play,' you know she's really mad," Candy
said, stepping out of the shower. The steam in the bathroom was
now so thick Lenore could hardly see to open the door. She opened
the door. A rush of cool hall air came in and cut the steam. Lenore
began to brush her teeth.

"I should shave my legs," she said. "My legs are making that
sound when I rub them."

"So shave."

"And then Candy what's with Vlad the Impaler? I think he must be sick. Rick said the lady in the store said cockatiels didn't really even talk that much, as a rule. Maybe he's dying, and this is like the huge burst of fireworks at the end, right before the fireworks are over."

"Clinty, the sex is great, you know the sex is great, I've told you how you fill me up, but sex is only like a few hours a day, you can't let it totally rule your life," said a raspy bird voice from down the hall.

"Little fucker sounds pretty healthy to me," Candy Mandible said, walking naked down the hall, Lenore in the bathrobe behind her. "If Mrs. Tissaw hears this stuff, we're really up the old fecal creek. We better start teaching him some Psalms or something."

Candy went into her room and Lenore into hers. In Lenore's room it was very pretty now. The floor and lower walls were liquid black, and dark tree shadows moved in the orange bath of sunset on the upper walls and ceiling.

"Sex is a few *hours* a day?" Lenore called to Candy.

"Clint, Clint, Clint, special-wecial," Vlad the Impaler crooned into his mirror.

"Jesus wept," Lenore said into Vlad the Impaler's cage. "The Lord is my shepherd. I shall not want."

Vlad the Impaler cocked his head and looked at her.

"Lenore, Clint is just something else, I have to tell you. He's super. He turns me inside out. He's a horse, a camel, a brontosaurus," Candy said from her door, demonstrating with her hands. "Like this."

"Yes, well, ummm," said Lenore.

"Inside out! Like this!" shrieked Vlad the Impaler.

"Shit on a twig," Lenore said.

"But he's so *possessive*," Candy continued. "He keeps asking me to marry him, and getting mad when I laugh. He thinks making me come gives him the right to my heart. How can such a big boy be such a little boy? My eye's on the president of the whole company, Mr. Allied." Candy stood on dancer's point in Lenore's doorway and let the last orange bits of sunset fall on her cheeks. She was a really pretty girl, all curves and ovals and soft milky shine, with thick dark hair, even darker now when wet. It lay like a blanket of chocolate over her breasts and back. A plane flew over, low, rattling the windows in their frames for a moment.

"Now let's have a night to remember, and remember each other always," Vlad the Impaler said to his reflection.

Lenore slipped a clean dress over her head. "When does this night to remember begin?"

Candy looked at the clock just as it clicked and buzzed a new minute. "Any time now. I'm just going to go over to his place for dinner, then I imagine we'll mate like animals for hours and hours and hours."

"A real romantic," said Lenore. "Jesus wept, Vlad the Impaler. The sins of the fathers. I shall not want."

"Jesus shall not want."

"Attaboy."

"I'm still waiting to hear about Rick, you know, mating-wise." Candy called from back in her room. "It's been months, after all, and if he's as super as you say . . . I'm waiting for minute anatomical tale-telling. Otherwise you'll just force me to find out for myself."

"Yes, well, ummm." Lenore put on clean socks.

"Just kidding. But really, we are partners in crime after all. And describing one can make you feel closer to it. I mean him. Really. Angles and bends and birthmarks and everything. It makes you intimater." Candy came in, in a pale old violet cotton dress that had been Lenore's for a long time, and was just perfectly too small for Candy, and clung to the not insignificant swell of her hips. She knelt at the window in the shadow and put mascara on, looking at her reflection in the black lower rectangle of the clear glass pane. Outside, crickets were starting.

"Making me come. Me as a person," said Vlad the Impaler. "Where is that ditzy bitch?"

"Sorry about that."

"May I please have a ride to Rick's? I left my car at the Building." Lenore finished tying her shoes and brushed out the curves of her hair. "I think Vlad the Impaler's going to be OK food-wise. He must not be eating much."

"Yes you may have a ride. Listen, you going to water that plant, or what?"

"It's like an experiment."

"The sins of the feathers!" screamed Vlad the Impaler. "Who has the book?"

"What book?" Lenore asked Candy.

"Search *moi*. Listen, I'm late. Shall we."

"Yes. Good night, Vlad the Impaler."

"Love has no meaning. Love is a meaningless word to me."

"Maybe we could get him on 'Real People.' "

" 'Real Birds.' "

"Thanks again for this dress. It may get torn, I'm warning you now."

"People should have wedding nights like your breakups."

"Women need space, need space!"

/c/

"Are you bothered by speculations about whether it bothers me that you never tell me you love me?"

"Maybe sometimes."

"Well you shouldn't be. I know you do, deep down. Deep down I know it. And I love you, fiercely and completely—you do believe that."

"Yes."

"And you love me."

". . . ."

"It's not a problem. I know you do. Please don't let it bother you."

". . . ."

"Thank you for telling me the Grandmother news. I apologize for being a pain in the ass at dinner. I apologize for Norman."

"Well, God, I wanted to tell you. Except I don't really even feel like it's telling. You tell facts, you tell things. These weren't things, they're just a collection of weirdnesses."

"Even so. Are you bothered by the book being gone, too?"

". . . ."

"The book is a problem, Lenore. The book is your problem, in my opinion. Hasn't Jay said you're simply investing an outside thing with an efficacy to hurt and help and possess meaning that can really come only from inside you? That your life is inside you, not in some book that makes an old woman's nightie sag?"

"How do you know what Jay's told me?"

"I know what I'd tell you in his place."

". . . ."

"Be legitimately concerned about a relative who'll turn up with a Mediterranean tan and a terse explanation from your father, Lenore. Is all."

"You fill me up, Rick, you know. You turn me inside out."

"Pardon me?"

"You turn me inside out. When we . . . you know. What we just did."

"I fill you up?"

"You do."

"Well thank you."

"A story, please."

"A story."

"Please. Did you get any today?"

"Oh, yes."

"Good."

"I actually began a journal today, too, really. Just jottings. Random, et cetera. It was interesting. I had wanted to ever since I was young."

"Well good. Can I read it, ever?"

"You most certainly cannot. A journal is almost by definition something no one else reads."

"I guess I'll just settle for a story, then, please."

"Got another interesting one today."

"Goody."

"Sad, though, again. Do you know where all the really sad stories I'm getting are coming from? They're coming, it turns out, from kids. Kids in college. I'm starting to think something is just deeply wrong with the youth of America. First of all, a truly disturbing number of them are interested in writing fiction. Truly disturbing. And more than interested, actually. You don't get the sorts of things I've been getting from people who are merely . . . interested. And sad, sad stories. Whatever happened to happy stories, Lenore? Or at least morals? I'd fall ravenously on one of the sort of didactic Salingerian solace-found-in-the-unlikeliest-place pieces I was getting by the gross at Hunt and Peck. I'm concerned about today's kids. These kids should be out drinking beer and seeing films and having panty raids and losing virginities and writhing to suggestive music, not making up long, sad, convoluted stories. And they are as an invariable rule simply atrocious typists. They should be out having fun and learning to type. I'm not a little worried. Really."

"So let's hear it."

"A man and a woman meet and fall in love at a group-therapy session. The man is handsome and jutting-jawed, and also as a rule very nice, but he has a problem with incredible flashes of temper that he can't control. His emotions get hold of him and he can't control them, and he gets insanely and irrationally angry, sometimes. The woman is achingly lovely and as sweet and kind a person as one could ever hope to imagine, but she suffers from horrible periods of melancholy which can be held at bay only by massive overeating and excessive sleep, and so she eats Fritos and Hostess Cupcakes all the time, and sleeps far too much, and weighs a lot, although she's still very pretty anyway."

"Can you please move your arm a little?"

"And the two meet at the group-therapy sessions, and fall madly in love, and stare dreamily at each other across the therapy room every week while the psychologist, who acts very laid-back and nice and wears a flannel poncho, leads the therapy sessions. The psychologist by the way it's important to know seems on the outside to be very nice and very compassionate, but actually it turns out we find out thanks to the omniscient narrator he's the only real villain in the story, a man who as a college student had had a nervous breakdown during the GRE's and hadn't done well and hadn't gotten into Harvard Graduate School and had had to go to N.Y.U. and had had horrible experiences and several breakdowns in New York City, and as a result just hates cities, and collective societal units in general, a really pathological hatred, and thinks society and group pressures are at the root of all the problems of everybody who comes to see him, and he tries unceasingly but subtly to get all his patients to leave the city and move out into this series of isolated cabins deep in the woods of whatever state the story takes place in, I get the feeling New Jersey, which cabins he by some strange coincidence owns and sells to his patients at a slimy profit."

" . . . ."

"And the man and the woman fall madly in love, and start hanging around together, and the man's temper begins miraculously to moderate, and the woman's melancholy begins to moderate also and she stops sleeping all the time and also stops eating junk food and slims down and becomes so incredibly beautiful it makes your eyes water, and they decide to get married, and they go and tell the psychologist, who rejoices with them and for them, as he puts it, but he tells them that their respective emotional troubles are really just on the back burner for a brief period, because of the distraction of their new love, and that if they really want to get cured for all time so they can concentrate on loving each other for ever and ever what they need to do is move away together from the city, I get the feeling Newark, into a cabin deep in the woods away from everything having to do with collective society, and he shows them some cabin-in-the-woods brochures, and suddenly the psychologist is here revealed to have tiny green dollar signs in the centers of his eyes, in a moment of surrealistic description I didn't really care for."

"Man oh man."

"Yes but the man and the woman are by now pretty much completely under the psychologist's clinical spell, after just a year of therapy, and also they're understandably emotionally soft and punchy from being so much in love, and so they take the psychologist's advice and buy a cabin way out in the woods several hours' drive from anything, and the man quits his job as an architect, at which he'd been enormously brilliant and successful when he wasn't having temper problems, and the woman quits her job designing clothes for full-figured women, and they get married and move out to their cabin and live alone, and, it's not too subtly implied, have simply incredible sex all the time, in the cabin and the woods and the trees, and for a living they begin to write collaborative novels about the triumph of strong pure human emotion over the evil group-pressures of contemporary collective society. And they almost instantly, because of all the unbelievable though emotionally innocent sex, have a child, and they have a close call at labor time because they barely get to the tiny, faraway hospital in their four-wheel wilderness Jeep, which the psychologist also sold them, they barely get to the hospital in time, but everything's ultimately OK and the child's a healthy boy and on the way back from the tiny hospital deep in the woods, though still very far from their even deeper and more secluded cabin, they stop in and have a talk with a retired nun who lives in a cabin in a deep valley by the highway and spends her life selflessly nursing retarded people who are so retarded even institutions don't want them, and the man and the woman and the retired nun dandle the baby on their knees and talk about how love can triumph over everything in general, and collective societal pressures in particular, all in some long but really quite beautiful passages of dialogue."

"Killer story, so far."

"Just wait. And they go back into the woods as before, and for a few years everything is great, unbelievably great. But then, like tiny cracks in a beautiful sculpture, little by little, their old emotional troubles begin to manifest themselves in tiny ways. The man sometimes gets unreasonably angry at meaningless things, and this sometimes makes the woman melancholy, and an ominous empty Frito bag or two begin to appear in the wastebasket, and she puts on a little weight. And right about then their child, who's about six, now, begins to have a horrible medical problem in which whenever he cries—which little children are obviously wont to do, they're always falling down and bumping into things and banging themselves up—in which whenever he cries, the child goes into something like an epileptic fit; his limbs thrash around and flail uncontrollably and he almost swallows his tongue, and it's just very scary, obviously, and the parents are extremely worried, even though they think and hope that it might be just a phase, but still they love the child so fiercely and completely that they're frantic. And the woman is now pregnant again. And all these little ominous things go on until, months later, they've gone in the Jeep all the way to the tiny far-off hospital for the woman to have the second baby, and as the baby's being delivered the older child happens to slip on a wet patch in the hall and falls and bangs his head, and he naturally begins to cry, and he immediately starts to flop around in a convulsive fit, and meanwhile the baby is being born, a girl, and when the kindly old country doctor slaps her bottom to get her to breathe she of course starts to cry, and *she* right away goes into a miniature epileptic convulsive fit of her own, so both children are at the same time having fits, and the quiet little backwoods hospital is suddenly a madhouse. But the kindly old country doctor quickly gets things back under control and examines both children on the spot and diagnoses them as suffering from an extremely rare neurological condition in which crying for some reason decimates their nervous systems, it harms their hearts and brains by making those organs disposed to swell and bleed, and he says that every time the children cry, as of course normal children can be counted on to do quite a bit, the fits will get worse and worse, and that more and more damage will be done, and that they will be in danger of dying, eventually—especially the older child, in whom the condition is more advanced and serious—unless, that is, treatment is administered to keep them really ever from crying."

"Wow."

"And the kindly old country doctor hands the man and the woman roughly a hundred little bottles of a certain special very rare and hard-to-make anticrying medicine, since it's such a prohibitively long and difficult trip from their secluded cabin to the tiny hospital, and he promises that as long as the children have a dose of the medicine whenever they look as if they might start to cry, to nip the crying in the bud and so prevent fits, they'll definitely be fine, and the parents are of course frantically worried but also relieved that it's at least a treatable condition, but also the strain is making their old emotional problems a little worse, and the man is ominously unreasonably angry at the universe for making his children have epileptic fits when they cry, and at the really unavoidably exorbitant bill for all the rare and hard-to-make anticrying medicine, and the woman is ominously yawning, and she makes them stop at the tiny deep-woods grocery store and buy virtually every junk-food item in the place, which clearly pisses the man off, because she's already put on some weight, even though she's still very pretty, and his being pissed off makes the woman even more sad and sleepy and hungry, and so on in what we can see has the potential to be a vicious circle."

"Would you like some of this ginger ale?"

"Thank you."

". . . ."

"And so they get back to the cabin, and things are more or less as they were before, although the woman is eating and sleeping a lot and gaining weight fast, and the man is so angry at the exorbitant price of the anticrying medicine that he vows to make a special effort to control his temper and be extremely nice to both children so they'll cry as little as possible. But of course meanwhile his old emotional temper problem is little by little getting worse and worse, and the strain of being artificially nice to the children is really telling on him, and at ever more frequent intervals he has to run deep into the woods to yell and punch trees with his fists, and he becomes involuntarily cruel to the sweet sad woman, and hisses at her about her steadily increasing weight late at night when the children are asleep at the other side of the tiny cabin, which hissing of course only makes the woman more melancholy and sleepy and hungry, and she quickly shoots up to her old pre-love weight, and then some. And this goes on for roughly a year, with some potentially really terrifying epileptic crying fits from the children, especially the older one, being averted only by administering the special medicine just in time."

"I'm engrossed, I admit it."

"Well, and now on the disastrous and climactic night of the story, symbolized by a really unbelievable rainstorm outside, with the wind screaming and big gelatinous globs of rain pelting the cabin, the four are sitting at dinner, and the woman's plate is piled almost to the ceiling with Hostess Cupcakes, and she's yawning, and the man, who is under enormous strain, is unbelievably pissed off, and struggling every moment to control his temper, and the older child, who's now about seven, whines a little bit about not wanting to eat his peas, which the woman had been too sleepy and gorged even to bother to unfreeze and cook, and the whine on top of everything else so angers the man that he involuntarily fetches the child a tremendous slap, purely involuntarily, and the child flies out of his chair, and falls, and knocks over a little table, on which are kept, in a place of honor, on a purple felt pad, all the precious bottles of the rare and hard-to-make anticrying medicine, and all the bottles are broken, and all the medicine in an instant ruined, and of course the child naturally starts crying from the tremendous slap and goes right away into a severe epileptic fit, and the baby, at all the negative commotion, begins to cry, too, and goes into a little fit of its own, and so suddenly the man and the woman have both children having epileptic crying fits, and no medicine to keep the fits from grievously harming the childrens' hearts and brains and maybe killing them. And they're frantic, and the kids are flopping around, and the woman finally manages to get the baby semi–calmed down by holding it and bouncing it and crooning to it, but the older child is in a very bad way indeed."

"Good God."

"So both parents are completely frantic, and they decide all they can do is for the man to take the older child in the Jeep and try to get to the tiny far-off hospital just as quickly as possible, while the woman calls ahead and gets them to make up an emergency batch of anticrying medicine right away, and that thus the woman should stay and try to call and keep the baby, who is now more or less stable in the mother's arms but who hates to ride in the Jeep and would certainly cry disastrously on the way to the tiny hospital, from crying and convulsing any more, until the father can get back with the medicine and the also hopefully saved older child. And so the man carries the flopping boy out to the Jeep in the gelatinously heavy rain and off they go, and the woman begins to try to call the tiny far-off hospital but can't get through because, as the narrator tells us, the hospital's lines have been hit by lightning, and so in desperation the woman finally calls their old psychologist in the city, because he'd told them when he'd sold them their cabin that if they ever needed anything not to hesitate to call, and she gets hold of him at his downtown penthouse and begs him to drive to the tiny far-off hospital and get some anticrying medicine for the baby and bring it down to the cabin right away. And the psychologist, after he's reminded of who the woman is—he'd forgotten—reluctantly says OK, he'll do it, even though it's raining gelatinously, and says he'll be right there, but as soon as he hangs up, who should stop by but a current patient, whom the psychologist had been trying to convince to buy a cabin and live out in seclusion, and so the psychologist delays for a bit while he stays and shows the patient brochures and tries to convince him to buy a cabin, and we're again rather irritatingly reminded that there are tiny green dollar signs in the centers of the psychologist's eyes."

"Bastard, though."

"No lie. And meanwhile the man is driving like mad in the Jeep toward the tiny far-off hospital, with the boy, who's no longer convulsing but now is sort of autistic and slack-jawed and still obviously in a very bad way indeed, and the man's driving like mad, but it's very slow going, in the dark and the gelatinous rain and the mud of the deep-woods roads, and the man is so incredibly angry at the universe for putting his family in this position he feels as if he's about to explode, but through enormous strength of will he keeps the lid on, and keeps driving, and eventually gets off the muddy deep-woods roads and onto the highway, where the going is at least a little faster. And the woman is meanwhile back at the cabin, waiting for the psychologist to arrive with the anticrying medicine, and she's so full and so upset and depressed at everything that's happened that she's yawning all the time, she's unbelievably sleepy, and it gets still worse as the hours go by and it gets late and the gelatinous rain drums rhythmically on the cabin roof, but the baby is meanwhile having small but severe convulsive attacks whenever it cries, and the only way the woman finds she can keep it from crying is to hold it against her enormous Frito-crumbed breast; whenever she puts the baby down, it cries and begins to have an epileptic fit. So she's staggering back and forth with the baby. And this goes on, some switching from scene to scene, the psychologist finally makes his sale and gets going, and he has an incredibly fast and expensive car, paid for out of cabin profits, and he gets to the tiny backwoods hospital in no time flat, and he talks to the kindly old country doctor, and after a brief wait while the kindly old country doctor practically kills himself making the anticrying medicine in almost no time, the psychologist gets the medicine, and says the man will pay for it, and starts jetting down the highway toward the deep woods and the far-off cabin, at incredible speed, and in an ironic and ominous twist he goes right by the Jeep, for obvious reasons headed in the other direction, while the Jeep is pulled over in the dark with a flat, which the man is in a rage in the storm

fixing, while the child slumps in the front seat in a bad way, and
the psychologist's incredibly fast car splashes a huge wave of rainwater on the man from clear across the highway and knocks the
jack handle out of the man's hand, and the jack handle hits something small but vital on the axle of the Jeep, and partially breaks
it, which the man doesn't notice, because he's so pissed off at the
psychologist's car for splashing water on him that he's jumping up
and down and screaming and giving the receding car the finger,
and just temporarily out of control."

"Jesus."

"And meanwhile back at the cabin the woman is almost passing
out, she's so melancholy and worried and sleepy, but she can't let
go of the baby or it will begin to cry and flop epileptically. And the
woman heroically and movingly holds out against sleepiness for just
as long as she can, waiting for the psychologist, but finally she's
simply physically unable to stay awake any longer, being awake is
just no longer an option, and so, as the only possible compromise
with circumstance, she lies down on her bed, still holding the baby
against her breast to keep it from crying and convulsing."

"Oh, no."

"And she falls asleep and rolls over on the baby and crushes it
and kills it."

"Oh, God."

"And she wakes up and sees what's happened and falls into an
irreversible coma-like sleep from grief."

"OK, that's enough."

"And the psychologist pulls up about ten minutes later and enters,
in his poncho, and he sees what's happened, and he calls the police
to report it. And the only police in such a remote area is the state
highway patrol, and the psychologist gives the patrol dispatcher a
description of the man and the Jeep, which he is of course familiar
with but just hadn't seen when he splashed it, and he tells the
dispatcher to have the patrol cars on the highway look for the Jeep
and give the man and the boy a fast ride to the tiny far-off hospital
if they're found, and meanwhile also to get over to the cabin and
have a look at the crushed baby and the comatose mother. And
the dispatcher relays all the psychologist's remarks to the troopers

by radio, and a cruiser starts speeding down the highway on the way to the cabin, and on the highway it encounters the Jeep, and does a fast U and pulls it over, and the officer in the cruiser gets out and goes to the Jeep in the gelatinous rain and offers to give the man and the boy a fast ride to the tiny far-off hospital, and the man accepts, and as he's getting the boy ready to be carried from the Jeep to the cruiser he asks the officer if it was his wife who had called the police, and the officer says no and then completely disastrously tells the man what he's heard has happened back at the cabin, and to the accompaniment of a huge ripping clap of thunder the man flips out completely with uncontrollable anger at the news, and starts involuntarily flailing around with his arms, and one of his elbows, by accident, hits the boy, slumped in the seat beside him, in the nose, and the boy starts to scream and cry again and immediately flops onto the floor of the Jeep and begins to convulse, and his head first knocks the gearshift out of neutral, then his head gets wedged next to the accelerator, and the accelerator gets floored, and the Jeep takes off, with the officer caught and holding on and riding along the side because he'd been reaching in the window trying to calm the flailingly angry man, and the Jeep starts heading for the edge of the highway, beyond which lies a deep valley, a cliff, really, and the man is so angry he can't see to steer, and the officer tries to grab the steering wheel from outside and steer away from the cliff, but the sudden tension on the wheel completely snaps the small but vital thing on the axle that had been broken by the jack handle's flying out of the man's hand earlier, and the steering fails completely, and the Jeep with the man, the boy, and the officer plunges over the cliff and falls several hundred feet onto the cabin where the old retired nun, you may remember, was nursing the prohibitively retarded people, and the Jeep falls onto the cabin and explodes in flames, and everyone involved is horribly killed."

"Holy shit."

"Indeed."

" . . . . "

"A thoroughly, thoroughly troubled story. The product of a nastily troubled little collegiate mind. And there were about twenty more pages in which the huge beautiful woman lay in a pathetic fetal

position in an irreversible coma while the psychologist rationalized
the whole thing as due to collective-societal pressures too deep and
insidious even to be avoided by flight to the woods, and tried to
milk the comatose woman's dead family's remaining assets through
legal maneuvers."

"Mother of God."

"Quite."

"Are you going to use it?"

"Are you joking? It's staggeringly long, longer than the whole
next issue will be. And ridiculously sad."

". . . ."

"And *atrociously* typed. That bothers me too. An unbelievably
involved story that some sad kid must have spent months dreaming
up and working out, and then he types it with his elbows. I'm going
to send a personal rejection slip in which I advise the kid first to
learn to type and then to go writhe to some suggestive music."

"I liked it. I thought it was a killer story."

"Yours is not a literary sensibility, Lenore."

"Gee, thanks a lot. Spunkless and non-literary."

"That's not what I meant at all."

". . . ."

"Come here. Come on."

"Go peddle your papers."

"Oh for Christ's sake, Lenore."

". . . ."

/d/

"Frequent and Vigorous."

"Fnoof fnoof."

"Frequent and Vigorous."

"What?"

"Operator. Frequent and Vigorous."

"Lenore."

"Gasp a similar ladder. Operator. Special-wecial food."

"Lenore! You're talking in your sleep! You're being incoherent!"

"What?"

"You're being incoherent."

"Fnoof."

"That's better."

/e/

"Holy cow!"

"Fnoof fnoof."

"What the hell!"

"Fnoof. What?"

"Rick, I don't own a walker."

"What?"

"I don't own a walker. I especially don't own Mrs. Yingst's walker, with that Lawrence Welk guy's picture on it. What was it doing in my room?"

"What walker?"

"And what did Vlad the Impaler mean special-wecial food, who's got the book?"

"What? That bird should be killed, Lenore. I'll kill it for you."

"Nobody's in Corfu, at all. I'm being messed with."

"Fnoof."

"Jesus."

8 **1990**

/a/

PARTIAL TRANSCRIPT OF RAP SESSION, THURSDAY, 26
AUGUST 1990, IN THE OFFICE OF DR. CURTIS JAY, PH.D.
PARTICIPANTS: DR. CURTIS JAY AND MS. LENORE
BEADSMAN, AGE 24, FILE NUMBER 770-01-4266.

DR. JAY: So it would be safe to characterize yesterday as just not a good
day at all, then.

MS. LENORE BEADSMAN: I think that would be a safe assessment, yes.

JAY: And how does that make you feel?

LENORE: Well, I think sort of by definition a day that isn't good at all
makes you feel pretty shitty, right?

JAY: Do you feel pressured into feeling shitty?

LENORE: What?

JAY: If a bad day is by definition one that makes you feel shitty, do
you feel pressured to feel shitty about a bad day, or do you feel natural
about it?

LENORE: What the hell does that have to do with anything?

JAY: The question makes you uncomfortable.

LENORE: No, it makes me feel like I just listened to a pretty meaningless
and dumb question, which I'm afraid I think that was.

JAY: I don't think it's dumb at all. Aren't you the one who complains
of feeling pressured and coerced into feeling and doing the things you
feel and do? Or do I have you confused with some other long/time
client and friend?

LENORE: Look, maybe it's just safe to say that I feel shitty because bad things are happening, OK? Lenore acts incredibly weird and melodramatic for about a month, then just decides to leave the place where she's supposed to live as a cold-blooded semi-invalid, and to take people with her, even though she's ninety-two, and she doesn't bother to call to say what's going on, even though they're obviously still in Cleveland, see for instance Mrs. Yingst's walker, which could only have gotten in my room at about six-thirty last night, and my father clearly knows what's up, see for instance having Karl Rummage tell Mr. Bloemker all this stuff yesterday morning before anybody knew, and he doesn't bother to let me know either, and takes off for Corfu, and I think someone may have given my bird Vlad the Impaler LSD because he's now blabbering all the time, which he never did before, and it's conveniently mostly obscene stuff that Mrs. Tissaw's going to flip about and evict me for if she hears it, and my job really bites the big kielbasa right now because there are like massive mess-ups in the phone lines and we don't have our number anymore and people keep calling for all sorts of bizarre other things, and of course no sign of anybody from Interactive Cable today, this morning, and then at the switchboard I get a lot of flowers and some supposedly humorously nearly empty boxes of candy, and it turns out they're from Mr. Bombardini . . .

JAY: Norman Bombardini?

LENORE: . . . Yes, who's our landlord, at Frequent and Vigorous, and who's unbelievably fat and hostile, and as a fringe benefit also clearly insane, and thinks he's doing me a huge favor, pardon the pun, by promising me a corner of a soon-to-be-full universe all for myself, and he claims he's infatuated with me.

JAY: And then there is of course Rick.

LENORE: Rick is Rick. Rick is a constant in every equation. Let's leave Rick out of this.

JAY: You feel uncomfortable talking about Rick in this context.

LENORE: What context? There's no context. A context implies something that hangs together. All that's happening now is that a thoroughly screwed-up life that's barely hung together is now even less well hung together.

JAY: So the woman is worried that her life is not "well hung."

LENORE: Go suck a rock.

Dr. Jay pauses. Lenore Beadsman pauses.

JAY: Interesting, though.

LENORE: What?

JAY: Don't you think? Don't you think it's rather an interesting situation? Set of situations?

LENORE: Meaning what?

JAY: Meaning very little. Only that if one is going to feel shitty, to continue your use of the adjective, about not having enough "control" over things, and we of course admit freely that we still haven't been able satisfactorily to articulate what we mean by that, yet, have we . . . ?

LENORE: God, the plural tense, now.

JAY: . . . that it's at least comparatively desirable to be impotently involved in an *interesting* situation, rather than a dull one, is that not so?

LENORE: Interesting to whom?

JAY: Ah. That matters to you.

LENORE: It matters to me a lot.

JAY: I smell breakthrough, I don't mind telling you. There's a scent of breakthrough in the air.

LENORE: I think it's my armpit. I think I need a shower.

JAY: Hiding behind symptomatic skirts is not fair. If I say I smell breakthrough, I smell breakthrough.

LENORE: You always say you smell breakthrough. You say you smell breakthrough almost every time I'm here. I think you must coat your nostrils with breakthrough first thing every morning. What does that mean, anyway, "breakthrough"?

JAY: You tell me.

LENORE: These seat belts on the chair aren't really for the patients' safety on the track, are they? They're to keep your jugular from being lunged for about thirty times a day, right?

JAY: You feel anger.

LENORE: I feel shitty. Pure, uncoerced shitty. Interesting for whom?

JAY: Whom might there be to interest?

LENORE: Now what the hell does that mean?

JAY: The smell of breakthrough is getting weaker.

LENORE: Well, look.

JAY: Yes?

LENORE: Suppose Gramma tells me really convincingly that all that really exists of my life is what can be said about it?

JAY: What the hell does that mean?

LENORE: You feel anger.

JAY: I have an ejection button, you know. I can press a button on the underside of this drawer, here, and send you screaming out into the lake.

LENORE: You must be about the worst psychologist of all time. Why won't you ever let me go with my thoughts?

JAY: I'm sorry.

LENORE: That's why I'm here, right? That's why I pay you roughly two-thirds of everything I make, right?

JAY: I'm honored and ashamed, all at once. Back to the Grandmother, and a life that's told, not lived.

LENORE: Right.

JAY: Right.

LENORE: So what would that mean?

JAY: In all earnestness I say you tell me.

LENORE: Well see, it seems like it's not really like a life that's told, not lived; it's just that the living is the telling, that there's nothing going on with me that isn't either told or tellable, and if so, what's the difference, why live at all?

JAY: I really don't understand.

LENORE: Maybe it just makes no sense. Maybe it's just completely irrational and dumb.

JAY: But obviously it bothers you.

LENORE: Pretty keen perception. If there's nothing about me but what can be said about me, what separates me from this lady in this story Rick got who eats junk food and gains weight and squashes her child in her sleep? She's exactly what's said about her, right? Nothing more at all. And same with me, seems like. Gramma says she's going to show me how a life is words and nothing else. Gramma says words can kill and create. Everything.

JAY: Sounds like Gramma is maybe half a bubble off plumb, to me.

LENORE: Well, just no. She's not crazy and she's sure not stupid. You should know that. And see, the thing is, if she can do all this to me with words, if she can make me feel this way, and perceive my life as screwed way up and not hung together, and question whether I'm really even me, if there is a me, crazy as that sounds, if she can do all that just by talking to me, with just words, then what does that say about words?

JAY: ". . . she said, using words."

LENORE: Well exactly. There it is. Lenore would totally agree. Which is why it sometimes just drives me nuts that Rick wants to *talk* all the time. Talk talk talk. Tell tell tell. At least when he tells me stories, it's up-front and clear what's story and what isn't, right?

JAY: I'm getting a scent.

LENORE: I don't think the armpit theory should be rejected out of hand.

JAY: Why is a story more up-front than a life?

LENORE: It just seems more honest, somehow.

JAY: Honest meaning closer to the truth?

LENORE: I smell trap.

JAY: I smell breakthrough. The truth is that there's no difference between a life and a story? But a life pretends to be something more? But it really isn't more?

LENORE: I would kill for a shower.

JAY: What have I said? What have I said? I've said that hygiene anxiety is what?

LENORE: According to whom?

JAY: Ejection remains an option. Don't misdirect so transparently. According to me and to my truly great teacher, Olaf Blentner, the pioneer of hygiene anxiety research. . . .

LENORE: Hygiene anxiety is identity anxiety.

JAY: I am gagging on the stench of breakthrough.

LENORE: I've been having digestive trouble, too, really, so don't. . . .

JAY: Shut up. So comparisons between real life and story make you feel hygiene anxiety, a.k.a. identity anxiety. Plus the fact that delightfully nice and helpful Lenore Senior, whose temporary little junket I must say does not exactly fill me with grief, indoctrinates you on the subject of words and their extra-linguistic efficacy. Do some math for me, here, Lenore.

LENORE: Wrongo. First of all, Gramma's whole thing is that there's no such thing as extra-linguistic efficacy, extra-linguistic *anything*. And also, what's with this throwing around words like "indoctrinates" and "efficacy"? Which Rick uses on me all the time, too? How come you and Rick not only always say the same things to me, but the same words? Are you a team? Do you fill him in on this stuff? Is this why he's so completely uncharacteristically cool about not asking me what goes on in here? Are you an unethical psychologist? Do you tell?

JAY: Listen to this will you. Aside from the me-being-terribly-hurt issue, why this obsession with whether people are *telling* all the time? Why is telling robbing control?

LENORE: I don't know. What time is it?

JAY: Don't you feel a difference between your life and a telling?

LENORE: Maybe just a little water out of that pitcher, there, in either armpit. . . .

JAY: Well?

LENORE: No, I guess not really.

JAY: How come? How come?

Lenore Beadsman pauses.

JAY: How come?

LENORE: What would the difference be?

JAY: Speak up, please.

LENORE: What would the difference *be*?

JAY: What?

LENORE: What would the difference be?

JAY: I don't believe this. Blentner would twirl. You don't feel a difference?

LENORE: OK, exactly, but what's "feeling," then?

JAY: The smell is overpowering. I can't stand it. Just let me tie this hankie over my nose, here.

LENORE: Flake.

JAY: *(muffled)* Who cares about defining it? Can't you feel it? You can *feel* the way your life is; who can feel the life of the junk-food lady in Rick's story?

LENORE: *She* can! *She* can!

JAY: Are you nuts?

LENORE: She can if it's in the *story* that she can. Right? It says she feels such incredible grief over squashing her baby that she lapses into a coma, so she does and does.

JAY: But that's not real.

LENORE: It seems to be exactly as real as it's said to be.

JAY: Maybe it is your armpit, after all.

LENORE: I'm outta here.

JAY: Wait.

LENORE: Hit the chair-start button, Dr. Jay.

JAY: Jesus.

LENORE: The lady's life is the story, and if the story says, "The fat pretty woman was convinced her life was real," then she is. Except what she doesn't know is that her life isn't hers. It's there for a reason. To make a point or give a smile, whatever. She's not even produced, she's educed. She's there for a reason.

JAY: Whose reasons? Reason as in a person's reason? She owes her existence to whoever tells?

LENORE: But not necessarily even a person, is the thing. The telling makes its own reasons. Gramma says any telling automatically becomes a kind of system, that controls everybody involved.

JAY: And how is that?

LENORE: By simple definition. Every telling creates and limits and defines.

JAY: Bullshit has its own unique scent, have you noticed?

LENORE: The fat lady's not really real, and to the extent that she's real she's just used, and if she thinks she's real and not being used, it's only because the system that educes her and uses her makes her by definition feel real and non-educed and non-used.

JAY: And you're telling me that's the way you feel?

LENORE: You're dumb. Is that really a Harvard diploma? I have to leave. Let me leave, please. I have to go to the ladies' room.

JAY: Come see me tomorrow.

LENORE: I don't have any money left.

JAY: Come see me the minute you have money. I'm here for you. Get Rick to give you money.

LENORE: Set my chair in motion, please.

JAY: We've made enormous strides, today.

LENORE: In your ear.

/b/

26 August

Monroe Fieldbinder Collection: "Fire."

Monroe Fieldbinder drew his white fedora over his eyes and grinned wryly at the scene of chaos all around him.

Monroe Fieldbinder drew his fedora over his eyes and grinned wryly at the chaos that surrounded him. The flames of the burning house leaped into the night air and cast long, spindly shadows of Fieldbinder and the firemen and the gawkers down the rough new concrete suburban street. Undulating shrouds of sparks whirled and glowed in the spring wind. As he stood on the running board of a fire engine, yelling instructions to his men, the fire chief spotted Fieldbinder.

"Thought you'd be here, Fieldbinder," said the chief, a grizzled old white-haired man with a rubicund face. "What took you so long?"

"Traffic." Fieldbinder grinned wryly at the chief. "Looks like a bit of a mess, here, Chief."

/c/

A Phase III Centrex 28 console with a number 5 Crossbar has features which greatly aid the console operator in the efficient performance of his or her duties. Six receiving trunks correspond to six Source Receiving Call lamps, which flash at 60 Illuminations Per Minute for Out-House calls and 120 Illuminations Per Minute for In-House calls, and which emit at 60 Signals Per Minute a pleasant yet attention-getting tone. Calls can be transferred in-house via the Start In button, the individual extension code, and the Release Destination button, with the Ready lamp and an audible "access-established" dial tone assisting the operator in a smooth transfer. A completed transfer circuit will occupy a trunk until one or both parties terminate the circuit. As in all fixed-loop operations, the Source- and Destination lamps will remain lit until appropriate parties disconnect. As in all fixed-loop operations, simultaneous occupation of all six trunks will result in an All Paths Busy signal and a 120 IPM flash in the console's Position Release button. The Position Release button allows the operator to exit all completed transfer circuits, and to abort any transfer circuit not yet completed. Other features include a HOLD option to be used when service-area conditions render its use appropriate, and a Position Busy button, an automatic all-trunk feed-lock that renders the console inaccessible from standard trunk circuits, and allows the operator to attend to urgent extra-console business when such arises.

Lunchtime, Bombardini Company and Frequent and Vigorous employees herding through the marble lobby and out the revolving door to lunch, the lobby a big box of noise for a few moments, Judith Prietht had depressed her Position Busy button and was reading a *People* magazine. Lenore Beadsman sat with wet hair over the Frequent and Vigorous console, answering calls.

"Frequent and Vigorous," she said.

"Fucking car won't start," said a voice.

"Sir, I'm afraid this is not Cleveland Towing, this is Frequent and Vigorous Publishing, Inc., shall I give you the correct number, though it may not work? You're very welcome." Lenore Released and then Accessed. "Frequent and Vigorous. Hi Mr. Roxbee-Cox, this is Lenore Beadsman, her roommate. She's supposed to be in again at six. I will. OK. Frequent and Vigorous."

The Position Release button gives the console operator a significant amount of control over any and all communication circuits of which he or she is a part. Depression of the button will immediately terminate any given active console circuit. Like hanging up, only faster and better and more satisfying. An additional and not explicitly authorized feature, introduced by Vern Raring, the night operator, with a trash-bag twistie and his son's Cub Scout knife, allows any and all abusive parties to be put in a HOLD mode unreleasable from that party's end and so rendering that party's telephone service inoperative until such time as the console operator decides to let him or her off the hook, so to speak. Exceptionally abusive calls placed in this mode can also, again thanks to Vern Raring, with the help of the Start Out button and a twelve-digit intertrunk reroute code and long-distance service number, be transferred to any extremely expensive long-distance service point in the world, with Australia and the People's Republic of China being particular favorites of operators inclined to exercise this option.

"I'm going insane," Lenore said. "This is nuts. This thing has hardly stopped beeping and ringing and shrieking once, and there's been like one semi-legitimate call all day."

"Now you know what it's like to work for a change," said Judith Prietht, thumbing through her magazine.

"Was it like this for Candy on my lunch hour?"

"How should I know, I'd like to know? I had affairs to attend to myself." Judith wet a finger and turned a page. A Tab can with red-orange lipstick around the hole and a bag of dull-colored knitting sat on the white counter next to Judith's console. Lenore had a ginger ale and four books, none of which she'd even gotten to open.

There was jingling and whistling out there. Out of the black line of shadow in front of the switchboard cubicle stepped Peter Abbott.

"*Hola,*" said Peter Abbott.

"*You,*" Lenore said over the beeping of the console, "you fix our lines this minute."

"An unbelievably nasty problem," Peter Abbott said, coming around the side of the counter and into the cubicle. Judith Prietht plumped up both sides of her hairdo with her hands. "The office is frantic," Peter said. "You might be interested to know that this is the worst problem since '81 and the ice storm in March and the all-Cleveland-numbers-mysteriously-busy-all-the-time problem, and the worst non-storm-related problem of all time, in Cleveland."

"What an honor."

"Pain in the ass, I'm sure, is more like it," Peter Abbott said.

Judith Prietht was looking up at Peter. "How are you today?"

Peter gave her the fish eye. "*Bueno.*"

"So is it the console?" Lenore asked, looking down at the console as if it might be diseased. "Is that why you're here, and not the tunnel man?"

"I'm here for P.R.," said Peter, eyeing Lenore's cleavage again. "I was just over at Big B.M. Cafe, and before that Bambi's Den, which by the way holy cow. And you should see Big Bob Martinez over at the cafe. He's *so* pissed. And I just now got done talking to your head guy upstairs, just now, Mr. Vigorous, the little fruit fly in the beret and double chin?"

"Ixnay," said Judith Prietht.

"So is it the console," said Lenore.

"We're assuming not," Peter Abbott said. "We're still assuming it's the tunnels. Otherwise why would targets outside your console-access field be affected?"

"Assuming? You're assuming?"

"Oh, an extra-special look back at the Olympics!" Judith Prietht said into her *People*.

"Well, yes," said Peter Abbott. He fingered a wire-stripper uncomfortably.

"The tunnel guy hasn't found anything?"

"Well, Tunnels is just having some problems of its own, really, that aren't helping Interactive Cable's ability to deal effectively with this service problem at all," said Peter Abbott.

"Problems."

"Tunnel men are flakey. Tunnel men tend to be drips. It looks like the tunnel guys have decided to just take off for a while, go fishing or whore-chasing or something. They even like haven't told their wives where they're going, and Mr. Sludgeman, who's the Tunnel Supervisor, is understandably really pissed off, also."

"So wait. We have a hideous tunnel problem that totally impedes our ability to conduct business. . . ."

Judith Prietht snorted.

". . . and Interactive Cable all of a sudden, whom we pay for service, doesn't have the staff needed to restore our service? Is that it?"

"P.R. isn't really my specialty, you know," said Peter Abbott.

"That really sucks," Lenore said.

"Could I just say in passing that you have incredibly beautiful legs?" said Peter Abbott.

"Fresh," said Judith Prietht.

"Fresh?"

"Go into our tunnel," Lenore said to Peter Abbott. The console was beeping insanely. Lenore had only recently gotten the hang of ignoring the console when she really had to. "Go and restore our

service this instant. I'm sure everyone would be grateful, especially
the apparently very busy girls over at Bambi's, if you get my drift.
Or get Mr. Sledgeman to go fix them."

"Sludgeman."

"Sludgeman."

"Mr. Sludgeman can't go, he's in a wheelchair. He broke his
spine in the ice-storm crisis of '81. And I can't go down. You can't
mess with the tunnels, they're real delicate. Think of them like
nerves, and the city's a body, with a nervous system. I go in and
clunk around, and mess things up even more, and then where are
we? Nerves cannot be messed with by the untrained. A tunnel man
needs incredible finesse."

"Even though they're drips."

"Right."

"Holy cow," Judith Prietht said into her magazine. "Holy cow.
Kid, listen to this."

"I'm sure Mr. Vigorous went on record as saying that Frequent
and Vigorous is collectively really ticked off about this," said Lenore.

"Kid, listen. Kopek Spasova. Kopek *Spasova*," Judith said. "The
superstar."

"Who?" said Peter Abbott.

"Kopek Spasova, the little kid from Russia that wins all the gold
medals all over the place in gymnastics. She's coming to Cleveland
next Friday, it says. She's going to exhibit."

"May I please see that?" Lenore said. The console was hushed
for a moment. "Holy mackerel," said Lenore. In *People* there was
a picture of Kopek Spasova, at the 1988 Olympics in Seoul, spinning
around the uneven parallel bars, holding on only by her toes. "She
was really great," Lenore said. "I watched that on television."

"It said she's coming to an exhibition sponsored by Gerber's Baby
Food in the lobby of Erieview Tower," Judith said.

" 'Kicking off a promotional campaign for the infant-food giant
will be hot gymnastic commodity Kopek Spasova,' " Lenore read
out loud, " 'whose father and coach, Ruble Spasov, just signed a
purportedly mammoth promotional and endorsement contract with
the firm.' That's just in few days."

"Endorsing baby food?" said Peter Abbott.

"Well, she's only something like eight, and really small," said Lenore. She looked back down at the magazine. "Dad's not going to be pleased at all. Gerber's done it again. And right here in Cleveland."

"How can a communist do endorsements in the U.S. of A., anyway?" asked Judith Prietht. "There are death-penalty rules against that, in Russia, I thought."

"She's not Russian anymore," said Lenore.

"Oh, right, she's the one whose father just defecated."

"Defected."

"That's the one!"

"Right."

"I gotta go. I gotta go do P.R. at Fuss 'n' Feathers Pets," Peter Abbott said. "The minute we get competent access to the tunnels, you're going to get satisfaction, I'm telling you straight out right now."

"How comforting."

"Take care."

"Kopek Spasova . . . goodbye!" called Judith Prietht.

"*Adios.*"

"I'd like to see that," said Lenore. "Frequent and Vigorous."

/d/

Every year in August Monroe Fieldbinder took a vacation and took his family deep into the woods to a lake in the Adirondacks. On this particular day Monroe Fieldbinder stood alone at the edge of the clear clean cold Adirondack lake, his fishing line limp in the clear water, and stared across the lake at a vacation house burning in the woods above the opposite shore. Fieldbinder listened to the distant crackle and watched the black plume of smoke spiral up into the crisp blue sky. He saw shrouds of twirling sparks and the tiny figures of the house's occupants running around yelling and throwing buckets of water onto the edge of the inferno. Fieldbinder pulled his white fishing hat over his eyes and grinned wryly at the chaotic scene.

and grinned wryly at the scene.

/e/

"Get him down! Get him down!"

"Got him."

"Get him down, Shorlit!"

"I gotcha."

"God, what a racket."

"God."

"We need Wetzel. Ring Wetzel."

"He's out of his mind."

"Just hold him, Wetzel'll be here."

"We're gonna have to wrap him."

"He's right, go get a wrap. Wetzel, go get a wrap, run!"

"Jesus."

"It's OK, it's OK."

"Is he gonna be OK?"

"Can you just stand back, please?"

"Got in the cab, wanted to go to the Loop, I says OK, I'm doin'
like he asks me, I get to Wacker and LaSalle and he starts screaming
like that. I didn't know what the hell to do."

"You did the right thing. Please go stand over there. Shorlit, how
you doing? You got him?"

"Barely. Shit."

"Strong little guy."

"Out of his mind."

"He flipped. He just totally fucking flipped out. Thought I was
gonna have an accident getting him here."

"It's OK, it's OK."

"He's gonna tear his throat out."

"Let's just get the wrap on him."

"Roll him over."

"Ow! Little bastard."

"Sshh, it's OK."

"Get the arm."

"Ow!"

"Roll him back. Wetzel, roll him back."

"I got him."

"Tighten it. Careful, his ribs. One more."

"Gotcha."

"Jesus God will you listen to that."

"Get him in. Wetzel, carry him. Shorlit, get a gurney with leg straps."

"I gotcha."

"Christ, he weighs about ninety pounds. He's a skeleton."

"Can't you make him stop?"

"You're going to have to get back out of the way."

"Thorazine?"

"I want Thorazine, 250 c.c.'s. Get a rubber, he may swallow his tongue. Shorlit, get the door."

"It's OK, sshh, listen we're here to help."

"How can he keep it up? He's gonna stroke."

"Get a rubber."

"Put him down."

"Jesus."

"Straps."

"Thorazine."

"Give me access to an arm, Shorlit."

"Come on."

"Forget the rubber till we get him out. He'll bite your finger."

"People are gonna think we're killing somebody down here."

"Been drivin' a cab seventeen years."

"Please wait outside."

"Never seen any shit like that."

"Wetzel."

"Let's go, pal. You can wait out here."

"Go with the orderly, please."

"It'll kick, wait a second."

"Jesus."

"Look at the eyes. They roll over. They'll roll back when it kicks."

"It's kicking."

"Thank God."

"My ears are ringing."

"Holy shit."

"You better get a drip ready. Call up on five and fill them in, Cathy, OK? First get the drip."

"Shit."

"Thanks, you guys. Shorlit, you want to see if he's got ID?"

"I'll roll him over."

"It's pretty much kicked."

"Christ, he wet his pants."

"I'm going to call up and let Golden know we didn't murder anybody."

"No ID."

"Check his chest. A necklace, tags."

"Umm . . ."

"Undo him. It's OK, it kicked."

"I'm gonna go call. Try to find ID, then take him over to Series Start."

"Jesus."

"Hell of a start to the night."

"Here's a necklace."

"Pretty nice one."

" 'To JB From LB.' "

"His eyes are back, anyway."

"It's OK."

/f/

Just a troubling flash of the Queen Victoria dream, last night. Just a strobe of a florid patch of red dough, curled in scorn. A new one, though. Sinister. Lenore is not unresponsible. This one should make Jay's day.

I am driving in Mexico, in a Lincoln. The air conditioner is broken. It is unbearably hot. I am wearing a wool suit. The suit is soaked with perspiration. The sand of the desert is black. I have reservations at a motel. I pull up to the motel and park by a cactus. There are scorpions. The motel sign says NO VACANCY, even though it's in Mexico. But I have a reservation, and I assert that I do to the desk clerk standing behind the counter in a lobby that smells like a burp. The desk clerk is an enormous mouse, with a huge handlebar mustache. The mouse is wearing a faded woolen Mexican poncho.

"I have a reservation," I say.

"*Sí*," says the mouse.

The mouse leads me through a hole in the wall (eat it, Jay, I defy you not to eat it up) to a room that is lovely and air-conditioned and perfect and complete in every way except that it has no sheets on the bed.

"Gee," I say, "there are no sheets on this bed."

The mouse looks at me. "*Señor*," he says, "if you sheet on my bed, I will keel you."

We both laugh, and the mouse punches me in the arm.

/g/

"Good morning."

"Good morning. How are you this morning?"

"I'm just fine, thanks, Patrice. Shall we begin?"

"Oh, please."

"Are you being sarcastic?"

"Oh, no."

"What is your name?"

"My name is Patrice LaVache."

"What is your married name?"

"My married name is Patrice Beadsman."

"How old are you?"

"I am fifty years old."

"Where are you?"

"I am at a sanitarium in Madison, Wisconsin."

"What is the name of the sanitarium?"

". . . ."

"Whom do you look like?"

"I look like John Lennon."

"Why?"

"I am sharp-featured and wear round John Lennon glasses and have brown hair in a ponytail."

"Why are you here?"

" . . . . "

"Why are you here?"

"Because I want to be."

"How long have you been here?"

"Years and years."

"What do you see?"

"I see a trellis I have to climb."

"Why do you have to climb the trellis?"

"Because I am at the top of the trellis and I have to climb it."

"What is wrong with the trellis?"

"West bids four hearts."

"What is wrong with the trellis?"

"The trellis is white, with vines with thorns. They scratch my stomach my stomach is fat."

"What is wrong with the trellis."

"The trellis has a crack at the top near the window and it pulls away from the wall and breaks off, the trellis breaks off, with vines that bleed when they break."

"How high."

"May I please breathe?"

"Yes."

" . . . . "

"How high?"

"Around . . . the sun. It's a doozy."

"Where are you hurt."

"My back is hurt. My collarbone is hurt. Like a blister I popped open. I gave birth to a blister in the flowers."

"How far did you fall?"

" . . . . "

" . . . . "

"I fell for years."

"Were you hurt."

"I am."

"What do you want."

"Punish me, please."

"Please tell me what you want to be punished for."

"For climbing, and falling, and breathing."

"Who was at the top of the trellis?"

"May I please breathe?"

"Yes."

". . . ."

"Who was at the top of the trellis."

"Nobody."

"Who was at the top of the trellis."

"A window."

"Whose window."

"John and Lenore's. Clarice's. Lenore's window."

"Lenore was in the window."

"It cracked."

"The trellis."

"Yes."

"Who was with Lenore?"

"I need to breathe."

"Breathe. Here, breathe. Let me wipe off your lip."

"Thank you. Lenore's governess was with Lenore."

"What was her name?"

"I don't know the name of Lenore's governess."

"Who was a prisoner?"

"Punish me, please."

"Was Lenore a prisoner?"

"It would be so fun to breathe."

"Was Lenore a prisoner?"

"My son is in horrible trouble, in the south. Higher than the trellis in the south. Smitten from afar. My son is burning in a white place. My son's eyes are white now. Needs something to make himself dark, in the game. Cut."

"Patrice. Breathe."

"I can't."

"Yes you can. You are. Watch yourself breathe, Patrice."

". . . ."

"Was Lenore a prisoner?"

"No she was not a . . . prisoner."

"Why not?"

"God."

"Why not?"

"My son."

"Who was the prisoner, Patrice?"

". . . ."

"Who was the prisoner, Patrice?"

". . . ."

". . . ."

"Good morning how are you this morning."

/h/

PARTIAL TRANSCRIPT OF RAP SESSION, THURSDAY,
26 AUGUST 1990, IN THE OFFICE OF DR. CURTIS JAY, PH.D.
PARTICIPANTS: DR. CURTIS JAY AND MR. RICK
VIGOROUS, AGE 42, FILE NUMBER 744-25-4291.

DR. JAY: Hell of a dream.

RICK VIGOROUS: Bet your ass.

JAY: Mice, again.

RICK: Hate mice.

JAY: Yes?

RICK: Yes.

JAY: Can we possibly articulate why?

RICK: Mice are small, soft, and weak. Mice scuttle. Mice get inside
things and gnaw. Mice tickle.

JAY: Pretty *unclean* animals, too, aren't they?

RICK: Dr. Jay, I swear to God, mention hygiene anxiety just once,
here, and I'm going to lunge.

JAY: The prospect of discussing hygiene anxiety makes you uncomfortable.

RICK: Lunge-alert.

JAY: Fine. Your comfort is after all our number one priority, here.

RICK: Damn well ought to be.

JAY: What would you like to talk about, then?

RICK: Lenore.

JAY: I rather think not, today, if you don't mind.

RICK: Pardon me?

JAY: It just so happens Lenore and I made enormous strides today. I smelled breakthrough, big time.

RICK: Christ, breakthrough again.

JAY: I'd just rather sit on the Lenore thing and see what comes out.

RICK: As it were.

JAY: The jealousy thing, still. You still think I'm sexually interested in Lenore Beadsman.

RICK: I—

JAY: When will you emotionally digest the information that jealousy is simply the stupid man's misdirected projection of insecurity? Of identity troubles? Of hygiene anxiety?

RICK: I am just so tired of you.

JAY: Sometimes you're such a clod, Rick. Think about last night's dream. After what I understand to be fulfilling coitus, then a story, then a fight. Then a dream. The dream. Let's do the dream. Black sand and scorpions. Where does that put us, now?

Rick Vigorous pauses.

JAY: *Awfully* tough to figure out. The G.O.D., where else? But Mexico, too. Which is to say here but not here. Which is to say the here of the dreaming unconscious. A luxurious Lincoln in the midst of a blasted region. Self and Other. Difference. Inside-Outside. Except the air conditioner is broken. The Outside is getting in. The heat is the Outside. It's getting in, because the Inside's *broken.* The Inside doesn't keep the distinction going. The Inside lets the Outside in. And what does it make you do? You *sweat.* You're hot and you sweat. What does the Outside do? It makes you *unclean.* It coats Self with Other. It pokes at the membrane. And if the membrane is what makes you you and the not-you not you, what does that say about you, when the not-you begins to poke through the membrane?

RICK: Look at this, you're drooling. I can see saliva on your lips.

JAY: It makes you *insecure,* is what it does. It makes *you,* the "you," *nonsecure,* not tightly fastened into your side of the membrane. So what happens? Communications break down. You get confused, cautious. Things don't mean what they mean. A Mexican motel sign that should be in Spanish says NO VACANCY. Another person, an Other, becomes a threatening animal, a kind that gets inside things and gnaws, to quote. The lobby smells like the nasty dross of digestion. There are language problems.

RICK: Christ, you can tell Lenore was here. How can you let patients dominate you?

JAY: Come on, Lenore and her particular troubles have nothing to do with it. What's the whole problem? The request you make for a clean, natural thing is interpreted by the Other/foreigner/threatening animal as a threat to *soil*, to dirty. The disturbance of your security on your interior side of the Self-Other membrane makes you an erratic and dangerous component of everyone else's Other-set. Your insecurity bleeds out into and contaminates the identities and hygiene networks of Others. Which again simply reinforces the idea of the hygiene-identity-distinction membrane being *permeable*—permeable via *uncleanness*, permeable via *misunderstanding*—which are ultimately, according to Blentner, not coherently distinguishable.

RICK: Blentner, Blentner. Is this all Blentner?

JAY: To a certain extent. So what? Most of what I've said comes out of the seminal Heidelberg Hygiene Lectures of 1962. I'd let you look at them, but they're—

RICK: I am so tired. You are deliberately unhelpful. I have a freakishly small penis. Attendant self-esteem and security problems. I want help with them. I want to hear about Lenore and her secrets. Instead I hear Olaf Blentner and membranes. Help me with my penis, Jay. Do something useful and help me with my penis.

JAY: Penis, shmenis. What can I do about your penis? You are not your penis. It's you I'm interested in.

RICK: Christ.

JAY: Are things so bad? You've got Lenore, a beautiful, bright, witty, largely joyful albeit troubled and anyway interestingly troubled girl, and she loves you.

RICK: But I don't have her. I can't. I never will.

JAY: The Screen Door of the Great House of Love, et cetera et cetera.

RICK: Christ.

JAY: Well, Rick, really, get mad if you want and no doubt will, but I think à la Blentner it all comes back to the membrane. I think the membrane is the breakthrough you want. I think it's membrane we're both smelling here. You want to use your penis to put what's inside of you inside an Other, to tear down distinctions the way *you* want them torn down. You want to have your membrane and eat it too, so to speak. Your desire to bring the Inside out is just an image of your fear of the Outside getting in . . . in short, hygiene anxiety.

RICK: Fuck this. Start the chair.

JAY: I'm your friend.

RICK: I have to go to the bathroom in the worst way.

JAY: We're making strides. You don't think we're striding? I insist that we're striding.

RICK: Schmuck.

JAY: The scent is everywhere.

RICK: You know who you'd get along with really well, is Norman Bombardini.

JAY: You know Norman?

RICK: Good God. I should have known. Let me out of here.

JAY: Come back on Monday. Give Lenore money so she can come back, too.

RICK: Schnook.

JAY: I'm here for you.

/i/

Lenore saw Mr. Bloemker through the window of Gilligan's Isle as she was passing by after work on her way to the bus stop. Gilligan's Isle was a little ways down from the Weight Watchers facility Norman Bombardini had pointed out from the restaurant the night before. In Lenore's purse was a note from Mr. Bombardini, with a smeared chocolate thumbprint in one corner, that had come with an almost empty box of candy to the Frequent and Vigorous switchboard today. The note said "Be my tiny Yin."

Gilligan's Isle was a very popular bar. The inside of the place was round, the walls were painted to look like the filmy blue horizon of the ocean, and the floors were painted and textured to resemble beach. There were palm trees all over, fronds hanging down ticklishly over the patrons. Sprouting from the floor of the bar were huge statued likenesses of the whole cast: the Skipper, the Howells, Ginger, and the rest, painted in bright castaway colors and all with uncannily characteristic facial expressions. The huge castaways were sunk into the floor at about chest level; their heads, arms, shoulders, and outstretched upturned hands were all tables for patrons. There was a certain amount of intertwining: Mr. Howell's arm was wrapped part way around Mrs. Howell's waist, Mary-Ann's long hair brushed the plastic top of Mr. Howell's forearm, the Professor's thumb hovered achingly close to Ginger's décolletage. The bar itself was made of that vaguely straw-like material that huts on the show were made of. Behind the bar at all times was one of a number of bartenders, all of whom resembled, to a greater or lesser degree, Gilligan. Once an hour the bartender would be required to do something blatantly cloddish and stupid—a standard favorite had the bartender slipping on a bit of spilled banana daiquiri and falling and acting as if he had driven his thumb into his eye—and the patrons would, if they were hip and in the know, say with one voice, "Aww, Gilligan," and laugh, and clap.

Mr. Bloemker was sitting at the back, at Mary-Ann's left hand, facing the front window. With him was a very beautiful woman in a shiny dress who stared blankly straight in front of her. Lenore saw them and came inside and went over to their table.

"Hi Mr. Bloemker," she said.

Mr. Bloemker looked up with a start. "Ms. Beadsman."

"Hi."

"Hello. Fancy meeting . . ." Mr. Bloemker looked strange and scooted a tiny bit toward Mary-Ann's wrist, away from the beautiful woman he had been sitting right next to.

"Well Frequent and Vigorous is just over in the Bombardini Building, over there," said Lenore, "which you can probably see, if you look over in the corner of the window, over there, with the lights on?"

"Well well."

"Hi, I'm Lenore Beadsman, I know Mr. Bloemker," Lenore said to the beautiful woman.

The beautiful woman didn't say anything; she stared straight ahead.

"Lenore Beadsman, this is Brenda, Brenda, may I present Ms. Lenore Beadsman," said Mr. Bloemker, his fingers in his beard. In front of both Mr. Bloemker and Brenda were drinks in plastic jugs shaped like pineapples, with straws coming out of holes in the top.

"Hi," Lenore said to Brenda.

". . . ."

"Please sit down," said Mr. Bloemker.

Lenore sat. "Is Brenda OK?"

"Please don't mind Brenda. Brenda is very shy," Mr. Bloemker said. He was slurring a tiny bit. He was apparently a bit tight. His cheeks were lit up above the tendrils of the top of his beard, his nose shone, his glasses were a little steamed, and he was uncombed, a huge, obscene Superman-curl of hair lying like a giant comma across his forehead.

"I tried to call you today," said Lenore, "except you weren't there, and then I could only try once, because we were incredibly busy, what with horrible line trouble and everything."

"Yes. It was a busy day."

"I couldn't have my father call you because he wasn't in. He's out for a couple of days, and apparently unreachable."

"Yes."

"But the minute he gets back."

"Fine."

"And the really big except also troubling news is that I think for sure Lenore and Mrs. Yingst and the other patients are at least still around, in Cleveland, because Mrs. Yingst's walker was in my apartment last night, and it wasn't before, and she left a message for me with my bird, who can suddenly talk."

"Your bird can suddenly talk?"

"Yes. Unfortunately mostly obscenely."

"I see."

"To be honest, it's not inconceivable that Mrs. Yingst gave him LSD."

"Oh, now, I don't think Mrs. Yingst would do something like that."

"But then what's going on, all these old patients just hanging around Cleveland, and not telling anybody, and staff and staff's families hanging around, too?"

"Residents."

"Residents, sorry." Lenore looked at Brenda. "Listen, are you sure Brenda's OK? Brenda like hasn't moved once, that I've been able to see, since I got here." Brenda stared straight ahead out of her beautiful eyes.

Mr. Bloemker looked blankly at Lenore. "Please," he said, "give Brenda not a thought. It takes Brenda a while to loosen up around strangers." He looked back down at his pineapple with bleary eyes and played with his straw. "Residents. We call them residents, you know, actually it's at my insistence that we not call them patients, we call them residents because we try very hard at Shaker Heights to minimize the medical implications of their being with the facility. We try to minimize the appearance of illness, the importance of illness. Without much success, really, I'm afraid."

"I understand," said Lenore.

There was a yelp and a crash and tinkle; the bartender lay sprawled over the bar with his head in a palm-tree pot, his legs in white cotton pants waving, beer on the floor. "Aww, Gilligan," everyone yelled and laughed, except Lenore and Mr. Bloemker and Brenda. Mr. Bloemker scratched under his beard with his straw.

"A troubling and disorienting position at the facility, mine," he said. He looked up at Lenore. "Why don't you help yourself to some of Brenda's Twizzler? Brenda's not drinking it, I see."

Brenda stared.

"Well, I don't really drink alcoholic stuff much," Lenore said. "It makes me cough."

"Here."

"Thanks."

"Troubling."

"I can imagine."

"The old . . . the old are not like you and I, Ms. Beadsman. As you no doubt know, having spent so much time around . . . at the facility."

"They're different, I agree."

"Yes."

"Yes." Lenore tried a bit of Twizzler, got a strong taste of gin and Hawaiian Punch, closed her eyes, discreetly spat the bit of Twizzler back out of the straw into the plastic pineapple jug.

"They are also Midwesterners," continued Mr. Bloemker. "As a rule, almost all of them are Midwesterners." He stared off. "This area of the country, what are we to say of this area of the country, Ms. Beadsman?"

"Search me."

"Both in the middle and on the fringe. The physical heart, and the cultural extremity. Corn, a steadily waning complex of heavy industry, and sports. What are we to say? We feed and stoke and supply a nation much of which doesn't know we exist. A nation we tend to be decades behind, culturally and intellectually. What are we to say about it?"

"Well, you're saying pretty good things, really; I sense some interest on Brenda's part, too, I think."

"This area makes for truly bizarre people. Troubled people. As past historians have noted and future historians will note."

"Yup."

"And when the people in question then become *old,* when they must not only come to terms with and recognize the implications of their consciousness of themselves as parts of this strange, occluded place . . . when they must incorporate and manage *memory,* as well, past perceptions and feelings. Perceptions of the past. Memories: things that both are and aren't. The Midwest: a place that both is and isn't. A volatile mixture. I have sensed volatileness at the facility for some time."

"Does this explain anything, do you think? Disappearance-wise?"

"I think it explains very little."

"I'm going to give Brenda back her Twizzler. Brenda, here's your Twizzler back, thanks a lot, I'm just not in the mood. Are you sure she's OK? Have I offended her somehow?"

"Brenda, don't be a stick in the mud."

Brenda was silent.

Mr. Bloemker massaged his chin. "The average age of the residents at the facility—I did some research today at the request of the owners—the average age of the residents at the facility is eighty-seven. Eighty-seven years of age. How old are you, Ms. Beadsman?"

"I'm twenty-four."

"So you were born in 1966. I was born in 1957. The average resident was born in 1903. Think of that."

"Boy."

"These people, think of the worlds they've been part of. The *worlds.* They've literally gone from horse and buggy to moonshot. The technological changes alone that they have stood witness to are staggering. How might one even begin to orient oneself with respect to such a series of changes in the fundamental features of the world? How to begin to come to some understanding of one's place in a system, when one is a part of an area that exists in such a troubling relation to the rest of the world, a world that is itself stripped of any static, understandable character by the fact that it changes, radically, all the time?"

"System?"

Mr. Bloemker looked at his thumb. "Have you ever been to the Desert, Ms. Beadsman? The G.O.D.?"

"Not for quite a while, like ten years. Lenore and I actually used to go. She had a Volvo that we'd take down, do a little fishing at the edge, do the wander-thing."

"Yes. I would like to go down and wander."

"Well it's easy. You can just buy a Wander Pass at any gate. They're only about five dollars. The really desolate areas can get pretty crowded, of course, sometimes, so it's good to get there early, get as much wandering as you can in before noon."

"Brenda and I may go down soon. I feel a need for . . . for sinisterness. I sense Brenda does, too. Am I right, plum petal?" Bloemker carelessly chucked Brenda's chin with his hand. Brenda tilted way back on the bench, beside Mary-Ann's hand, until her legs hit the bottom of the table, then sat rapidly up again, vibrating a little. Lenore narrowed her eyes.

"Hmmm."

"Another thing I must in all frankness admit to finding . . . amusing," Mr. Bloemker said, sucking for a moment on the straw in his jug, drinking at something that smelled to Lenore like another Twizzler, "although I hesitate to use that term, because it sounds as if I mean to be derogatory, which I do not. Our residents, the people who are very old now, have really made our culture what it is. And now by culture I mean this country's culture, not Ohio's culture, which I do not profess even to begin to understand. Particularly the women, it seems to me. We like to think the sexual revolution is a creation of our generation. That's a crock, pardon my language. The women who are now old invented it all. Everything we profess to enjoy. The women who reside in facilities now were the first American women to cut their hair short. The first to drink. To smoke. To dance in public. Shall we discuss voting? Making money? Being economic entities? They were pioneers, these people in wheelchairs with blanketed laps."

"Listen, are you absolutely sure Brenda's OK?" Lenore asked. "Because the thing is I haven't really seen Brenda move once on her own, which it occurs to me now includes seeing her chest move to breathe, or seeing her blink. What's with Brenda?"

"The cutting of hair. That particularly fascinates me. It freed these women from a prison. An aesthetic prison. It freed them from the one-hundred-brushstrokes-a-night tyranny of the culture that . . . obtained."

"The not blinking really bothers me, I've got to tell you. And what's this on her neck, here? On Brenda's neck?"

"Birthmark. Pimple."

"Is this an air-valve? This is an air-valve! See, here's the cap. Are you sitting with an inflatable doll?"

"Don't be ridiculous."

"You're sitting with an inflatable doll! This isn't even a person."

"Brenda, this isn't funny, show Ms. Beadsman you're a person."

"My God. See, she weighs about one pound. I can lift her up." Lenore lifted Brenda way up by the thigh. Brenda suddenly fell out of Lenore's hand and her head got wedged between the bench and Mary-Ann's hand, and she was upside down. Her dress fell up.

"Good heavens," said Mr. Bloemker.

"One of *those* dolls. That's just sick. How can you sit in public with an anatomically correct doll?"

"I must confess, the wool seems to have been completely pulled over my eyes. I thought she was simply extremely shy. A troubled Midwesterner, in an ambivalent relation . . ."

"Nice doll," remarked another patron, at Mrs. Howell's elbow.

"I think Brenda and I should be going," Mr. Bloemker said. He struggled with Brenda's plastic legs. Brenda was wedged. Lenore helped Mr. Bloemker pull. Brenda came out, but her dress got caught on Mary-Ann's thumbnail and ripped and fell off.

"Holy shit," said Lenore.

"Holy cow," said the patron at Mrs. Howell's elbow. "Where'd you get that? Are those expensive?" Other people at different tables turned to look. Things got quiet.

"How excruciatingly . . . ," Bloemker muttered.

"Probably wise to go now," Lenore said.

"Certainly nice to have seen you, anxiously await your father's . . ." Mr. Bloemker covered Brenda as best he could with his sportcoat and made for the door. There were whistles and claps. Bloemker broke into a run and ran suddenly into the bartender, who was coming around the side of the bar with a tray of creamy White Russians. There was an enormous crash and tinkle, and the bartender flipped over backwards and drove his thumb into his eye, and White Russian went everywhere, and a shard of broken White-Russian glass hit Brenda and punctured her and she flew out of Mr. Bloemker's arms and went whizzing around the room, twirling, losing air, finally to land limply but beautifully in a palm-tree pot, with one leg wrapped around her neck. Mr. Bloemker flew out the door. Lenore sniffed at his Twizzler. The patrons laughed and clapped,

"Aww, Gilligan."

/a/

"Come in. Waiting long? Busy day. I get back, am unable even to see my desk, for all the messages. Foamwhistle, leave. Remember Pupik, in Lids, and Goggins, in Jars, have to be brought to see me at the *same time*. Attend to it. I've asked you repeatedly before. A company that cannot coordinate its lids and its jars is a bad company. I do not run a bad company. Go now. Come in. Don't jump at her, Foamwhistle, you can whisper and giggle together later. This is my time. Come in. For whatever part of your wait was my fault I apologize, although none of it was my fault. You like this? You don't like this? I caught it. I had it stuffed. Still looks wet, to me. You? I caught it in Canada. Went up to Canada, with Gerber. Did a little fishing. Little fishing with Gerber up in Canada. Got a tan, a natural one, tell your sister that. Not there, up here, closer. Light's terrible in here today. Why Foamwhistle can't arrange an office that doesn't have to depend for its light on a window is beyond me. At least I can see you up here. Are you really gray, or is it just the light? Although I like the rain on the window, I like to look out, when I find myself with a second, which is of course never. Lake looks good in the rain. Rain cleans the lake up. The sound of the rain on the window . . . You like it? No? Yes? Down to business. Stonecipher got off to Amherst satisfactorily, I assume. How long has it been, three weeks? You can't spare an hour in three weeks? I know what you're going to say, but the Canada thing just came up. Gerber just came up with the idea. We can't plan these things, or it looks as if we're price-fixing or something. You, on the other

hand, you have no free time? This is not simply one indefinitely
broad interval of free time? How is your job? How much money do
you have? Do you have money? If you do not say anything, I automatically assume you have money. Further thoughts on the issue
we discussed at length the last time I saw you? No? No further
thoughts? Planless, still? Distinguished graduate of Oberlin? Most
highly educated receptionist and telephone operator in Cleveland
history? And the firm. I anxiously await the appearance of the firm's
first book. Has the firm published a book yet? Norslan? That's not
a book, that's advertising. Still, production is production, as I well
know. Up to four-ten yet? Still four big dollars an hour? How long?
No. Perfectly natural to want some sort of interval without school,
without a real job or any responsibilities, I won't even say marriage
because my glasses will break, but *how long*? The reasonable question.
Followed by the reasonable point. Wait. Wait. To love a non-
nuclear relative is a good thing. To be connected . . . excuse me,
to be connected is good. But to imitate that relative . . . in all
facets . . . is not good. To try to be that relative is unnatural. Thus
bad. Not fair? Not true? Then, really, why purposely invite comparison, accusation? Is that the appropriate question? Why the hair,
which you must know I loathe that way? The ancient dresses? What
is the function of those shoes? Yes, function. I know. Wait a moment. The aimlessness after a self-consciously dazzling college career. Gramma Lenore leaves her child, my father, your grandfather,
at Shaker School and flies off to England. England. Yes, I know
where function comes from, after all. Yes. The irreponsibility. Your
refusal, *a*, to go to school; your refusal, *b*, to put your expensive
degree to renumerative use. Your refusal even to live at home. No,
not really, of course there is understanding, but perceive simply that
on my end too there is embarrassment and sadness. Except in the
daytime . . . excuse me . . . except in the daytime there are only
Miss Malig and myself, in that huge house. Why that look? I seethe
with anger at that look, and will not even condescend to deny
anymore. Your mother's child. The aimlessness. A mindless job,
punching numbers and making connections for other people. Still
no romantic involvement? No? No, that doesn't point up an important difference. Aimlessness and irresponsibility simply take on
new forms as time goes by. Besides, there is Mr. Vigorous. No,

don't bother to deny involvement, bother to deny extent. I see. No real point in discussing it, is there? So then, Lenore. Right. With regard to the issue I strongly suspect has understandably brought you here, just let me say everything's largely under control and thoroughly explainable. The thing with Gerber was incidental. The thing with Gerber just came up. Rummage did call Bloomfield. Bloemker. At my instructions. Yes. Not at all. Your not knowing what's going on was purely accidental. The big picture and so on. I'd assumed Gramma, not to mention very probably Foamwhistle, had been keeping you filled quietly in, all along. What was going on was that some time ago Gramma Lenore summoned me to her greenhouse of a room to discuss a project. A project. A business project. Just wait. She had concepts she wanted to bounce off me. They bounced, and I was intrigued. I brought in one of our men, one of our researchers, one of our chemists, the Obstat kid? Neil Obstat, Jr.? I know you went to Shaker with him. The little lizard still has your picture in his wallet, apparently. In any event, he was intrigued, too. Gramma Lenore's friend, the Yingst woman? Had had a husband who had done research. Pineal research. The pineal gland? No? A little round gland at the base of the brain? P-i-n-e-a-l? Remember Descartes thought it was where mind met body, way back when, the point of mediation, where the body's hydraulics were adjusted and operated according to the . . . ? Right. Certain you must have done it in class. Yingst had theories, certain theories, in which Gramma Lenore was not uninterested, for predictably self-oriented reasons. A mutually beneficial transaction was proposed."

/b/

From Advertising Age, 28 August 1990, "Ear to the Ground" Column, pp. 31–32:

INFANT-FOOD MARKET HEATS UP THANKS TO UNPRECEDENTED PRO-MOTIONAL AGGRESSIVENESS, ENTREPRENEURIAL CAJONES.

Cleveland, Ohio, is the unlikely site for what insiders say is the next real industry battle in the production of infant food, with giants Gerber's Quality Brands and Stonecipheco Baby Food Products lining up toe to toe for a market-share struggle that could very well leave third-place Beech-Nut Infant Division out in the cold.

As Gerber's ties up loose ends and prepares to mount an unprecedented pan-media advertising and consumer-good-will operation, featuring the highly prized and high-priced services of ex-Soviet hot commodity Kopek Spasova, Stonecipheco, say *A.A.* sources and analysts, is preparing to announce and capitalize quickly on the market implications of a research advance unprecedented in food service history, a cattle-endocrine derivative that, when added to an infant's (Stonecipheco!!!) food on a regular basis, can significantly speed up the development of powers of speech and comprehension. "Kids are talking months, maybe years before they normally would have, in limited tests," whispered an inside Stonecipheco source. "We're talking not only eventual market domination, but a potentially really significant insight into the relation between nutrition and mental development, between what the body needs and the mind can do."

Is Gerber's in on the research? No one's saying, but the coincidence of Gerber's opening its promotional bonanza in downtown Cleveland, a stone's throw from Stonecipheco's main facility and headquarters, has been noted. The plot also thickens when we recall that company chiefs Robert Gerber and Stonecipher Beadsman III are old school chums, both attending tiny highbrow Amherst College in Massachusetts in the fifties.

The interest of nutrition-market enthusiasts in the whole downtown Cleveland scene heightens when we take note again of last week's *E.T.G.* item concerning genetic-engineering giant Norman Bombardini's wild and apparently successful forays into . . . (continued on page 55)

/c/

". . . that, to repeat what I heard for years and years and suspect you've been hearing over and over, yourself, something's meaning is nothing more or less than its function. Et cetera et cetera et cetera. Has she done the thing with the broom with you? No? What does she use now? No. What she did with me—I must have been eight, or twelve, who remembers—was to sit me down in the kitchen and take a straw broom and start furiously sweeping the floor, and she asked me which part of the broom was more elemental, more *fundamental*, in my opinion, the bristles or the handle. The bristles or the handle. And I hemmed and hawed, and she swept more and more violently, and I got nervous, and finally when I said I supposed the bristles, because you could after a fashion sweep without the handle, by just holding on to the bristles, but couldn't sweep with just the handle, she tackled me, and knocked me out of my chair, and yelled into my ear something like, '*Aha*, that's because you want to *sweep* with the broom, isn't it? It's because of what you want the broom *for*, isn't it?' Et cetera. And that if what we wanted a broom for was to break windows, then the *handle* was clearly the fundamental essence of the broom, and she illustrated with the kitchen window, and a crowd of domestics gathered; but that if we wanted the broom to sweep with, see for example the broken glass, sweep sweep, the bristles were the thing's essence. No? What now, then? With pencils? No matter. Meaning as fundamentalness. Fundamentalness as use. Meaning as use. Meaning as use. Excuse me? You're asking me why? Lenore, please. What do you talk about all the time, then, 'why'? She feels useless. She feels, felt, as if she had no function, over there, in the nursing home. Wait, I'll get to that. Uselessness is the key, here. Well now Lenore of course she had to be there, nursing care, ninety-eight point six, and she wasn't happy in the house, which she said if you remember dripped with memories of lost capacity. No, there was no choice, and we did buy the Shaker Heights facility, even though it was a poor investment. If that's not love, what is? But for someone who feels that meaning is use then to feel that she has no use, well then. She told me she was unhappy. She came to me and told me that. Didn't tell you all this? I find that passing strange. Recall appropriately now when I refer to my own mother's section, for those with Alzheimer's. This bothered Gramma Lenore deeply. How Bloomfield noticed that the patients there couldn't remember the names for things, televisions, water, doors . . . and so under Gramma Lenore's influence he had them identified with their function? With the gilt letters, the little use-vocabulary handbook, with Lawrence Welk on the cover? So the door is 'What we go from room to room though'? Water is 'What we drink, without color'? Television is 'What we watch Lawrence Welk on'—Lawrence Welk being primitive, undefined, even in syndication, no problem with Lawrence Welk. How my mother and all the rest came after a fashion to relearn the words they needed, via function, via what the things named were good for? And then Gramma Lenore noticing that the one component of the facility this method couldn't be applied to was the patients themselves, because they *had* no function, no use, weren't good for anything really at all? No? She told me this drove her up the wall. They had no use at all. What? No, the derivative comes from the pineals of cattle. We use cattle pineals. Rather we would if we could. Now, just wait, please. So Gramma Lenore perceived loss of identity without function. She wanted to be useful, she said to me. As did Gretchen Yingst, of course, and that Mr. Etvos, the whole pseudo-Wittgensteinian mafia over there. Mrs. Yingst had results from her late husband's projects—the really interesting ones, by the way, done on his own, not for his company. Consolidated Gland Derivatives, in Akron? Now C.E.O.'d by Dick Lipp, best serve on the corporate tennis circuit? On his own, though. Took much of it to his grave, apparently, but left some pineal results written down . . . on Batman tablets, the coincidentality of which I don't care to comment on, right now, for reasons that you'll hear in approximately six minutes. Now just wait. There is of course too the fact that pineal-efficacy in nutrition is, it's turning out, verifiably mostly linguistic, as I mentioned, speech understanding et cetera, the dreary and tiresome importance of which to certain parties I won't even bother to allude to, but the understandable importance of which to potentially proud and ambitious parents I both understand and rub my hands over, not to mention the importance in all sorts of general scientific areas from which benefits should begin to accrue in no small measure, should things get on track. . . . So that Gramma Lenore, Mrs. Yingst, and Mr. Etvos agreed to turn over results from Mr. Yingst's work to me, and I bounced them off Obstat, a pain in the rear but a fine chemist, and Obstat's eyes bugged out, and away we went. Or rather now away they've gone, which is to say they've apparently decided to withdraw their support from the project, and to take back the Yingst Batman tablets, which is regrettable though OK, but also to filch all of Obstat's samples and results and notes, which he in an attempt to be clever was keeping in Batman folders and Batman lunchboxes in the laboratory fridge, and apparently the day before I left for Canada to do some fishing with Bob Gerber Mrs. Yingst and Etvos got in here and got to Obstat, and Etvos amused Obstat with card tricks, which is unfortunately not hard to do, while Mrs. Yingst put the fruits of many many dollars of research into that kangaroo-pouch pocket of her nightie, under her robe, which Obstat helpfully remembers as being pink terry cloth. Obstat, why don't you just come out. Why don't you just come on out, Obstat. Why don't you just come out from behind the curtain.

Lenore could see your shoes, anyway, couldn't you? Come out, Obstat. Obstat is here representing the technical angle on the whole problem. Neil you remember my daughter, Lenore, Neil. Yes. And they've made off with the all-important Batman items, which includes the only existing jars of the prototype food mentioned in this *Advertising Age*, here, and if I ever find out who leaked to that magazine I will kill, kill. Are you listening on the intercom, Foamwhistle? If you're listening make no sign that you're doing so. I thought so. And they have it all. And who knows what they're doing, who really knows what the food can do. Cattle pineal derivative is phenomenally if mysteriously powerful, we're finding out. Isn't that right Obstat. And they have seen fit to leave the nursing home, and have others join them, one shudders at the persuasive force probably brought to bear, to leave the nursing home, on who knows what sort of quest for function, or symbolic rejection of their life as they've come to understand it, who knows? Worried? Am I worried? What kind of worry? In all honesty not particularly. She's surrounded by followers, which is of course her favorite sort of situation. Warmth must have been arranged somehow. They could be at anyone's home, some nursing home janitor. . . . Yes, we have checked. Still, though. At the house? You thought she might be at the house? You didn't call Miss Malig to see? I see. I'm seething. Let's not discuss it. She's not at the house, rest assured. Frankly I'm more worried, and here I apologize not a whit, frankly I'm more worried about the pineal-derivative situation, the potential embarrassment and revenue-loss of not following through with the product for the market year, especially now that that bastard Gerber is starting his ridiculously expensive attack, with the gymnast, et cetera, I'm sure you've heard. Yes, I'd like to go too, actually, but appearances. . . . You and that Vigorous person go and report. No that will not make you an employee. So who knows where they are, who knows what they're doing. No. I do not think the police need to be involved. Especially at this point. Police mean press means publicity about missing material means Gerber and Beechnut. No. Look, I rationalize it this way, and invite you to do the same. Their leaving is connected with a project connected with the Company. The Company owns the Home. Therefore their leaving is connected with the ownership of the Home, which makes their leaving almost like a nursing-home field trip. Unless of course they don't come back with the pineal material pretty soon. Or unless they give it to Gerber, or to Erv Beechnut, the thought of which deeply chills me, especially with Gerber's being in Cleveland next week, knowing Gramma Lenore's long antipathy for the Company that's given her everything she has and enjoys. No, that's beside the point. Although it really, I hope, doesn't ultimately matter, because Neil here feels he can reconstruct the relevant research and follow through with the delivered goods, eventually, even without the filched material. *Eventually*, though, and meanwhile there's Gerber, drooling over the aforementioned material. But we can do it, and hopefully, barring Obstat's being wrong which is scarcely possible in such an important regard is it Neil, or lid-and-jar screw-ups which are as of today unthinkable are you listening Foamwhistle, to be ready to run market-tests by Thanksgiving. Test small bits of the potential global market. We're thinking Corfu. Corfu is what we're thinking, for the first distribution, right now. Small, isolated, contained. Corfusians breed like hell, infants crawling all over. We hope to be ready to hit Corfu with Stonecipheco Infant Accelerant by November. Care for a Corfu nut, by the way? No? They're quite good. I got them in Canada, fishing. Eat a nut, Obstat."

/d/

FROM THE RECORDS OF THE FIRST UNITED CHURCH OF ONE GOD FOR ALL MEN, CHAGRIN FALLS, OHIO: PARTIAL TRANSCRIPT OF WEDDING OF MR. STONECIPHER BEADSMAN III, OF SHAKER HEIGHTS, OHIO, AND MISS PATRICE ANDLEMOTH LAVACHE, OF MADISON, WISCONSIN, 26 MAY 1961.

MINISTER: Where is everyone?
PATRICE LAVACHE: Here I am, your honor.
MINISTER: And where is the groom?
STONECIPHER BEADSMAN III: We are here.

ROBERT GERBER, BEST MAN: Here we are!

MINISTER: Are we all here?

MRS. LAVACHE: What's that on his tuxedo?

STONECIPHER BEADSMAN III: Can we get on with this? We have a reception to go to, after all.

MRS. LAVACHE: There is a lady's undergarment fastened to that man's tuxedo.

ROBERT GERBER: "O, first she gave me whiskey, then she gave me gin, then she gave me crème de menthe for kissing her on the chin."

MINISTER: This man is intoxicated.

PATRICE LAVACHE: Oh, Stone.

STONECIPHER BEADSMAN III: Shut up, Patrice. Father I personally am not intoxicated, Mr. Gerber is here for ring-duty only, all pertinent parties are functional, let's do the thing.

MRS. LAVACHE: I insist that that man remove the underwear from his tuxedo.

MINISTER: We really must insist, sir.

ROBERT GERBER: You have any idea, *any* idea, what this panty signifies?

MRS. LAVACHE: I shudder to think. I'm shuddering, Edmund.

MRS. LENORE BEADSMAN: Get on with it!

ROBERT GERBER: "O, first she gave me whiskey, then she gave me scotch, then she gave me crème de menthe for kissing her . . ."

MRS. LAVACHE: Oh, Edmund.

MR. LAVACHE: There there. The family's loaded.

MRS. LENORE BEADSMAN: This is ridiculous, get on with it. Stonecipher, what are you doing?

STONECIPHER BEADSMAN III: Shall we, Father?

MINISTER: Ahem. Miss LaVache, I understand you have composed your own vows, to be read to Mr. Beadsman.

PATRICE LAVACHE: Yes, sir.

MINISTER: And Mr. Beadsman?

STONECIPHER BEADSMAN III: I'll just be going with the standard. If the standard's good enough for the rest of the Judeo-Christian world, it's good enough for me.

PATRICE LAVACHE: Oh, Stone.

MINISTER: Is that man going to be all right?

MRS. LAVACHE: He doesn't look well at all.

MINISTER: What's that ring he's holding? Is that supposed to be the wedding ring?

STONECIPHER BEADSMAN III: Of course not. Bob, show the minister the monstrously expensive ring I've purchased.

ROBERT GERBER: Here it is.

PATRICE LAVACHE: But that's a Lone Ranger decoder ring!

ROBERT GERBER: Surprise!

STONECIPHER BEADSMAN III: Where is the monstrously expensive ring I've purchased?

ROBERT GERBER: I lost my head. I gave it to Paquita, to my little Amazon flower. A madness, last night, in the fulgent bath of the Midwestern moon. The night air, spring in Cleveland. And she in return . . . oh Paquita, my little Amazon flower!

MR. LAVACHE: So that's where that came from.

STONECIPHER BEADSMAN III: This is beyond unforgivable.

ROBERT GERBER: "O, first she gave me whiskey, then she gave me grass . . ."

MRS. LENORE BEADSMAN: God damn it.

MINISTER: Ahem. Most dearly beloved, we are . . .   sight of God . . .   union, spiritual . . .   speak now or . . . Miss LaVache . . .   lovely vows . . .   commit . . . Mr. Beadsman . . .   forever   . . . ?

STONECIPHER BEADSMAN III: Of course I do.

MINISTER: I now pronounce you man and wife. You may kiss the bride.

STONECIPHER BEADSMAN III: Come here, Patrice. Are you ready to be kissed?

PATRICE BEADSMAN: Yes.

STONECIPHER BEADSMAN III: Good.

ROBERT GERBER: Yay!

MRS. LENORE BEADSMAN: About time.

STONECIPHER BEADSMAN III: We're going to be late for the reception. Please go to the car immediately, Patrice.

ROBERT GERBER: Hell of a deal, guy. Congratulations.

STONECIPHER BEADSMAN III: You bastard. You wore a panty to my wedding, and I had to use a ring out of a box of Ralston. I'll get even with you in corporate struggle.

ROBERT GERBER: Oh, yeah?

STONECIPHER BEADSMAN III: Damn fine ceremony, Father. Rewards will accrue. I must go. Goodbye, everyone!

EVERYONE: Goodbye!

MRS. LENORE BEADSMAN: Officious little pissant.

/e/

". . . that at this point who Bloomfield chooses to spend his time with is of less than no concern to me. Bloemker. Dolls might be the very best thing for him, nervous little moth of a man, always scratching at his beard, makes me itchy. Obstat, sit down, you're getting on my nerves. Other item, yes. Disturbing, too, so brace. Your brother is apparently temporarily missing. John. John is missing, in Chicago. Just wait. What would have been the point of telling you right away? It would have served no purpose. I found out just this morning, just two hours ago. Beal called me from Chicago. Seems there was a lecture John had wanted to go to, so he called a taxi from his office. A friend talked to him immediately before he called the taxi, but that's the last. . . . No, not at the lecture. Apparently not seen since. Now, really. I am inclined to think John simply elected to drop out of sight for a while. He's dropped before, God knows. Holiday Inn, anywhere, what difference would it make? I could call Steve Holiday, yes, but that's not the point, that was just an example. Calm down. I'm also inclined to suspect that it is not impossible that John is somehow privy to, maybe even involved in, Gramma Lenore's whole little adventure. No, not really. But he's always been against the Company, we both know that, and there was the constant doting. His sentiments, her sentiments. It's not inconceivable. No, I called Wisconsin, not a peep, and your mother is in a not-well period right now. Even more not-well. No, but just not in a position to be useful to anyone. So wait. What could I do? I'm prepared to give him a few weeks, and if he still hasn't turned up, at least to teach his classes, to begin worrying in earnest. Yes, his colleagues did call the police. No, I've not called Clarice, who knows which of her . . . places she's at today. I did call Al in here, and I told Al, and he'll tell Clarice. Alvin is part of the family, too, Lenore. Stonecipher is not reachable, as I've said. Stonecipher, no doubt following your personal lead, has opted not to have a telephone. The best and brightest of my children cannot be reached by me. Interpret that in whatever way you wish. Obstat, if you want another nut, take one, do not play with the jar. Go see Clarice if you wish; obviously your sister can be seen by you. Discuss whatever you wish. No? I'm ignoring everything you imply. Go to her. I am also now going to ask you for a favor. Go to Stonecipher and speak to him and see if he has been communicated with in any way. By either of them. Very possibly, I think. You'll have to see him personally. It's now become clear that he represents the future of the family, of the Company, that it is he on whom the mantle of power and control will devolve. Gramma Lenore knows this, she has been a witness to, if not even more likely a cause of, John's default and then your default. All the tests for nothing. No, I never see irony, Lenore. Irony is a meaningless word to me. The point here is that Stonecipher must and will know that he is connected to this family, which is to say the Company. Not at all. Go, see him, autumn in New England. Take a vacation from your vacation, some time off from your time off. Tell him what obtains here, including the story of Gramma Lenore, et cetera, and be told of any and all involvement on his part. No. That's ridiculous. You cannot possibly be fired for taking one or two days off for a family emergency. Who? Peahen? No. I am prepared to allow you, to insist that you take the Company jet, to minimize the time factor. A friend could be taken along. You see what you can do. In the next three or four days. Yes. I am prepared to wait and do more or less . . . nothing. My worry is present but manageable. Do this for me. Help the family, Lenore. See what you can do about getting off. Obstat, perhaps you'd better be getting back to the lab. I . . . heavens, I have a tennis date. Did you bus over? I more than understand. I've always hated your car, as you should recall vividly. Did I or did I not try to give you a car? But no. Let Foamwhistle drive you back. Oh come now . . . Foamwhistle, come in here at once. Think about what I've said. Please be in touch. Foamwhistle, drive Lenore to Erieview Plaza. Pardon me?

What do you mean Pupik refuses to be in the same room with Goggins? Get me Pupik. You two may go free. Please call me soon. Hello, Pupik?"

/f/

Ideas for Monroe Fieldbinder Story Collection, 27 August

1. Monroe watches a house burn down. Or Monroe's house burns down, symbolizing destruction of the structure of his life as estate attorney, a plunging into chaos and disorientation, etc.

2. Monroe has enormous sex organ—the adoration of women only sharpens and defines by opposition his sense of self-loathing and disgust.

3. Monroe Fieldbinder sees psychologist to bounce ideas off him. One of Fieldbinder's ideas is that the phenomenon of modern party-dance is incompatible with self-consciousness, makes for staggeringly unpleasant situations (obvious resource: Amherst/Mt. Holyoke mixer '68) for the at all self-conscious person. Modern party-dance is simply writhing to suggestive music. It is ridiculous, silly to watch and excruciatingly embarrassing to perform. It is ridiculous, and yet absolutely everyone does it, so that it is the person who does not want to do the ridiculous thing who feels out of place and uncomfortable and self-conscious . . . in a word, ridiculous. Right out of Kafka: the person who does not want to do the ridiculous thing is the person who is ridiculous. (Idea: Kafka at an Amherst/Mt. Holyoke mixer, never referred to by name, only as "F.K.," only one not dancing . . .) Modern party-dance an evil thing.

4. Monroe Fieldbinder's psychologist has movable chair like that idiot Jay. Lampoon Jay unmercifully in Fieldbinder collection. Make Jay look like an idiot.

/a/

The reason Lenore Beadsman's red toy car had a spidery network
of scratches in the paint on the right side was that by the driveway
of the home of Alvin and Clarice Spaniard, in Cleveland Heights,
lived a large, hostile brown shrub, bristling with really thorny branches.
The bush hung out practically halfway across the drive, and scratched
hell out of whatever or whoever came up. "Scritch," was the noise
Lenore heard as the thorns squeaked in their metal grooves in the
side of her car, or rather "Scriiiiitch," a sound like fingernails on
aluminum siding, a tooth-shiver for Lenore.

The only other thing even remotely irritating about the Spaniard
home was the fact that the front doorknob was right in the middle
of the door, rather than over on the right or left side, where door-
knobs really should be, and so the door never seemed to swing open
so much as just fall back, when someone opened it. There was also
the very incidental fact that the house had a funny smell about it,
on the inside, as if something not quite right were growing on the
underside of some of the carpets in some of the rooms.

But it was on the whole a very nice home, a two-story brick home
with a huge elaborate antenna on the roof, a home in which lived
Alvin Spaniard, Clarice Spaniard, Stonecipher Spaniard, and Spatula Spaniard (the latter named for Ruth Spatula Spaniard, Alvin
Spaniard's mother).

Alvin Spaniard, Vice President of Advertising in Charge of Gauging Product-Perception, Stonecipheco Baby Food Products, opened
the door to Lenore's ring and stepped nimbly aside as the door

seemed to fall back at him, and asked Lenore in, calling to Clarice
and the kids that Lenore was here. Alvin immediately offered Lenore
gin.

"No thank you," Lenore said. "Gin makes me cough."

Alvin Spaniard liked gin a lot. Lenore asked for a seltzer-and-lime.

"You do know it's family theater night," Alvin said quietly as
they moved in the direction of the living room.

"Clarice told me on the phone. I really need to talk to her,
though. I sort of hoped I could grab her during intermission or
something."

In the living room, under hanging Mexican Aztec woven tapes-
tries featuring suns and bird-gods with their heads at angles inappropriate with respect to their necks, Stonecipher, who was five,
and Spatula, who was four, were playing Chutes and Ladders with
Clarice, who was twenty-six, and who was only ostensibly playing
Chutes and Ladders, while really watching an Olympic recap on
television, in preparation for family theater, with a gin-and-tonic.
It was quarter of eight.

"Hey guys, here's Aunt Lenore to play Chutes and Ladders with
you," said Clarice. She winked at Lenore.

"Super," said Lenore.

Chutes and Ladders was perhaps the most sadistic board game
ever invented. Adults loathed the game; children loved it. The
universe thus dictated that an adult invariably got snookered into
playing the game with a child. Certain rolls of the dice entitled you
to certain movements on the board, some of which movements
entitled you to move up ladders toward the base of the golden ladder
at the top of the board (the climbing of which ladder represented
the ultimate telos and reward-in-itself of the whole game). Moving
up ladders was desirable because it saved time and spins and tiresome
movements on the board, square by square. Except there were chutes.
Certain rolls of the dice got you into board positions where you fell
into chutes and slid ass-over-teakettle all the way down to the
bottom of the board, where the whole process started all over again.
The chances of falling into chutes increased as you climbed more
ladders and got higher and higher. A long and tedious climb up
ladder after ladder until the End was in sight was usually nixed by
a plummet down one of the seven chutes whose mouths yawned

near the base of the golden ladder at the top. The children found this sudden dashing of hopes and return to the recreational drawing board unbelievably fun. The game made Lenore feel like throwing its board at the wall.

"Super," said Lenore.

"Here's that seltzer," said Alvin.

"Frozen pea?" asked Clarice.

"Thanks."

"Treat you right around here or what?"

Spatula accused Stoney of sneakily moving his game piece—a laughing little plastic Buddha of a baby with a pencil-sharpening hole in its head, given out by the gross at Stonecipheco stockholder meetings—from a position in which a chute-fall was imminent to a position in which a ladder-climb was imminent. There ensued unpleasantness, while Lenore ate some frozen peas. Clarice soothed Spatula while Alvin worked on the vertical hold of the giant-screen television.

Order was restored, and the vertical hold was looking good. Alvin rubbed his hands together.

"So how's CabanaTan?" Lenore asked Clarice over her drink. Clarice owned and managed five Cleveland franchises of a tanning-parlor chain called CabanaTan. She had bought in originally by selling the Stonecipheco stock she'd gotten for a graduation present, something which had pissed Lenore and Clarice's father off, a lot, at first, but he had calmed down when Clarice married Alvin Spaniard, whom Stonecipher Beadsman liked, and respected, and whose father had been at Stonecipheco all his life, too, and things were especially good now that Clarice, who obviously worked, and Alvin, who obviously also worked, had made an arrangement whereby they left the children during the day in the care of Nancy Malig, at the Beadsman home in Shaker Heights, the same Nancy Malig who had been Lenore and Clarice's governess when they were children.

"CabanaTan is thriving," Clarice said. "It's been a cloudy summer, you know, and people feel the need to supplement. We're gearing up for the fall rush. There's always a fall rush, as people start losing the summer tan and get tense. We should have most of Cleveland roasting nicely by November."

"And Misty Schwartz?"

"Can't talk about it. Legal stuff. Other than Schwartz problems, it looks like a banner fall coming up."

"Terrif."

"And how about you? How's the switchboard? How's the bird?" Clarice asked. Lenore saw that Alvin was holding Spatula high over his head in the center of the living room, while Spatula laughed and kicked her legs.

"Sort of need to talk to you, for a bit, if we could break away, here, maybe Chutes and Ladders later . . ."

"Family theater in ten minutes, is the thing."

"Maybe after, then, we could just sort of . . ."

On the big-screen television, shots of people running in slow motion ended. Stoney threw a Buddha-baby at Spatula. It missed, rang out against a bronze flowerpot. An announcer's head filled the television.

"We'll be back with a look at . . . gymnastics, and a live conversation with a . . . certain someone," the announcer grinned mysteriously.

"Kopek Spasova," said Lenore.

Alvin looked up. "You sure?"

"I feel in my marrow they're going to have Kopek Spasova," Lenore said.

"Holy shit," said Alvin, "I've got to get a notebook."

"Alvin, family theater in eight minutes."

"I have to take notes. This is supposed to be Gerber's nuclear weapon."

"It is pineal-extract, you might say," said Lenore.

"Jesus," said Alvin, rummaging through his briefcase. Stoney and Spatula had been sucked into the television's intake; they sat, Indian-style, staring at the screen. Lenore nonchalantly nudged the Chutes and Ladders game under the sofa with her foot.

"I'm going to go get the props, so we can start just the minute she's done," said Clarice. Lenore drank some seltzer and ate a bit of lime pulp floating on top.

Ed McMahon came on the television, doing a commercial for a line of tiny vaccum cleaners that were alleged to suck even the stubbornest lint out of your navel. "Sell it, Ed!" yelled Alvin Spaniard, grinning admiringly at the television.

"Is that regular, or cable?" Lenore asked.

"I think it's network. I think that's Curt Gowdy, doing the recap. OK, all set." Alvin sat with his glasses and a yellow legal pad and a pen.

"You've sure got a lot of equipment on that television," said Lenore.

"We're a family that takes its home entertainment very seriously," Alvin said. Stoney looked up at Lenore and nodded, and Alvin ruffled his hair.

"We're back live," said the announcer on television.

"Hurry Mommy, we're back live!" shouted Stoney.

"Sshh," Alvin said.

"I'm standing here with the brilliant Soviet—former Soviet gymnastics coach Ruble Spasov," said the announcer, "and with the equally brilliant former Soviet gymnast and certainly not former Olympic and World Championship gold medalist Kopek Spasova, Mr. Spasov's daughter." The camera panned down from the adults' heads to their stomachs to get Kopek Spasova in the shot. She was a thin, blond-haired, hollow-cheeked girl with enormous black circles under her eyes.

Clarice came in with a load of masks and cardboard cut-outs and some personal items in a box.

"Well, at least she's not pretty," said Alvin.

"Sshh," said Spatula.

"Ruble, Kopek, how did it feel to win all the big ones?" asked the announcer.

"Who is this person?" asked Ruble Spasov, looking to someone behind and off to the side of the camera.

"It felt good to win," said Kopek Spasova.

/b/

3 September

Monroe Fieldbinder, a successful six-foot estate attorney with a fine lawn and a two-hundred-pound body as fit and taut as it was exceptionally attractive, returned one Wednesday night from the home of his gorgeous

Wednesday mistress to find his house in flames and his house surrounded
by the pulsing lights of fire and police engines
of fire engines and police cars and saw that his house was in flames
on fire and that his bird, Richard the Lionhearted, who lived inside, was
probably dead, in his iron cage.

As Monroe Fieldbinder watched his house burn, he felt all the order
and unity of his life melt away into chaos and disorder. He grinned
wryly.

How explicit need we make this burning? Need we a reference,
or just a picture? "Grinned wryly" seems most potent when used in
reference to a picture. Pictures do things. Show, don't tell.

Do pictures tell? I have a color Polaroid of Vance at seven and
Veronica at twenty-nine traversing a ricket^v dry-gray dock in Nova
Scotia to board a fishing boat. The water is a deep iron smeared
with plates of foam; the sky is a thin iron smeared with same; the
mass of white gulls around Vance's outstretched bread-filled hand
is a cloud of plunging white V's. Vance Vigorous, as he holds out
his white little child's hand, is surrounded and obscured by a cloud
of living, breathing, shrieking, shitting, plunging incarnations of
the letter V; and I have it captured forever on quality film, giving
me the right and power to cry whenever and wherever I please.
What might that say about pictures.

A truly, truly horrible dream, last night. Don't even want to talk
about it. I am fresh out of bed. Urinating. I look down. Just a lazy
stream of early-morning maple-syrup urine. Suddenly the single stream
is a doubled, forking stream. Then a tripled trident stream. Four,
five, ten. Soon I am at the node of a fan of urine that sprays out
in all directions, blasting the walls of the bathroom, plaster shooting
everywhere, currents swirling at my feet. When I awoke—alone,
Lenoreless, hence the dream—I was really afraid I had wet the bed,
the windows, the ceiling. I may murder Jay over this one.

/c/

". . . have asked Kopek to recreate that stunning uneven-parallel-
bar routine that won her the all-around gold, and we'll remind the
audience that her performance is now made possible by the gen-

erosity of the folks over at Gerber's Quality Brands, the infant food that helps your child chew."

"Yes," said Ruble Spasov. He and the announcer, trailing a snake of black microphone cord, accompanied Kopek over to the bars as she mounted and began to twirl and spin and let the bars bend her into strange shapes.

"Ruble, I notice you've got that cattle-prod, there, in your hand, while your brilliant daughter and pupil does her really superb routines," said the announcer. "Any story behind that."

Ruble Spasov pulled his eyebrows up. "Is what you call a blanket of security. Kapelika feels more secure and confident and happy to know that when she performs routines cattle-prod is always nearby her."

"And what a performer she is," said the announcer.

"Guy's nuts," Alvin Spaniard said. "Guy's a fascist."

"She's just super, though," said Lenore. "Watch her do the thing with her toes . . . *there*. Wow."

"So she's got prehensile toes, big deal," said Alvin. "Take you to a zoo, show you cages full of prehensile toes."

"I smell sour grapes," said Clarice.

Lenore sniffed at her armpit.

"Family theater in one and a half minutes," Clarice said.

"She's almost done anyway," said Lenore. "It's the dismount where she lands on just one finger that's the killer . . . right there. Believe that? And she's coming to Erieview in like a week."

"Tell me about it," said Alvin.

"I'm anxious to go," said Lenore.

"Spatula sweetie, you want to get the audience-disc? Any questions from anybody about any lines? Alvin, think about your job on your own time." Clarice moved the coffee table out of the center of the living room.

"Ruble and Kopek Spasov and Spasova: quite a team, and just if I may interject a personal note a fine addition to this great country," said the announcer. "Ruble and Kopek Spasova."

"Please go away now," Ruble Spasov said. Ed McMahon reappeared. Stoney got up and switched the television controls to Laserdisc input.

Clarice distributed masks. There was a Clarice-mask for Clarice,

an Alvin-mask for Alvin, a Stonecipher-mask for Stonecipher, a
Spatula-mask for Spatula. The masks were very good and very lifelike. Clarice made them out of plaster molds and papier-mâché and
Reynolds Wrap, in a workshop in the basement. Clarice was in
many ways an artist, Lenore thought, CabanaTan notwithstanding.
She was particularly good at making things with people's faces on
them. Every year she gave her father, Lenore's father, cans of tennis
balls in which each ball was an eerie likeness of the head of Bob
Gerber or Erv Beechnut. Stonecipher Beadsman III loved to play
tennis with these balls. Clarice also on the sly made some Stone-
cipher-Beadsman-III-head balls that she and Alvin batted around
from time to time. During a dark period, about a year before, there
had appeared a can of Alvin-head balls.

The audience-disc was inserted, and on the huge television screen
there appeared a view, as that from a stage, of rows of theater seats,
being filled by people dressed to the nines, with programs. As the
house filled up on the screen, Clarice got masks on the children.
Life-size cardboard cut-outs of Alvin, Clarice, Stoney, and Spatula
were positioned on either side of the television, so as to form part
of the audience.

"Is this the last time we're going to do this one, Mom?" Stoney
asked, his voice a bit muffled. "We've done this one five times in
a row."

There was pleasant pre-performance mood music playing for the
audience on the television screen. The house was now nearly full.
The cardboard cut-outs were the standing room.

"Last time. Next week a new thing."

The rubber band that attached Spatula's Spatula-mask to her head
got twisted and snagged in her hair, and she began to cry. Alvin
soothed her from behind his Alvin-mask. The audience on the
television made murmured noises; according to Laserdisc timing,
family theater had already started. Clarice reinserted the disc and
got an earlier point, in which the theater seats were just filling up.
She distributed a Spiro Agnew watch to Alvin, a Richard Scarry
cut-out book to Stoney, English Muffin the teddy bear to Spatula,
and Clarice herself brandished a Visa Gold Card. Lenore took her
seltzer and peas to an easy chair next to the television and sat down
beside the Alvin cut-out.

Clarice checked the watch on the underside of her wrist. "Go ahead, babe," she said to Stoney. Stoney moved closer to the television as Clarice and Alvin and Spatula grouped in close tight behind him.

The audience stopped coughing and looked on attentively. Clarice prodded Stoney in the back with her finger.

"There once existed," Stoney recited behind his mask, "a unit called the Snapiard family. The family was close and very tightly bound together by feelings of family love." All four Spaniards now kissed each other through their masks and hugged each other. "What is more," Stoney continued to the television screen, "the people who were in the family thought of themselves more as . . . more as . . ."

"Members of the family," Clarice whispered behind him.

"More as members of the family than as real people who were special individual people. All they thought about was the family, and all they thought of themselves as was family-parts."

Clarice picked up from the floor four red masks that had just generic features and the words FAMILY-MEMBER stamped in white across the forehead, and the Spaniards all put one of the masks on, which was cumbersome, given the presence of the original masks, too.

Stoney stepped back and Alvin stepped to the television. "This was both a good thing and a bad thing, apparently. It was a good thing because each family member felt a strong and secure sense of identity and identification with a unit larger than he. Or she. His or her concerns were not his or her concerns alone, and he or she could count on the things and ideas and feelings he or she valued as having value not merely for him or her, but also for the whole organic/emotional unit of which he or she was a part. There was sense of identification, of unaloneness, in short one of security and warmth, emotional shelter. Four individual people were a unit." The audience applauded warmly.

Spatula stepped forward. "But it was a bad thing, too. Because everybody in the . . . family felt like all they were were parts of the family. So in case anything bad happened that was bad and made the family not as much a family anymore, it also made the people in the family not as much people anymore, and then they were alone and invisible and unhappy, and things exploded very fast in bad ways." The Spaniards took off the FAMILY-MEMBER masks and put on plain white featureless masks with red cracks down the middle, and very tiny holes for breathing, and they all took three steps away from each other and turned their backs. The audience whispered. Lenore began to eat her lime. She could see Stoney discreetly picking his nose under his mask.

/d/

I am in receipt of the following communication, dated 1 September 1990, from a Mr. Karl Rummage, of the legal firm of Rummage and Naw, Cleveland, acting at the corporate behest of Mr. Stonecipher Beadsman III, President and Chief Executive Officer of Stonecipheco Baby Food Products:

Dear Mr. Vigorous:

Having been exposed to and in admiration of Frequent and Vigorous Publishing Inc.'s performance with respect to the publications "Norslan, Big Iron, and You" and "Norslan: The Third-World Herbicide That Likes People," etc., for some time, Mr. Stonecipher Beadsman III, President and Chief Executive Officer of Stonecipheco Baby Food Products, Cleveland, Ohio, has authorized me to extend to you an offer to undertake for us the publication of three product-information packages concerning a new infant benefit service currently in the final stages of development at Stonecipheco Baby Food Products. Initial drafts of said informational packages have been composed and compiled by Stonecipheco's Division of Advertising and Product-Perception-Gauging, and are enclosed under separate cover.

Mr. Beadsman has authorized me to extend to you an offer of significantly generous compensation for the firm of Frequent and Vigorous, and an even more significantly generous personal bonus for you, Richard Vigorous, for the acceptance of and satisfactory realization of the goals set forth under the proposed contract (see also enclosure).

Stipulations attached to the tender of such an offer include, but are not necessarily exhausted by, the following: (1.) The retention by the firm of Frequent and Vigorous of some personnel familiar with the culture and language of the inhabitants of the island of Corfu (see enclosure); (2.) The withholding of information concerning the tendering of and details concerning any part of the proposed contract from Ms. Lenore Beadsman, East Corinth, Ohio, with whom you are known to enjoy some personal connection, until such time as such withholding is deemed inadvisable by Mr. Stonecipher Beadsman III; (3.) The firm of Frequent and Vigorous's granting Ms. Lenore Beadsman a leave of absence of two (2) days from switchboard duties, for a trip to see her brother, Mr. Stonecipher Beadsman IV, on Beadsman family business at Amherst College, Amherst, Massachusetts, an institution of which I am given to understand you are an alumnus. Your accompanying Ms. Beadsman on this trip, with travel accommodations provided and all legitimately incurred expenses absorbed by Stonecipheco, Inc., would be welcome, but should not be regarded as a stipulation attached to the tendering of the original contract offer. Etc. etc. etc. etc.

What are we to make of this? I have yet to open the enclosure. I can feel the Erieview shadow creeping over and through the lamps behind me, at the licorice window. It is noon. Today Lenore and I do not lunch. Tonight she goes to visit her sister. Another day of missing.

/e/

Stoney was addressing the television audience. "Since every member of the Snapiard family thought of themselves just as family-members, it meant that if there was less of a family, they were less people, and if there wasn't a family, they weren't people."

". . . in the full sense."

"Weren't people in the full sense."

Alvin stepped to the television. "Each family-member, then, in a natural and understandable attempt to preserve individual identity and efficacy of will . . ."

Spatula made knee-motions indicating that she needed to go potty. Lenore continued eating her now not quite so frozen peas.

". . . sought to restore identity, and a sense of belonging, by attaching themselves to things in the world, extrafamilial objects and pursuits; they sought identity and shelter in things." Alvin held up his Spiro Agnew watch; Spatula hugged English Muffin the teddy bear to her chest as she bobbed; Stoney made motions as if to kiss his Richard Scarry cut-out book, while Clarice made as if to tango with her Visa Gold Card. The cracked white faceless masks came off, and so everyone was back to his or her original mask. The audience made soft sounds. And now extremely tiny but still accurate Clarice-, Alvin-, Stoney-, and Spatula-masks were affixed to the objects by their owners.

"Hell of a lot of masks, here," Lenore muttered.

"The problem, again, however," Alvin continued, "was that in making their own sense of self and rightness-with-themselves-as-people depend on things outside them, the family-members were letting themselves in for riskiness and trouble. Things couldn't be people, not even the people they belonged to." The tiny masks on the objects were taken off and discarded with wide arm-motions. Alvin said, "And now a lost or a misplaced thing meant what, for the Snapiard family?"

"What?" shouted the audience on the television.

There was silence. Alvin took Clarice's Visa Gold Card, and she the watch, and they traded masks. Alvin's nose had been sweating heavily, and Clarice was clearly less than pleased about putting his mask on. Clarice took English Muffin and gave Spatula the Alvin-mask. Soon each member of the family was wearing an incorrect mask and was twirling around, symbolizing disorientation and despair, although the despair-effect was compromised somewhat by the fact that Spatula really liked to twirl, and was giggling.

/f/

Lenore's sister is ravingly lovely, if one likes the ravingly lovely type, with soft honey hair and dark blue eyes and breasts like artillery; but she is cocky and serious and dull and utterly (and unattractively unaware that she is utterly) dependent on the Latest Thing for her sense of direction and worth. Her husband is a civil man, though that he lusts after Lenore I do not for one second doubt. Alvin Spaniard is randy. My understanding—which is arrived at via Lenore and so is of course vague—is that on four occasions early last year Alvin Spaniard had sexual intercourse with his Georgia peach of a receptionist. Clarice Spaniard found out about the incidents from Sigurd Foamwhistle, Stonecipher Beadsman III's executive aide and possibly the half brother of Lenore's younger brother, and in any event a man about whose unsavory desires with respect to Clarice and Lenore both I am in no doubt whatsoever. So Clarice found out, and there were, for a while, various kickings of emotional ass. They subsided, and Alvin and Clarice finally sat down and conferred, and it was decided marriage therapy was needed, Alvin agreeing vigorously, obviously—loving his wife, also liking his job. Marriage therapy degenerated into family therapy. God knows what all went on. I know there were stages concerned with human sculpture, in which each member of the family molded the others into those positions reflecting perceived relationships, etc. There were fights involving toy clubs made of Nerf material. The Spaniard vogue now is apparently drama, carried on in front of a fabricated audience; rather, at least tonight, at least one real person—regardless of what that person herself may happen to think. Lenore and Clarice are not close. As are not Monroe and I. She says she avoids going over. But where does she go, then?

A bad day. The urine dream has so upset me that I find it hard to function. As it were. I miss Lenore. I feel physical pain, now, when I am absent or apart from Lenore Beadsman. Which is, of course, always. Too bad a day to think actively of what her father might be trying to do. On the face of it I must say that it seems to me that whatever I can do to establish connections with Lenore's family, to deepen and strengthen the personal bonds that join Lenore and me, can only hasten that day when I am able truly and completely and finally to take Lenore Beadsman inside myself.

A bad, bad day. Dark, soaring feelings of important tasks yet undone. Yet unknown. I am afraid to go to the bathroom.

/g/

All the excitement of the twirling and giggling, and the tension of live performance, but especially the twirling, had been responsible for a slight crisis with respect to Spatula. Things were quickly put right again, though, with Lenore helping with paper towels, and the audience was put in a FREEZE mode, and finally unfrozen, and things got back underway.

Stoney: "Disorientation and sadness resulted when the family-members tried to depend on things that weren't them and weren't the family for their own happiness and being-themselves-ness."

"Sense of self."

"Sense of self. So they . . . they . . ."

Clarice stepped forward and gently pushed Stonecipher out of the way:

"So they did what any smart family-members would do. They talked with one another, and aired the things they weren't comfortable with as people right then, and meaningful dialogue and personal interaction was established, and the family-members began to grow emotionally both as individuals and as members of an emotional network of shared interests and values and emotional commitments, and then the growth and development and dialogue was facilitated by their going and seeing an outside party whose whole life was directed toward helping family-members grow and see themselves clearly both as selves and members, and so come to a fuller and happier sense of self."

The invisible orchestra on the television now struck up a tune, and in the living room in Cleveland Heights there took place a sort of dance, with involved connections and motions and gestures, each directed by family-members at other family-members, while the audience clapped its hands. The dance would have been better, except Alvin wasn't participating with full enthusiasm, and kept gravitating back to the sofa and looking down through his mask at his notes from the Kopek Spasova interview.

The dance ended. Lenore looked at the clock on the mantel. Spatula, damp but cheerful, stepped forward.

"And after a long time of trying, the Snapiards . . . ," she giggled, ". . . discovered the easiest thing in the whole world. They all discovered that they couldn't try to depend for their feelings of being themselves on just the whole family, because they each weren't the whole family." The Spaniards all went and stomped on their FAMILY-MEMBER masks. "And they couldn't get their feelings of themselves from things, because they weren't things." They all pretended to stomp on their things, but didn't really, especially Alvin and his Spiro Agnew watch. "They found out that what they needed to get their feelings of being themselves from was *themselves* . . . ," Spatula smiled wonderfully at the television as a murmur went through the crowd, ". . . because that's what they were. The easiest thing in the world is what they saw." And

Alvin, Clarice, Stoney, and Spatula took off their Alvin-, Clarice-, Stoney-, and Spatula-masks, and stared deeply into the empty eyeholes of their own faces. Through one of her eyeholes Spatula said to the television, "The End." The television audience rose as one.

/h/

"Dum de dum de dum de dum."

". . . ."

"La de da de da de da."

"Jesus shall not want."

". . . ."

"Jesus shall not want."

"What?"

"Pardon me?"

"What in the Lord's name?"

"The Lord is my supper. Jesus shall not want."

"Sweet Mother McCree."

"You fill me up."

"It's a miracle."

"Lay your sleeping head, my love."

"Dear Father in heaven."

"Human on my faithless arm."

"The bird has been touched by God."

"The bird has been touched by God."

"Yes."

"I have to do what's right for me as a person."

"Thank you Lord. Thank you for touching this house. Oral, I did, I expected a miracle."

"The sins of the fathers."

"*Charlotte's Web*. It's like *Charlotte's Web*."

"A camel, like this."

"Dare I touch you?"

"Women need space, too."

"Ow! Well, the dear little thing still bites."

"Clint Clint Clint. It's like *Charlotte's Web*."

"Oh Martin Tissaw, why aren't you here?"

"Maybe we could get him on 'Real People.' "

"What?"

"Maybe we could get him on 'Real People.' "

"Is that what You direct me to do, God? To get this bird, this animal through which You have chosen to make Yourself heard, on 'Real People'?"

"Anger is natural, let it out."

"To deliver Your message of anger and love?"

"Human on my faithless arm."

"Then that is what I shall do. Get up off your knees, woman!"

"Get up off your knees, woman!"

"Go forth and do the work directed."

" 'Real People.' "

"Yes, 'Real People.' Disgusting mirror and all. But first I call Martin."

" 'Real Birds.' It may get torn, I'm warning you. Care for a mint?"

"Forget dusting."

"What's with Vlad the Impaler?"

"I've been called."

"Make me come."

"Come you shall. We shall go together, but first let me call 'Real People.' "

"Goodbye."

"Thank you, Lord."

/a/

"I think maybe it's time for me to just hop on my horse and git."

"What the hell does that mean?"

"It means I feel like I need to get the fuck out."

"Out of what?"

"How much time we got here, Melinda-Sue?"

"You said you loved Scarsdale. You said you loved me."

"I think it's turning out there's problems with that analysis. I think what I unfortunately meant is that I loved fucking you, is basically all. And I just don't think I love fucking you anymore."

". . . ."

". . . my razor . . ."

"Why not?"

". . . ."

"How come?"

"I'm not sure I really know. I'm hopin' to give it some more thought. It's just not wonderful anymore. Nothing personal. It's just not wonderful."

"Not wonderful? What do you mean, not wonderful?"

"Well, look at your leg."

"What's the matter with my leg? I'm only twenty-seven. I've got nice legs. I happen to know for a fact they're nice."

"You irritate all kinds of hell out of me when you don't listen to what I say, Melinda-Sue. I never said you didn't have nice legs. All I said was to just look at your goddamn leg."

". . . ."

"We're just missing the wonderfulness. Your leg, for an example. It's all smooth and firm and shapely and all. It looks good and it feels good and it smells good. God knows you keep it real well shaved. It's all beautiful and artistic and all that shit. But see, it's just a leg. That's all it is for me, now, is a fucking leg. It could be *my* leg, if I shaved my leg."

"What difference does that make?"

"It makes all kinds of difference, honeypot. You put your thinkin' cap on about it for a while."

"You're being immature. You're being totally unrealistic. You're deliberately trying to hurt me."

"No, what I'm deliberately trying to do is say fuck off, is what I'm deliberately trying to do."

"Well then what am I supposed to do?"

"It's weird how I'm not at all worried about that. You got your work, if I get to use loose terms. You got your goddamned voice, still. I know that for a undeniable fact. It comes at me forty times a day. I can't get the fuck away from you. I get in the car and there you are. I feel like all the air I breathe you've already breathed."

". . . ."

"Is cryin' supposed to make me feel bad? 'Cause it don't. I don't feel bad. I just feel like I need to get the fuck out, still."

"You're just drunk."

"I'm a tinch drunk. No bones about it. But I'm sincere, here, ma'am. No more fucking, no more love."

". . . ."

"Take your robe off a second."

". . . ."

"Take it *off* please I said."

"Ow! God, what are—?"

"*Thank* you. Don't worry, no rape on the horizon this morning, ma'am. Look, mine comes off too, to be fair. Let's just have us an objective look at the situation, here."

"The curtains are open."

"My analysis of the problem, if you want my analysis of the problem, is that you've just run out of holes in your pretty body, and I've run out of things to stick in them. My pecker, my fingers, my tongue, my toes . . ."

"Oh, God."

". . . my hair, my nose. My wallet. My car keys. So on. I've just run the fuck out of ideas. And this crying shit is starting to piss me off. I'm askin' you right now to stop crying, 'cause it's not working, and it only pisses me off."

". . . ."

"I'm getting pissed off."

"Daddy . . ."

"Well there we go. Daddy. I think maybe he's just what you need right now. You can help him fuck his lawn."

"I *hate* you."

"All I'm tryin' to do is say fuck off."

"I love you. Please. Here . . . see?"

"Now let's don't be misled here. What we got here is just purely perverse excitement at seein' you upset. It's just the reaction of a bored old soldier in the game of love. It's not wonderfulness. And if we did do it, it'd be like two animals in the fucking forest."

". . . ."

"You care to hear how many women I've blasted since we got married?"

". . . ."

"I've personally blasted over a dozen women since I married you. Since I committed to you forever and ever, I have fucking betrayed you, hundreds of times. There's been times in the last year when I haven't with you, 'cause I was savin' it up for somebody else. That ought to make you feel better about me taking a indefinite vacation."

"Oh, God."

"Have a Kleenex."

". . . ."

"And please don't think I don't know you've fucked around too. I know about you and Gluskoter. The only reason I haven't kicked his ass is that it would just be too fucking boring. I know you're not any better than me, don't worry. But I'm talking about doing it on a grand, grand fucking scale."

"How can you be so ugly to me?"

" 'Cause I'm bored, and when a man gets bored enough he gets like an animal. I'm an animal now, feels like. I'm sick of this shit, your work, my work, worryin' about other people's taxes, hearing about your Daddy's fucking fertilizer strategies every day. I got to get out. When animals get so they feel trapped, they get ugly. You want to watch out for trapped animals, Melinda-Sue, I'm tellin' you that for future reference."

"I can't take this. I don't know what's come over you."

"It sure ain't you, don't you worry."

"I think I want a divorce."

"Christ, even my clothes smell like you."

"There's no way you can hate me the way you're trying to convince me you hate me."

". . . ."

"Oh, God."

". . . car keys . . ."

". . . ."

"One drink for the road and I'm gone, like a desert breeze."

"You're contemptible."

"We out of ice *again*? Shit on fire. You eat ice, or what? Do you go around takin' the ice out of here after I make it? If you do, just admit it."

"Just leave, if you're going to leave."

"Let me just take a quick squirt, if I may. One for the road."

"Wait. I think you shouldn't go."

"Say please."

"Please."

"Too bad. Fooled you."

"You're drunk."

". . . ."

"Where are you going to go?"

"I think first I'm gonna go home."

"You're going to drive to Texas? Now?"

"No, you very very dumb woman. I said I'm going the fuck *home*. Home."

"I love you."

"Then you're a confused little specimen."

"And you love me."

"You are an amazing woman if you think that's today's message. You amaze me, Melinda-Sue. I'd take my hat off to you, except I think I left it next door. And hey, you should probably either get out of the window, or else put something on."

" . . . . "

"No sense givin' it away."

/b/

A bright day, in very early September, everything dry, the sun an explicit thing, up there, with heat coming right off it, but a flat edge of cool running down the middle of the day. A jet airplane stood at lunchtime on Runway 1 at CHA, pointed west to go east, a red-ink drawing of a laughing baby on its side, guys with earmuffs and orange plastic flags torn at by the wind off the flatness taking iron prisms out from under the airplane's wheels, the air behind the engines hot and melting the pale green fields through it, the engines hissing through the dry wind like torches, fuel-shimmers. The guys slowly waving the orange flags. The sun glinting off the slanted glass of the windshield, behind which there are sunglasses and thumbs-ups. One of the flag-guys is wearing a Walkman, instead of earmuffs, and he twirls with his flag.

/c/

"There is an ominous rumbling in my ears."

"That's the engine, right outside the window."

"No, the engine is a piercing, nerve-jangling, screaming whine. I'm talking about an ominous rumbling."

" . . . . "

"My ears are going to hurt horribly on this flight, I know. The change in pressure is going to make my ears hurt like hell."

"Rick, in my purse are like fifty packs of gum. I'll keep shoving gum in your mouth, and you'll chew, and swallow your saliva, and your ears will be OK. We've discussed this already."

"Maybe I'd better have a piece now, all unwrapped and ready to go in my hand."

"Here, then."

"Bless you, Lenore."

"A story, please."

"A story? Here?"

"I'm really in the mood for a story. Maybe a story will take your mind off your ears."

"My ears, God. I'd almost begun to have hopes of forgetting, what with the gum in my hand, and you go and mention my ears."

"Let's just have a minimum of spasms, here in public, on the plane, with a pilot and stewardess who're probably going to tell my father everything we do and say."

"How comforting."

"Just no spasms, please."

"But a story."

"Please."

". . . ."

"I know you've got some. I saw manila envelopes in your suitcase when I put stuff in."

"Lord, they're getting ready to take off. We're moving. My ears are rumbling like mad."

". . . ."

"Ironically enough, a man, in whom the instinct to love is as strong and natural and instinctive as can possibly be, is unable to find someone really to love."

"We're starting the story? Or is this just a Vigorous pithy?"

"The story is underway. The aforementioned pre-sarcastic-inter-ruption fact is because this man, in whom the instincts and incli-nations are so strong and pure, is completely unable to control these strong and pure instincts and inclinations. What invariably happens is that the man meets a halfway or even quarterway desirable woman, and he immediately falls head over heels in love with her, right there, first thing, on the spot, and blurts out 'I love you' as practically the first thing he says, because he can't control the intensely warm feelings of love, and not just lust, now, it's made clear, but deep, emotionally intricate, passionate love, the feelings that wash over him, and so immediately at the first opportunity he says 'I love you,' and his pupils dilate until they fill practically his whole eyes, and he moves unself-consciously toward the woman in question as if to touch her in a sexual way, and the women he does this to, which is more or less every woman he meets, quite understandably don't react positively to this, a man who says 'I love you' right away, and makes a bid for closeness right away, and so the women as an invariable rule reject him verbally on the spot, or hit him with their purse, or worst of all run away, screaming screams only he and they can hear."

"Look down a second, Rick. Out the window."

"Where?"

"Right down there."

"Heavens, I know her! That's . . ."

"Jayne Mansfield."

"Jayne Mansfield, right. What's she doing as a town? Is that East Corinth?"

"I'll explain later."

"My God, will you look at that west border. That 271. That's the Inner Belt. I've driven over that."

"Meanwhile, back with the lover whose love drives the lovee away with silent screams."

"Right. So the man is understandably not too happy. Not only is he denied the opportunity to love, but it's the very strength and intensity of his own love-urge that denies him the opportunity, which denial thus understandably causes him exponentially more sadness and depression and frustration than it would you or me, in whom the instincts are semi-under-control, and so semi-satisfiable."

"More gum?"

"And so the man is in a bad way, and he loses his job at the New York State Department of Weights and Measures, at which he'd been incredibly successful before the love-intensity problem got really bad, and now he wanders the streets of New York City, living off the bank account he'd built up during his days as a brilliant weights-and-measures man, wandering the streets, stopping only when he falls in love, getting slapped or laughed at or hearing silent screams. And this goes on, for months, until one day in Times Square he sees a discreet little Xeroxed ad on a notice board, an ad for a doctor who claims to be a love therapist, one who can treat disorders stemming from and connected to the emotion of love."

"What, like a sex therapist?"

"No, as a matter of fact it says 'Not A Sex Therapist' in italics at the bottom of the ad, and it gives an address, and so the man, who is neither overjoyed with his life nor overwhelmed with alternatives for working out his problems, hops the subway and starts heading across town to the love therapist's office. And in his car on the subway there are four women, three of them reasonably desirable, and he falls in love in about two seconds with each of the three in turn, and gets hit, laughed at, and subjected to a silent scream, respectively, and then eventually he looks over at the fourth woman, who's conspicuously fat, and has stringy hair, and Coke-bottle glasses, and an incredibly weak chin, weaker even than mine, and so the fourth woman is prohibitively undesirable, even for the man, and besides she's very hard to see because she's pressed back into the shadow of the rear of the car, with her coat collar pulled up around her neck, which neck is also encased in a thick scarf. Did I mention it was March in New York City?"

"No."

"Well it is, and she's in a scarf, pressed back into the shadow, with her cheek pressed against the grimy graffiti-spattered wall of the subway car, clutching an old Thermos bottle that's jutting half-way out of her coat pocket, and she just basically looks like one of those troubled cases you don't want to mess with, which cases New York City does not exactly have a scarcity of."

"You're telling me."

"And then on top of everything else the fat stringy-haired woman with the Thermos has been watching the man telling the other three women that he loves them, and making bids for closeness, out of the corner of her eye, as she hugs the wall of the car in shadow, and then so when she sees the man even look at her, at all, she obviously flips out, it really bothers her, and she bolts for the door of the subway car, as fast as she can bolt, which isn't too fast, because now it becomes clear that one of her legs is roughly one half the length of the other, but still she bolts, and the car is just pulling into a station, and the door opens, and out she flies, and in her excessive haste she drops the old Thermos she'd been clutching, and it rolls down the floor of the subway, and it finally clunks against the man's shoe, and he picks it up, and it's just an old black metal Thermos, but on the bottom is a piece of masking tape on which is written in a tiny faint hand a name and an address, which he and we assume to be the woman's, in Brooklyn, and so the man resolves to give the woman back her Thermos, since it was probably he and his inappropriate emotional behavior that had caused her to drop it in the first place. Besides, the love therapist's office is in Brooklyn, too.

"And so the man arrives at the love therapist's office, and actually wouldn't ordinarily have gotten in to see the love therapist at all, because she's apparently a truly great and respected love therapist, and incredibly busy, and her appointment calendar is booked up months in advance, but, as it happens, the love therapist's receptionist is a ravingly desirable woman, and the man immediately and involuntarily falls head over heels in love with her, and actually begins involuntarily reciting love poems to her, then eventually sort of passes out, swoons from the intensity of his love, and falls to the carpeted floor, and so the receptionist runs in and tells the love therapist what's happened, that this is obviously a guy who really needs to be seen right away, out here, on the rug, and so the love therapist skips her lunch hour, which she was just about to take, and they pick the man up off the reception-area rug and carry him into the office and revive him with cold water, and he gets an appointment right away.

"And it turns out that one of the reasons why this love therapist is so great is that she can usually hew to the bone of someone's love-problem in one appointment, and doesn't keep the patient stringing along month after expensive month with vague predictions of breakthrough, which we are both in a position to appreciate the desirability of, I think, and so the love therapist hews to the bone of the man's problem, and tells the man that surprisingly enough it's not that his emotional love-mechanism is too strong, but rather that some of its important features are actually too *weak*, because one of the big things about real love is the power to discriminate and decide whom and on the basis of what criteria to love, which the man is very obviously unable to do—witness the fact that the man fell deeply and intricately for the receptionist without even knowing her, and has already said 'I love you' to the love therapist, herself, about ten times, involuntarily. What the man needs to do, the love therapist says, is to strengthen his love-discrimination mechanism by being around women and trying not to fall in love with them. Since this obviously will be hard for the man to do at the start, the love therapist suggests that he begin by finding some woman so completely and entirely undesirable, looks-wise and personality-wise, that it won't be all that hard to keep from falling in love with her right away, and then proceeding to hang around her as much as he can, to begin to strengthen the mechanism that lets men hang around with women without necessarily falling in love with them. And the man is dazed from the one-two punch of the ravingly desirable receptionist and the wise and kind and obviously exceedingly competent and also not unerotic love therapist, but the back part of his brain, the part that deals with basic self-preservation, knows that things cannot keep going as they have been, and he resolves to give the love therapist's advice a try, and then he happens to look down at the Thermos he's still holding, and he sees the piece of masking tape with the name and address of the Thermos woman on it, and he has an epiphany-ish flashback to the subway, and sees that the Thermos woman is just a prime candidate for non-love, stringy-hair-and-uneven-leg-wise, and clearly-troubled-personality-wise, and as the scene ends we see him looking speculatively at the Thermos and then at the love therapist."

"How's the gum doing?"

"New piece, please."

"Here."

" . . . . "

"Is the gum working?"

"Do you hear me complaining yet?"

"Good point."

"And so as the next scene opens it's a few days later, and the man and the Thermos woman are walking in Central Park, or rather walking and limping, respectively, and they're holding hands, although for the man it's just a friendly platonic hand-holding, although we're not sure what it is for the Thermos woman, and it's made clear that the man had gone to the Thermos address and had talked to the woman and had, after a reasonably long time and many visits, broken down some of her really pathological shyness and introversion, though only some. And they're walking hand in hand, although it's inconvenient, because the woman clearly has a pathological need always to be in shadow, and so they keep having to veer all over Central Park to find shadow that she'll be able to walk in, and she also has a pathological need to keep her neck covered, and keeps fingering at one of the seemingly uncountable number of scarves she owns, and she also strangely always seems to want to have only her right side facing the man, she keeps her left side turned away at all times, so all the man ever sees of her is her right profile, and as he turns from time to time and moves relative to her she keeps moving and positioning herself like mad to keep only her right side facing him."

". . . ."

"And she also seems really aloof and not emotionally connected with anyone outside herself at all, except her family, who live in Yonkers, but as the man works to exercise his love-discrimination mechanism and starts hanging around the woman and beginning to get to know her better, it seems clear to him that she actually *wants* to be connected with people outside herself, very much, but can't, for some strange reason that he can't figure out, but knows has something to do with the shadows, the scarves, and the profiles."

". . . ."

"And a funny thing happens. The man begins to like the Thermos woman. Not love, but *like*, which is something the man has never experienced before, and finds different, because it involves directing a lot more emotional attention to the actual other person than the old uncontrollable passionate love had involved, involves caring about the whole other person, including the facets and features that have nothing whatsoever to do with the man. And now it's implied that what has happened is that the man has for the first time become really *connected* to a person other than himself, that he had not really ever been connected before, that his intense-love tendency, which might at first glance have seemed like the ultimate way to connect, has really been a way *not* to connect, at all, both in its results and, really, as a little psychological analysis is by implication indulged in, in its subconscious intent. The inability to bring the discriminating faculty of love to bear on the world outside him has been what has kept the man from connecting with that world outside him, the same way the Thermos woman has been kept from connecting by the mysterious shadow-scarf-and-profile thing.

"Which thing, by the way, really begins to bother the man, and makes him intensely curious, especially as he begins to feel more and more connected to the woman, though not exactly in a passionate-love way, and thinks he feels her yearning to connect, too. And so he gradually wins her trust and affection, and she responds by starting to wash her hair, and dieting, and buying an extra thick shoe for her obscenely short leg, and things progress, although the Thermos woman is still clearly pathologically hung up about something. And then one night in very early April, after a walk all around the quainter parts of Brooklyn, the man takes the Thermos woman back to her apartment and has sex with her, seduces her, gets her all undressed—except, compassionately, for her scarf—and he makes love to her, and it's at first surprisingly, but then when we think about it not all that surprisingly, revealed that this is the first time this incredibly passionate, love-oriented man, who's about thirty, has ever had sex with anybody, at all."

" . . . . "

"Um, first time for the Thermos woman, too."

" . . . . "

" . . . . "

"What's the matter?"

"My ear! Shit! God!"

"Try to swallow."

" . . . . "

"Try to yawn."

" . . . . "

" . . . . "

"Good God. I so hate airplanes, Lenore. I can think of no more convincing demonstration of my devotion to you than my coming on this trip. I am flying for you."

"You're going to get to see Amherst in the very early fall. You said early fall in Amherst used to make you weep with joy."

" . . . . "

"You're less pale. Can we assume the ear is better?"

"Jesus."

" . . . . "

"So they have sex, and the man is able to be gentle and caring, which we can safely intuit he couldn't have been, passion-wise, if he'd really been hopelessly in love in his old way with the Thermos woman, and the Thermos woman weeps tears of joy, at all the gentleness and caring, and we can practically hear the thud as she falls in love with the man, and she really begins to think it's possible to connect with someone in the world outside her. And they're lying in bed, and their limbs are unevenly intertwined, and the man is resting his head on the little shelf of the Thermos woman's weak chin, and he's playing idly with the scarf around her neck, which playing pathologically bothers the woman, which the man notices, and curiosity and concern wash over him, and he tries tentatively and experimentally slowly to undo the scarf and take it off, and the Thermos woman tenses all her muscles but through what is obviously great strength of will doesn't stop him, although she's weeping for real, now, and the man gently, and with kisses and reassurances, removes the scarf, throws it aside, and in the dimness of the bedroom sees something more than a little weird on the woman's neck, and he goes and turns on the light, and in the light of the bedroom it's revealed that the woman has a pale-green tree toad living in a pit at the base of her neck, on the left side."

"Pardon me?"

"In a perfectly formed and non-woundish pit on the left side of the Thermos woman's neck is a tiny tree toad, pale green, with a white throat that puffs rhythmically out and in. The toad stares up at the man from the woman's neck with sad wise clear reptilian eyes, the clear and delicate lower lids of which blink upward, in reverse. And the woman is weeping, her secret is out, she has a tree toad living in her neck."

"Is it my imagination, or did this story just get really weird all of a sudden?"

"Well, the context is supposed to explain and so minimize the weirdness. The tree toad in the pit in her neck is the thing that has kept the Thermos woman from connecting emotionally with the world outside her: it has been what has kept her in sadness and confusion, see also darkness and shadow, what has bound and constrained her, see also being wrapped in a scarf, what has kept her from facing the external world, see also staying in profile all the time. The tree toad is the mechanism of nonconnection and alienation, the symbol and cause of the Thermos woman's isolation; yet it also becomes clear after a while that she is emotionally attached to the tree toad in a very big way, and cares more for it and gives it more attention than she gives herself, there in the privacy of her apartment. And the man also discovers that all the scarves the woman wears to cover up and hide the tree toad are full of tiny holes, air holes for the toad, holes that are practically invisible and that the woman herself makes via millions of tiny punctures of the cloth with a pin, late at night."

"My ear even hurts a little. We must be really high."

"So that the very thing that has made the woman unconnected when she wants to be connected and so has made her extremely unhappy is also the center of her life, a thing she cares a lot about, and is even, in certain ways the man can't quite comprehend, proud of, and proud of the fact that she can feed the pale-green tree toad bits of food off her finger, and that it will let her scratch its white throat with a letter opener. So now things are understandably ambiguous, and it's not clear whether deep down at the core of her being the Thermos woman really wants to connect, after all, at all. Except as time goes by and the man continues to hang around, exercising his non-love love-mechanism, being gentle and caring, the woman falls more and more for him, and clearly wants to connect, and her relation with the tree toad in the pit in her neck gets ambiguous, and at times she's hostile toward it and flicks at it cruelly with her fingernail, except at other times she falls back into not wanting to connect, and so dotes on the tree toad, and scratches it with the letter opener, and is aloof toward the man. And this goes on and on, and she falls for the man on the whole more and more. And the man begins to be unsure about his formerly definitely non-love feelings for this strange and not too pretty but still quite complex and in many ways brave and in all ways certainly very interesting Thermos woman, and so his whole love-situation gets vastly more complicated than it's ever been before."

"Listen, would you like a Canadian Club? I can get Jennifer to bring you a Canadian Club."

"Not too tasty with gum, I'm afraid, of which I would however like another piece."

"Coming right up."

"And so things are complicated, and the man earns the Thermos woman's trust more and more, and finally one night she brings him to her family's home in Yonkers, for a family get-together and dinner, and the man meets her whole family, and he knows right away something's up, because they all have scarves around their necks, and they're clearly extremely on edge about there being an outsider in their midst, but anyway they all sit around the living room for a while, in uncomfortable silence, with cocktails, and Cokes for the little kids, and then they sit down to dinner, and right before they all sit down, the Thermos woman looks significantly at the man, and then at her father, and then in a gesture of letting the family know she's clued the man into her secret condition and initiated some kind of nascent emotional connection, she undoes her scarf and throws it aside, and her tree toad gives a little chirrup, and there's a moment of incredibly tense silence, and then the father slowly undoes and discards his scarf, too, and in the pit in the left side of his neck there's a mottle-throated fan-wing moth, and then the whole rest of the family undo their scarves, too, and they all have little animals living in pits in their necks: the mother has a narrow-tailed salamander, one brother has a driver ant, one sister has a wolf spider, another brother has an axolotl, one of the little children has a sod webworm. Et cetera et cetera."

"I think I feel the need for context again."

"Well, the father explains to the man, as the family is sitting around the table, eating, and also feeding their respective neck-tenants little morsels off the tips of their fingers, that their family is from an ancient and narratively unspecified area in Eastern Europe, in which area the people have always stood in really ambiguous relations to the world outside them, and that the area's families were internally fiercely loyal, and their members were intimately and thoroughly connected with one another, but that the family units themselves were fiercely independent, and tended to view just about all non–family-members as outsiders, and didn't connect with them, and that the tiny animals in their necks, which specific animal-types used to be unique to each family and the same for each member of a particular family, in the old days, were symbols of this difference from and non-connection with the rest of the outside world. But then the father goes on to say that these days inbreeding and the passage of time were making the animal-types in the necks of the family-members different, and that also, regrettably, some younger members of the fiercely loyal families were now inclined to resent the secrecy and non-connection with the world that having animals in their necks required and entitled them to, and that some members of his own family had unfortunately given him to understand that they weren't entirely happy about the situation. And here he and all the other members of the family stop eating and glare at the Thermos woman, there in her glasses, who is silently trying to feed her tree toad a bit of pot roast off the tip of her finger. And the man's heart just about breaks with pity for the Thermos woman, who so clearly now stands in such an ambiguous relation to everything and everyone around her, and his heart almost breaks, and he also realizes in an epiphany-ish flash that he has sort of fallen in love with the Thermos woman, in a way, though not in the way he'd fallen for any of the uncountable number of women he'd fallen in love with before."

"Look down a second, if it doesn't hurt your ear. I think we're over Pennsylvania. I thought I saw a hex sign on a barn roof. We're past Lake Erie, at least."

"Thank God. Drowning in sludge is one of my special horrors."

". . . ."

"And so things are complicated, enormously complicated, and the man feels he's now experiencing the kind of strong discriminating love the love therapist had been recommending, so he's pleased, and also maybe I neglected to mention he's long since toned down his head-over-heels-in-love-in-public inclinations, things are now much more under control, and with all his professional weight-measure experience, plus his new-found amorous restraint, he manages to land a fairly good job with a company that makes scales, and he's doing pretty well, although he does miss that exciting head-busting rush of hot feeling he used to get from being madly, passionately, non-discriminatingly in love. But the Thermos woman is clearly undergoing even more complicated changes and feelings than the man; she's obviously fallen in love with him, and her nascent connection with him is obviously arousing in her a desire to begin to connect emotionally with the entire outside world, and she gets more concerned with and attentive to her own appearance; she loses more weight, and buys contact lenses to replace the Coke-bottle glasses, and gets a perm, and there's still of course the problem of chinlessness and leg-length, but still. But most of all she now noticeably begins to perceive the green tree toad in the pit in her neck as a definite problem, and ceases to identify herelf with it and non-connection, and begins instead to identify herself with herself and connection. But now her perception of the tiny toad as a definite problem, which is, remember, a function of her new world view and desire to connect, now paradoxically causes her enormous grief and distress, because, now that she feels a bit connected to the world, she no longer feels that she *wants* to stay in shadow and present only profiles—so far so good—but that now even though she doesn't want to hide away she feels more than ever as though she *ought* to, because she's got a reptile living in a pit in her neck, after all, and is to that extent alienated and different and comparatively disgusting, with respect to the world she now wants to connect with."

"Aren't tree toads amphibians, really?"

"Wise-ass. Amphibian in a pit in her neck. But she suddenly and ominously gets even more fanatical about being in shadow and wearing the scarves, even though these are obviously alienating things: the more she wants to be accepted by the world, the more she's beaten back by her heightened perception of her own difference, amphibian-tenant-wise. She becomes absolutely obsessed with the green tree toad, and gives it a really hard time with her fingernail, and cries, and tells the man she hates the toad, and the man tries to cheer her up by taking her out dancing at a nightclub that has lots of shadows. Gum, please."

". . . ."

"And things get worse, and the Thermos woman is now drinking a lot, sitting in her apartment, and as she's drinking, the man will look at her sadly, as he sits nearby working on the design for a scale; and the tree toad, when it's not busy getting flicked by a fingernail, will look at the man and blink sadly, from the lower lid up, there in the pit in the Thermos woman's neck."

". . . ."

"And now, disastrously, it's late April. It's the height of spring, almost. Have you ever been around someplace that has tree toads, in the spring, Lenore?"

"Oh, no."

"They sing. It's involuntary. It's instinctive. They sing and chir-rup like mad. And this, I rather like to think, is why the tree toad looked sadly at the man as the man was looking sadly at the drinking Thermos woman: the tree toad has its own nature to be true to, too. The toad's maybe aware that its singing will have a disastrous effect on the Thermos woman, right now, because whereas in the past she always just used to keep herself hidden away, in the spring, in the singing season, now she's clearly torn by strong desires to connect, to be a part of the world. And so maybe the tree toad knows it's hurting the Thermos woman, maybe irreparably, by chir-ruping like mad, but what can it do? And the singing clearly drives the Thermos woman absolutely insane with frustration and horror, and her urges both to connect and to hide away in shadow are tearing at her like hell, and it's all pathetic, and also, as should by now be apparent, more than a little ominous."

"Oh, God."

"And one day, not long after the toad began singing in the apartment, as the air is described as getting soft and sweet and tinged with gentle promises of warmth, with a flowery smell all around, even in New York City, the man gets a call at work from the Thermos woman's father, in Yonkers: it seems that the Thermos woman had thrown herself in front of the subway and killed herself that morning in a truly horrible way."

"Sweet Jesus."

"And the man is obviously incredibly upset, and doesn't even thank the father for calling him, even though it was quite a thing for the Eastern European father to do, what with the man being an outsider, et cetera, and so but the man is incredibly upset, and doesn't even go to the funeral, he's so frantic, and he discovers now—the hard way—that he really was connected to the Thermos woman, really and truly, deeply and significantly, and that the severing of an established connection is exponentially more painful than the re-jection of an attempted connection, and he wallows in grief, and also disastrously his old love problem immediately comes roaring back stronger than ever, and the man is falling passionately in love with anything with a pulse, practically, and now, disastrously, men as well as women, and he's perceived as a homosexual, and starts getting regularly beaten up at work, and then he loses his job when he tells his supervisor he's in love with him, and he's back out wandering the streets, and now he starts falling in love with children, too, which is obviously frowned upon by society, and he commits some gross though of course involuntary indiscretions, and gets arrested, and thrown in jail overnight, and he's in a truly horrible way, and he curses the love therapist for even suggesting that he try to love with his discriminating-love-faculty."

"May I please ask a question?"

"Yes."

"Why didn't the Thermos woman just take the tree toad out of her neck and put it in a coffee can or something?"

"A, the implication is that the only way the animal-in-neck people can rid themselves of the animals in their necks is to die, see for instance the subway, and b, you're totally, completely missing what I at any rate perceive to be the point of the story."

" . . . . "

"And the man is in a horrible way, and his old love problem is raging, together with and compounded by his continued grief at the severed Thermos-woman-connection, and his desire never ever to connect again, which desire itself stands in a troublingly ambiguous and bad-way-producing relation to the original love problem. And so things are just horrible. And they go on this way for about a week, and then one night in May the man is lying totally overcome by grief and by his roughly twenty-five fallings in love and run-ins with the police that day, and he's almost out of his mind, lying in a very bad way there on the rug of his apartment, and suddenly there's an impossibly tiny knock at the apartment door."

"Oh, no."

"What do you mean, 'Oh, no'?"

" . . . . "

"Well he opens the door, and there on the floor of the hall outside his apartment is the Thermos woman's tiny delicate pale-green tree toad, blinking up at him, from the lower eyelid up, with its left rear foot flattened and trailing way behind it and obviously hurt, no doubt we're to assume from the subway episode, which episode however the toad at least seemed to have survived."

"Wow."

"And the story ends with the man, bleary-eyed and punchy from grief and love and connection-ambiguity, at the door, staring down at the tiny pale-green tree toad, which is still simply looking up at him, blinking sadly in reverse, and giving a few tentative little chirrups. And they're just there in the hall looking at each other as the story ends."

"Wow."

"I think I'd like to try two pieces of gum at once, please."

". . . ."

"It's clearly not right for the *Frequent Review*, but I'm going to write a personal rejection note in which I say that I personally liked it, and thought it had possibilities, though it was not as yet a finished piece."

"Another troubled-collegiate-mind submission?"

"That's the very strong sense I get, although the kid tried to pass himself off as much older in his cover letter, and included what I have now determined to be a phony bibliography of published material."

"Lordy."

"I'm suddenly monstrously hungry, Lenore."

"I know for a fact there are sandwiches. Let me buzz Jennifer."

". . . ."

"Well, it's about time somebody wanted something around here."

"Hi Jennifer. I think Mr. Vigorous would like a sandwich."

"Well, sure. Sir, what would you like?"

"What sorts of sandwiches do you have, please?"

"We have ham, today, and also turkey."

"Does the turkey have mayonnaise?"

"I think so, sir."

"Miracle Whip, or Hellman's?"

"Sir, I'm afraid I'm not sure. Lenore, I'm sorry."

"That's OK, Jennifer. Hellman's makes Rick's throat itch, is the thing."

"How perfectly awful!"

"Perhaps I'll have the ham, provided it's mayonnaiseless, with the crusts removed from what I'll naturally assume to be rye bread."

"Yes, sir."

"Please, and understandably again given the above it's vital that there be no mayonnaise, though I would like a smidgeon of mustard, and also a Canadian Club with a splash of distilled water."

"Lenore?"

"May I please have a ginger ale?"

"I'll be right back."

"Thanks, Jennifer."

"Beautiful girl."

"Trying to make me jealous?"

"Don't I wish."

". . . ."

"Speaking of which . . . I saw Norman, yesterday, Lenore. He asked about you."

"Really? I think we're getting close to Bradley Field. I know we're over New York state, anyway. See the traffic?"

"Norman asked about you."

"Really."

"Norman claims to be in love with you."

"Why that tone, Rick?"

"What tone?"

"An obese, hideous, insane, aspirations-to-be-infinite person, who's off his rocker, expresses a necessarily-given-his-universe-view temporary interest in someone who made every effort to be explicitly rude to him, and who clearly has no interest in him, and you get that tone."

"I almost attacked him on the spot. I just had no idea where to begin hitting. He's much larger than he was a week ago."

"That seems longer ago than a week, doesn't it?"

"Besides, his palanquin carriers were all quite burly. Otherwise I really would have lunged."

". . . ."

"Norman hasn't communicated with you directly, has he? Expressed things to you?"

"I'll handle it, Rick."

"Handle what?"

"Whatever needs to be handled."

". . . ."

"I get to handle things too, you know. I'm a person."

"What has he said?"

"Nothing even the tiniest bit interesting, and nothing that's really any of your business."

"None of my business?"

" . . . . "

"None of my business?"

" . . . . "

"Aren't *you* my—? Thank you. Thanks."

"Looks super, Jennifer, thanks. Are we getting close?"

"I know we're over New York. Captain says about half an hour."

"Thanks."

"Just buzz if there's anything at all, you two."

"She didn't take the crusts off."

"Give me your knife. I'll do it."

"We're her only responsibility, the one thing she has to do, and she doesn't take the crusts off."

" . . . . "

"You're not my business? I'm confused about what's my business and what isn't?"

"Got a knife, here, remember."

" . . . . "

"I'm your friend. Your girlfriend. I'm not your business."

"My *girlfriend?*"

"Whatever you want to call it. May I please eat these crusts, or do you want them for some reason?"

"The things I love are my business."

"That's just untrue. The things you love and the people you love are the things and people you love. Your business is you."

" . . . . "

"Just like my business is me."

" . . . . "

"Which I'll handle, Rick."

"My, aren't we assertive and confident and sure of ourselves all of a sudden."

"I don't think this is the place for this. When you start using the plural tense, I sense spasm-potential."

"This ham is far too salty."

"You did take your gum out, right?"

"I'm losing you, Lenore. My ears were rumbling ominously at impending loss. That's what that rumbling really was."

"Why do you perceive everything in terms of having and losing? Have you ever for about one second thought of how that makes me feel? You haven't 'lost me,' whatever on God's green earth that means. I'll handle the people who might happen to be temporarily infatuated with me on my own, is all."

"*People?*"

"Sweet shrieking mother of God! Listen to yourself! You're not even insanely jealous, you're just . . . *pathetically* jealous."

"So now I'm pathetic."

"No more. I'm going to sleep. May I please put my ginger ale on your tray?"

"You may not go to sleep, Lenore."

". . . ."

"At least have the decency to give me some gum, to have, for the landing, which I might tell you I'm not looking forward to one bit."

"Here."

". . . ."

". . . ."

"You are too my business."

"Fnoof."

"Christ."

/d/

EXCERPT FROM DUTY LOG OF DR. DANIEL JOY, ASSISTANT DIRECTOR FOR EMERGENCY SERVICES, CHICAGO DEPARTMENT OF MENTAL HEALTH, CHICAGO, ILLINOIS, FRIDAY, 3 SEPTEMBER 1990.

10:40 a.m.   Arrive Lake Lady Medical Center, Chicago.
10:42   Arrive Floor 5. ID check complete. Station log verifies assignment to observe patient "JB," Room 573, admitted p.m. of Thursday, 26 August.

10:45 *Arrive Room 573. ID check complete. Occupants of 573
as of 10:45: Joy; patient "JB"; Dr. Robert Golden, Supervisor Emotional/Psychological Services, Lake Lady
Center; Dr. Daniel Nelm, Staff Physician, E/P S, L.L.C.
Observe patient "JB." Patient male, Caucasian, fair,
dark hair, height appr. 5' 9'', weight appr. 100 lbs.
Prominent features: eyes. Exceptionally large, black.
Condition skin around eyes indicates lack of/difficulties
connected with sleep. Patient conscious but sedated.
Medication indicated Golden to be 110 Thor. Pcm #7
drip ver. saline × 2 hrs.; increased to 220 Thor. Pcm
#7 post shift #3 (11 p.m.–7 a.m.).
Observe filming apparatus on tripod at foot of patient's
bed. Observe director's chair. Observe sunglasses worn
by Drs. Golden, Nelm. N explains patient delusion e.g.
admittance, believes he is contestant on television
"quiz-" or "game-show," refuses/unable to give correct
name, refers to himself only as "The Contestant," variously under heavy post-#3 sedation "He Who Smites
From Afar" (per report Golden, Nelm). Patient "JB" refuses to speak unless believes being filmed, recorded;
refuses to acknowledge questions posed by any but those
representing selves as "game-show" personnel (per G,
N). Food refused 27 August, thereafter; Drip Class 7 initiated 27 August, thereafter.
Malnutrition advanced but not sufficient for exhaustive
explanation condition (Golden, concurrence Joy).
Nelm explains camera is Motorola home-movie outfit
owned by Mrs. Nelm. Patient appears to ignore. Patient
stares into camera. Am handed by Nelm pair sunglasses,
director's bullhorn. Am instructed to address patient as
"Contestant, Baby." Sit in director's chair. (Here see E/
P S L.L.C. reports 8-28, 8-29, 8-30, 8-31, tag 573,
L.L.M.C.) Am introduced as "Mr. Barris of Screen Gems,
Inc." Patient response noticeable. Difficulty observing
patient from behind sunglasses judged acceptable, offset
by desirability patient response. Delusion observed. Delusion constant only with respect to television. Patient*

*appears confused as to whether appearing on game show
or being interviewed for/about appearance game show.
Nelm suggestion (positive impression Nelm, unorthodox
vs. highly competent, formally noted 9-3) Mr. "Barris"
ask "prospective contestant" for previous "game-show
experience." Patient's voice exceptionally raw, scratchy;
intelligibility inconstant. Hoarseness see admission report JB-L.L.M.C. 8-26, Nelm report 8-27 tag 573. Patient responds request "experience" (from tape, N):*

*"The experience I have had was on
the . . . (unintelligible) . . . In the Desert? And I
was . . . where we were I was contestant. I am the
contestant. The host opened the showcase and from
where I was the audience screamed. It was the most
desirable prize imaginable. The prize impossible to
conceive of a more desirable prize. The totally desirable prize. And the audience had to be restrained
with electrified wire mesh. And where I was I was
not restrained. And . . . " (unintelligible). "And the
host in the robe set the clock and shots of Dad
and . . ." (unintelligible) "and wires affixed. Host in
robe says . . ." (here patient adopts different voice,
possibly one of game-show quizmaster [N], pain at
vocal effort obvious):*

*" 'And the contestant will of course receive in
which he receives the most widely desirable prize
imaginable, on the condition that he, here we are,
not want it, for the next 60 seconds.'*

*"Contestant, where I was, did not receive prize.
Shouts from audience: 'Don't think about it.' 'Re-
nounce all desire.' Shouts from audience behind
electrified wire mesh. To receive totally desirable
prize by not desiring prize I did not receive prize.
Failure occurred at 50 seconds. Per the rules of the
game received the electric shocks, on the tip? Every
2 seconds? For the 50? And the audience com-*

> *pletely howled, threw water from behind the wire*
> *mesh, were thrown back . . ."*

Patient emits screams, rhythm appr. every 2 seconds,
over 20 seconds, throat condition prohibits excessive
noise or potential for harm (G, N). Dosage increased
Nelm × 1.5; patient now conscious but heavily sedated.
Eyes roll white.
Here c.f. formal report Joy CDMH 9-3-90 tag L.L.M.C.
#573: identity patient sought via standard police, media
procedure. Initials J.B., relative (?) L.B., established by
jewelry worn date admittance. Nelm emphasis mention
"Dad." Reference to Desert, together with accent, estab-
lishes experience (residence?) in Ohio post-1972. Direc-
tive Nelm; proceed through all missing persons reports
male Caucasion—Illinois,Ohio—past 30 days.
Observation assignment Nelm. Observation continued
through 9-10 authorized (see Joy, 9-3 tag 573
L.L.M.C.). Follow-up assignment Nelm authorized. Use
of equipment authorized through 9-10. For following
refer Joy formal 9-3 tag 573 L.L.M.C.
Overall impressions none. Parallel/Precedent impression
none.
11:30   Leave Lake Lady Medical Center, Chicago.   dj/hvs

/e/

"It sure is weird having it be Monday and no telephones. You were awesome with Walinda, Rick. I never would have believed it."

"My ears still hurt like hell. It was as if the takeoff merely softened my ears up for the landing. It was beyond belief, Lenore."

"I'm so sorry. What can I do?"

"Oh, *Route* 9. Here it is. We're on Route 9. God, the memories I have of Route 9. Good Lord, the Coolidge Bridge."

"Haven't you ever been back here, for reunions or stuff like that?"

"You must be joking."

". . . ."

"The plane isn't simply going to idle and wait for us at Bradley Field, Lenore, is it?"

"No way. That's Stonecipheco's one jet."

"How thrifty."

"I think it took off again almost right away. I think it had to get back home."

"Places to go and people to see."

"I'm not even sure. You hustled us into this limo in like four seconds."

"The law of the East Coast. You see available transportation, you grab it immediately."

"The plane's supposed to be back for us by lunchtime tomorrow . . . eleven-thirty."

"Plenty of time to talk to LaVache."

"Which is obviously going to be a waste of time, in terms of Dad, I predict. There's no way Lenore's talking to LaVache if she hasn't talked to me. LaVache and Lenore hate each other. And he doesn't even have a phone. And he and John hate each other, too. Or rather at least he hates John."

"So much hating."

"Well, it's just family hating. It's not like real hating."

"My God. The Aqua Vitae restaurant. I thought that had been torn down. I haven't thought of the Aqua Vitae in years. Good God. We used to pile in the car and go on down to the Aqua Vitae for monstrously huge hamburg pizzas."

"Hamburger."

"Ah, regional linguistic clash. I love it. It all comes flooding back."

". . . ."

"I really do have to pee, though."

"Should we pull over? We can pull in really quick at this mall, here."

"God, no, not a mall. We're nearly there. We're nearly here. I think perhaps it's just excitement. Amherst is rife with restroom facilities, anyway. At least it used to be. I knew them all."

"Hang in there, soldier."

"At least you can watch the putative future of Stonecipheco in academic action. You can issue a full report to your father, back at his lair."

"I'm not going to tell Dad anything except what I want to tell him. Dad told me like ninety lies in his office. I'm beginning to think Dad is maybe a compulsive liar. He lies pathologically, even sort of pathetically, when it comes to Miss Malig. And he had this guy who works for him, who I used to go to school with, spying on us. And he didn't even tell him to come out until it was obvious that I'd seen his shoes under the window curtain."

"Who is this person you went to school with? Have I been told about him before?"

"Look, an absolute moratorium on spasms is declared, here, Rick, OK? I'm just not in the mood at all."

". . . ."

"And you should know I'm not my father's messenger, or spy."

"Relax. You're among friends. You're with the one person who places your interests above his own. Remember that."

"Oh Rick."

"I love you, Lenore."

"But I have to admit I am sort of anxious to see what LaVache is like at school. He's really smarter than John, I think. In terms of pure smarts, he's the one person in the family who's smarter than John. He never had to work a bit at Shaker School, I know. And at home in the summer he's just a waste-product. He just sits around all day in the east wing, getting flapped and watching soap operas, and stuff like 'The Flintstones,' and carving designs in his leg."

". . . ."

"And at night, every night, he just goes out drinking with his spooky buddies, in their cars where the back is higher off the ground than the front."

"Jacked-up."

"Jacked-up cars. And Dad never knows what he's doing, because Dad's hardly ever around, or when he is he's like tiptoeing around ever so discreetly with Miss Malig. Dad thinks LaVache works. He thinks LaVache is another him."

"We're almost there. This hill. We're going to crest this hill, and we'll be there."

"I'm sure he must work, now, in college. I know I sure did."

"And . . . ahh, there it is. Good heavens."

"Your eyes are misting."

"Bet your ass. I make no bones about it. I haven't been back here in exactly twenty years. This is my alma mater."

"Well, of course it is, you silly."

"Alma mater."

". . . ."

"Shall we just proceed right to Stone, Lenore? That is where LaVache lives, correct?"

"Right."

"Driver, please take us directly to Stone Dormitory, Amherst College. You are, I'm afraid, on your own in terms of finding it. It's one of the new ones, with which I'm not familiar, not having—"

"No problem, buddy."

"How nice. Good heavens. How truly eerie, seeing all this. The trees are just barely hinting at beginning to turn, see? You can see it in some more than in others. Look there, for instance."

"Pretty, all right."

"Have you ever been here?"

"I've been to Mount Holyoke. I went there once, when Clarice was there."

"Did you find it pretty?"

"It was March, but it was pretty. The campus was really pretty."

"I've always liked Mount Holyoke, in a general sort of way."

"What does that mean?"

"God, I really must pee, Lenore."

"You can pee in LaVache's room."

". . . ."

"Oh, God, no! Rick, those *shoes*, still."

"Pardon?"

"Those shoes. See those shoes, on those people? The boat shoes? With the leather shoe and white plastic sole?"

"Well, yes."

"See those two girls and that guy? God, everybody's still wearing them out here. Boy do I hate those shoes."

"They, umm, seem all right to me. They seem harmless enough."

"I have what I'm sure is this totally irrational hatred for those shoes. I think a big reason is that everyone at school wore them with no socks."

" . . . . "

"Which meant that they weren't just wearing sneakers without socks, which would have been plenty repulsive enough, they were wearing nonsneakers without socks. Which is just incredibly . . ."

"Unhygienic?"

"Make fun if you want, smart guy. You're the one who's dumb if you pay Dr. Jay all that money and then don't even listen to him. It's not just that it's unhygienic, it's downright sick. It stinks. At school, I can remember, I'd be sitting in my carrel, in the library, doing homework or something, minding my own business, and somebody would sit down in the next carrel, with those shoes, and then they'd take them off, and I'd all of a sudden be smelling somebody else's feet."

" . . . . "

"Which did not smell good, let me tell you, from constantly being in shoes without socks. I mean I really think foot-smell should be a private thing, don't you?"

" . . . . "

"What are you grinning at? Are those ridiculous feelings? Does that make no sense at all?"

"Lenore, it makes perfect sense. It's just that I'd never given the matter that much thought. Never much thought to the . . . socio-ethics of foot-smell."

"Now I can tell you're being sarcastic."

"You completely misread me."

" . . . . "

"Is that why you always wear two pairs of socks? Under constant and invariable sneakers?"

"Partly. Partly because it's comfortable, too."

"Stone Dorm, pal."

"Which one of these is Stone?"

"The one we're right in front of, pal."

"I see . . . . Lord am I stiff."

"You want to just bolt right in and pee?"

" . . . ."

"Rick?"

"I rather think not, now that the moment has arrived."

"What does that mean? You did nothing but talk pee, in the car."

"Have you the bags?"

"You know perfectly well they're in the trunk."

"The question really meant, do you suppose you could manage getting them inside yourself, making absolutely sure to take my bag in, too, with my underwear and toothbrush and Old Spice and all essentials?"

"I suppose so, but I don't get it."

"Meter's still running, ace."

"I think with your permission I will simply leave you, here, for a bit. I feel emotions and feelings washing over me that are perhaps best confronted alone."

"What?"

"I'm going to go wander among the blasted crags of memory, for a while."

"Pardon me?"

"I'm going to go take a look around."

"Oh. Well, OK."

"Till later, then."

"You want to just come back here and meet me? We can check in at Howard Johnson's at five and then go to dinner?"

"Fine. Goodbye."

"It's room 101, remember."

"Righto. See you soon."

"Are you OK?"

"Yes. Goodbye. Thank you ever so much, driver."

" . . . ."

"Can you please help me with the bags?"

"I guess so, lady. What's with him?"

"He gets this way, sometimes, when he has to go to the bathroom."

/f/

6 September

The sudden strength with which the desire to go see whether the initials I'd carved so long ago in the wood of the stall in the men's room of the Art Building were still there, the sudden and unexpected and overwhelming strength with which these feelings had washed over me, there at the dormitory, with Lenore, was a frightening thing. As I joined the serpentine line of students walking up the ungentle hill to the Art and Science Buildings, all of us falling into the vaguely floppy, seal-like gait of the hurried hill-climber, most of us seals apparently late for class, one of us late for an appointment with a tiny ocean of his own past, stretching away and down beside the carved dock of his childhood, an ocean into which this particular seal was going to pour a strong (hopefully unitary) stream of his own presence, to prove that he still is, and so was—that is, provided of course the bathroom and toilet and stall were still there—as I joined the line of seals in short pants and loose short-sleeved shirts and boat shoes and backpacks, and as I felt the fear that accompanied and was in a way caused by the intensity of the wash of feelings and desires and so on that accompanied even the thought of a silly men's room in a silly building at a silly college where a sad silly boy had spent four years twenty years ago, as I felt all these things, there occurred to me a fact which I think now as I sit up in bed in our motel room, writing, the television softly on, the sharp-haired object of my adoration and absolute center of my entire existence asleep and snoring softly in the bed beside me, a fact which I think now is undeniably true, the truth being that Amherst College in the 1960's was for me a devourer of the emotional middle, a maker of psychic canyons, a whacker of the pendulum of Mood with the paddle of Immoderation.

That is, it occurs to me now in force that in college things were never, not ever, at no single point, simply all right. Things were never just OK. I was never just getting by. Never. I can remember I was always horribly afraid. Or, if not horribly afraid, horribly angry. I was always desperately tense. Or, if not tense, then in an odd hot euphoria that made me walk with the water-jointed jaunt of the person who truly does not give a shit one way or the other. I was always either so unreasonably and pointlessly happy that no one place could seem to contain me, or so melancholy, so sick and silly with sadness that there was no place I could stomach the thought of entering. I hated it here. And I have never been as happy as when I was here. And these two things together confront me with the beak and claws of the True.

One of the trees at the top of the hill, which I stopped to look at as I played with my hat and recovered from the climb, the line of students forking past either side of me and disappearing into buildings to the sound of bells, one of the trees was just beginning to burn, a bit, with color, a flush of hesitant red suffusing the outline of the tree against the southerly sun, the tree's blood draining out of those leaves most distant from the heart first; and I looked at the flush of crinkled red crowning a body of soft green, with the sunlight winking through the branches as they moved and creaked in the breeze, until I was drawn away by the twin urges to remember and to pee.

And the initials were still there, the tiny carved "R.V.," near the bottom of the stall. Someone had filled in the carving with ballpoint pen. Near the initials were another set of initials, "S.U.X.," which I come to see now were to be a joke at my expense. And, near the joke-at-my-expense initials, someone, some tiny soul, probably during exam time, in a gesture the emotion behind which I could completely understand, had put the single word, "Mommy"—which predictably, someone else, a mean person, had altered in a slightly different color to become "Your Mommy hates you."

"She does *not*," I put—still being a really incorrigible graffiti man, I'm afraid—under the cruel alteration, although I had to get on hands and knees in the scum-laden stall to do it, and managed to dip my tie neatly in the toilet bowl in the process; let Jay and Blentner have a look at this. And my present bubbled and frothed in my past, and was borne naturally away.

Out the door of the Art Building and through the courtyard I pass into a quad, the quad, where loosely clothed barefoot boys with liquid wrists are playing Frisbee under the lying leaves, running like deer, throwing the plastic plate every which way. We dinosaurs used to play a similar game here, with trays taken from the dining hall, metal trays back then, with sharp digit-removing edges, so that, I remember, the trays had to be caught in midair by the tweezer of finger and thumb. . . . We would play and bleed. Now they are only high-tech and beautiful, and the bright disc hangs motionless in the air while earth and trees and lithe slippery boys slide underneath as if on oil to receive it again. I clap my hands a bit, hem and haw, throw my cap into the air, practice some motions, make it clear that I want to be invited to play, but I am ignored.

I walk around the quad, kicking at exposed tree roots, listening to snatches of conversation in languages with which I am unfamiliar. I stay well clear of North Dormitory, to be sure. I make a giant detour around it. Out of the corner of my eye I can see its windowshades fluttering. I can see its tree-fingers pointing. North Dormitory. Scene of perhaps the single most disastrous, unthinkable moment of my life, thus far.

Actually probably second to my wedding night.

Whom do I see, here, in the quad? Can the present of a past fail to be ugly? But it isn't so. As I really should have remembered, ugliness is absent from the College. I have visions of it, bound and muffled, its walleyes rolling helplessly, stuffed into the darkest closets and boiler rooms in the deepest basements of the thickest buildings. I think I can hear its soft cries for help. The crazy relative everyone ignores, and denies, and feeds. Ugliness is absent from the quad.

Whom do I see, here? I see students and adults. I see parents, obvious parents, the ones with name tags. I watch the students, and they watch back. Ability To Handle Oneself, elaborate defense structures, exit their eyes and begin to assemble on the ground before them. But the eyes and faces are as always left bare. In the girls' faces I see softness, beauty, the shiny and relaxed eyes of wealth, and the vital capacity for creating problems where none exist. For some reason I see these girls also older, pale television ghosts flickering beside the originals: middle-aged women, with bright-red fingernails and deeply tanned, hard, seamed faces, sprayed hair shaped by the professional fingers of men with French names; and eyes, eyes that will stare without pity or doubt over salted tequila rims at the glare of the summer sun off the country club pool. The structures spread out, grow, wave at me with the epileptic flutter of the film-in-reverse. The boys are different, appropriately, from the girls. From each other. I see blond heads and lean jaws and bow-legged swaggers and biceps with veins in them. I see so many calm, impassive, or cheerful faces, faces at peace, for now and always, with the context of their own appearance and being, that sort of long-term peace and smooth acquaintance with invariable destiny that renders the faces bloodlessly pastable onto cut-outs of corporate directors in oak-lined boardrooms, professors with plaid ties and leather patches at the elbows of their sport jackets, doctors on bright putting greens with heavy gold shock-resistant watches at their wrists and tiny beepers at their belts, black-jacketed soldiers efficiently bayoneting the infirm. I see Best faces, faces I remember well. Faces whose owners are going to be the Very Best.

I see the faces of those who belong and those who do not belong. The belonging faces appear in rows, like belts of coins. The coins bob up and down, because belongers swagger. The belonging faces are tiringly complex, the expression of each created and propped up, through processes obscure, by the faces on either side of it. These structures intertwine and mesh, have not yet begun to tear at one another. And the nonbelongers. Of course the faces of those who do not belong are the adjustable dark-eyed faces of Vance Vigorous. Many of these faces are tilted downward, for fear of trip-ping on a root, for fear of being seen tripping on a root. These are the ones who do not sleep, sleep badly, sleep alone, and think of other things when they hear the sounds through the walls of their rooms. I intuit that the Frisbee players, whom I continue to watch, are nonbelongers. The Frisbee traces faint lines between them, strands that are swept and snapped like spidersilk by the wind off the Me-morial Hill and athletic fields to the south. The nonbelongers' faces are the unfirm faces that are really firm, the self-defined faces, the faces defined by not belonging in a place defined by belonging. These alone are the faces that stare out, protected and imprisoned, from behind the barbed borders of their own structures, the faces that know that, but for the grace of a God distinguished for the arbitrariness of his grace, it is they who would be bound and muffled in the College closets. The faces that are unreachable from this far away, and that look through you and digest you in a moment, against everyone's will.

Who knows how long I watch. My pantcuffs fill with leaf bits and clippings of hollow-stemmed grass. Parents go by with their name tags. Older men, for whom bellies are burdens wrapped and hefted in checked sportcoats. Older women I have already seen and known in the faces of their daughters. Seals on hills, bright discs in the air. Lovers on stomachs, legs up, ankles lazily crossed against the fluttering approach of the odd falling leaf. The sun moves out over the mountains. I am able to feel it. The ellipse of my quad-orbit absorbs the indentation of North Dormitory.

Oh, why the hate? Why, when a horrible, worse-than-worst thing happens to you, when in all honesty *you* do something horrible, why is it the situation in the context of which the thing happens, the physical place where it happens, the other people whom it involves, that you hate, the thought of which and whom sends organs leaping inside you and corridors in your brain clanging shut against the assault? Why is it not yourself whom you hate, the mirror away from which you reel in horror? Can Jay explain this? What an entirely inappropriate question. How very far I've come.

On 2, soon to be 3, March 1968, North Dormitory, of which I was a resident, sponsored a mixer for the junior class, of which I was a member, and for the residents of our sister dormitory at Mount Holyoke College, an all-women's institution ten miles away, the institution Lenore's sister and grandmother—mother, too, I think—had all passed through. In attendance at this mixer was a Mount Holyoke sophomore named Janet Dibdin, a small, quiet, curved girl, straight red hair and blue eyes with tiny, fluffy white diamonds in the irises. Really. A girl about whom I was privately wild. A girl I met at another mixer, another of the year's endless string, this one at Mount Holyoke; and at this mixer I had met her, and had survived the agony of dancing with her. And so. And so this was a girl in whose presence I was stupid, damp, tongue-tied, and comparatively huge. One of the three females in my life to whom I have been overwhelmingly sexually attracted, the others being Lenore Beadsman and the daughter of my next-door neighbor in Scarsdale, Rex Metalman's daughter, an objectively erotic young thing who undulated her way into my heart in the summer of her thirteenth year while ostensibly playing with the sprinkler in the lawn.

In any event, there were we, grouped in blue suits and gray suits and slicked-back hair and shiny nervous noses, and there were they, a sweet shifting miasma of wool, shaped hair, cashmere, eyes, cotton, calves and pearls, in the midst of which she stood, by the hors d'oeuvre bar, in a skirt and monogrammed sweater, talking quietly with friends, conspicuously danceless all night, and it was close to twelve, and there were we, in suits, gathering our saliva for the final assault. And there we were, moving through geologic time, impossibly slowly, imperceptibly, across the cedar floor, the fire in the fireplace doubtless and not inappropriately reflected and dancing in the centers of our eyes. We moved, and I was suddenly beside her, talking to her, good heavens hello, pretending it be by accident lest all dissolve, one or two of her friends standing with towering hairdos off to the side, wary lest they be caught in the ropes of sexual tension that snapped and crackled in the air between Janet and me, the friends watching us, me, for the tiniest error, the Beatles on the record player playing "Eight Days a Week," and my hands prepared some sort of hors d'oeuvre, what do I mean some sort, a fastened cylinder of bologna on a Ritz cracker, and she declined it, and stared at me kindly, telling me with her eyes that she was willing to play the elaborate and exhausting game, that it was all right, and I put the hors d'oeuvre into my mouth, and the cracker seemed to explode into deserts of dust, and there was meat, and I recall she was talking about the upcoming election, and the unavoidable and untalkaboutably horrible invitation to dance began its salmon's migration from my intestine up toward my brain, and my hand was in the pocket of my slacks, soaking through the wool, and in a disastrous flash I thought of something witty to say, to delay the invitation, and my heart leapt, and my throat constricted, and I turned convulsively from myself to say the thing to Janet Dibdin, as she stared with undeserved trust into my eyes, and I tried to say the thing, and as I opened my mouth there somehow flew out of my mouth an enormous glob of the chewed hors d'oeuvre, the Ritz cracker and bologna, chewed, with saliva in it, with shocking force, and it flew out and landed on the fleshy part of Janet Dibdin's nose, and stayed there. And the friends were blasted into silence, and the rest of the hors d'oeuvre in my mouth turned to

ice, adhered forever to my palate, and the Beatles sang, "Guess you
know it's true," and Janet stopped all life processes, virtually killed
with horror, which she out of a compassion not of this earth tried
to hide by smiling, and she began to look in her purse for a Kleenex,
with the obscenely flesh-and-bone-colored glob of chewed food on
the end of her nose, and I watched it all through the large end of
a telescope, and then the world ceased mercifully to be, and I became
infinitely small and infinitely dense, a tiny black star twinkling
negatively amid a crumple of empty suit and shoes. This was my
taste of hell at twenty. The month following that night is an ir-
retrievable blank in my memory, an expletive deleted. That portion
of my brain is cooked smooth.

An unprecedentedly enormous veer around North Dormitory,
effected with hands over ears, flings me out past Memorial Hill and
into the bleeding forests south of the campus, and I wander, crunching needles and the weak leaves already down, as I used to wander
alone for hours as a student, elbowing through the throngs of other
students wandering alone, as I elbow students and parents aside now
and head for the really isolated, natural part of the New England
forest, beyond the road, past dry fields of baking, screaming crickets,
out through the wind, elbowing, to find the really secluded places
already full, lines of belongers cracking like whips around the sap-
sprung trees, sending nonbelongers spinning into the brush. I am
outside. And I wait my turn for admission, and smoke two clove
cigarettes under the angry eye of a blue-haired mother in a yellow
Bonwit pantsuit unfortunately right downwind from me, hissing into
the ear of a son with a note concerning laundry pinned to the sleeve
of his brand new AMHERST jacket. I buy a hot dog from a vendor
and watch the sun glitter faraway against the windows of the buildings on the southern face of the broad ridge, the southern wall of
the citadel. One of my "R.V.'s" was still here, and I had, in the
back of my mind, one other place where I might still be, and these
things somehow made me unreasonably happy—as happy as seeing
the immoderate curve of Lenore's hip under her scratchy Howard
Johnson's blanket, here, next to me. I love you, Lenore. There is
no hatred in my love for you. Only a sadness I feel all the more
strongly for my inability to explain or describe it. My ears rumble
still.

/g/

There was simply no getting around the fact that Stonecipher LaVache Beadsman looked satanic. His skin was a dark, glossy red, his hair an oily black and swept back without care over a deep widow's peak, his eyebrows Brezhnevian in thickness and starting up high off to the side to slant down evilly over his eyes, his head small and smooth and oval and not too securely attached to his neck and tending to flop, like the head of a shoe tree. An OBERLIN sweatshirt and corduroy shorts and a hurricane of hair on his foot, beside his black hightops. A clipboard with a pen hanging by a string was attached to his leg as he sat in an easy chair, watching television, his profile to Lenore, at the door. On television was "The Bob Newhart Show." In the big social room with LaVache were three boys who all seemed to look precisely alike, although Lenore wasn't completely sure about this, because the heavy window curtains were drawn against the afternoon sun and the room was dim. The room smelled of, in descending order, pot, Mennen Speed Stick, hot alcohol, feet. The three identical guys all sat sockless beside tumbled empty pairs of those shoes.

"Lenore, this is Cat, this is Heat, this is the Breather," LaVache said from his chair in front of the television. "My sister Lenore, guys."

"Hi," said Cat.

"Hello," said Heat.

"Hi," said the Breather.

Heat and the Breather were on a spring-sprung sofa, sharing what was obviously a joint. Cat was on the floor, sitting, a bottle of vodka before him, and he clutched it with his bare toes, staring anxiously at the television screen.

"Hi Bob," Suzanne Pleshette said to Bob Newhart on the screen.

"Merde du temps," Cat said. He took a swig from the bottle.

LaVache looked up from his clipboard at Lenore. "We're playing Hi Bob. You want to play Hi Bob with us?" He spoke sort of slowly.

Lenore made a place to sit on the luggage. "What's Hi Bob?"

The Breather grinned at her from the sofa, where he now held the bottle of vodka. "Hi Bob is where, when somebody on 'The Bob Newhart Show' says 'Hi Bob,' you have to take a drink."

"And but if Bill Dailey says, 'Hi Bob," said Cat, tending to the joint with a wet finger, "that is to say, if the character Howard Borden on the show says 'Hi Bob,' it's death, you have to chug the whole bottle."

"Hi Bob," said Bill Dailey, on the screen.

"Death!" yelled Cat.

The Breather drained the bottle of vodka without hesitation. "Lucky it was almost empty," he said.

"Guess I'll probably pass," said Lenore. "You're out of vodka, anyway."

"The duration of a game of Hi Bob is according to the rules determined by the show, not the vodka," the Breather said, getting another bottle of vodka from a rack behind the sofa and breaking the seal. The liquor-rack was a glitter of glass and labels in the sun through a gap in the curtains. "The serious Hi Bob player makes it his business never to run out of vodka."

LaVache drummed idly on his leg with his pen. "Vodka gives Lenore lung-troubles, anyway, as I recall." He looked at Lenore. "Lenore, baby, sweetheart, how are you? What are you doing here?"

The Breather leaned close to Lenore and told her in a hot sweet whisper, "It's a Quaalude day, so we all have to be accommodating."

Lenore looked at LaVache's lolling head. "Didn't you get my message? I left this detailed message about how I was coming today. I left it with one of your neighbors, next door, a guy from New Jersey. The college operator connected me to him."

"Wood, yes," LaVache said. "He's actually coming by real soon. He and the leg have an appointment. Yes, I got the message, but why didn't you just call me?"

"You told Dad you didn't have a phone, Dad told me."

"I don't have a phone. This isn't a phone, this is a lymph node," LaVache said, gesturing at a phone next to the television. "I call this a lymph node, not a phone. So when Dad asks me do I have a phone, I can in all good conscience say no. I do, however, have a lymph node."

"You're horrible," said Lenore.

"Hi Bob," said someone on the screen.

"Zango," said LaVache, and took a big drink.

"Dead bird, here, A.C.," Heat said to LaVache.

LaVache detached the clipboard and slid out a drawer in the plastic of his artificial leg and tossed a white new joint to Heat.

"You have a drawer?" said Lenore.

"I've had a drawer since high school," said LaVache. " I just wear long pants, at home, as a rule. Come on, you knew I had a drawer all the time."

"No I didn't," said Lenore.

"Crafty girl."

There was a knock at the outside door.

"*Entrez!*" Cat yelled.

In came a tall thin guy with glasses and an adam's apple and a notebook and a baggie.

"Clint Wood," Heat said from over the bottle, which he was blowing into like a jug, sounding a deep note.

"Guys," said Clint Wood. "Antichrist."

"What can we do for you, big guy?" LaVache said, slapping the leg affectionately.

"Introductory Economics. Second quiz. Bonds."

"Feed the leg," said LaVache.

LaVache opened the drawer in his leg and Clint Wood put the baggie inside. LaVache slapped the drawer shut and patted it. "Professor?"

"Fursich."

"All you need to remember for Fursich is, when the interest rate goes up, the price of any bond already issued goes down."

"Interest rate . . . up, price . . . bond . . . down." Clint Wood wrote it down.

"And when the rate goes down, the price goes up."

"Down . . . up." Clint Wood looked up. "That's it?"

"Trust me," said LaVache.

"What a guy," said the Breather. "A little Hi Bob, Wood?"

Clint Wood shook his head regretfully. "Can't. I got class in like ten minutes. I gotta go memorize what the Antichrist told me." He looked over at Lenore and smiled.

"Well, hey, good luck," Cat said.

"Thank you very much for taking my message, if you were the person who took my message," said Lenore.

"Oh, OK, you're the Antichrist's sister," said Clint Wood, sizing Lenore up. "Can't do enough for the Antichrist, no problem. Thanks again, guys." He left.

"Hi Bob."

"Oomph."

"This is a deadly one. There've been like twenty 'Hi Bobs' in this one."

"What's the leg got there?"

"Looks to be three j-birds. Poorly rolled."

"None of you guys have classes?" Lenore asked. Ed McMahon came on the television.

"I have classes," LaVache said. "I know I do, because it says on my schedule I do." He cleaned under his fingernail with the corner of his clipboard clasp.

"He's going to go to a class this semester, he told me," Heat said to Lenore, doing a handstand in the middle of the floor, so that his shirt fell over his face. "He's determined to go to at least one class."

"Well I'm *disabled*," LaVache said. "They can't expect a disabled person to hobble to every faraway, top-of-the-hill class of the semester."

Lenore looked at LaVache. "You don't work, here, do you?"

LaVache smiled at her. "That was just work, what I did. I do lots of work."

"He literally does the work of like forty or fifty guys, and even more girls," said Heat. "He does all our work, the big lug."

"What about your own work?" Lenore said to LaVache.

"What can I tell you? I've got a leg to support, after all."

"Dad thinks you work."

"Surely you of all people didn't come all the way out here after seeing me only a few weeks ago to tell me what Dad thinks. Or to find out what I think and do and then scuttle back to Dad."

"Not exactly," Lenore said, shifting because her suitcase handle was digging into her bottom. "There's stuff we need to talk about, that's sort of come up." She looked around at Cat, Heat, and the Breather.

"Well goody. Stuff." LaVache looked back at the television. "We have a game of Hi Bob to finish, and then there's an episode of 'The Munsters' on Channel 22 I particularly want to see, and then we can go conversationally wild."

"He'll be asleep by then, though, I predict," the Breather whispered into Lenore's ear as his elbow brushed her chest.

"Hi Bob," said Bill Dailey, the character Howard Borden, on the screen.

"Death, big time," said LaVache, looking at Cat and the nearly full bottle of vodka on the floor in front of him. "See you tomorrow, Cat."

"À l'enfer," Cat muttered. He began sucking on the bottle. He had to stop almost immediately.

"You've got five minutes to finish that," LaVache said to Cat.

"He's going to be really sick," said Lenore.

"We don't get sick here anymore," said LaVache. "This Amherst guy, this legendary guy a few years back started this tradition where, instead of getting sick, we pound our heads against the wall."

"You pound your heads?"

"Really hard."

"I see."

The phone rang. "Breather, you want to get the lymph node?" LaVache said, returning to writing on his clipboard. The Breather stepped over Cat, who was crawling on the gray carpet, and got the phone. The Antichrist was writing something.

"Antichrist, it's Snadgener," the Breather said after a bit, putting his hand over the phone. "Evolution as Cultural Phenomenon Paper Number One. Were Darwin's critics right about the theory of natural selection being deeply dangerous to Christianity."

"Tell Snadge the leg is wondering what he has for it," said LaVache.

"Mushrooms, he says."

"Professor?"

"Summerville."

"Tell Snadge the interesting answer for Summerville is yes," LaVache said. The Breather whispered into the phone. LaVache continued, "After the Origin, the Bible has to retreat, he thinks. The Bible ceases to be a historical record of actual events and instead becomes a piece of moral fiction, useful only as a guide for making decisions about how to live. No longer purporting to tell what was and is, but only what ought to be." LaVache opened his eyes. "Summerville'll lap it up."

The Breather talked into the phone. Cat had a third of the bottle to go and was green and moist. Heat sat cross-legged with the joint on the sofa.

"Snadge says it sounds kick-ass," the Breather said. "Snadge says thanks, Antichrist."

"Tell Snadge the leg and I look forward to seeing him and his fungal fee sometime tonight," said LaVache.

Lenore leaned as far as she could over toward LaVache. "*Antichrist?*" she said.

"What can I tell you?" said the Antichrist. "We can't deny I look satanic. Heat, you want to clear a space on the wall for Cat?"

Heat got up slowly and began to move posters.

"Mother," moaned Cat.

"The really sadistic aspect of this game," the Breather whispered to Lenore, leaning over her so she had to lean way back and almost fell off her suitcase. "is that if someone else on the show says 'Hi Bob' before Cat has discharged his vodka-responsibility, Cat has to drink a whole 'nother bottle in another five minutes."

"Does Cat know that?" Lenore asked, looking at Cat. Cat sat slumped on the floor, the back of his head resting and intermittently pounding weakly on the wall behind him, the bottle of vodka in his lap and a thin rope of spittle joining his lip and the lip of the bottle.

"I think at this point Cat knows what's up in a sort of ganglial sense," the Antichrist said, "although he'd have a hard time actually articulating the rule if you asked him to."

"Mommy," Cat squeaked faintly.

"You can do it, you great big enormous guy," the Breather said, massaging Cat's shoulders.

Ed McMahon came on the television screen. "Sell it, Ed!" yelled the Antichrist.

Heat put aside the corpse of the joint and sipped thoughtfully at a beer. He turned dense red eyes and looked at Lenore for so long that Lenore felt uncomfortable. Heat then looked at LaVache, who ignored him. Then back at Lenore. "Hey Antichrist," he said. "You care if I ask your sister a question?"

"Be my guest," the Antichrist said, alternately watching the screen and Cat's attempts to finish the bottle, attempts that were at this point pretty pathetic, because there was just a little bit of vodka left, and Cat kept trying to get it in his mouth, but it kept somehow bouncing off, or at any rate not staying in, and sliding back inside the bottle and down the outside and onto the rug and his shirt.

Heat looked at Lenore as the Breather massaged his shoulders, now, from behind. "Lenore, how did the Antichrist lose his leg?"

"Well, now, hey, that's not fair, because it's not a question, because I've already answered it," the Antichrist said. Lenore looked at him. His head rested on his shoulder. "I've already told you it was a dancing accident. I had such an unreasonably happy childhood that I simply danced, all the time, for joy, and one day the dancing just got to be too much, and I had an accident. *Quod est demonstratum.*"

Lenore laughed.

"Is that true?" Heat said to Lenore. "Are you going to back him up?"

"By all means," Lenore said, not looking at LaVache, who was not looking at her.

LaVache turned to Heat. "And don't you know disability etiquette? You don't discuss a disability in the presence of a disabled person unless the disabled person brings up the disability. For all you know I could be reeling, from hurt, on the inside. How'd you like to do your own Calculus homework for a while?"

"Antichrist," Heat said with an easy grin, "I hereby tender a sincere apology for my gaucheness, and also take the opportunity to point out that another joint seems to have expired, here."

"Harumph," the Antichrist said, sliding open his drawer. "Clint Wood and bonds to the rescue."

"Five minutes is up, Antichrist," said the Breather.

Cat's chin was resting on his chest. One of his arms was incongruously outstretched, with a finger pointing at the stairs leading up to the social room's bathroom.

"Has he done it?" asked LaVache.

The Breather held up the bottle. "The merest smidgeon left."

"More than a smidgeon on his shirt, though, I see," Heat said, lifting up Cat's head to have a look at the dark field of vodka-soaked shirt on his chest.

The Antichrist rubbed the leg thoughtfully. "I say if Cat consents to suck on his shirt for the rest of the show, which is about five more minutes, he'll have acquitted himself in his usual thoroughly admirable way."

"Congratulations, big kitty," the Breather said softly, tucking part of Cat's shirt in Cat's mouth, caressing a cheek under fluttering eyelids. "Still the undisputed prince of Hi Bob."

"Did you come alone?" LaVache asked Lenore. "Did you come by plane, or by toy?"

"I came via the Company jet," said Lenore.

The Antichrist's eyebrows went up, so it looked like he had more hair.

Lenore continued, "I came with a friend, who's also sort of my boss at Frequent and Vigorous."

"Mr. Vigorous." The Antichrist nodded his head. "The one Candy told me about."

"What did Candy tell you, when?" asked Lenore.

The Antichrist looked away, drew a smile-face on the plastic of his leg with his pen, wiped it away with a moist finger. "That your boss was also your friend, so you were lucky. In July. Please don't have a spasm; I sense Cat really not feeling well at all."

"Is Candy the Mandible babe you blasted?" Heat asked the Antichrist with a grin.

Lenore looked at her brother with wide eyes. "You and Candy? Blasting?"

LaVache turned slowly and rested absolutely icy eyes on Heat. Heat's clothes seemed suddenly to get roomier, as if he'd developed a slow leak. "Sorry," he muttered. He closed his eyes.

The Antichrist looked at Lenore. "Heat knows not whereof he speaks, as I will no doubt be explaining at considerable length later. Heat, don't you have some math you better do?"

"Shit," Heat whispered. He sucked on the Antichrist's joint.

Lenore stood up. "May I please ask a favor?"

"Yes."

"I'm sure it's an imposition, but Rick and I don't get to check in at the motel till five, and it's been a really long day, and also sort of a dirty one, what with travel. . . ."

"I understand entirely," the Antichrist said soothingly. The "Bob Newhart Show" credits came on. The Breather went to the television and changed the channel. LaVache beamed at Lenore. "There is a clean, neatly folded towel for you in the bathroom, a bathroom which you'll be happy to know you can secure for a brief period with the hanger on the door, although in a crisis Cat may find himself forced to impose, and there is on the towel, for your personal use, a crisp new bar of soap."

"What, is she going to take a shower?" the Breather asked from the television, where he was twidgeling the vertical-hold controls.

"If it's OK," said Lenore.

"Hubba-hubba," said the Breather.

"Steady, big guy," said the Antichrist. "Lenore's traveling companion is, I understand, fanatically jealous."

Lenore looked at her brother.

"Where is this Mr. Vigorous, anyway," LaVache asked quietly, looking back down at the leg.

The phone rang. The Breather reached over and picked it up. "It's Nervous Roy Keller for you, A.C.," he said to LaVache.

The Antichrist's eyes lit up. "May I please have the lymph node?" The Breather handed him the phone. Lenore, not sure if she should stay around to explain where Rick Vigorous was, stood awkwardly, hefting her suitcase, hurting for a shower. Heat lay curled up on the sofa, apparently alseep. The Breather quietly went over and removed the red eye of the burning nubbin of the joint from between Heat's fingers. Cat lay crumpled against the wall under the window, his shirt in his mouth.

"Nervous Roy Keller," the Antichrist said into the phone. "Is it possible that I have not yet seen you this year? Are you spending all your time in the library again? In spite of what we talked about last spring?"

Nervous Roy Keller said something.

"Nervous, Nervous Roy," laughed LaVache. "OK. I sense that a certain limb and I can do something for you. Right. You're what? You're taking Hegel? With Professor Huffman? I thought that got canceled for lack. He turned it into a tutorial? Just you and Huffman, and Hegel? That's going to be death and destruction, you huge guy you. Well I'm sure sorry, is all. Uh-huh. Obliteration of Nature by Spirit? That's the first assignment? What's he going to do for an encore I wonder." The Antichrist looked up at the Breather from the phone. "Breather, you want to be a good Sancho and go get me my *Phenomenology of Spirit?*"

The Breather went up the little set of stairs from the social room into the bedroom/bathroom area. On the television, marred only by a few vertical flutters, Marilyn Munster was bringing a date home, and the date saw her father, Herman, and ran away and climbed a telephone pole in sped-up motion, which Herman and Lily interpreted as a reflection on Marilyn's seductive charms, and the audience laughed. The Breather reappeared and handed the Antichrist the book.

"Obliteration N by S, let's see," LaVache said, thumbing through. He stopped. "Bingo. Let's see. . . . OK, look, N.R., why don't you come by the room right before dinner, and we'll talk Sublation Through Concepts. OK? Right. The leg will of course be positively growling with hunger by that time. *Verstehen Sie?* Right. See you then, then."

The Antichrist hung up the phone and put it on the floor. "A tutorial on Hegel with Huffman," he said to the Breather. "The leg likes that."

The Breather grinned and manipulated his eyebrows at Lenore.

"Rick's taking . . . walk around . . . alumnus . . . intense emotions washing . . . ," Lenore was muttering.

The Antichrist looked at her. "Why aren't you in the shower this very moment?" he asked. "Take until four, and 'The Munsters' will be over, and my catharsis will be effected, and away we'll go, leaving Heat to his homework."

"Right," said Lenore. She undid the straps of a suitcase and dug through Rick's underwear and got her washcloth and toothbrush, and headed for the stairs.

"Need any help, don't hesitate to call," said the Breather.

"Thanks," Lenore said. She shivered.

"Guess I might as well have a Quaalude, too, A.C., since there's going to be no one left to play with," the Breather said to LaVache.

Lenore unhooked the wire hanger bent and fastened to keep the bathroom door open and closed the door against the noise of the television and low voices and the sliding of the drawer.

/h/

I'm not exactly sure how I arrived at the Flange, at three o'clock, and I really have no idea when the Flange became a gay bar, although I do know it was sometime after 1968, during which year a group of marginal Psi Phi fraternity brothers—including myself—would come every Wednesday to hoist a few and play pool and try, in our tweed jackets and white socks and Weejun loafers, to blend in with the public-university- and townie-crowd. A crowd that I can say with all confidence was at this point not the least bit gay.

But the bead curtain at the inner room clicketed and in I came, feeling warm from my walking and with a sneezy, burning afterdust of dry leaves in my nose. The place was relatively empty on this Monday, apart from some couples dancing and a group sitting at one end of the bar watching an episode of "The Bob Newhart Show," a program I'd always enjoyed. The place did not scream gay bar, as so many gay bars seem to, not of course that I've personally been to many. In any event, here the choice and placement of posters and mirrors, the planty, velvety decor, the male bartender with orange mascara, the dancer-gender situation, told me all I needed to know. I didn't care. My plans were simple. I wanted a Canadian Club with distilled water, then I would go initial-hunting in the restroom. I was sure I had left myself here. I sat on a stool, away from the television crowd, feeling a bit childish. Barstools make me feel a bit childish, because my feet do not quite reach the supports; they dangle, and sometimes swing, and my thighs plump out from the weight of the dangling and swinging legs, and my feet sometimes go to sleep.

I slipped unconsciously into my bar mode. I looked at people. The people at the actual bar were easy, because of the huge mirror we were all looking into. The mirror revealed that the young bartender's hair became a mohawk in back. I was given the Canadian

Club and immediately tasted tapwater, to which I am acutely sensitive.

The man nearest me, a few stools away, even farther than I from the "Bob Newhart" audience, was the best-looking man in the room. He had a strong face, a chin I admired wistfully over my whiskey, his high features stronger for the fact that he was engagingly in need of a shave. Hair a kind of deep, dark blond, cut short and almost brushed up. The muscles of his jaw worked as he chewed peanuts. He drank beer; he had a small brown forest of bottles around him. The eyes were bright green, but bright and still soft, somehow, plant-green as opposed to emerald-green, so that he still looked like a human being, and not a product of technology, as so many green-eyed people in my opinion do. Look like products of technology. His chin, his generous chin was cleft. Enough about chins. I'm certain this person felt the stares of all the men in the room, but he didn't seem to notice, simply sat hunched on his stool, legs reaching the supports and then some, in designer jeans and sportcoat and dress shirt opened at the neck, eating nuts and drinking beer at an impressive rate. I somehow smelled Amherst College.

The only Approach I had the misfortune to witness personally came from a big, sleek, blue-eyed man in a rugby shirt and white cotton pants. How he slid in between the man and myself, then slid the upper part of his body down the bar toward the man, hiding him a bit, so that I had to make exclusive use of the angle of the mirror above the glitter of the bar's arsenal of bottles to watch. I shivered. I shivered only because the Approach looked so troublingly familiar. I had seen it at every single one of the singles bars, heterosexual singles bars I'd attended during the first desolate Lenoreless year after my hegira to Cleveland. It was indeed an Approach.

"Hi there," said the Approacher to the man, in the mirror. "Do you come here often?"

I shivered.

"Nope," said the man, popping a handful of nuts in his mouth. His eye caught mine in the mirror.

"No, I didn't think so," said the Approacher, gauging the man's bicep under his sportcoat. "I come here fairly regularly, and I *certainly* would have noticed you, but I haven't noticed you here before." He played with his daiquiri glass.

The man looked the Approacher in the eye through the mirror, considering something. His green eyes grew liddy, sleepy, amused. "I think you're probably barking up the wrong tree, here, guy," he said to the Approacher. "I'm here as a rememberer, not a patron."

The Approacher looked down at the man's hands, around his beer glass, on the bar. "A rememberer?"

"Yup," said the man. "I used to go to school around here. A few years ago." A nut, into his mouth. "I used to come to this bar, a lot, before it changed."

"Oh?" The Approacher cupped his chin in his hand, looked at the side of the man's chewing face. "The Flange changed? I never heard about any change."

"Sure enough." The man looked levelly at the Approacher through the mirror. "Now, I'm sorry to say, it looks to be a place for faggots." He said this slowly and distinctly. I looked down at my drink and my handkerchief. When I looked up the Approacher was gone, back at the television, and the man was placidly ordering what appeared to be his tenth beer, patiently repeating the order until the bartender could no longer pretend to ignore him.

Careful to make it in no way resemble an Approach, I came over to the man and sat on the stool beside him, my feet dangling.

"Look, I'm not a homosexual either," I found myself saying, though thank God quietly. "In fact I too am here as a . . . rememberer and not a patron. But I think if one comes to a place like this, for whatever reason, it behooves one not to be overtly rude to the people for whom coming here is . . . entirely appropriate." My ice snapped suddenly in my drink.

The man looked at me in the mirror, chewing. We waited while his mouth cleared of peanuts. "I got nothing against homosexuals," he said. "They can go around being homosexuals amongst themselves all they want, far as I'm concerned. It's just when it's my own personal ass that they start sniffin' after and checkin' out, I find my tolerance level really plummets, for some reason." He took some beer. "As for coming into this place, I was coming into this place when these old boys were all out kneeling in alleys in the rain." He gestured slightly through the mirror at the Approacher and his friends. "This is more my place than theirs. I used to spend hours here, when it was a real bar. I used to talk to the whores here. They were real nice. I got educated here. My house used to come down here, en-fucking-masse, on Wednesday nights."

"Wednesdays?" I asked. Wednesdays. "House as in . . . fraternity house?"

His green eyes were on mine in the mirror. I thought I could see something, in those eyes. "Yeah," he said. "Why?"

"Not . . . Amherst College fraternity house."

"Yeah, I went to Amherst," he said.

"Not . . . Psi Phi fraternity at Amherst," I said.

He swiveled on his stool to face me. "*Yeah.*" I felt the jealous stares of the "Bob Newhart" crowd.

"My Lord," I said. "Myself as well. Psi Phi. Class of '69."

The man grinned widely. " '83 here," he said. Then his eyes narrowed; he held out his hand, each finger pointing in a different direction. Testing me, I knew. After only the briefest hesitation, I joined him in the Psi Phi handshake. I had not done it in so, so long. My throat ached a little bit. I found my arm tingling. "Quaaaango!" we yelled in unison at the end, and grabbed each other's wrists, and tapped elbows. I felt eyes.

"Sheeit."

"Heavens."

I held out my hand in the conventional way. "I am Richard Vigorous of Cleveland, Ohio."

The man took it. "Andrew Sealander Lang," he said, "of Nugget Bluff, which is to say really Dallas, Texas, and lately of Scarsdale, New York."

"Scarsdale, Andrew?" I said. "I lived in Scarsdale, myself, for a good while. Mostly in the seventies."

"But you moved," Andrew Lang said, smiling. "I can understand, completely and entirely. Yes."

What am I to say, retrospectively, here? Perhaps that I felt myself in the presence of a kinsman. Not simply a fraternity brother: I had been a completely marginal Psi Phi, and had actually moved out of the place in some haste in the middle of my sophomore year, when the House upperclassmen cut our stairs off halfway and fashioned a crude diving board and cut open the House's living-room floor and filled the basement with beer and called the entire creation a swimming pool, into which it was dictated that all sophomores were to be required to dive and then drink themselves to safety. I was marginal. And I sensed in Lang a really hard-core Psi Phi: he had had at least ten beers, was entering into negotiations for the eleventh, and didn't seem the slightest bit tipsy; nor, even more important, had he been to the restroom once since I arrived. This was collegiate manhood as I had come to know it.

No, but still I felt affinities, elective or otherwise. I sensed somehow in Lang another inside outsider, another lonely alumnus here at an alumniless time. Surrounded by insiders, now: children, swaggering and belonging, with their complicated eyes. Lang's eyes, eyes the color of plants, were not complicated. I looked at them in the mirror. They were like my eyes. They were the eyes of a man gone back to the house where he grew up, to watch new children play in his yard, a new Rawlings Everbounce pass through a new basketball hoop over his garage, a new dog diddle on his mother's rhododendrons. Sad, sad. Perhaps it was only the whiskey, and the beer, but I sensed sadness in Lang. His bar was my college. They were the same. And we simply no longer belonged, now.

"Why are you in town?" I asked Lang. "Is '83 having some function?"

"Naw," said the Texan. " '83 never has functions. I just felt like I had to . . . to get the heck out of Scarsdale. Just get out for a while. Plus I really like it up here in the fall. 'Course it's not really fall yet. Too goddamned hot."

"Still, though."

"Right. Exactly. Now but I bet you didn't come all the way out here from Ohio just to get out, though, right?"

"No, you're right." I shook my head. I asked the now explicitly hostile bartender for another drink. The bartender glared at Lang. Lang ignored him. "No," I said, "my fiancée is here visiting her brother, '93, and I just came along on a bit of a lark. I hadn't even been back before."

Lang stared into the mirror. "Naw, I haven't been back much either. 'Course I only been out a few years. And I've come back for a couple Homecomings. Those kick ass."

"I remember they were fun."

"You bet."

"Are you married, in Scarsdale?" I asked. I must here confess that

I asked the question for an admittedly immature and selfish reason. I instinctively and involuntarily regard all other men as potential threats to my relationship with Lenore. One more married man was one fewer member of the great threat-set.

"Yeah, I'm married." Lang looked at his reflection in the mirror.

I giggled sympathetically.

"Is the wife up with you?" I asked.

"No she is not," said Lang. He paused to belch. "The wife . . . ," he looked at his watch, ". . . the wife is at this second indubitably out in the back yard, on the lawn chair, with a martini and a *Cosmopolitan*, reinforcin' the old tan."

"I see," I said.

Lang looked at me. "I really don't know why the hell I came up here, to tell the truth. I just . . . felt like I needed to come home, somehow." He drummed his knuckle on the bar.

"Yes, yes." I almost clutched at his arm. "I understand completely. Trying to come back inside . . ."

"What?"

"Nothing," I said. "Nothing. What do you do, Andrew? May I call you Andrew?"

"Sure you can, Dick," he said. He turned back toward me, and there was peanut-smell. His eyes went dull. "Right now I'm in accounting. My wife's Daddy's an accountant and all, and so I do some work for him. I mostly fuck off, though. I'm gonna quit. I think I in effect quit today, by not showing up." He gulped beer and wiped his lip, looking faraway. "When I got out of school, I worked overseas for a while, for my Daddy. My Daddy owns this company, in Texas, and I worked for them overseas, for a couple years. That was the balls."

"But then you got married."

"Yup." Peanuts. "You married, Dick? That's right, you said you're engaged."

"I . . . I am engaged. To a wonderful, wonderful girl." He was married, after all. "I was married before. I got divorced."

"And engaged again now. Whooee. A glutton for punishment, Dick."

"Please call me Rick," I said. "My friends call me Rick. And an entirely different situation, this time, fortunately." I felt a bit uncomfortable. Lenore and I were, after all, not explicitly engaged, although it was only a matter of waiting for the combination of the right moment and sufficient saliva.

"Well good for you. What's the lucky little lady's name?"

"Ms. Lenore Beadsman, of East Corinth, which is to say Cleveland, Ohio," I said.

Lang speculatively sucked the salt off a peanut. He looked in the mirror and removed something from his lip. "Beadsman. Beadsman." He looked at me. "Hmmm. She didn't go to school around here, did she? Or more exactly Mount Holyoke?"

"No, no," I said, excited, feeling connection potential—'83, after all. "But her sister did. Ms. Clarice Beadsman. Now Mrs. Alvin Spaniard, Cleveland Heights, Ohio."

"Well I will be goddamned," said Lang. "Clarice Beadsman was one of my wife's roommates, one year. My sophomore year. I knew her. Christ in a camper, that seems like just too goddamned long ago. My wife and her didn't get along too good."

"But they knew each other. Really. Really." I squirmed with excitement and a full bladder. No possible way I was going to the men's room before Lang, though. "What is your wife's name, pray, so I can tell it to Lenore and she to Clarice?"

"My wife's maiden name was Miss Melinda Metalman," said Andrew Lang to the mirror.

The earth tipped on its axis. The spit was vacuumed from my mouth and disappeared out the back of my head. Melinda Metalman. Mindy Metalman, perhaps the most erotic girl I have ever seen in person. Rex Metalman's daughter, who had done things around a lawn sprinkler no thirteen-year-old should be able to do. Sweat leapt to my brow.

"Mindy Metalman?" I croaked.

Lang turned again. "Yeah." His eyes were old, dull.

I looked at my whiskey. "You don't perhaps know whether her father might by any chance live on . . . Vine Street, in Scarsdale," I said.

Lang grinned to himself. "Yeah, you're from Scarsdale, that's right. Well, yup. 14 Vine Street. Except he don't anymore, 'cause he gave the house to me and Mindy last year. He lives in an apartment now. One supposedly without a lawn. Having a lawn fucked with old Rex's mind. But except now he's starting a lawn at his building, he says. Just a real tiny one. Hardly a lawn at all, he says. Who the hell knows." Lang looked at the mirror. "I live at 14 Vine now, more or less."

"I used to live at 16 Vine," I said quietly. Lang turned to me. The "Bob Newhart" crowd must have thought we were in love. Our eyes shone with the thrill of apparent connection. It was something of a thrill, given the context. I tingle a bit even now, in the motel. "My ex-wife still lives there, though I've been led to believe she's preparing to sell," I said.

"Mrs. Peck?" Lang's eyes opened wide. "Veronica?"

"Ms. Peck," I said, clutching for real now at Lang's sportcoat sleeve. "Peck was her maiden name. And I used to play tennis with Rex Metalman, long ago. I used to watch Rex go at his lawn almost every day. It was a neighborhood event."

"I will be dipped and fried and completely goddamned," said Lang. "I just had no idea Ronnie'd been married to an Amherst alum. Sheeit." He thumped the bar with his hand again. I noticed his hand, suddenly. It was heavy, and brown, and strong. A hard hand.

"Ronnie?" I said.

"Well, I know her pretty good, her living next door and all." Lang looked down to play with the ring of moisture his beer glass had made on the dark wood of the bar.

"I see," I said. "How is Ronnie?"

We looked at each other in the mirror. "Last time I saw her, she was just fine," Lang said. He poured more beer into the suds at the bottom of the glass. I saw salt, from the peanuts, on the rim. "What exactly do you do, Rick? In Cleveland."

"Publishing," I said. "I manage a publishing firm in Cleveland. Frequent and Vigorous, Publishing, Inc."

"Hmmm," Lang said.

"What about Mindy?" I asked. "I knew her, slightly, as a girl. Is Mindy well? Does Mindy have a career of her own?"

"Mindy does have a career," Lang said after a moment. "Mindy is a voice."

"A voice?" I said. My head was filled with visions of Mindy Metalman. Her bedroom had been directly across the fence from my den.

"A voice," said Lang. He played with a cocktail napkin decorated with a huge lipstick-kiss design. "You ever been in a grocery? And when you pay for your items and all at the cash register, the girl pushes the items over the scanner thing, that beeps, and then this voice in the register says the price? Or do you have one of them late-model cars that says to please fasten seat belts when you didn't fasten your seat belts? Melinda Sue is the voice in things."

"That's Mindy Metalman?" I shopped. I drove a late-model car.

"Mrs. A. S. Lang herself, now," said Lang. "The big voice used to be this lady in Centerport, on Long Island? But she's getting old, scratchy. Melinda Sue's pretty much pushin' her out of the business."

"Heavens," I said, "That certainly sounds like an enormously interesting career. Does Mindy enjoy it?"

"Sure she enjoys it. It's easy as shit. She just sits around like once a week, with a drink and a million-dollar tape recorder and a script with lines like 'Change due, four dollars.' It's easy as hell. But she's ambitious now, all of a sudden. Her and her manager." Lang swallowed half his beer. "Alan Gluskoter, her manager. Ambitious Al. They're ambitious, now." More beer. "She wants television."

"Television?"

Lang stared at himself. "You know the voice that says 'This is CBS,' or 'This is ABC,' or 'Stay tuned to CBS, please'? She wants to be that voice. That's her great aspiration."

"Good heavens."

"Yeah."

I was about to wet my pants. The only pair of pants I'd brought on the trip.

I slid off my stool, stretched, pretended to yawn. "Think I'll just dash into the men's room," I said. "I want to see something. I think I may have left my initials in the wood of the stall here."

Lang smiled at both of us. "I know I did. I carved hell out of everything when I was a student here." He stood. "Hell, I'll go with you. Could use a squirt myself."

"Quite," I said.

In the men's room Lang ranged expertly over the urinal, aiming for the deodorant disc. "Room for two, here, big guy," he said.

I muttered something and hurried into the stall, ostensibly to hunt for initials, really so that I could shut the door. I tried to last just as long as I could. Long after my last tinkle had ceased to sound, I could still hear the roar of Lang's jet. This was an Amherst man.

I looked for my initials. All I can say at this point is that I must have been confused. I was sure I'd left another R.V. in the Flange's stall, up over the door latch, to the left, actually I even thought I could remember the occasion of the carving, but here in the spot I remembered was, instead of an R.V., a deep, wickedly sharp set of W.D.L., long since filled in with violet pen. I pored over the wooden surfaces of the stall until I saw Lang's boat shoes under the door.

"Not there," I said, opening the door. "My initials don't seem to be there."

"Maybe they went ahead and changed the door sometime since '69," said Lang, coming into the stall with me and swinging the door shut, so that I had to sit on the toilet to give him room to look at the door.

"Same door as '83, though, 'cause here are mine, still," he said, pointing at the deep W.D.L. over the latch. He brushed at the letters with a big thumb, removing a smidgeon of God knows what.

"W.D.L. for Andrew Sealander Lang?" I said.

"I got called Wang-Dang Lang all through school," said Lang, grinning. "Actually I still get called Wang-Dang Lang, by my real good friends. You can call me Wang-Dang, if you want." He stared lovingly at his initials.

"Thank you," I said. I had to pee again, already, I felt.

There were sounds of the restroom door opening. Snickering. I thought I recognized the Approacher's voice. They must have been looking at our four shoes in the crowded stall. The group attended to business, noisily, and eventually left, after teasing us by flicking the lights off and on several times. I was lost in thought, for the most part, trying to account for my memory of my initials in the Flange's door, which memory was clear and distinct, in the face of the evidence. It certainly looked like the same door. Lang studied the door with me, thinking.

"Is your girlfriend Clarice's younger sister?" he suddenly asked.

I looked up at him from the toilet. "Yes," I said. "Yes, Lenore is two years younger than Clarice."

"You know, I'm pretty sure I've met her, then," said Lang, absently digging with his finger at some peanut in a molar, extracting some beige material. He looked at it. " 'Cause Clarice had a sister visiting her the night I met my wife. Or was it that other girl had a sister up?" He scratched. "No, I'm real sure it was Beadsman. I think I remember for sure she said her name was Lenore Beadsman." He looked faraway.

"So you probably met my fiancée before I did," I said.

Lang grinned down at me. "And you knew my wife before I even met her, when she was a little girl."

I grinned back. "Not all that little."

"I know what you mean," Lang laughed. Spontaneously, out of the sheer odd warmth of the moment, we did the Psi Phi handshake again. "Quaaaango!" We laughed.

I got off the toilet. We left the restroom and went back into the bar. There were stage titters from the Approacher's little television coterie. Wang-Dang Lang ignored them and clapped his arm around my shoulders.

"Ah, Rick, Rick," he said. "I just don't know what the hell to do." He looked around. "I just feel like I need to . . ."

"Get outside," I said. For us inside outsiders, the only real place to go was outside.

"Well, yeah. Exactly." He looked me in the eye. "I feel like I need to get out. Just . . . out, for a while." He ordered another beer as I chewed the whiskey out of my ice.

"Are things not well with you and the wife?"

In the mirror Lang said, "Things are the same as ever, fine and Daddy—excuse—fine and dandy as ever. I just feel . . . constricted, like I can't breathe. Like I'm breathin' used-up air. I'm living in the bitch's town, in her house, working for her Daddy, hearing her voice when I get in my freaking car. I think we need a slight vacation from each other. Things are just less than wonderful right now. I think I just need to get out, for a period of time."

"Establish other connections," I said. "Hence the utter appropriateness of your little trip up here. It'll do you a world of good." God, there was a time when I would have given limbs to be constricted by Mindy Metalman.

"Eggzackly," Lang said. He punched me affectionately in the arm. I struggled not to rub my shoulder.

"And so just one hell of a buzz, meetin' you," Land said to me in the mirror. "A House brother, a neighbor, damn near a relative. Like an uncle or something. Shit on fire. *Ti symptosis.*"

"What was that?" I asked.

"What was what?"

" 'Tea' something," I said.

"*Ti symptosis?*" said Lang. "It's just this expression. '*Ti symptosis*' is idiomatic modern Greek for, like, 'What a hell of a coincidence.' Which this is, sure enough, let me tell you."

"Greek?" I said. "You speak modern Greek?"

Lang laughed loudly. "Does a bear make skata in the woods?" I intuited that even such as he was beginning to feel the lake of beer inside him. "Yeah," he said, "I picked up Greek real well after college. I told you I was overseas? I was working for my Daddy's company? This really kick-ass company called Industrial Desert Design, Dallas?"

I stared at Lang. "Your father owns Industrial Desert Design?"

"You know Industrial Desert Design?" said Lang.

"Jesus Christ," I said, "I live in Ohio. Just north of your *magnum opus.*"

"I will be slapped, pinched, and rolled," Lang said, pounding the bar with his fist. "This is just too goddamned great. Is that thing great or what? I worked on the crew for that, in the summer, when I was just eleven, twelve years old. I planted cactuses. That was a fucking blast."

"So then you travelled for I.D.D. after college?" I said.

"Yeah," said Lang. "Best couple years of this little life, so far. I more or less oversaw this one whole project, this real tasteful little desert—nothing fancy, mind you, but small, solid, tasteful, and sinister. This really kick-ass desert project on the west side of Kerkira, near Italy."

"Kerkira?" I said.

"Yeah. Beautifulest goddamn place I ever seen. This island. I loved it there. I was all over it, did all kinds of wild shit. Why, one time, me and Ed Roy Yancey, Jr., who was more or less my right hand, we took this goat, and about ten pounds of butter, and we . . ."

"Kerkira?" I said.

"Y'all probably know it as Corfu," said Lang. "Kerkira is the Greek name for Corfu. Corfusian, too, since Greek is their language, too, over there."

I stared at the mirror. The bartender was fingering his mohawk and looking at Lang. On the television some sort of obscene Frankenstein figure was lumbering around to the accompaniment of canned laughter.

"Let me review this for a moment," I said, trying to collect my thoughts. "You, who were in my fraternity, at college, and are married to my former next-door neighbor, who was roommates in college with the sister of my fiancée, whom you have met, are intimately familiar with the culture and language of the inhabitants of the island of Corfu, and are furthermore as of now probably unemployed, and chafing for some sort of at least temporary change in your geographical, professional, and personal circumstances right now. Is all that correct?"

Lang looked at me in the mirror. His eyes were sleepy again. But simple. He was knocking at the door. Our houses, our rhododendrons were fundamentally the same. "Not at all sure what it is you're tryin' to drive at, Dick," he said. The jukebox broke suddenly into "Eight Days a Week"; I fancied I saw the Approacher grinning at me from the machine. I felt an overwhelming urge to wander, to take Lang with me back to the admission line for the forests, as the sun began to die.

"*Ti symptosis,*" I said.

Lenore is sleeping, unusually soundly tonight, under her scratchy Howard Johnson's blanket. Her breath as it comes up to me is soft and sweet; I feed on it. Her lips are moist, with the tiniest bits of the white paste of sleep at the corners.

I do not know a horizontal Lenore. Lenore in her bed is an otherworldly, protean thing. Lying on her side, defined by the swell of a breast and the curve of a hip, she is an S. A chance curl around the pillow she holds to her stomach, and she becomes variously a question mark, a comma, a parenthesis. And then spread out before me, open, wet, completely and rarely vulnerable, her eyes looking into mine, she is a V. I will confess that her shoe is in my lap as I write this. The soft light of the lamp bolted into the wall over my shoulder blends with the inconstant grainy gray of the television's cold flicker to cast for me a shadow of Lenore's chin, down her throat, to cover her tiny adam's grape, just caressed by the razor point of a hair-mandible, in a soft black various as breath. Who knows how long I watch. The whine of an Indian-head test pattern brings me around. I find that sitting up in bed for any length of time makes my bottom terrifically numb.

/i/

Cat, Heat, and the Breather all lay around the room they shared with the Antichrist, in various states of distress, in the sun, which now came through the big windows in the west wall, because the Antichrist had opened the curtains at four, at Lenore's suggestion, and the sun washed the room in late heat, and lit up the systems of dust moving in the air. The sun itself, in the sky, slowly lowered on its wire, swelling and getting inflamed, soon to drop behind the Art Building and leave the room in cool black again. Cat's preemptive head banging had unfortunately not been able to keep things from becoming very unpleasant indeed in his corner.

While all this happened, Lenore and the Antichrist walked outside, and Lenore let the warmth of the big sun and the motion of the breeze dry her hair, and LaVache got some badly needed exercise. They talked while they walked, some. It took a long time for Lenore and LaVache, with Lenore helping LaVache, to get up to the Art Building, orbit the quad, amid tree roots and Frisbee players, and come out on Memorial Hill, to look south at the forests and the bird sanctuary behind the sprawling space of the athletic fields, the fields themselves covered with writhing wind-influenced jets of water from the industrial sprinklers, the mist from the sprinklers' plumes hanging low over the wet fields and breaking into color as the sun lowered to touch it, some tiny fine wind-blown water bits migrating north and gently dotting Lenore's eyelids and lips as she and the Antichrist settled on the hump of the hill, as she helped the Antichrist lower himself to the ground and stretch the leg out before him in the curve of the grass. They looked out at the fields, and the forests, and the mountains beyond that, purple and vaguely gauzy in the faraway heat.

With Lenore and the Antichrist on the crest of the hill, nearby, was a family: a father in checked sportcoat and white leather loafers, a mother with a red cotton skirt and high hair and blue broken veins in her calves, a tiny red-haired girl, maybe five, with great green eyes and shiny black shoes and silky white socks, beneath a tiny white dress, and also two older children of indeterminate gender who were struggling and wrestling on the curve, trying to shove each other down the hill. While the father and mother worked with their camera to take a picture of the view off the hill, really stunning in the strange light of late afternoon, with the wash of watery red mixed with gymnasium shadows spilling in like ink from the right, the west, and while the two older children struggled, the little girl watched LaVache, who noticed her and detached the leg and played with it, a bit, to amuse the girl, who stared with huge eyes, and tugged at the hem of the mother's red skirt, and was ignored.

Lenore watched LaVache lean back and put the foot of the leg on his nose and balance the leg with no hands. The little girl, who had come closer, sat down heavily with her legs out in front of her, staring at Lenore and the Antichrist and the leg. The Antichrist took the leg off his nose and manipulated his heavy eyebrows at the little girl, grinning. The little girl rolled up to her feet and ran to her mother's hem, hiding behind a calf.

Lenore laughed. "You're horrible," she said.

LaVache removed some grass from between the toes of the leg. "Yes." Lenore's hair felt lovely and light and soft, clean, dried by the hot wind off the fields. The two older children suddenly shrieked in unison and rolled away down the hill, becoming small.

"Did Candy really seduce you?" Lenore asked her brother.

The Antichrist scratched at his hip. "No, Lenore, she didn't. I lied to Heat and the Breather." He looked at the leg. "A really important part of being here is learning how to lie. 'Strategic misrepresentation,' we call it. I've been wildly infatuated with Candy for a long time. To be honest with you, it was really her breasts that launched me into puberty, that time she came home with you for spring break, I think four years ago. Last summer was just particularly bad, in terms of the infatuation. I simply presented fantasy as fact to Heat and the Breather. Heat has a huge mouth. My latest theory is that Heat isn't busy enough with homework, a situation you can be quite sure I'll be remedying."

"Oh," Lenore said. She felt the grass. "You know, to be honest, I don't much like the Breather, either, I'm afraid. The Breather seems awfully touchy-feely to me."

The Antichrist didn't say anything.

"What's his name, anyway?" said Lenore.

"His name's the Breather."

"I mean his real name."

"Who cares. Mike something."

"Hmmm."

The Antichrist was staring out into the thin twisting fountains in the fields, and the forests, all in the reddening shadowy light. "Do you still drink a lot of Tab?" he said, out of the blue.

Lenore looked at him. She decided he was high. "I don't drink Tab much anymore," she said. "I mostly drink seltzer water now. Tab tastes to me like some little kid made it with his chemistry set."

The Antichrist laughed and hefted the leg. His hightop was with Lenore's hightops, out in front of them in the grass. The little girl was peering around her mother's leg at the Antichrist, who pretended to ignore her.

"Where's your friend Mr. Vigorous? What's he supposed to be doing?"

"I don't really know. I think he's wandering around. I think he sort of has some internal catching up to do. He hasn't been back here, ever, since he graduated."

"I see."

The two older children had stopped rolling and now started to trudge heavily back up the steep hill. The father and mother hissed at each other over the camera's light meter. Around the woman's calf were green eyes and wisps of red hair. The Antichrist put part of the leg inside his shirt.

"Are you pretty sleepy?" Lenore asked. "From the Quaaludes, I mean?"

LaVache looked at the trees. "The Breather told you this was a Quaalude day? What a garrulous room-group, today. It was a very small Quaalude. And no, not really, Quaaludes don't make me sleepy, anymore, really."

"How do they make you feel?"

The Antichrist looked at his ankle. "Like I'm elsewhere."

Lenore looked at the little girl.

"Elseone," LaVache said to his ankle. "Besides," he looked up, "the old cortex is a flurry of activity now, because I have to get all prepared to talk Hegelian sublation with Nervous Roy Keller, which will be a bitch, because Nervous Roy is far too nervous to assimilate any but the most clearly presented information. Clear presentation is not Hegel's strength."

Lenore tugged at a blade of grass. It came out of the ground with a faint squeak. "How come you do everybody else's work for them, Stoney?"

"Where do *you* think Lenore is?" the Antichrist asked the leg.

"Why do you do other people's work and not your own?" said Lenore. "You're the smartest person I've ever met. John included."

"Speaking of which . . ."

"How come you're doing this? You're flapped here all the time, aren't you?"

The Antichrist brought a joint out of the drawer. "I have a leg to support."

"How come?"

The Antichrist lit up with practiced ease in the wind and looked at his sister from behind his cloud. "It's my thing," he said. "Everybody here has a thing. You have to have a thing here. My thing is being the Antichrist, more or less being a waste-product and supporting my leg. A tragically wasted intellect. So to speak. You can't be thingless, Lenore. Mr. Vigorous notwithstanding."

"What the hell's that supposed to mean?"

LaVache looked over Lenore's head, at the sun. "Let's pause for just a moment to let me try to get all this straight." He scratched at an eyebrow. "You came all the way out here, to the very most tangential of Beadsmans, to inform me that you don't know where certain people are, and to ask me whether I know where certain people are. And you did so at Dad's request."

"What Dad wants me to find out is whether you've heard or have any idea where exactly Lenore or John are. Is. Especially Gramma, for Dad."

"Of course."

"And you say you have no idea."

"Right."

"Did you know about the stuff Gramma was doing with Dad?" Lenore asked. "The nursing home stuff?"

"More or less. More less than more."

The little green-eyed girl was cautiously approaching Lenore and LaVache, moving inside her mother's long late shadow. The Antichrist, still pretending to ignore her, nevertheless enticed her with the leg.

"How come?" Lenore said.

"How come what?"

"How come you knew?"

"I believe Lenore told me, in her own unique epigrammatic way."

"Well, when?"

"A while ago. Actually I did some math for her and Mrs. Kling."

"Yingst."

"Yingst. Some multiple regression. Last Christmas. Really more John's area than mine, but since dear John is, or was, busy starving himself, and the leg quite obviously isn't, it cheerfully gobbled up the hundred clams with nary a qualm."

"Have any thoughts of how come Lenore told me exactly nothing about any of this, by any chance?"

"Nothing even remotely resembling a thought," LaVache said. When Lenore looked up from her blade of grass, she saw that the little girl was now sitting next to the Antichrist, her small soft legs with shiny black shoes out in front of her. The Antichrist was letting her touch the leg. To Lenore he said, "I really must confess to wondering, in the dark part of the night, what you and Lenore actually talk about all the time. You were over there constantly, this past summer."

"Well, I was reading to Concarnadine, some of the time, too."

"I'm glad someone can stand to see her."

"Who says I can stand to see her?"

"She still likes *Old Mother West Wind*? Ollie the otter and Sergio the snake and all that?"

"I really haven't seen her in a while. She liked it the last time I read it to her. At least she made what I interpreted as liking-sounds."

"How lovely," LaVache said. "You better go see her. She must get really lonely. You think?"

The little girl was looking at the side of the Antichrist's dark shiny face, Lenore could see. The girl tugged on the sleeve of his sweatshirt.

"Are you the devil?" she asked in a loud voice. Her parents didn't seem to hear her.

"Not right at the moment," the Antichrist said to the little girl, turning the leg over to her completely, for a bit.

"I don't want to go there anymore, at least until Lenore gets back," Lenore said softly, shaping a hooked curve of hair under her chin. "I'm afraid I really and truly hate Concarnadine. I don't know if your theory is right, but I'm afraid I do. And that Mr. Bloemker who's constantly around gives me even more big-time creeps than he did before, for reasons I don't feel like going into right at the moment. And plus of course now Lenore's just gone, for over a week, and after working awfully hard to make really sure I'd care about her, she now doesn't even bother to say where she is. She should know I'm not Dad. Just like you, of all people, should know I'm not Dad."

The Antichrist played with the floppy empty leg of his corduroy shorts.

"I'm beginning to think Lenore's dead," said Lenore. "It's horrible to think that and still not be able to really grieve. I think she maybe even died in the nursing home, and Mrs. Yingst did something to her, when she wasn't busy giving innocent animals LSD or pineal-food."

"You know, in my opinion, if you want my off-the-top-of-my-head opinion, I think Lenore's maybe dead, too," the Antichrist said, amusing the little girl by guiding her hands so as to make the leg dance on the ground, his joint held easily between two fingers. "She's about a hundred, after all, isn't she? I think she's just gone off somewhere to die. Somewhere where no one could see her being for the briefest second defenseless. I think that would be her style. Either that or she's down at Gerber's right now, preparing to give Dad an incredible kick in the corporate groin. To which I say go for it."

The little red-haired girl laughed loudly as the leg performed a particularly tricky dance step. The man in white loafers and the woman with veins turned from the field.

"Brenda!" the mother yelled. The little girl looked up from the leg at her mother. "Come away from there right this minute!" The mother bore down.

"Just a quick anatomy lesson, here, ma'am," said the Antichrist.

"Come *away* from there I said." The little girl was lifted away by a wrist. The leg lay in the grass. The two older children were struggling on the curve again. A shadow in a sportcoat fell over Lenore and LaVache. Lenore made a visor out of her hand. The father stared down, his complicated camera obviously really heavy around his neck. Lenore looked at his shoes. They had networks of tiny black cracks in the white leather.

The father sniffed the air, his hands on his hips. "Is that one of those funny cigarettes?"

LaVache held up the nubbin of joint and looked at it reflectively. "Sir," he said, "this is a deadly serious cigarette."

"You ought to be ashamed, using drugs in a public place, around little children, who are impressionable," the mother said. Lenore resisted the impulse to touch the mother's stockingless calf. She considered the fact that the veins in some older women's calves are a blue found nowhere else in nature. A nicotine blue, almost.

"I think I'm so ashamed I suddenly don't feel like being around people, right now," the Antichrist said slowly, squinting up into the two shadows. There were "Hmmphs," and the parents came away, calling to the struggling children to come this instant. Lenore heard Brenda's tiny shoes on the cement of the War Memorial, above them, a moment later. They were alone on the curve of the hill. The Antichrist was scratching at his hip, Lenore saw. No he wasn't: he was reaching into his pocket. He pulled something out. It was a Stonecipheco label. Veal purée. He finished unfolding it and turned it over and smoothed it against his hip, then gave it to Lenore. Lenore noticed that LaVache's nails really needed cutting.

On the white, slightly fuzzy back of the label was an ink drawing of a man walking up a hill, as seen from the side. The man's profile was smiling. The hill looked sandy. It was the same sort of doodle Lenore had found in Lenore's room at the Shaker Heights Nursing Home.

"Hmmm," she said. She looked at the Antichrist. She took out of the zippered compartment at the side of her vinyl purse the drawing of the barber with the exploded head. She gave it to LaVache. LaVache laughed.

"Ah, the barber," he said. "Boy, she may be a ring-tailed bitch, but I do get a kick out of Lenore. I really sort of hope she isn't dead, after all, to tell the truth."

Lenore looked at the Antichrist. "How unbelievably decent of you, seeing she's your relative." She reached way out with her foot into the grass and gave the leg an angry little kick.

"Ow," said LaVache.

Lenore wiped a couple of tiny sprinkler-droplets from the skin under her eyes. "When did you get this?" she asked. "I thought you said you had no ideas about Gramma. Or does 'idea' mean 'toenail,' for you, or something?"

The Antichrist tore at some grass, looked at his sister. "No, 'idea' means 'idea,' but that, you may have noticed, is not an idea, but rather a sort of drawing. An infamous Lenore Beadsman drawing, right out of her infamous school of stick-figure symbolist art." He smiled, did something to his hair. "You remember the drawing of John and Dad, that one Christmas? The time John had said something about Miss Malig, something pretty funny, and Dad had said that if you can't say anything nice, you shouldn't say anything at all, and John pointed out that that thing itself that Dad had just said to him really wasn't by any stretch of the imagination 'nice,' and so shouldn't itself have been said, and so was, interestingly, internally contradictory? And Lenore gave us that drawing of John and Dad, and Dad's exploded head, and the corn-cob suppository? A really deadly drawing, I thought."

"But when did you get this one?" Lenore asked, looking at the veal label. She thought she could make out a cactus in the splatter of ink surrounding the incline of the hill in the drawing.

"It was waiting in my p. o. box when I got here," LaVache said. "Return-address-less, I might add, and interestingly not in Lenore's distinctive indecipherable hand. That was ten . . . eleven days ago. I got it eleven days ago, Lenore." The Antichrist suddenly hawked and spat white.

Lenore ignored the spitting, and the fact that the Antichrist's head was lolling quite a bit now. "Do you know what it is?" she asked.

"Oh, very much so, don't we, precious," the Antichrist hissed to his leg.

"Then maybe you'll be good enough to tell me, because I'm afraid I seem to be clueless on this one," Lenore said, staring at the label.

The Antichrist sucked at the red eye of the corpse of his joint. Lenore saw that he held the nubbin delicately in his very long fingernails, avoided getting burned. He grinned at Lenore. "What would you do if I demanded that you first feed the leg?" he asked.

Lenore looked at her brother, then at the leg. She said, "I'd propose a deal. You tell me the thing you know, the thing that clearly bears on the well-being of a relative we're both supposed to love, the thing that it looks like I came all the way out here to find out; you tell me, and in return I don't throw the leg all the way down to the bottom of the hill, leaving you with a long and possibly dangerous and certainly very embarrassing retrieval-hop."

"Oh, now, don't be that way," smiled the Antichrist, casually reattaching and strapping the leg, which took a minute. When he was attached, he said, "The drawing is of a sort referred to in the *Investigations*, as I'm sure you, the hotshot major, would remember a lot better than I, if you thought about it for about three seconds. I seem to recollect the reference being page fifty-four, note *b*, of the Geach and Anscombe translation. We're presented with a picture of a man climbing a slope, in profile, one leg in front of the other as he progresses, marking motion, walking up the incline, facing the top, eyes directed at the top, all the standard climbing-association stuff. Et cetera et cetera. So it's a picture of a man walking up a hill. But then remember Gramma Lenore's own Dr. Wittgenstein says hold on now, pardner, because the picture could just as clearly and exactly and easily represent the man sliding *down* the slope, with one leg higher than the other, backwards, et cetera. Just as exactly."

"Shit," said Lenore.

"And then we're invited to draw all these totally fecal conclusions about why we just automatically assume from just looking at the picture that the guy's climbing and not sliding. Going up instead of coming down. Complete and total dribble, and really actually heart-rending psychological innocence, as far as I'm concerned, which you should remember, given this certain conversation we all had in the Volvo when you were in school, when Gramma decided I was evil and said I needed to be 'stamped out,' declared her intention to stop giving me Christmas presents. Anyway . . . "

"Well and then here, on the other hand, we've got this antinomy," Lenore said, looking at the barber drawing.

"Right," the Antichrist said, throwing away the tiny dot of black joint. He paused for a moment, looking out into nothing. Lenore looked at him. "Brenda," she heard him say loudly, "you should go back to your parents immediately. Try not to be at all impressionable, at least while you're around here."

Lenore twisted around and looked. The little girl with green eyes was standing behind them, above them, on the cement rim of the Memorial, looking down at their heads. The wind ruffled her silky socks. She stared at the Antichrist.

"Shoo, love of mine," LaVache said.

The girl turned and fled. Her shoes clicked on the cement, fading.

Lenore looked at her brother. More grass squeaked in his hands. The sprinklers suddenly all went off, stopped hissing, the water sucked back inside itself, in the pipes, down in the fields. The fields looked great. They shone fire in the red light, deepened to twinkle in the glossy black of the gym shadows. "So then here I guess I'm supposed to ask what you think the two together might be supposed to mean," Lenore said.

LaVache laughed like a seal. His head lolled. "Gramma would be disappointed in her minion," he said. "They obviously . . . *mean* whatever you want them to mean. Whatever you want to *use* them for. Ms. Beadsman . . . ," he pretended to hold a microphone under Lenore's nose, ". . . how would you like the drawings to function?

Audience, please just hold off on that input . . ." The Antichrist made tick-tock noises with his tongue. "Function," he said. "The extreme unction of function. Function. From the Latin 'func,' meaning foul-smelling due to persistent overuse. She has crawled off. She is either dead, or functioning furiously. Speaking of functioning furiously, you might help me up, here, for a moment, please."

Lenore helped her brother up. He limped behind a bush at the side of the hill. Lenore heard sounds of him going to the bathroom into the dry bush.

"I have an idea," the Antichrist's voice came over the bush to Lenore. "Let's do the natural Beadsman thing. Let's play a *game*. Let's pretend just for fun that Lenore hasn't expired, that Mrs. Yingst hasn't chopped her up and fed her to Vlad the Impaler, that Gramma actually does give a hoot about your being potentially worried, and might actually be trying to use that worry in some nefarious way." He came back over, slowly, keeping his balance on the incline. "Now, under this game-scenario, how might we wish to see the drawings as functioning, here?" He settled back down with Lenore's help, looked at her. "The sliding-man drawing, under this scenario, might say, hey, ho, watch how you go. *Perceive* how you—we— perceive Lenore's being . . . 'missing.' Don't just look at it; think about *how* to look at it. Maybe it . . . *means* the opposite of what you think it does, of the way it . . . looks." LaVache was having leg trouble, on the hump of the hill. Lenore helped him get more comfortable. She held the baby food labels in her hand.

LaVache continued, "See, maybe Lenore isn't gone at all. Maybe you're who's gone, when all is said and done. Maybe . . . this one I particularly like . . . maybe Dad's gone, spiralled into the industrial void. Maybe he's taken us with him. Maybe Lenore's *found*. Maybe instead of her sliding away from you, you've slid away from her. Or climbed away from her. Maybe it's all a sliding-and-climbing *game*! Chutes and Ladders, risen from the dead!" The Antichrist was having trouble talking, because his mouth was all dry from the joint. He got the last of Clint Wood's fee from his drawer and lit it.

"Hmmm," Lenore was saying.

"Except don't think about yourself, in this game, at all," said the Antichrist. "Because in this game, the way we're playing, the barber drawing means don't think about yourself, in the context of the game, or your head explodes into art deco. Just think about other people, if you want to play. Which means that family-members have to be treated as explicitly Other, which I must say I find attractively refreshing."

"What the hell does that mean?" Lenore said.

The Antichrist exhaled. "Let's pretend just for fun that it's the late seventies, and Lenore is in her blue period, and is still keeping exclusively to her study, and snapping at anyone who comes near, including poor old Grampa, who was getting ready to die, and being generally pathetic . . ."

"Get on with it. My bottom hurts."

"And anyway, in this game-context, that Lenore is still Skeptical as hell, or at least strenuously adopting the pose, and ostensibly convinced that all she is is the act of her thinking, à la the Frenchman, although Lenore would say all she is is the act of speaking and telling, but that's so bullshitty it makes my tongue hurt, and anyway luckily unnecessary, and so we say that all she is is the act of her thinking; that's the only thing she can be sure of, is just her being her thinking."

"Is this real, or are you saying all this because you're flapped?" asked Lenore.

"Please hush," LaVache said. "I'm hard at play. So all Lenore is is her act of thought, nothing else can be 'assumed.' " He lay back and looked at the reddening sky, the joint resting in a carved initial in the leg. "So she's her thinking. And, as we know, all thinking requires an object, something to think of or about. And the only things that can be thought about are the things that are not that act of thought, that are Other, right? You can't think of your own act of thinking-of, any more than a blade can cut itself, right? Unless you're the guy who's significantly lowering Nervous Roy Keller's quality of life, but I refuse to think about that until the leg demands that I do so. So, we can't think ourselves, if all we are is the act of thinking. So we're like the barber. The barber, if I recall, shaves all and only those who don't shave themselves. Here Lenore thinks we think all and only those things which do not *think* themselves, which aren't the act of our thought, which are Other."

"Hell of a game," Lenore muttered.

"But then we remember that all we are is our act of thought, in the game, for Lenore," LaVache said, fast, now, and slightly slurry. "So if we think about ourselves with respect to the game, we're thinking about our thinking. And we decided the one thing we couldn't think about was our thinking, because the object has to be Other. We can think only the things that can't think themselves. So if we think ourselves, see for instance conceiving ourselves as thought, we can't ourselves be the object of our thinking. *Q.E.D.*"

Lenore cleared her throat.

"But if we can't think ourselves," the Antichrist continued to the sky, trying to lick his lips, "that means we, ourselves, are things that can't think themselves, and so are the proper objects for our thought; we fulfill the game's condition, we are ourselves Other. So if we can think ourselves, we can't; and if we can't, we can. *KA-BLAM*," LaVache gestured broadly. "There go the old crania."

"Dumb game," said Lenore. "I can think of myself any time I want. Here, watch." Lenore thought of herself sitting in the Spaniard home in Cleveland Heights, eating a frozen pea.

"Dumb objection, especially from you," the Antichrist said to the sky. " 'Cause do you really think of yourself? What do you think of yourself *as*? Shall I recall some of our more interesting and to me more than a little disturbing conversations of the last two years? If you don't think of yourself as real, then you're cheating, you're not playing fair, you're chute-hopping, you're not thinking of yourself."

"Who says I don't think of myself as real?" Lenore said, looking past the Antichrist at the bush he'd gone to the bathroom in.

"I'd be inclined to say you say so, from your general attitude, unless that little guy with the big mustache and the movable chairs has conked you on the head or something," said the Antichrist. "It's my clinical opinion that you, in a perfectly natural defensive reaction to your circumstances, have decided you're not real—of course with Gramma's help." LaVache looked at her. "Why is this all so, you ask?"

"I haven't asked anything, you might have noticed."

"It's because you're the one on whom the real brunt of the evil—shall I say 'evil'?—the brunt of the evil of this family has fallen. Evil in the form of these little indoctrination sessions with Lenore, which I've got to tell you I've always regarded as pathetic in the extremus. Evil in the form of Dad, who, having totally fucked with our mother's life, for all time, is trying to fuck with your life in all kinds of ways I bet you don't even know about, or want to know about. Think now of the circumstances leading up to my own particular birth. The same way Dad's tried to fuck with my life, everybody's. Just as he was fucked with in his turn, by fools in old-style hats and coats." The Antichrist laughed. "That's a poem. Anyway, you've borne the brunt. John was off to Chicago with his slide rule and a whole lot of masochistic baggage by the time he would have been any use to Dad or Lenore; I've had a limb and a thing to fall back on; Clarice was clearly inappropriate in terms of disposition— we needn't discuss all that. But so you're it. You are the family, Lenore. And in Dad's case, go ahead and substitute 'Company' in the obvious place in the above sentence."

Lenore reached under and removed a bit of stick she'd been sitting on.

"But Lenore has fucked up your life even further, sweetness," the Antichrist said, sitting back up with the joint and looking at Lenore. "Lenore has you believing—stop me if I'm wrong—Lenore has you believing, with your complicity, circumstantially speaking, that you're not really real, or that you're only real insofar as you're told about, so that to the extent that you're real you're controlled, and thus not in control, so that you're more like a sort of character than a person, really—and of course Lenore would say the two are the same, now, wouldn't she?"

"I wish it would rain," Lenore said.

"You just had a shower a little while ago," LaVache laughed. "You're a nervous wreck, sis. Don't be so nervous. Here. Kiss the bird for a second." The Antichrist was holding up the joint, which Lenore saw was burning down one side much faster than the other.

"I don't want any," Lenore said. She glanced at the sun, which was now sticking Kilroyishly over the top of the gymnasium. "How about if we just spontaneously abort this line of conversation, Stoney, OK? Since, if I were maybe to ask you to help me out with respect to this supposed evil-and-reality-as-opposed-to-telling problem, what you'd do is obviously just *tell* me something, so that the whole thing would—"

"Don't call me Stoney," said LaVache. "Call me LaVache, or the Antichrist, but no more Stoney."

"You don't mind Antichrist, which I have to say is just about the most disturbing nickname I've ever heard? But you mind Stoney?"

"Stoney is *everybody's* name," the Antichrist said. He spat white again. "Everybody in the family with male genitals is Stoney. Stoney reminds me I'm probably just a part in a machine I wish I wasn't part of. Stoney reminds me of deeply annoying expectations. Stoney reminds me of Dad. As Stoney I'm more or less just educed . . ."

"What?"

". . . but as the Antichrist I just *am*," said the Antichrist, waving the joint grandly at the red and black horizon. "As the Antichrist I have a thing, and it's gloriously clear where I leave off and others start, and no one expects me to be anything other than what I am, which is a waste-product, slaving endlessly to support his leg. I've also just sort of helped you, here, I think, if you bothered to notice." With his finger the Antichrist wet the side of the joint that was burning too fast, to make it burn slower.

Lenore wasn't looking at her brother, but at the gym shadows, which were visibly moving across the fields. A shadow from a different part of the gym began to edge up the west side of the hill, to their right.

"Do you hate Dad?" Lenore asked. "Do you think I hate Dad?"

"Well, now, seeing as how you're *you* . . . ," the Antichrist playfully pretended to punch Lenore in the arm, "I can't speak for you, but only for me, regardless of what I might say *about* you. *Verstehen?*"

"Pain in the ass."

"I don't hate Dad," said the Antichrist. "Dad just makes me millenially weary. I find Dad exhausting. The stump aches, horribly, whenever I'm around Dad."

Lenore hugged a knee to her chest.

"The one who hates Dad is Mom," LaVache continued, "or, that is, she would if she were Mom. The person I saw last month resembled a mom in no way whatsoever. John Lennon, yes. A mom, no."

"You miss Mom."

"I miss a mom. Mom's been in that place practically my whole life. Certainly at the beginning. My whole life is to an extent why she's in there, right? Although I do remember that one year when I was nine. And then Dad and Miss Malig sent her right back again."

"Well, she was trying to climb again. You can't just have somebody trying to climb up the side of your house all the time."

LaVache didn't say anything.

"But it's a shame you never got to really know her. I thought she was a good person. Really good." Lenore moved her head to make the fields sparkle in the half-light.

"I just feel an affinity, is all, probably," LaVache said. "No, for sure I do. Mom's head and my leg were taken out in the same dancing accident, after all. At least I got left with a thing. Mom's thingless." He picked the sliding-man label up from where it lay on Lenore's leg near the lacy hem of her white dress. "Interesting thing here is that it looks like this guy is climbing up dash sliding down a sort of sand dune. See the way his feet sink? And see this sort of cactus? I feel the implication of Desert, Lenore. Food for thought, in my opinion—no pun intended."

"But since his feet sink in the sand, then we know for sure he's climbing and not sliding," Lenore said, taking the drawing. " 'Cause if he had slid, there would have to be slide tracks all the way down from the top."

LaVache looked at the label and fingered his red chin. "But if he's climbing, then there ought to be footprints leading up from the bottom, in the sand, which there aren't."

"Hmmm."

"Looks like Gramma screwed up, unless perhaps the guy was dropped from a helicopter into this exact position; that's one possibility Dr. W. never fathomed. I guess there were no helicopters back in his day. Technology does affect interpretation, after all, doesn't it?"

"Hmmm."

The Antichrist gave Lenore the drawing back. "Can Vlad the Impaler really talk now?"

"You should hear it. His language was getting worse, too, over the last week or so, although I haven't been home in a couple days." Lenore saw that the man in the drawing was smiling broadly, in profile, and had what seemed to be a shadow, unless it was just the sand.

"What does he say?"

"Unfortunately mostly really obscene stuff, because he's around Candy all the time."

The Antichrist groaned. "I'm tingling all over. The leg may spontaneously detach."

"Except we've been teaching him stuff out of the Bible, so Mrs. Tissaw hopefully won't evict me if she hears him," Lenore said. "She's already ticked off because Vlad tends to chew the wall."

"Can't wait to hear him."

"My bottom really hurts," Lenore said. "I think I'd like to go back. Rick might be back at your dorm and wondering where we are. Would you like to come to dinner with us? I predict Rick's going to want to go to the Aqua Vitae."

"Let me just gather my resources for the trip back, for a second," said LaVache. He massaged the leg with a hand. "If I can drive a stake through the heart of Nervous Roy's Hegel problem without making you guys wait too long, I'll gladly come."

"Look, by the way, do you mind if I tell Dad you have a phone?" Lenore said. "Dad is crazy about you."

"All sorts of different truths in that statement."

"He's pinned all his hopes on you, he says."

"Pins tend to smart, I've found," LaVache said.

"At least you should tell him you call a phone a lymph node."

"Well, gee, then I might as well call it a phone," the Antichrist said sulkily.

They both looked at the athletic fields and the forests behind them. Long spears of shadow were moving across the breadth of the grass. Shadow-gaps sparkled with sprinkler-dew. Two very tiny figures emerged from the edge of the trees of the bird sanctuary, far away, and started walking across the wet fields toward the hill. One of the figures, the shorter one, wore a brown beret.

"Hey," Lenore said quietly.

She saw the two figures stop. The taller one, whose hair looked red in the red sun between the gym-shadows, bent over and felt the wet grass with his hand. The two figures slipped off their shoes and socks—the taller one merely his shoes, because he wore no socks underneath—and continued walking. They got to the bottom of the hill.

"Well that's Rick right there," Lenore said to the Antichrist, pointing to the man in the beret. She waved. Rick looked up at her for a bit, his hand to his hat, confused, then finally smiled broadly and waved back. He said something to the other man, pointing at Lenore.

"Who's that other guy?" asked LaVache. He tossed away his roach and struggled to get to his feet.

"I don't think I know," Lenore said. She stared at the taller man, who walked the hill well, one hand holding boat shoes, the other helping Rick Vigorous, who was having trouble, sliding back in his bare feet in the wet grass of the bottom of the steep hill. The taller man grinned at his efforts, and some of the last bits of fiery sunset over the gym hit his teeth, which shone red.

"Do I look all right?" Lenore said to LaVache.

"Nut," LaVache said. "Help me up, please."

Lenore helped her brother up. The two men got close to the curve of the top of the hill, where the grass became dry and brown. Rick no longer needed help. There were voices, back and forth. The Antichrist was having balance problems. The very last of the sun sucked itself down behind the gymnasium, to the west. A cool shadow filled up the field, then climbed the hill all the way to the Memorial. The shadow covered the four figures, as they came together, and they were gone.

PART TWO

12 → 1990

/a/

"Perhaps I'll try another crustless Hellman's-less ham sandwich, with you taking whatever steps might be possible to minimize the saltiness of the ham."

". . . ."

"And a Canadian Club and distilled water."

"Sure. How about Lenore? Is Lenore asleep?"

"Fnoof, fnoof fnoof."

"So it would seem."

"Sir, how about you? Would you like anything?"

"Ma'am, while I take a minute to formulate a suitable answer to that, you could bring me a beer. I don't need a glass."

"All righty."

"Thank you, miss."

". . . ."

"Who the hell is that?"

"I think her name is Jennifer. She's the Stonecipheco stewardess."

"Hang me upside down if that's not the beautifulest goddamn stewardess I ever saw. Would I like anything, she says."

"Ahem. Lenore has given me to understand that Jennifer is married to the Stonecipheco pilot, in whose hands our lives at the moment happen to rest."

"Uh-huh."

"Would you care for some gum?"

"Not if I got beer coming. You sure chew a lot of gum, R.V."

"I have ear trouble on planes. Normally I loathe gum."

"Uh-huh."

"Not to mention planes themselves."

"Ho there, Lenore. You up?"

"Fnoof."

"I so envy people who can sleep on planes, Andrew."

"She sure is a nice sleeper. My wife, when she sleeps, sometimes her mouth hangs open. Sometimes a little bit of spit comes out of her mouth and gets on the pillow. I hate that."

"Lenore is a lovely sleeper."

"Look, R.V., does Lenore remember me or not? Like I said, I'm just positive it was her I met that night I met my wife. I was a little bit trashed, but still."

"She hasn't said anything to me. An appropriate context for discussing the issue didn't arise, last night. She fell asleep almost immediately."

"Those Howard Johnson's beds are comfortable all right. Howard Johnson's kicks ass. I appreciated the room, and the dinner, and the use of the razor. The Flange just about cleaned me out. I can't believe I was too stupid to bring more money up with me."

"Not a problem at all. Stonecipheco will absorb it. Consider it an advance."

"Except the thing is, I've been thinkin' about it . . . hey, thanks, looks great. The beer, too. Heh-heh."

". . . ."

"Thank you, miss. I believe that will be all for now."

"Just ring if you want anything."

"Thank you."

"Just ring, she says. She's a tease, ain't she? Lord, though, look at that. That's a first-rate pooper, under that skirt."

"Crusts, again. The girl seems incapable of removing crusts."

"What?"

"Nothing. Please go on with what you were saying."

"Well, I was thinkin' about the night I think I met Lenore, the night I met Melinda-Sue, and what happened was me and this other guy, who turned out later on to be a real loser, we went over to Mount Holyoke, and kind of barged on into these girls' rooms, for a kind of fraternity thing. I don't quite remember what."

". . . ."

"And I remember I think Lenore got pissed off. She was real young and I don't think she knew the whole story. I remember she threw a shoe at the guy I was with."

"A shoe?"

"Yup. And she told Melinda-Sue she had ugly feet."

"Shoes and feet, again."

"Yup. So I don't know what to do. I don't know how to act, if I should just pretend like I don't know her, either, or what. I can't tell if she's still pissed off after all these years or not."

"Real, sustained anger in Lenore is quite rare, I've found. Embarrassment, though, is not. I would be willing to bet that Lenore is simply embarrassed. When she's embarrassed about something, she tends to pretend it doesn't exist."

"You think that's why she sort of acts like she don't remember me, from that night, or Melinda-Sue?"

"It's very possible."

"You say she works at Frequent and Vigorous too? So I'll be workin' with her?"

"Not directly. As of before we left, she answered telephones, at the Frequent and Vigorous switchboard, in the lobby, downstairs. But on this trip I've had a bit of an inspiration, I think."

"An inspiration?"

"Yes. I think I've come to see that the switchboard is not a full-time place for a woman of Lenore's capacities. She is chafing, I'm almost certain."

"Chafing?"

"Yes. I've come to see that it all adds up. The context is right. Lenore is chafing. She likes stories. To the extent that she understands herself, it's as having something like a literary sensibility. And you and I, here most significantly I, will at least for a while be occupied with the Stonecipheco project account. The crux is that I plan to put Lenore on my personal staff, part-time, as a reader."

"A reader?"

"Yes, of pieces submitted to the high-quality literary review of which I am editor, the *Frequent Review*. She can weed out the more obviously pathetic or inappropriate submissions, and save me valuable weeding-time, which you and I can spend on the Corfu project."

"Hell of an idea, R.V."

"I rather think so myself."

"Yes indeedy."

"Of course I'll have to make sure that her sensibilities are keened to precisely the right pitch for the *Review* . . ."

"So we'll be workin' with her, but not exactly with her."

"As far as you go, that is right."

"Which works out good, because I'm not supposed to say what it is I'm workin' on, to her."

"Yes, unfortunately."

"And if she asks, I have to say I'm . . . let me look at this . . . I'm supposed to say I'm translating this thing called 'Norslan: The Third-World Herbicide That Likes People' into idiomatic modern Greek."

"Correct."

"But except we still haven't come to why exactly I have to say all this shit if she asks. If she's just an employee, how come it matters? And what does she care if we're tryin' to sell nuclear baby food on Corfu?"

"This is unfortunately not entirely clear to me, Andrew, and just let me say I'm far from qualmless about the whole situation."

" . . . ."

"You are of course already aware that Stonecipheco is controlled by the Beadsman family, to a nearly exhaustive extent, and I'll now inform you that Mr. Stonecipher Beadsman has stipulated in our contract that Lenore not know what is up in terms of Frequent and Vigorous involvement in the project until he wishes her to."

"And you don't find that just a tinch unusual?"

"Charitable speculation about Mr. Beadsman's reasoning might suggest that he doesn't want to involve Lenore in any more unpleasantness than is necessary. Suffice to say that the whole Corfu marketing venture is bound up with some family turbulence that's worrying Lenore a lot, right now. Which turbulence is the main reason she and I came to Amherst, at all, so that Lenore might speak with her brother . . ."

"The kid we had dinner with at Aqua Vitae."

"Yes. Stonecipher LaVache Beadsman."

"He was pretty goddamn wild, I thought. 'Course I have to admit I was kind of wasted. We drank all that in the Flange, and then you dragged me all over hell's half acre through those crowds in the forest. Shit I drank went to my head and roosted. He was wild, though, I could tell."

"He's had rather a rough time of it."

"Satanic little dung beetle, too."

"Dung beetle?"

"Little dude looked like the devil. And what was all that about talkin' about his leg like it was another person? He would like address comments to his fucking leg. What was all that about?"

"Lenore's brother has only one leg. One of LaVache's legs is artificial."

"No shit."

"None whatsoever. Couldn't you tell?"

"He limped some, and he sat weird, but no."

"He was wearing slacks at dinner. But he was wearing shorts when we first met him, on the hill. You didn't see his leg then?"

"R.V., that hill got blacker than a panther's ass when we got up top. The sun went right the hell down. It was darker than shit. I was wasted, too. I wouldn't have been able to even see Lenore, if she hadn't had that white dress on. And plus then I had to run right down to get my car over to Coach's, so I never really saw the sucker in shorts. I sure am sorry, though."

"No need to be sorry. I was simply informing you of a fact."

"Christ. What happened to his leg, then? How come they chopped it off?"

"No one chopped his leg off. LaVache was minus a leg from birth."

"No shit. What, like a birth defect or something?"

"Not exactly."

"What, then?"

"God, we're over Lake Erie, now. This is my least favorite part of the trip, by far. My ears are also hurting like hell."

"Too bad. That's Lake Erie, huh?"

"Unfortunately."

"Water's kind of a funny color."

"I'm sure whatever percentage of the lake is water is a perfectly lovely color. The percentage is however unfortunately quite small."

"How come there's no waves? How come the water doesn't move?"

"You don't want to know."

"So what's this about the kid's leg, then? Legs don't just disappear for no reason."

"That's obviously true."

" . . . . "

"Lenore is still asleep, isn't she?"

"Fnoof."

"Yup."

"Lenore hates to be told about."

"The leg story isn't about her, though, is it?"

"What happened was that after the first three Beadsman children were born, Mrs. Beadsman's health apparently got a bit ticklish. Nothing physically major—just a touch of anemia, or something like that. Mr. Stonecipher Beadsman III, Lenore's father, however, through a troublingly ambiguous process of reasoning, came to the conclusion that Mrs. Beadsman was no longer entirely able to care for her children adequately, so at a certain point he hired a governess, a Miss Malig, a stunningly beautiful woman—she's now an unbelievable battle-ax, with calves like churns, but back then she was apparently stunningly beautiful—which hiring itself represented a significant corporate coup, because Miss Malig had only the year before been named Miss Gerber in the annual Gerber Quality Brands beauty pageant, and Mr. Robert Gerber, Mr. Beadsman's old college friend—Amherst, by the way, '61—and sworn corporate enemy, had been wild about her, and there had been rumors that he was going to divorce his striking Brazilian wife Paquita to devote all his time to the pursuit of Nancy Malig, but Mr. Beadsman, somehow, through maneuvers to this day unclear, spirited her away, and installed her in his home, at an exorbitant salary, ostensibly to take care of Clarice and John and Lenore."

"What does all this have to do with legs?"

"What happened was that this hiring of Nancy Malig—with whom by the way Mr. Beadsman almost certainly began having an immoderate sexual affair that may very well continue to this day—

and the at least partial separation from her children such a hiring represented and entailed, made Mrs. Beadsman, who had always been naturally rather melancholy, intensely sad. And the intense sadness had further non-good consequences for her health, now by implication emotional health, as well as physical. And so Mr. Beadsman, by now inarguably to some extent under Miss Malig's erotic spell, and in any event naturally disposed to be very weird indeed about his children, and obsessed with the future of the family, and of Stonecipheco, Inc., even though at that point he was still only a vice president, since his father had not yet died in a Jell-O accident, and in any event disposed to be constantly giving his three children all sorts of specially developed standardized tests, academic and psychological, to begin the process of determining on whom the mantle of corporate power would someday devolve, became convinced somehow that Mrs. Beadsman's mere presence was a harmful thing for the children, and thus the family, and thus the Company, and he began to take active steps to keep the children away from her altogether, which steps consisted of, *a*, expanding and combining the three children's rooms into an immense impregnable combination nursery and playroom and bedroom and dining room, et cetera, with a heavy boltable iron door, and its own restroom facilities, and a dumbwaiter link to the kitchen, and so on, a maneuver which in intended effect isolated the children and Miss Malig in one wing of the Beadsman home in Shaker Heights, the east wing, an almost tower-ish extension of the house, with a lovely white trellis draped with dusky green vines running up the outer wall to the windows, a wing I've obviously personally seen, given this description. So the children, under Miss Malig's malevolent eye, were isolated from the rest of the house, through which the now more than a little troubled Mrs. Beadsman would roam, in a flowing white cotton dress, often in the company of Mrs. Lenore Beadsman, Mr. Beadsman's grandmother, who usually as a rule kept to her study, poring over meaningless tomes she'd been exposed to in her days as a student, which she still in effect was, a student, that is Mrs. Lenore Beadsman kept to her study until the mother-separated-from-children situation began really to assert itself, and old Lenore began to perceive the evilness of the Stonecipher-Malig liaison, and so would roam the house with Mrs. Beadsman, Patrice, also in a flowing white dress, trying to help Patrice think of ways to get in to see the children."

". . . ."

"That is they roamed until Mr. Beadsman took step *b*, which consisted of demanding that Patrice Beadsman become a world-class contract bridge player—she'd been quite a spectacular bridge player in college—so as to get her out of the house and away from the children and him and Miss Malig. And so he arranges to have built a special little bungalow in the back of the house, for Patrice to by and large live in, and to practice bridge in, every moment, and he enters her in all sorts of world-class bridge tournaments, and hires a coach and partner for her, Blanchard Foamwhistle, a world-class contract bridge player, and, interestingly enough, the father of the man who is now Mr. Beadsman's executive secretary at Stonecipheco. And Foamwhistle is paid an exorbitant salary, and he and Patrice are confined for days at a time to the bridge bungalow, ostensibly working on bridge strategy and bridge theory, and soon Patrice becomes mysteriously once again pregnant, and it is to me unclear whether she became pregnant by Foamwhistle or by Mr. Beadsman, although Mr. Beadsman gave no indication that he suspected anything sexually amiss, and in any event announced his intention to name the baby—which baby would without a doubt, he maintained, be a boy—Stonecipher, and he instructs Miss Malig to set up another crib in the impregnable east wing fortress."

"You got this shit down, don't you?"

"You want your question answered or not?"

"I guess."

"Well that's what I'm attempting."

". . . ."

"And so by this time Mrs. Beadsman's pregnancy, with its attendant hormonal and general chemical consequences, together with the original unhappiness and troubles, together with the continued isolation of the children, who are as a matter of routine hustled right up to the east wing tower after school, while Foamwhistle, on Mr. Beadsman's high-paid instructions, keeps Patrice confined as best he can in the bridge bungalow, together with the obviously planned additional isolation of the baby, too, when it's born, all combine to make Mrs. Beadsman understandably even more intensely unhappy, and frantic, and disoriented, and emotionally not a little unwell. And this has truly disastrous consequences for her contract bridge, a game which you may or may not know demands a clear undistracted mind and nerves of steel and absolute emotional soundness, and Patrice and Foamwhistle lose in the first round of every single world-class bridge tournament they enter, even though Foamwhistle is acknowledged to be one of the world's very finest contract bridge players, which gives you some idea of the truly pathetic state of Patrice's bridge, and soon they no longer even legitimately qualify for the world-class tournaments, because they get annihilated all the time, but Stonecipher Beadsman persistently bribes and coerces various tournament officials into continuing to admit Patrice and Foamwhistle to the tournaments, which the already frazzled Patrice finds excruciatingly embarrassing, and so becomes even more frazzled, and so on."

" . . . . "

"And this goes on until about the eighth or ninth month of Patrice's pregnancy, and finally she and Foamwhistle get absolutely demolished in the preliminary round of a marginally world-class tournament in Dayton, by two eight-year-old contract bridge prodigies who wear matching beanies with propellers on top, and who deny Patrice and Foamwhistle even one trick, which represents a true thumping of ass, in bridge, and Patrice comes home, huge with child, and wildly frazzled, and deeply humiliated, and immediately on her arrival she runs into the east wing and up the tower stairs and pounds on the iron door of the children's impregnable ward, pleading for entry, and apparently little Lenore on the other side pounds back, but Stonecipher Beadsman appears at the door and says that Patrice is obviously in no condition to have anything but a bad effect on the children, who are at this point undergoing a battery of intricate standardized psychological tests administered by Miss Malig to help see which one is best suited to assume control of Stonecipheco one day, and the tests are at the final and most critical stage, Stonecipher says, and so he demands that Patrice return to the bridge bungalow with Foamwhistle, to practice, and he orders Foamwhistle to keep her confined as best he can, and so she's installed back in the bungalow with only a card table and some decks of cards, and of course Foamwhistle.

"And to Foamwhistle's enormous consternation and pity Patrice begins beating her head against the edge of the card table, crying out that if she can't see the children she's going to die, and she's totally hysterical, and in a very bad way, and Foamwhistle's heart almost breaks—that there is some sort of ambiguous emotional connection between Patrice and Foamwhistle is by this time hardly open to doubt—and his heart is breaking, and he decides to do his best to help Patrice see the children, at least for a moment, and he asks her what he can do to help. And Patrice looks at him with doe-like gratitude and trust, and tells him that she's been thinking, and that if he can just somehow arrange to get one of the outside windows of the children's east-wing nursery fortress unlocked, she can scale the white trellis running up the outer wall of the east wing and pop in to see the children, and touch them, if only briefly, before anyone can stop her. A really bad idea, for a woman huge with child, and actually, you are probably beginning to intuit, an ominous and disastrous idea. But Foamwhistle, who is vicariously frazzled by Patrice's clear emotional distress, unwisely agrees to do it. And so he waits until the children's nap time, and then goes to the nursery fortress and shouts through the door to Miss Malig that Patrice is asleep, too, and that he wants to come in and give Miss Malig a contract bridge lesson, and also maybe fool around, a bit— who knows what all was going on by that time—and Miss Malig lets him in, and at some point, when her attention is diverted, Foamwhistle goes to the window and unlocks it and opens it ever so slightly—this was in May, by the way, of '72, just as I was moving to Scarsdale—and but anyhow Foamwhistle slips out of the ever-so-slightly opened window a card—the Queen of Spades—which is the pre-arranged signal to Patrice that all is set, and the card flutters down through the soft May air to Patrice, there in her white dress at the bottom of the trellis."

"Are you bullshitting me, here, R.V.? I mean come on."

"Since I sense impatience on your part, I'll make a long story short by saying that Patrice attempts to scale the trellis to the open window, and that, near the top, her pregnant weight pulls the troublingly weak and unsteady trellis away from the tower wall, and the trellis breaks, and, with a shriek, Patrice falls a significantly and disastrously long way to the ground, and lands on her pregnant belly, and spontaneously gives explosive birth to LaVache, which is to say Stonecipher, who lands several yards away in a flowerbed, minus a leg, the leg in question, which was torn off in LaVache's explosive ejaculation from Patrice's womb, and both infant and mother are grievously hurt, and in a horrible way, but Foamwhistle hears Patrice's shriek and runs to the window and looks down and bites his knuckle in grief and relocks the window and calls ambulances and fire engines and rushes down to administer the appropriate sustaining first-aid, and Patrice and LaVache are rushed to the hospital, and both survive, but Patrice is now hopelessly emotionally troubled, out of her head, to be more exact, and she has to be institutionalized, and spends the rest of the time between then and now in and out of institutions, and is as a matter of fact in one now, in Wisconsin."

"Shit on fire."

"In any event, hence LaVache's leglessness."

"Holy shit."

"And once Patrice is psychologically out of the picture—about which Stonecipher the father apparently feels little guilt, since he, presumably through the filter of Miss Malig's erotic spell, had already perceived Patrice as off her nut for some time—once she's out of the house, more or less for good, the physical and emotional isolation of the children gradually stops, and Miss Malig eventually lets them live semi-normal, childish lives, including Little League and Brownies and slumber parties, et cetera, when they're not busy being tested, but in all events by this time all sorts of damage has been done, to the family and the individual family-members."

"Not to mention the poor little satanic sucker's leg."

"Right."

"Christ on a Kawasaki."

"Fnoof."

" . . . . "

"Lenore tell you all that?"

"I think we're getting close. I sense the closeness of Cleveland. Can you smell that? A smell like removing the lid from a pot of something that's been left in one's refrigerator just a little too long?"

"Can't say as I smell anything but beer and Wrigley's Spearmint, R.V."

"I'm just acutely sensitive to the odor of Cleveland, I suppose. I have a monstrously sensitive sense of smell."

". . . ."

"Though not as sensitive as some people I could name."

"So what books have y'all published? Have I likely read some books you put out?"

"We're definitely getting close. See all the dead fish? The density of the fish goes up significantly as we approach shore. It looks as if I'm to be spared a sludge-death yet again."

"Uh-huh."

". . . ."

"So you think I can get a temporary room at this house Lenore lives at, right?"

"I'm practically positive. The young lady who lives directly below Lenore and her roommate Ms. Mandible will be involuntarily out of her apartment for at least three months, guaranteed. Mrs. Tissaw will be predictably anxious to ensure occupancy and so rent payment for that period."

"How come you know for sure the little lady's gone for three months?"

"She works for Lenore's sister, Clarice, who now owns a chain of tanning parlors in the area. There was a horrible accident. The girl will be all right, but will require at least three months of hospitalization and continual Noxzema treatments."

"You mean . . . ?"

"Yes. Tanning accident."

"Bad news."

"Yes. But at least an available apartment, cheap. And your assignment with the firm cannot possibly last for more than three months, barring utter disaster."

"OK by me."

"Andrew, listen, may I ask a question?"

"Shoot."

"Will Mindy be coming out to join you? You have told her the developments—she does know where you're going to be, doesn't she? What exactly is the Mindy situation?"

"R.V., look and listen. It's like I told you, I just felt like I had to get out for a while. Breathe some temporarily Melinda-Sue-free air. She and I had a bit of a tiff before I drove up to school, I make no bones. But it's more'n that. To my mind there's just this temporary lack of wonderfulness about our whole relationship."

". . . ."

"So things are just temporarily up in the air."

". . . ."

"And no, I didn't exactly call her from school, I didn't tell her I'd run into y'all and was coming out here to do some work. But she'll be able to find out when she wants. I had to leave my car with Coach Zandagnio, who was my lacrosse coach, and sort of my mentor, at school, and I told him the whole story. And Melinda-Sue knows that if anybody knows where I would have gone from school, it's old Stenetore, 'cause she knew him too, he went to our wedding when she got out of school; he gave us a gravy boat."

"You played lacrosse at Amherst?"

"I was a lacrosse-playing fool."

"Always struck me as a staggeringly savage game."

"A truly and completely kick-ass game. A game that kicks ass."

"I see."

". . . ."

"Lenore darling, are you awake?"

"Fnoof."

"Girl can do some serious sleeping."

"May I be explicit, here, for a moment, Wang-Dang?"

"Draw and fire, R.V."

"I am passionately, fiercely, and completely in love with Lenore. She is not quite as explicitly my fiancée as I may have inadvertently led you to believe in the Flange, but she is nevertheless mine. I have a bit of a jealousy problem, I'm told. My setting in motion the process of your possibly temporarily sharing a building with Lenore, actually, to be honest, my inviting you to come and temporarily enter our lives and work for Frequent and Vigorous, at all, was predicated on the understandable assumption that you were

emotionally involved with and attached to Mindy Metalman, a
woman who, just let me say in all candor, strikes me as the sort of
woman an attachment to whom on, for example, my part would
leave me completely uninterested in any and all of the world's other
females. Do you get my drift?"

"Go on."

"Then the drift now becomes a tide, and I say that, in light of
what I now know, given what seems to be at least a partial and
temporary unattachment to your wife, Mindy, a past that includes
an acquaintance with Lenore, under whatever circumstances, prior
to my own, and at least clear verbal evidence of vigorous hormonal
activity on your part, I feel I can be truly comfortable only in the
context of an explicit recognition on your part of the fact that
Lenore is mine, and thus out of bounds, that as I am to be regarded
as a sort of brother, or uncle, whatever you will, so Lenore is to be
regarded by you as a sort of sister, or aunt, with whom any sort of
attempted romantic involvement is and would be entirely unthinkable."

". . . ."

"There."

"Damned if you're not the most articulate little rooster I ever
heard crow."

". . . ."

"I'd be lying if I said I wasn't a tiny bit hurt by the idea that I
might do something like what you're afraid of to a Psi Phi brother,
to an Amherst uncle. But to put your mind at rest . . . your mind
isn't quite at rest, here, is it?"

"It can be put so with utter ease, by you."

"OK, then let me just say, right here, that I give you my word
of honor as an alumni of the single finest undergraduate institution
in the land that I will not harbor any but the most honorable of
thoughts toward your woman."

"I'm all too aware that it's silly, but could you promise not to
take her away?"

"R.V., I promise not to take her away."

"Thank you. Well there. That's out of the way."

"You all right? Your forehead's wet as hell. You want to use my
hankie?"

"No thank you. I have my own."

"Gentlemen, the captain asks that you please refasten your seat belts for landing."

"My ears are rumbling like mad."

"You wouldn't by any chance want to help me with my particular belt, here, ma'am, would you?"

"Ixnay—ilotpay."

". . . ."

"Fnoof."

"Lenore."

"Fnoof. What?"

"Damned if you can't sleep up a storm, Lenore."

"What time is it?"

"We're apparently preparing to land."

"Boy am I tired."

"Sweet dreams?"

"I'm not sure. My mouth tastes like a barn. I would kill for a shower."

"Have some gum."

"Want to try some Skoal?"

"Not for anything in the world."

"Lenore, my ears are in their own private hell."

"Poor Rick. What can I do to help?"

"Perhaps a bit of a temple massage . . ."

"Let me just get my big old carcass out of the way, here . . ."

/b/

By the time Rick dropped Lenore and Wang-Dang Lang off near the Tissaws' it was almost four, and beginning to mist a little, so that even though it wasn't very cold Lenore could see her breath, and Lang's. Rick dashed off to attend to some affairs at Frequent and Vigorous, but promised, as he dropped them a few hundred yards from the oral surgeon's big gray house, to be back as soon as possible to take them both to dinner.

"Super," said Lenore.

"Straight up," said Lang.

The reason Rick had to drop Lenore and Lang off near, rather than at, the Tissaws' was that the street all around the house was totally clogged with cars, and especially vans. A lot of the vans were white, with the ornate letters P.W.G. on the sides, in red. Lenore had never seen the street so crowded.

"I've just never seen the street so crowded," Lenore said.

"Don't suppose all these folks are here to try to sublet Misty Schwartz's room, do you?" said Lang.

"Not a chance."

"Must be a really bitching party going on around here, then," said Lang.

"On a Tuesday afternoon?"

"My kind of neighborhood."

As they went up the walk, Lenore saw that the Tissaws' front door was propped partly open by a network of thick black cables that led out from the backs of two of the white P.W.G. vans— vans parked halfway onto the grass of the Tissaws' lawn—and disappeared into the house. Lenore all of a sudden heard what was unmistakably Candy Mandible shout something from her third-story window, a window that looked strangely lit up, right now, and actually had a bit of a tiny rainbow-doughnut around it in the cool wet air, and then from the front porch Lenore heard Candy running down the stairs of the house to meet them at the door.

"Lenore I swear to God you will just not believe it," said Candy.

"What the heck is going on here?" Lenore said, looking around. "Are we having sewer trouble?"

"Not exactly, come on, it's Vlad the Impaler," Candy said, starting to try to pull Lenore toward the stairs, up which the black cables from the vans ran and disappeared from sight. Candy was wearing that violet dress.

"Hey, ho, and hello," Lang said to Candy. He hefted the suitcases.

"Hi," said Candy, barely looking at Lang. "Lenore, come *on*. You'll flip and die!"

"What can Vlad the Impaler have to do with vans and letters and cables?"

"Mrs. Tissaw heard him say things, God knows what, really, and she just freaked *out*." One of the shoulder straps of the violet dress had slipped off Candy's shoulder. Lang hefted the suitcases again.

"She's getting him on television. Well, religious television, on cable. But still, television."

"Television?"

"Vlad the Impaler?" said Wang-Dang Lang.

"My bird," Lenore said. "Who is now troublingly and also obscenely able to talk." She turned to Candy. "Who gave permission for him to get put on television?"

"Mrs. Tissaw says it's in lieu of the bill for the chewed wall and the guano-damage to the floor, which she knows you can't pay because she talked to Prieth at the board and Prieth very helpfully told her you're broke . . ." Candy stopped and looked up the staircase. There was noise from the third floor. Lots of it. "But look," she said, "come on, they're going to make him a *star*, they say. They say *literally*."

"Literally? A star? Of what?"

"Come *on*."

Lenore let herself be pulled. Lang followed her and Candy up the stairs with the suitcases, watching their bottoms.

/c/

"Friends, as subscribing members of the Reverend Hart Lee Syke's Partners With God Club you can expect the entry of the Almighty into your own personal life in twenty-four hours or less," Vlad the Impaler was saying, staring blankly into a lavishly unfamiliar little unsmeared mirror perimetered with tiny light bulbs. Lenore's own personal room was full of television cameras and towering metal lamps, and bright-white light. The room was cruising at about a hundred degrees. Thick black cables, and panels with colored lights winking on and off, and sunglasses were everywhere. The brown velvet chair, the uneven-legged desk chair, the bed, and all the black corduroy cushions on the windowsills were occupied by people holding various sorts of electronic equipment, or thick sheaves of paper, and all smoking, and all tapping cigarette ashes onto the floor. Vlad the Impaler was in his cage, his enormous feet hooked over the arms of a tiny director's chair, licking tentatively at the hot surface of his lit-up mirror. A truly enormous gray box of a television camera, with a little red light on top, was trained on him. Pushed back onto Vlad's spiky pink mohawk Lenore thought she could see a tiny pair of sunglasses. Vlad the Impaler's old smeared mirror, on its chain of Frequent and Vigorous paper clips, was gone.

"Holy shit," said Lenore.

"You wouldn't believe what's been happening," said Candy.

"One hell of a dress, there, ma'am," Lang said to Candy. "A. S. Lang, here."

"Perfect! *Perfect!*" came shouts from a huge man with a white leather body suit, and an enormous beehive of sculptured black hair, and several chins. Red sequins on the chest of his body suit formed the letters P.W.G.

"Love it! Love that bird!" the man was yelling.

"Cut!" yelled somebody else, from the middle of the mob near the windows. The windows were smeared with steam, from breath.

"Twist my major limbs if that's not Hart Lee Sykes himself," Wang-Dang Lang said, staring at the man in white leather.

"Who?" said Lenore.

"It is, that's Hart Lee Sykes," said Candy. She got close to Lenore's ear to make herself heard. "He's this truly enormous wheel at CBN, the Christian Broadcasting Network? He used to host this show called 'Real People and Animals of Profound Religious Significance,' a sort of religious spin-off of 'Real People.' But now he hosts this incredibly successful show on cable called 'The Partners With God Club.'"

"He's A-OK," Lang said to Lenore, setting down the suitcases amid a litter of Styrofoam cups and candy wrappers and butts. "My Daddy watches his show all the time. My Daddy thinks Hart Lee's the spiritual balls."

"Who are you?" Candy said to Lang.

"This is Andrew Sealander Lang," said Lenore, "a friend of Rick's and now a very temporary F and V employee. I'm supposed to get Mrs. Tissaw to rent him Misty's room while she's in the hospital."

"And a friend of you fine ladies, now, too, I hope," said Lang. "I—"

"Inside out! A camel! The bird has been touched by Auden!" shrieked Vlad the Impaler. A sound-man yelped and tore off his headphones.

"No, no, *no*!" screamed Hart Lee Sykes, stamping a pointy-toed cowboy boot on the wooden floor. "The next line is 'All contributing subscriptions are tax-deductible.' Cindy honey . . . where's Cindy?" Hart Lee Sykes spotted Candy by the door with Lenore and Lang and made his way over as all heads turned toward them. Lenore began to edge toward the door. Sykes towered over all of them, even Lang. To Candy he said, "Cindy honey, you've simply got to make the miraculous little incarnation behave. Now if you'll—"

"Reverend Sykes, this is finally Lenore Beadsman, who owns Vlad," Candy said, preempting Lenore's flight with an iron hand at the small of her back.

The Reverend stopped, turned to Lenore, seemed almost to be getting ready to bow. "Miss Beadsman, at ever so long last. The owner, to the extent that any single man can be called the owner, of this animal—dare I say animal?—touched by the Lord and guided by His hand to His humble servant, me." Sykes's voice had risen from whisper to shout. A murmer went through the room from the people looking through scripts and checking equipment.

"Jesus knew the sex was great!" squawked Vlad the Impaler.

"A pleasure to meet you, and a sincere expression of the pro*found*est gratitude for allowing us into your home and into the presence of an animal of vital theological importance," Sykes was saying to Lenore, ignoring Lang's outstretched hand. "Our friend Mrs. Tilsit has told me all about you and your profound relationship with your profound pet."

"Tissaw," said Candy Mandible.

"Tissaw." Sykes smiled. "A bird through which the voice of the Lord has been personally heard by me to cry out for exposure to the American people, through the medium of, again, to my profound and humble honor, me."

"Hmmm," Lenore said.

"Lenore, Lenore," twittered Vlad the Impaler. "Make me come. I need space, as a person. Let's get rid of this disgusting unprofessional mirror. You will be a star in the electronic firmament of American evangelical theology! Like *Charlotte's Web*!"

"Boy, he's gotten even worse," Lenore said to Candy.

"Worse?" cried Hart Lee Sykes. "Worse? The lady jests with us all, friends. Miss surely you are aware that your feathered companion has been touched by the hand of the Lord Himself."

"Probably bit it, then," muttered Lenore.

"Mmm-hmmm," the crowd of technicians was rumbling at Sykes.

". . . that he represents a theological development of the very highest order, a manifestation of the earthly intervention and influence of the Almighty comparable in significance to the weeping fir tree of Yrzc, Poland, and the cruciform tar-pit formations of Sierra Leone! Worse, she jests!"

The crowd of technicians laughed.

"Hart Lee, sweetheart," crooned Vlad the Impaler.

"You live here too?" Lang whispered to Candy.

"Sshh," Candy hissed. Lang grinned and put his finger to his lips, nodding.

"Mrs. Tissaw told you to put Vlad the Impaler on religious television?" Lenore was saying to Reverend Sykes. Vlad the Impaler was going to the bathroom on his little director's chair.

"My little friend, the directive to afford this creature exposure to an American populace crying out for divine direction and reaffirmation came from a source far, *far* higher than Mrs. Tyson, or you, or I!" cried Sykes, standing on tiptoe in his pointed boots.

Lenore stared at Sykes. "Not my *father.*"

"Exactly, young Miss. The *Father* of us all!" Sykes looked around him. "I am the recipient of the mandate which all true humble servants of the Lord pray for, all their miserable lives. Thank you. Thank you." Sykes made motions toward trying to kiss Lenore's hand.

"It's *Tissaw,*" Candy said wearily. Sykes gave her the fish-eye.

"Andrew Sealander Lang, here, padre," Lang said to Sykes, taking the Reverend's pudgy hand from Lenore's and shaking it. "One of Ms. Beadsman's closest friends and a deep admirer of her bird, and of your show, sir."

The Reverend shook Lang's hand without looking at him. He stared into Lenore's eyes. Lenore could smell his breath. "Miss Beadsman, you are in a position to aid us in delivering to the American people and to the world the Lord's true contemporary message, through His chosen feathered vehicle."

"Look, I'm afraid I just don't understand what you're talking about," said Lenore. "There's a pretty troubling explanation for Vlad's talking, I'm afraid, that shouldn't—"

"The only even remotely problematic problem is that the Lord is moving in such very mysterious ways through your pet that the miraculous little thing isn't saying quite what requires to be said, quite as quickly as he might, given the extreme expense involved in delivering the message of the Lord these days," said the Reverend. "The bird in its secular aspect seems to be so understandably caught up in the ecstasy of the Lord's verbal presence within him that he goes far beyond what actually needs and is proper to be said, given the import of the mission."

"Little fucker sounds pretty healthy to me," said Vlad the Impaler, crunching a sunflower seed.

"A case in point," the Reverend said solemnly to Lenore. "What you find yourself in a position to do is to help the bird deliver the message intended and required. His next line in the relevant initial message is, 'All contributing subscriptions are tax-deductible.'" The Reverend's smile reached almost to his ears. "If you could simply use your privileged position to reemphasize to the bird the vital importance of his mission, and prompt him to deliver the lines he's directed by our Father through me to deliver, and also perhaps get him to stop biting the makeup-man . . ." Sykes gestured toward a pale man with a bandaged hand.

"I still don't get it," said Lenore.

"May I, Reverend?" Candy said, trying to ignore something Lang was whispering into her ear.

"By all means." Sykes folded his arms and tapped a pointed boot on the floor. The director looked at his watch.

"What apparently happened was that Mrs. Tissaw was in here dusting," Candy said, "two days ago, the day you went right from the switchboard to Clarice's and then I guess to Rick's, 'cause you sure weren't around, and I was out too, because Nick Allied and I finally . . ."

"Ahem," said the Reverend.

"Anyway," Candy said, "Mrs. Tissaw was in here, and she heard the little . . . the bird, and he I guess was saying religious stuff . . ."

"Of the profoundest importance," Sykes added.

". . . and she just had a complete spasm, from excitement, and she called 'Real People,' to try to get them to come have a look at him, because he'd supposedly been squawking something about 'Real People' . . ."

"Well Candy you know how come he was saying that," Lenore said.

"We *all* know tonight," said Sykes, nodding solemnly. Affirmation-noise swelled from the cigarette smoke above the technicians' heads.

Candy rolled her eyes. "And I guess 'Real People' figured he wasn't their cup of tea, weird-mixture-of-Biblical-and-obscene-stuff-wise, but the guy in charge told the guy on the phone to tell her to call CBN . . ."

"Which is of course me," Sykes said.

"And she did, and they flew somebody out here from the Reverend's office," Candy said. "And this was yesterday, when you were obviously totally out of town, and your Dad's office said your brother didn't have a phone, and that you were unreachable."

"LaVache and his stupid lymph node," muttered Lenore.

"But anyway the guy came and had a look, and I guess Vlad was just in incredible form, that day."

"As was of course meant from the beginning to be," said the Reverend.

"And but anyway the guy from 'Partners With God Club' saw him, and I guess just did a spiritual back-flip, and spasmed his way over to the phone, with Mrs. Tissaw like wringing her hands for joy beside him . . ."

"No need to embellish, Cindy," said Sykes, looking with annoyance over at Wang-Dang Lang, who was at the cage, poking at Vlad the Impaler through the bars with a section of Styrofoam cup, while Vlad eyed him beadily.

"And first the guy tried to call me, at work, to get me to try to call you, at Mrs. Tissaw's surprisingly considerate suggestion, but I guess they never could get through, because the phone-situation at F and V is still really biting the big wazoo . . ."

"Ahem," said Sykes.

"But obviously if you were phoneless I wouldn't have been able to reach you anyway, but anyway they tried, and then the guy of course called 'Partners With God Club' headquarters, and more or less told Father Sykes the story, and I guess they all decided old Vlad was much hotter stuff than just for 'Real Religious People' or whatever, and the Reverend hightailed it up here from Atlanta . . ."

"And the rest you can of course glean from what you see and feel here tonight," said Sykes. "So then, if you'll simply indicate to the bird its appointed lines, we can—"

"So it looks like Mrs. Tissaw is who I ought to talk to," Lenore said. "Because if she thinks she can just put a drugged bird on television, without even—"

"Drugged with the intoxicating overdue message of the very Lord Himself!" Sykes cried. Lang suddenly yelled as Vlad latched onto his finger. The sound-man rushed over to get him loose.

"So where is Mrs. Tissaw, is the big question," said Lenore. "Maybe I could grab a quick shower, and then she and I could just sit down, and—"

"Mrs. Tissaw is out shopping," Sykes beamed.

"Father Sykes's agent gave her a really disturbing amount of money, as like an advance," said Candy.

"We sow to reap, here in America," Sykes said, drawing the loudest affirmation yet from the technicians.

"She's out buying clothes, and girdles, and getting her hair tinted," Candy said. "She's getting ready to take Vlad the Impaler down to Atlanta with the Father."

"She's going to *what?*"

"The bird will be the first cohost in the history of the 'Partners With God Club'!" Sykes cried, pointing a finger at the ceiling. Lang, who was back by Candy with a Kleenex around his finger, looked up to see what Sykes was pointing at.

"Sow to reap!" shrieked Vlad the Impaler.

"Mrs. Tissaw says she gets the bird temporarily in return for the chewed wall, and damage from Vlad pooping on the floor, which she says is more damage than you can pay for," said Candy. "So she says she'll temporarily just take Vlad instead. Her husband's backing her up, just to get her out of town for a while, I think."

"The bird belongs to the ages, now," the Reverend said quietly.

"Not legally, though, if you guys want to have things get unpleasant," Candy said, putting her arm around Lenore, who continued to edge toward the door.

"Of course, Mrs. Simpson needn't come at all, if you wish as would be only natural to accompany the chosen vehicle yourself into the new epoch it's made possible," Sykes said to Lenore.

"Does this mean I don't get the apartment?" said Lang.

"Bathroom," Lenore squeaked faintly in Candy's ear.

"All contributing subscriptions are deductible! Like this!" said Vlad the Impaler.

"At last!" Sykes cried. He flew to the cage.

"Action!" yelled the director.

"Lay your sleeping head, my deductible love!"

"Miss Beaksman, hear the mandate!" thundered Sykes. The camera zoomed in, filling everything.

The hallway was cool and empty, after her room. Lenore wedged the bathroom door shut with the toe of a sneaker. She looked at the painted parrots on the shower curtain.

"You say one word, and there's going to be lunging like nobody's ever seen."

13 1990

"So you're upset, then."

"I think I'm too tired to be upset. I don't know why I'm so tired."

"Like your brother."

"Which brother? The one who's flapped all the time, or the anorexic one who we've had to watch go around the bend for years and now just disappears and is maybe dead for all I know? I just want to sleep. Just put your arm . . . like that. Thank you."

"I thought you said the thing with John was that he was so reluctant to be in any way involved with anything's death that he usually refused to eat, since every eating entails a death. That's not anorexia."

"It is, sort of, if you think about it."

"And that he had a horizontal proof of the indisputability of the proposition that one should never kill, for whatever reason."

"A diagonal proof."

"Diagonal proof."

"I guess."

"He . . . want it published, maybe?"

"I doubt he ever wrote it down, since that would involve paper, and so trees, et cetera."

"Quite a fellow. A certain nobility."

"I don't really even know him. He's like this stranger who drops in from Auschwitz every Christmas. He's also lately been very weirdly religious. He told me he wants to write this book arguing that Christianity is the universe's way of punishing itself, that what Christianity is, really, is the offer of an irresistible reward in exchange for an unperformable service."

"Obvious problems involved in actually writing the thing, of course."

"I think I'm even more worried about John than I am about Lenore."

"I certainly know one particular feathered animal I wouldn't mind him eating."

"That's not even a tiny bit funny, Rick."

"I'm sorry. To be honest, though, I think it will be good for you, to have the bird out of your hair, so to speak, until this nursing-home and thin-brother business gets cleared up."

"Poor Vlad the Impaler. All he ever wanted was a mirror and some food and a dish to go to the bathroom in."

"A dish he used with distressing infrequency, remember."

"I just can't believe Mrs. Tissaw was saying he'd done thousands of dollars of damage to the room. That's just a lie. She was standing there lying to me."

"She's clearly in some sort of religious ecstasy. People in religious ecstasies put live snakes in their mouths. Mate with the eyesockets of rotting skulls. Smear themselves with dung. Bird-damage delusions are small potatoes."

"I've never had a shower feel any better than that shower did."

"You must have been in there quite a while, for them to have time to spirit the bird away before you returned."

"No one spirited anyone away. They just had him down in a van. And actually I guess that was sort of good, because it at least in a way took the decision out of my hands, right then. So I didn't have to make any split-second decisions with those white-hot TV lights on me, which would have been spasm city."

"But you laid down the law that it's just for a month."

"Candy and I squeaked faintly that it's just for thirty shows as they all peeled away in their dumb vans, with the antennas. I told Mrs. Tissaw that if it's more than a month without my permission I'll take legal action. But I don't think she was too impressed."

"We will take action, if necessary. We can use that man F and V has on retainer. God knows he owes us some sort of work for his fee. Or I'll get us one on our own, and pay for it. The bird is after all legally mine, remember."

"What do you mean? You gave him to me for Christmas. I said

that was the best Christmas present I'd ever gotten, remember?"

" . . . . "

"And plus you hate Vlad the Impaler. You make that clear all the time."

"I'll admit I regret buying him for you. But, legally speaking, I have the receipt from Fuss 'n' Feathers pet shop. And, more to the point, as you may recall, on the relevant Christmas I did give you what you asked for, while you did *not* give me what *I* asked for. Had there been some sort of emotionally fulfilling Christmas exchange, that would have been one thing. As it was, it was one-sided. I never received my gift. Thus in some emotional dash legal deep sense the bird remains technically mine."

"You said you liked the beret I gave you."

"But it's not what I *asked* for."

"Look, we've been through this. I told you I just won't do that stuff. If you cared in any non-creepy way, you'd only want to do what I want to do. And I *don't* want to be tied up, and I'm *sure* not going to hit your bottom with any paddles. It's just sick."

"You don't understand. Any possible sickness is obviated by the motivation behind it, as I tried—"

"Incredibly dangerous territory, Rick. Let's abort."

"If you really loved me you'd let me."

"That's not even going to get dignified."

"You do love me."

"Let's not do this."

" . . . . "

" . . . . "

"Anyway, the point is that my emotional and economic and legal resources are behind you all the way. As it were. And don't think this has anything to do with any royalties. You can keep all the royalties Swaggert promised you, though I must say I think the figure's got to be a little inflated."

"Sykes."

"Sykes. He really wore white leather, with letters on the chest?"

"It would have been funny if it hadn't been so obscene. And I hated his cowboy boots."

"Footwear, again."

"And Lang was being incredibly obnoxious to Candy, I thought.

His tongue was swinging down around his knees, practically. God knows what all happened after we dropped him back off."

"Nothing she won't want to happen."

"You're mean. Anyway she's snagged the president of Allied Sausage Casings himself, now, she told me. Nick Allied. She finally bagged him, she said. She wore that violet dress about a week in a row. That dress is way too small for her."

"And of course when push comes to shove Lang is married, as well, to your—"

"The worst thing about the Vlad thing is going to be the embarrassment. The money, well I don't know what to think about any money-promises. But Sykes's career is going to be shot for sure when Dad and Neil Obstat come out with the pineal food and the talking business becomes clear and people make the connection that he's my bird, and I'm related to Dad. And eventually the police are just going to have to get called about Gramma, and the other residents and staff, and then there'll be newspapers. It's going to look like Sykes tried to put something over on all those poor people who like send his club their medicine money every week so they can be partners with God or whatever. It's going to look like I maybe helped him perpetrate a fraud."

"You tried to tell him, Lenore."

"It was totally impossible. He was incapable of listening. I'd mention the word 'father,' and off he'd go, stomping his foot and pointing his finger at the ceiling. And he had horrible breath. I think maybe the worst breath I've ever smelled, on anybody. He absolutely dwarfed Judith, who was the previous champion."

"I loathe Prietht."

". . . ."

"At least Lang got the room. He'll be of help to me."

"And you know I'm going to miss him. I liked bitching about his mirror with Candy. I didn't mind vacuuming his seeds and his gunk. And I really didn't even mind hearing him say obscene stuff. His talking was almost sort of nice."

"What are your thoughts on Lang, overall?"

"Although there was something cruel about it—it was almost like Gramma was being deliberately cruel. She got me all used to hearing her talk to me all the time . . ."

"He's not what we're used to, but I do feel affinities."

". . . and then off she goes, and takes off, and won't talk to me, but fixes it so that now Vlad talks to me, except all Vlad can really do is repeat what I say to him, and even that not too well . . ."

"Not precisely sure why I feel affinities, but I do. Two inside outsiders . . ."

". . . so that it's like I'm sort of talking to myself, alone, now, except even more so, because there's now this little feathered pseudo-myself outside me that constantly reminds me it's just myself I'm talking to, only."

"Except of course not anymore, now, right? Thanks to Mrs. Tissaw and the evangelist."

"I guess so."

"And what am I, Lenore, in terms of talking? Am I a mannequin? Am I a Bloemker-doll?"

"You know what I mean, Rick. I'm grateful for you. You know I am."

"So you do love me, then. I do have you, after all."

"You know I hate this 'having' stuff."

"So I'll settle for the fact that you love me."

"All right, you can settle for it."

"So you do love me."

"What did I just say?"

"What *did* you just say, Lenore? As usual I'm really not sure. I certainly didn't hear the word 'love' exit your mouth."

". . . ."

"Some words have to be explicitly uttered, Lenore. Only by actually uttering certain words does one really *do* what one *says*. 'Love' is one of those words, performative words. Some words can literally make things real."

"You and Gramma Lenore should get together, is who should get together. I'm sure she'd hit you with all the paddles you want. Bats, mallets, boards with nails in them . . ."

"For Christ's sake, Lenore."

"I do the best I can, Rick."

"So you do love me."

"I do the best I can."

"Meaning exactly what?"

" . . . . "

"So then why do you love me?"

"Oh, gee. I'd *really* rather not do this now."

"No, I'm serious, Lenore, why? On the basis of what? I need to know, so that I might try desperately to reinforce those features of me on the basis of which you love me. So that I can have you inside myself, for all time."

"You could just stop the having-talk, for one thing."

"Please, please. Oh, please."

" . . . . "

"I know I'm more than a little neurotic. I know I'm possessive. I know I'm fussy and vaguely effeminate. Largely without chin, neither tall nor strong, balding badly from the center out, so that I'm forced to wear a ridiculous beret—though of course a very nice beret, too."

" . . . . "

"And sexually intrinsically inadequate, Lenore, let's please both explicitly face it, for once. I cannot possibly satisfy you. We cannot unite. The Screen Door of Union is for me unenterable. All I can do is flail frantically at your outside. Only at your outside. I cannot be truly inside you, close enough only for the risk of pregnancy, not true fulfillment. Our being together must leave you feeling terribly empty. Not to mention of course more than a little messy."

" . . . . "

"So why, then? List the features on the basis of which you love me, and I will exercise them unmercifully, until they grow and swell to fill the field of your emotional sight."

"What is with you?"

"Please tell."

"Rick, I don't know. I think you and I maybe just have a different conception of this, you know, this 'love' thing."

" . . . . "

"I think for me there gets to be a sort of reversal, after a while, and then mostly things don't matter."

"Reversal? Explain, explain."

"This is embarrassing."

"Please."

"At first you maybe start to like some person on the basis of, you know, features of the person. The way they look, or the way they act, or if they're smart, or some combination or something. So in the beginning it's I guess what you call features of the person that make you feel certain ways about the person."

"Things are not looking at all good, here."

"But then if you get to where you, you know, love a person, everything sort of reverses. It's not that you love the person because of certain things about the person anymore; it's that you love the things about the person because you love the person. It kind of radiates out, instead of in. At least that's the way . . . oh, excuse me. That's the way it seems to me."

"Oh God. And that's what's happened with me? There's been the reversal?"

"Well Rick it's just dumb for you to go to like a features-gym and start exercising features. That's just dumb."

"So things have indeed reversed, then."

". . . ."

"Lenore?"

"Stop trying to *pin* me, Rick. I feel like a butterfly on a board."

"But if such a propensity-to-pin is a feature of me, then you must love that feature, if there's been the reversal."

"I guess I'm not saying it right. I'd really rather not do this now. I feel all public, saying this stuff."

"What about, for example, Lang? Do you suppose a Lang-love involves a reversal? Does a Lang ever stop loving on the basis of features and qualities?"

"*Especially* don't want to talk about him, OK?"

"Why not?"

". . . ."

"Don't just grit your teeth, tell me why not. It's vital that I know, and surely you see why."

"No, Rick, I don't."

"Why, if the reversal issue remains ambiguous, how am I to feel about you and me and, for instance, just to take an instance, Lang? For here we have, in Lang, a male creature surely far more worthy of love than I, features-wise, if we're to be objective. Tall, feet easily reaching bar-stool supports, wincingly handsome, easy, loose, mildly funny, widely travelled, wildly wealthy, muscular, intelligent, though in my perception not threateningly so . . ."

". . . ."

"And in uncountably many other respects features-love-deserving, Lenore. I've been in a men's room with the man. Do you hear me? I've been in a men's room with the man."

"I feel like bundling you into the car and rushing you to Dr. Jay's right this minute. I think new plateaus of spasmodic weirdness are being reached."

"I must know things, Lenore. You must begin to tell me things, or I will implode. I must know whether I have effected the reversal in you. I must know how Lang fits in."

"What does fitting in have to do with anything?"

"I must know. Lang doesn't even know whether you remember him or not. He expressed doubts and anxieties on the plane, to me, while you were into your twentieth consecutive hour of sleep."

"Oh I remember him all right. Don't worry about my not remembering him."

"So what's the problem?"

"I really just don't want to talk about it. What are you, trying to sell him to me or something? I just would rather not discuss it, and a feature I'd love to see in you right now would be your not wanting to discuss things I don't want to discuss."

"The next sound you hear will be that of implosion. Say I've effected the reversal in you, Lenore. Please."

"There a towel around here?"

"No showers, until you tell me things. I'll do something to the water main."

"Look, Lang's a big reason why I got my whole family really mad at me by not going to Mount Holyoke, OK? The time I visited, he and this other guy, with an adolescent, Amish, armpitty beard, came and barged in and banged their heads on the wall and made people sign on their bottoms, bare, and Lang practically molested Mindy Metalman on the spot."

"They're married, now, you know."

"I heard you two talking about it at the Aqua Vitae, Rick. I heard. I heard everything you guys said, when I wasn't busy keeping Stoney's head from plopping into his pizza."

"So there's been a reverse reversal with Lang. You anti-love him, in the face of all the features that seem to cry out for and necessitate love. And yet through the reversal you love a man approximately one twentieth the man he is . . ."

"You want to know what I really definitely don't love? I don't love this sick obsession with measuring, and demanding that things be said, and pinning, and having, and telling. It's all one big boiling spasm that makes me more than a little ill, not to mention depressed."

"So you don't love me, after all."

"Maybe I'll just go down to Atlanta and be with Vlad the Impaler and get my royalty checks while you soak your head for like the next month, OK?"

". . . ."

"What do you need him for, anyway? What's his function in all this?"

"Translation, I told you."

"Norslan herbicide stuff into idiomatic modern Greek? That makes no sense at all."

"Unfortunately, we're not always in control of the decisions on the basis of which business is conducted, life lived."

"How encouraging. But why him? You met him in a bar, is all. Cleveland must be crawling with actual Greeks, from Greece, if you want stuff translated."

"I'm really not sure why. There are affinities: Amherst, fraternity, the Scarsdale connection. But something . . . I simply felt . . . I don't know how to describe it. That was a strange day."

"You're making no sense at all."

"Please note that what we have here is an inability, rather than an unwillingness, to tell."

"I just think it will be weird to have him at Frequent and Vigorous. He's just going to add to the chaos. Walinda will be retroactively on the ceiling about my being gone, once you're upstairs, and plus Candy was dropping ominous hints about the phone situation."

"More than a hint-matter, I'm afraid. One of my tasks at the office while you and Lang were ostensibly settling in was to check phones. The story is not a happy one."

"What do you mean, 'ostensibly' settling in? Did I detect a tone?"

"I was referring to the unexpected and troubling Vlad matter."

"Oh."

" . . . "

"If poor Vern's been working double shifts to cover for me, he must not even have a stomach left. You really ought to hire somebody extra, at least to cover, at least while the phone deal is the same."

"From the payphone near the Cleaveland skeleton, I was in communication with a Mr. Sludgeman at Interactive Cable. He promises the very promptest possible action."

"I think it's possible to be prompter than eight days, which is what it's been. I don't see what kind of phone company lets all its tunnel people go off fishing or wherever just when there's a hideous tunnel problem. And that guy who looks like a negative, who refuses to do tunnels, and says tunnels are nerves, is about zero help."

"Mr. Sludgeman claims new avenues are being explored. Highly sensitive equipment is being rented, to be brought to bear on the tunnel below the Bombardini Building. Sludgeman alleges the locus of the problem has been identified as Erieview Plaza."

"Super. Just not at all thrilled about the prospect of answering Den of Pain calls for the next six months."

"Which brings us to the really central issue of the night."

"Rick, sleepiness is shooting out of every pore in my body."

"No chance you'd want to hear a story, then."

"Time just doesn't seem right, somehow."

"A number of interesting ones on my desk right now."

" . . . "

"For instance, a man is completely faithful to his wife, but only because he is impotent with all of the truly staggering number of women he tries to be unfaithful with, although he is not at all impotent with the wife. We're invited to speculate about whether he's a good man, or a bad man, deep down. Interested?"

"Not . . . pretty sleepy."

"You don't enjoy stories anymore?"

"That's not it. You do awesome . . . stories. I'm just either going to sleep or die, here."

"Well, you may or may not be interested to know . . ."

"Fffnoof."

". . . that I've had a not insignificant inspiration."

". . . ."

"Bearing directly on you."

"Fnoof."

"And so of course on me."

". . . ."

"What an anticlimax."

/a/

At the Frequent and Vigorous/Bombardini Company switchboard at 10 A.M. on Wednesday were Lenore Beadsman, Candy Mandible, Judith Prietht. Under the switchboard counter, with only his boots visible in the cubicle, was Peter Abbott. Just leaving was an anonymous delivery boy, having delivered to Lenore an enormous enclosing wreath of flowers, red-and-white roses arranged in an interlocking Yin and Yang. The wreath sat atop the switchboard wastebasket, being too big to fit inside. Definitely in the wastebasket, though, was the note that had come with the flowers: "Miss Beadsman. Time grows short. One way or the other you will be part of me."

There was just no way Lenore was going to sit in her chair with Peter Abbott right under her. She and Candy Mandible stood off, by the door to the cubicle, Candy smoking and making rings. Judith Prietht was frantic at the Bombardini Company board, but she did find time to keep darting looks over at Peter Abbott's boots as they jiggled with his mysterious efforts. Peter was apparently attaching something to the Frequent and Vigorous switchboard console. Something long and intricate, and expensive, Candy had said. He had had to shut off the F and V console temporarily, which was just fine by Lenore.

Candy was smoking a clove cigarette, which are particularly good for rings, and she also from time to time dropped ashes into the opened bloom of one of the Yin-blossoms. "He is rich, you know," she said to Lenore.

"That's not nearly funny," Lenore said, eyeing the flowers. "I'm thinking of maybe having Dr. Jay call the net people about him for me. At least he's too big to get down in here anymore. I think. I hope."

"Rich is not to be dismissed lightly, kiddo," said Candy. "You may not want to be Stonecipheco-rich, but you can still not mind richness per se."

"Is that why you're with Mr. Allied now? Is he going to take you away from all this?" Lenore laughed and gestured.

"Well, we haven't gotten past the just plain taking stage, yet." Candy gave a smoky laugh. "This is a real man, Lenore." She looked at her. "The world is turning out to be full of real, real men."

"What's that supposed to mean?"

Candy lowered her voice, and Lenore could see her pupils spread. "I don't know where you found that Lang guy, but good God."

"Don't want to hear about it." Lenore looked away, at the back of Judith's head, with a phone attached. "And anyway I'm possibly rich per se now, anyway, thanks to Vlad-royalties. We still need to talk at length about that, Candy. You're supposed to be my friend. Vlad the Impaler's friend."

"Vlad's probably got a cage entirely lined with full-length mirrors now. Vlad's probably in a state of constant bird-orgasm."

"Shit!" came Peter Abbott's voice from under the console counter.

"Gesundheit," Judith Prieht said among console-beeps.

"If things don't work out in a month, Rick and I are going to get him back legally," Lenore said. "Rick says he'll hire a lawyer. It turns out Vlad the Impaler is legally his, because he's got the receipt. He was being weird about Vlad last night."

Judith Prieht swiveled in her chair; she had hit her Position Busy button. "Listen, Lenore honey . . ." She blinked and smiled. "Can I call you Lenore?"

"I'm not too sure about Lenore *honey*, Judith," said Candy.

Lenore turned to Candy. "How come she's being so nice today?"

"She wants you to get her Hart Lee Sykes's autograph," Candy said, tapping ashes. "She's a God-Partner, apparently. Big time."

"If you wouldn't mind . . ." Judith started to croon.

"I'm hopefully not going to see Sykes again, Judith," said Lenore.

"But you could write him," Judith Prietht said. "You could call him, right from here, and I'd even pay for it if you wanted."

"Oh, you wouldn't have to—"

"And could you also ask him to . . . maybe to . . . ?" Judith looked imploringly at Candy Mandible.

Candy rolled her eyes. "She wants you to get him to say a blessing over a picture of her cat." Judith came out with a Polaroid and waved it at Lenore, as if Lenore were very far away.

"Judith, how about if I say I'll do what I can. Maybe I can get Rick to talk to him; he's going to deal with CBN people, he said." Lenore stared absently at the soles of Peter Abbott's boots.

Judith's Position Release button started flashing that flash that means there are just too many calls piling up. She Accessed and Started In and waded back, blowing a kiss to Lenore.

"We've found the way to her heart, at least," said Candy, making a fist to look at her nails.

Lenore was looking at Candy. "Listen," she said. "What did you mean good God about Lang? You guys didn't . . . ?"

Candy watched herself make and unmake a fist. "Yes and no," she said. "I mean I'm afraid yes we did, and did, and very definitely yes good God." She saw Lenore's look. "What can I tell you? I was bored, and Nick was meeting with supermarket chains, and he'll never know. But no we won't, probably, ever again, I don't think. First because Nick and I are really serious, and I think I've got a shot at richness per se, not to mention that Nick is almost a Lang, himself. Did Andy tell you his old college nickname, by the way?"

Lenore dug a bit of stone out of the tread of her sneaker.

"I died laughing," said Candy.

"Lang is rich per se himself, you might want to know," Lenore said. "His father owns a mammoth company in Texas. His father is supposedly more or less responsible for the G.O.D." She looked up at Candy. "And then what about Clint Roxbee-Cox? Clint must be insane with jealously, over you and Mr. Allied."

"Clint is admittedly not a happy man right now," Candy said, arranging things in her purse on the switchboard counter. "But he's a company man. And Nickie is the company. Clint told him he wishes us all the best, although Nick did say he didn't much care for the way Clint was looking at his throat when he said it."

"If you want to call Mr. Vigorous now, you can use my phone," Judith shot over.

"Well Judith I'm supposed to go up and see him after lunch, anyway," said Lenore. "He's getting Vern to come in for me this afternoon, for some unclear reason."

Candy looked over at the back of Judith's head, then at Lenore. "The thing is—" She put a hand on Lenore's arm and guided her into the line of Erieview shadow that creased the edge of the white cubicle. "The other reason why the Lang thing was just one night I think is that it was pretty darn clear he has his eye on somebody else, in a big way." She looked at Lenore.

Lenore looked at her own wrist, pretended to study it. "Listen, how did you snag Mr. Allied, anyway? You were in despair last week. I want to hear."

"He wants you, Lenore, really, is who he wants," Candy said, making sure that Judith couldn't be listening and then forcing Lenore to look her in the eye. "It was far too clear."

"*Really* don't want to go into it," Lenore muttered, looking out into the lobby.

"It was just incredibly obvious," said Candy. "He kept asking all about you, when we could talk. Talked about having met you once, how sorry he was about that, although I never got clear on just what he was sorry for and you're going to have to fill me in sometime, I'm dying to know. Kept talking about you and Rick, and laughing. Saying stuff about strategic misrepresentation, whatever that is. And even weirder stuff about how he noticed on the plane coming back that your leg wasn't at all like his leg, wasn't really even like a regular leg, at all, he said."

"That was a really leggy trip," Lenore laughed, edging for the cubicle door. "Listen, maybe I'll just go up and see Rick right now."

"Sweetie, it was just too obvious he thought he was using me," said Candy. "Not that we didn't have big fun. Not that Schwartz's room will ever be the same. But I could see how he thought he was trying to get at you through me. And he could do it, Lenore. You get me? He could literally get at you through me. You get me?"

"Ummm . . ."

"Rick just better be something entirely else, in his own right, is all I can say," said Candy.

Lenore looked at her. "Except I thought you said Mr. Allied was unattainable, hence part of the charm. I thought you said he was engaged to some Australian lady."

Candy laughed and drew on her cigarette, made an oval in the air and speared it. "I sense a sudden shift in the conversation. Well I just saw my big chance, is all. At a company party three days ago. Was it three? When you were in the Heights? I used Clint mercilessly to get to the executive side of the room. The violet dress came through. It got Nick, over hors d'oeuvres. The dress did it. He was helpless. The dress was awesome."

"You're awesome, is who's awesome."

"*Vidi, vici, veni*, is all I can say," said Candy. "Which is what you could say, too, with a really spectacular specimen, if you wanted. I'd think about it."

"Rick and I are supposed to be in love, you forget," Lenore said quietly, back at her wrist.

"What would Vlad the Impaler have to say to that, I wonder," said Candy. She put out her cigarette in the middle of Yang.

"What a bitch," Peter Abbott said, emerging stiffly from beneath the console.

"I beg your pardon?" said Candy.

"I'm gonna have some words for those tunnel drips when they get back, is all I can say," said Peter. He bent and with a grunt dragged an enormous box of exotic tools and cables and wires out from under the white counter. Began arranging items on the box's shelves.

"I hardly even dare to hope that you just fixed our lines," said Lenore. The console began to beep the minute Peter plugged it back in; Candy took the call.

Peter was hooking some things onto his belt. "What I've done here is to take the first step in Interactive Cable's plan to restore service and get you some satisfaction."

"He didn't fix anything," Candy shot over. "He just attached something weird and deeply Freudian to the underside of the console, so they can do a tunnel-test or something. In case you're in any doubt about the phones, I just talked to a Bambi's Den of Discipline customer wanting to know about inflatable dolls."

"Inflatable dolls?"

"The first step in a really expensive but ingenious plan Mr. Sludge-man came up with," Peter Abbott was continuing, bent over his box on the counter. "We're gonna do tunnel-tests. We're gonna test your tunnel like nobody's business."

"Big whiff," said Candy Mandible.

"Hey, lady, it is a big whiff," Peter said. "A really big and nasty whiff, if you're the one that's gotta do it. Try to imagine having to test a whole nervous system by trying to stick all sorts of shit in the nerves."

"You are really the master of the yummy image," said Lenore.

"Just tell your supervisor, that hen lady, so I don't have to tell her, 'cause she scares the stuffing right out of this guy," said Peter Abbott, jingling his belt nervously, "that what we're doin' is hooking all the consoles that utilize lines in your tunnel, the one under this building, hooking all the consoles into this network of testing cable, this cable that we're gonna feed into the tunnel, to test it. If it's one of the consoles that's infecting all the others, we're gonna know. If it's something in the tunnel infecting all you guys, we'll know. We're gonna like feel the tunnel's pulse."

"Feel the pulse of a nerve?"

"Testing's gonna hopefully start in a few days," Peter said, picking up the last of his things and hooking them onto his belt. Lenore bent and saw a brightly colored spaghetti of new wires leading down from the base of the console to a plug in the cubicle's floor. The wires pulsed with a strange sort of violet light.

"That stuff looks really hard to put in," she said to Peter.

Peter turned and stared into her eyes. Lenore looked back innocently. Peter sighed. "Yeah, it's a bitch. The tests can't start till I get all you guys hooked into the test circuit. It's a son of a bitch. I can only work so fast, and it's just me, and I'm only gettin' scale for it."

"Well, we certainly don't want to keep you," Candy said without looking up, handling a request for a wheel of Stilton.

"I'll see ya. I gotta go insert the exact same stuff over at Bambi's Den of Discipline now," Peter said, moving toward the door of the cubicle. "You take it easy."

"Happy inserting," said Candy. The jingle of Peter's belt receded.

"Peter, goodbye!" called Judith Prietht, sitting up a bit to get her head over the top of the cubicle. Peter was gone. The shadow in the huge lobby had almost seemed to move toward him to take him, Lenore saw.

"I'm going to talk to Rick about getting some smaller windows in this lobby," she said to Candy. "This shadow stuff is starting to really give me the creeps. I don't like the way the shadow is handling people's exits."

"You know who you have to talk to about the Building." Candy smiled, winked at Lenore, gestured at the flowered wreath on the wastebasket. "The big *fromage. El Grandé Yango.*"

"Not even potentially funny. Humor not even possible in that." Candy laughed and bent to the console.

/b/

"So is all clear, here?"

"No problem I can see, R.V."

"Can't possibly take more than two or three months."

"Less, if we haul ass."

"If this is ready for distribution by Thanksgiving we're supposedly in line for a mammoth bonus."

"Kick-ass."

"So then, no questions?"

"None I can see, except maybe who that skeleton guy is, out front."

"Who?"

"That skeleton guy, out front, in the sidewalk, under that mesh?"

"Oh. Well that's Moses Cleaveland, Andrew."

"Who?"

"General Moses Cleaveland, the founder of the city of Cleveland."

"The founder of the city?"

"Yes."

"With a 'Reserved Parking' sign sticking out of his eye?"

"What shall we say? Shall we say that reserved parking respects no man?"

"Say whatever you want. Just seems a tinch disrespectful, is all."

"Fits with the whole concept, then."

". . ."

/c/

8 September

Vance.

Is there any skin, any substance at all, softer than the cheek of a young child as it yields under a late-afternoon caress at the swimming pool? When the child is caped in a towel, thin calves emerging whitely and trailing away into feet with their temporary stains. The skin is so soft, all defenses, all color washed away, white as shell, loose, lips bright red tinged with blue, trembling; the child shivers, in the summer, at the pool, as the sun hints at becoming only implicit, and the hard-haired mothers stare without pity. And the trembling skin is almost translucent, new.

The pool gives birth to clean new red-eyed children, trembling in cotton capes, and then the slightest wetting of any part of the renewed white skin sends up into space a rebirth of the fragrance of rebirth, a clean that survives until the next bath. The new children are to kiss. And the red sun lowers to melt into the blue bath of clean chlorine, and the red-eyed children are lifted out and leave themselves in prints on the paved deck, shrinking. And suntan oil yields to the sterile scent of a new start, at the end of the day, always a new start. And, as with every newness, ears that pain, and eyes that sting and water.

"Lenore, where are you?" Fieldbinder wrote in his journal, a Batman notebook lifted from the toychest of his absent son. "Evelyn, where are you? Bring my Plain Dealer when you come."

I've had a look at the little bastard who apparently has Lenore's picture in his wallet. He is in the Stonecipheco staff directory sent me by the phenomenally thorough Mr. Rummage. This Obstat person, this person who went to high school with Lenore, and whose father was a force behind our absurd Desert and is now in Washington aspiring to some greater sillinesses; this young Obstat who is himself an improbable force behind this whole increasingly troubling Corfu-food project. I've had a look at him, here in the directory, and I feel ever so much better. Looks to be almost as short as I, and thin, eminently breakable, with watery colorless hair retreating from a head positively dominated and defined by the shape of the skull underneath. The skin stretched tight over that skull. A skull that seems to me perhaps even to threaten to burst through and end the whole charade. Yecch.

So a head the shape of a skull. And tiny little lifeless brown eyes, eyes like little anuses.

I have nothing to fear from an anus-eyed skull-head.

He and Lang are apparently lunching. He and Lang enjoy some sort of connection through Industrial Desert Design. Lang came close to insinuating that he had had congress with Mandible last night, this morning. I must approach him carefully on the subject of the reversal. My ears still hurt me, from the flight, and there are sounds when I swallow.

For once Fieldbinder was actually looking forward to seeing his pathetic psychologist, Dr. J_____, with his ridiculous moving chairs, the next day. Fieldbinder had been having a dream that was troubling him a lot. that was troubling him no end.

My father was a large, soft estate attorney who dressed exclusively in flannel in his off-hours. Broad and pale. With boots. And a small boy's persistent love for throwing stones into deep, empty places, and listening. He spanked. He was one of those parents who spanked. I never once laid an angry hand to Vance Vigorous's bottom. Maybe that is part of the trouble.

It is a windy day. Clouds scud. The wind whips at Lake Erie, the shaggy lake. My office window is sliced neatly in black. Half. In the lit half, the wind makes Lake Erie shaggy. In the shadow-half it all looks like rotten mayonnaise, there in the distance, squelching brown and white between the pudgy fingers of the wind. What a hideous view.

And where on earth does Norman Bombardini get off putting a sign through the eye of the founder of Cleveland?

Ten minutes, at the outside. I'll simply keep time on the wall of my office. When the shadow reaches the diploma, she will be here.

/d/

"Is this place great or what?" Neil Obstat, Jr. was saying to Wang-Dang Lang. "Just wait. The bartender sticks his thumb in his eye once an hour. It's in his contract."

"And look at the gazongas on that Ginger," Lang said, tilting his beer bottle. "Never seen any shit like this."

"We can come back here tonight," said Obstat. "They've got even wilder shit at night. Cleveland at night can get pretty wild." He sucked at his Twizzler. "Cleveland gets underrated. You guys in the East forget that significant cultural stuff goes on in the Midwest."

"Nothing insignificant about those gazongas, I'll tell you that right now."

Lang and Obstat were in Gilligan's Isle. It was almost lunchtime. This was lunch. Lang had spent the morning with Rick Vigorous, determining that he would be able to do all his translation work in a week, if he worked at all hard. Lang was looking forward to the next three months. He'd been given the rest of the day off. He'd called Neil Obstat the minute he'd happened to see Rick Vigorous staring at Obstat's picture in some of the material from Stone-cipheco.

"I can't get over seeing you again, and here in Cleveland," Obstat was saying. They were at the Professor's thumb. "And you say you're not in deserts anymore."

"Temporarily."

"Temporarily. You've been doing accounting? Just can't see you as an accountant, big guy."

"The story behind that has to do with this girl who was just such hot shit that I let her run the show, for a bit of time," Lang said, crossing and uncrossing his legs on the plastic bench.

"Not Lenore Beadsman."

"No, course not Lenore Beadsman." Lang signalled for another beer, and the bartender over there in his white hat gave him a thumbs-up. "My wife," Lang said to Obstat. "The girl who's my wife."

"Really hot, huh?"

"Don't want to talk about it."

"Sure." Obstat sipped his Twizzler. "But you mentioned something about Lenore Beadsman, when you called."

"Did I?"

"Positive."

"Huh. Well she works at the place I'm workin' at, translating your wild shit for you."

"Stuff is wild, isn't it?" Obstat squirmed on his seat. "Boy I'm excited, is all I can say. This is the sort of thing a corporate chemist just dreams of. I thought I'd be spending all my time testing pH levels in creamed fruit."

"I just can't believe the shit works. Does it really work at all like y'all are havin' us say in this ad?"

"Really looks like it does, guy. The Chief has been ga-ga for months. Kids are talking months, maybe years before they would have, in limited tests. We're talking not only eventual market domination, but a potentially really significant insight into the relation between nutrition and mental development, between what the body needs and the mind can do."

The bartender, coming over with Lang's fourth beer, slipped on a strategically placed maraschino cherry and pitched headlong into Ginger's chest. He missed his eye with his thumb, but did manage to crack his head nastily on the plastic table. Beer flew everywhere.

Obstat laughed and clapped with everyone else, "Aww, Gilligan." He bent and quickly tied the bartender's shoelaces together.

"What about my beer?" Lang was saying.

"Coming right up," the bartender murmured. He was on his feet and moving when the shoelaces got him. He somersaulted into and off of Mrs. Howell's hair, ending up draped over her pince-nez.

Obstat giggled.

"Immature fucker," Lang grinned.

"Got to get into the spirit of the place."

Lang sucked off the last bit of beer in his bottle. "But you say you do know this Beadsman girl, then," he said to Obstat.

Obstat got serious. "Do I ever," he said. "I went to high school with her, when we were kids. I've had a crush since I was this high. She's maybe even a reason why I went to work for Stonecipheco. Unconscious or something. Except I had no idea she didn't like her Dad and didn't want to go into the Company. I'm pissed. I only got to see her in person again the other day, when we were all in the Chief's office. The Chief is her Dad. And one of their relatives got us going on the whole pineal project, and now she's trying to rip us off. But I can still pull it off. Except I think Lenore's frigid. I made a bit of a dick of myself over her in school, and I was going for heavy eye contact, in the Chief's office. But she always just looked right through me. I think she's frigid."

Lang accepted another beer without looking up. "But hot, though, too."

Obstat fingered his tie. "Don't know what it is about her, Wanger. The girl's just always slayed me. The way she dresses, the not incidental gazonga factor. And her legs. The single most out-of-this-world pair of legs I've ever laid eyes on."

"I was noticin' those legs," Lang said, nodding.

"I've had this wild fantasy, for who knows how long, about doing her out in the G.O.D.," Obstat said, looking faraway. He looked back at Lang and blushed a bit. "You been back out there, lately, at all? I've been dying to go. I still remember when we planted cacti."

"We can go any time you want," said Lang. "I'm gonna buy some sort of car for out here tomorrow, I decided. Lenore's little boyfriend's paying me like the money hurt his hand."

"Boyfriend?"

"This guy named Vigorous, owns the firm we're at, or at least part of it." Lang looked off over Obstat's shoulder, at the Skipper.

"I remember the Chief saying something to her about a Vigorous, in his office," Obstat said, narrowing his little brown eyes. He dug at his Twizzler's plastic pineapple jug with a straw.

"He's a interesting little dung beetle. Doublest chin I ever did see on a human being." Lang drank deeply. "How'd he get hold of Lenore, I wonder, if she's so all-fired hot as you say."

"There is no God in the universe, Wang-Dang," Obstat said, shaking his big head.

"So I keep getting told. Even though the girl herself owns this wild-ass bird that's gonna be on religious TV, with padre Sykes, who's my own personal Daddy's favorite." Lang held up a bandaged finger. "Little Fucker damn near took my digit off, yesterday."

"You were at Lenore's house, with her bird?"

Lang stared silently at Obstat.

"Well, we know all about the bird thing," Obstat said, looking away and shaking his head. "We're shitting all kinds of different bricks over that one. We think what happened was this relative who got us going on the project slipped the thing a pineal mickey. Which means maybe they're going around slipping it all over the place. Which means other companies could get hold of it. Which has the Chief shitting bricks, believe you me—that along with the fact that the retards in Jars have made something like three times as many jars as we need, or have lids for, even, so the Chief has to try to sell some jars to this chain of medical laboratories, and he's—"

"This crap can make animals talk?" Lang interrupted.

"Well, our understanding is the bird doesn't talk, so much as just repeat."

". . . remember Candy did say something about that."

"Who?"

"They got peanuts in this bar, at all?" Lang said. They both looked around. "What kind of self-respectin' bar doesn't have peanuts?"

"Coconut I know they've got. It's a mood place."

"Shit on fire."

"But anyway we don't really know what it can do. You ought to hear some of these kids. They can sing like birds."

"Some joke."

"No pun intended."

Lang stared absently into Ginger's décolletage. "So she's hot, then, and things with her Daddy aren't too good."

"My impression is they aren't close at all."

"Uh-huh."

"Listen, you want to see a picture of her?" Obstat dug for his wallet in the back pocket of his Chinos.

"I know what she looks like," Lang said. Then he looked up at Obstat in surprise. "You carry her picture?"

"The little lady has smitten me from afar, since way back who knows when," Obstat said, shaking his head and flipping through his credit cards. "I admit it's a pitiful situation."

"This an old picture you got?"

"High school yearbook."

"Give it here, then."

Obstat handed over the little wallet photo. In the picture Lenore was sixteen. Her hair was very long. She was smiling broadly, looking off into the nothing reserved especially for yearbook photos.

Lang stared down at the picture. He brushed away a bit of beer foam from the border with a thumb. Lenore smiled at him, through him.

"Looks to be her, all right."

Obstat was bouncing up and down in his seat. "Listen, stay a few more minutes. It'll be time for another gag in a while. And have a look at that one over there, at Mary-Ann, with the little guy in the beard and steamed glasses. Looks a little spacey, but talk about your basic gazongas."

Lang kept looking at the photo. He seemed to be about to say something.

/e/

"Maybe even inclined to say big mistake here, Rick."

"Don't be silly. It's an absolute inspiration. I was positively writhing with excitement at the prospect of telling you, last night. And then of course you conked out. Again."

"But I like the switchboard. You know that. And it even looks like the lines are going to get fixed soon. They're going to do tests."

"Lenore, you are in a position to do me a favor. Actually to help both of us, I think. This will be deeply interesting, I promise. I've seen that you're chafing, at the switchboard, deep down."

"Beg pardon?"

"You can save me valuable weeding-time."

"How can Norslan translations take so much time? That's not a long thing."

". . . ."

"And what's with the light in here right now? This is creepy."

"Frigging shadow . . ."

"We need to have a serious talk about the windows in the lobby, too, mister. I'm starting not to care one bit for the way the—"

"Come here a moment. See the way the lake looks like rotten mayonnaise in the shadow-half of the window? Doesn't that look like rotten mayonnaise?"

"Oh, that's just sick."

"But doesn't it?"

"It really does."

"I thought so."

"OK, so what does this involve, then?"

"What?"

"This hopefully very temporary *Review* job."

"It simply involves screening a portion of the back submissions to the quarterly, for a time, the time I'm to be frantically busy with the herbicide thing. You'll be weeding out the more obviously pathetic or inappropriate submissions, and putting asterisks on those that strike you as meriting particular attention and consideration on my part."

"Hmm."

"We'll need to make sure your tastes are keened to the proper pitch for our particular publication, of course . . ."

"You're going to keen the pitch of my tastes?"

"Relax. I'm simply going to have you read briefly through a batch I've already exposed myself to, and we'll just see what happens, taste-pitch-wise. You'll be having a preliminary look at . . . these."

"All those are submissions?"

"I shall say that most are. Some few might for all you know have been sent to me by friends for scrutiny and criticism. But I've effaced all names."

"So it's not all just troubled-college-student stuff?"

"The bulk of it is, to my ever-increasing irritation and distress. But the average collegiate material you should be able to spot a mile off."

"How come?"

"Oh, dear, many reasons."

" . . . "

"What shall we say? Perhaps that it tends to be hideously self-conscious. Mordantly cynical. Or, if not mordantly cynical, then simperingly naive. Or at any rate consistently, off-puttingly pretentious. Not to mention abysmally typed, of course."

" . . . "

"It tries too hard, is really all we can say about most of it. There is simply an overwhelming sense of trying too hard. My, you're looking particularly lovely in this half of the light."

"Rick, how am I supposed to know if something's mordant, or simpering? I don't know anything about literature."

"A, the vast majority of the material that passes through here is not even potentially literature, and b, good!"

"What's good?"

"That you 'know nothing about literature,' or at least believe that you don't. It means you're perfect: fresh, intuitive, shaking the aesthetic chaff out of your hair . . ."

"There's something in my hair?"

"It's when people begin to fancy that they actually know something about literature that they cease to be literarily interesting, or even of any use to those who are. You're perfect, take it from me."

"I don't know . . ."

"Lenore, what's with you? Isn't this the person who sees herself as almost by definition a word person? Who snarls when her literary sensibility is even potentially impugned?"

"I just want to try to keep my personal life and my job as separate as I can. I don't need Walinda going around saying I got a cushy deal because of you."

"But here's your chance to be out of Walinda-range for whole periods of time."

"And plus, Rick, I just have a bad feeling about the whole thing."

"Trust me. Help me. Look, let's take a couple of examples. How about this pathetically typed little item right here? Why don't you just read the very first bit of it, here, and we'll . . ."

"This one?"

"Yes."

"Let's see: 'Dr. Rudolph Carp, one of the world's leading proctologists, was doing a standard exam one warm July morning when he suddenly remembered that he had forgotten to put on an examination glove. He looked down with horror at . . .'—oh, gak."

"Gak indeed. Material like this can simply immediately be put in the rejection pile, on Mavis's desk, and she will Xerox a terse little rejection slip to go with the returned manuscript."

"What's with these titles? 'Dance of the Insecure'? 'To the Mall'? 'Threnody Jones and the Goat from Below'? 'The Enema Bandit and the Cosmic Buzzer'? 'Love'? 'A Metamorphosis for the Eighties'?"

"That last one is actually rather interesting. A Kafka parody, though sensitively done. Self-loathing-in-the-midst-of-adulation piece. Collegiate, but interesting."

" 'As Greg Sampson awoke one morning from uneasy dreams, he discovered that he had been transformed into a rock star. He gazed down at his red, as it were leather-clad, chest, the top of which was sprinkled with sequins and covered with a Fender guitar strapped tightly across his leather shoulders. It was no dream.' Hmmm."

"Read it over at your leisure. There are some interesting ones. There's one about a family trying to decide whether to have the grandmother's gangrenous feet amputated—you should vibrate sympathetically with that one. There's one about a boy who puts himself through prep school selling copies of the *Physicians' Desk Reference* in the halls. One about a woman who hires herself out at exorbitant rates as a professional worrier and griever for the sick and dying . . ."

" 'Elroy's problem was that he had a tender pimple, on his forehead, right in the spot where his forehead creased when he looked surprised, which was often.' Gak. Rejection. 'So it finally happened. Bob Kelly, busy checking out the rear end of his neighbor Mrs. Ernst as she bent to retrieve a mitten, ran over his son, Miles, with the snowblower.' Double gak. Double rejection."

"Like those instincts, kiddo."

" 'Santo Longine, having learned to shift with a cigarette in his hand, now smoked while he drove.' 'The morning that Monroe Fieldbinder came next door to the Slotniks' to discuss Mr. Costigan was a soft warm Sunday morning in May.' These seem prima facie OK."

"Why not start with those. Why not go ahead and start with

those—start with that last one. Read through about half the stack . . . like so. You can use Mavis's desk until her return from lunch, then you can come in here. I have to run to the typesetter's this afternoon, and I may be gone for some time. You can have free rein."

"This one looks sort of interesting, at least potentially. At least it's not overtly sick."

"Which one?"

" . . . ."

"Just see what you think. Go with your feelings, is the vital thing."

"Do I get switchboard scale for this?"

"Readers make ten dollars an hour."

"I'll just be outside, reading."

"Have things reversed, Lenore?"

"Hmmm?"

"Nothing. Go. Have fun. Be intuitive."

" . . . ."

/f/

"Come in."

"Good heavens."

"Come down."

"Dear me."

"This way."

"I've got to confess, I thought this was some sort of joke at—"

"It wasn't. It isn't."

"My God, it's boiling in here. How do you people live? And how am I to walk?"

"Bent over. This way. Hunch your shoulders."

"Lord."

"You notice I'm not complaining. We all bend this way naturally. Mrs. Beadsman told me to tell you that as space is bending you now, so time has bent us."

" . . . ."

"The pain of which you have no idea, God willing. God forbid you should ever be in our state."

"Rather hope to be in just your state, actually, at some point in the very distant future. Otherwise I . . . Ow! Otherwise I expect I'll be even worse off—specifically dead."

"Well now that's a very interesting point, which you can take up with Mrs. Beadsman."

"Am I perhaps going to have a chance to speak to Mrs. Beadsman, then?"

"No."

"Mrs. Yingst!"

"Hello, Dr. Jay."

"Well, I must say it seemed difficult to conceive of, but this is —"

"Cut the guano."

". . . cozy, I must—"

"Here are the sessions' transcripts back. Here is your money. Lenore instructs me to tell you you're doing a competent job."

"Competent?"

"That's what she said."

"And how long is this to go on? This is eventually going to kill her. You people and I are killing a person from the inside out."

"That's exactly wrong. It's we who are keeping her alive. Can't you read? You're even more of an idiot than Lenore maintains."

"I refuse to submit to this sort of abuse, madam. I am a distinguished professional, a graduate of Harvard University, a respected member of—"

"You're a pathetic phobic neurotic whom Lenore used her influence to rescue from institutional commitment by your wife, who if you recall objected to being scrubbed with antiseptic every night before bed. We set you up and keep you in soap and peroxide and deodorant. You'll do what Lenore tells you to do for precisely as long as you're needed."

"But this simply cannot keep on indefinitely. The Vigorous aspect, especially. He's the real problem. Spoken things anger him beyond belief, and I know he's eventually—"

"Lenore instructs me to instruct you simply to take care of Mr. Vigorous vis à vis Lenore. He's getting on everyone's nerves. Do it. You'll find some material here on a person who—"

"Listen, though. This will only make it worse. He's going to want to read something by Blentner. He's a reader. He's going to want to lay eyes on Blentner's actual texts. And he'll ask me for them, and he'll find out that there is no Blentner, and then what am I to say?"

"There can be a Blentner if you want there to be, if you need there to be."

"How's that?"

"You'll write something, you ninny. You'll make something up and attach a name to it. What could be simpler? Are you completely dense?"

"Really, I see no need for this sort of—"

"Take your money and go. Here is the material on Vigorous. Go away."

"Do you two notice anything smelling the tiniest bit peculiar down here? I—"

"Take your nostrils and go."

"How am I to turn around? It's too cramped to turn around."

"Back up. Go backwards. Mrs. Lindenbaum will help you."

"This way, dear."

"Good God."

LOVE

The morning that Monroe Fieldbinder came next door to the Slot-niks' to discuss Mr. Costigan was a soft warm Sunday morning in May. Fieldbinder moved up the Slotniks' rough red brick front walk, through some damp unraked clippings from yesterday's first-of-the-season bagless mow, and prepared to press their lighted doorbell, one with a "Full Housepower" decal beneath it, just like the former decal on Fieldbinder's former home, and then paused for just a moment to extract a bit of grass from his pant cuff.

The Slotniks sat in their dining room, in robes and leather slippers and woolly footmuffs, amid plates with bits of French-toast scraps loose and heavy with absorbed syrup, reading the Sunday paper, with maple stickiness at thumbs and mouth-corners.

The melody of the Slotniks' doorbell took time. It was still playing when Evelyn Slotnik opened the front door. Fieldbinder stood on the stoop. Evelyn's hands went involuntarily to her hair, her eyes to her feet, in woolly footmuffs, beneath unshaved ankles. And then context came in, and she looked away from herself, at Fieldbinder.

Fieldbinder was dressed to harm, in a light English raincoat and razor slacks, black shoes, subway shine. There was a briefcase. Evelyn Slotnik stared at him. All this took only a second. There was a sound of the newspaper from back in the dining room.

"Good morning Evelyn," Fieldbinder said cheerily.

"Monroe," said Evelyn.

When some more seconds passed during which Fieldbinder still stood outside, smelling the inside of the Slotniks' home, he smiled again and repeated, louder, "Good morning, Evelyn. Hope I'm not . . ."

"Well come in," Evelyn said, a little loud. She opened the door wider and stepped back. Fieldbinder wiped off the last of the dewy lawn clippings onto Donald Slotnik's joke of a welcome mat, that read GO AWAY, and came in.

"Come on in, Monroe," Evelyn was babbling, even louder. Her puffy eyes were wide and confused on Fieldbinder's. "He's *home*," she mouthed.

Fieldbinder smiled and nodded at Evelyn. "By any chance is Donald home," he said loudly. "I'm sorry to intrude. I need to speak to you and Donald."

From farther in, there was a chair-sound. Donald Slotnik came into the living room, where Evelyn and Fieldbinder stood, looking past each other. Evelyn manipulated the belt of her robe. Donald Slotnik wore some sort of shiny oriental wrap over his pajamas. He had leather slippers, and the sports page, and a cowlick. From the dining room came the rustle of funnies, to which Scott Slotnik was applying Silly Putty.

"Monroe," said Slotnik.

"Hello Donald," said Fieldbinder.

"Well hello," Slotnik said. He looked at Evelyn, then back at Fieldbinder, then at the easy chair Fieldbinder stood next to. "Please, have a seat, I suppose. You'll have to excuse us, as you can see we weren't really expecting anyone."

Fieldbinder shook his head and raised a stop-palm at Slotnik. "Not at all. I'm the one who should apologize. Here I am, barging on a Sunday morning. I apologize."

"Not at all," Slotnik said, looking at Evelyn, who had her hands in the pockets of her robe.

"I'm here only because I really felt I should talk to you," Fieldbinder said. "I felt a need to talk to you both. Now." One of Evelyn's hands was now at her collar.

"Well all right then, sure," said Slotnik. "Let's all have a seat. Honey, maybe Monroe would like some coffee."

"No thanks, no coffee for me," said Fieldbinder, taking off his coat, which Slotnik didn't offer to hang up for him, and folding it onto the arm of his chair.

"Well I'd like some more," Slotnik said to Evelyn. She went into the dining room. Fieldbinder heard Scott say something to her.

Slotnik sat on the love seat across from the living room window and Fieldbinder's chair and crossed his legs, so that one leather slipper threatened to fall off. Fieldbinder refused to believe he saw tiny ducks on Slotnik's pajamas.

"So," Slotnik said. "How are Estates?"

"Estates are fine. How are Taxes?"

"Taxes are one hell of a lot better than they were two months ago. Returns are all in, the worst of the post-deadline bitching is petering out . . . thanks, honey." Slotnik took a sip from a mug of coffee and put it on the coffee table in front of him. Evelyn sank into the little gap next to Slotnik on the love seat, opposite Fieldbinder. "You remember how seasonal Taxes tends to be," Slotnik continued, smacking his lips a little over the coffee in his mouth. Slotnik had always struck Fieldbinder as the sort of man who enjoyed the taste of his own saliva.

"I remember all too well." Fieldbinder smiled at Slotnik. "Fred's not riding you too hard over there, is he?"

"Not at all. Not at all. Fred and I get along well. We played tennis just yesterday. Fred's a fine man."

"Fred rode us hard."

"Maybe he's mellowing."

"Could be."

The silence that followed was broken only by the sound of Scott doing something to a dish in the kitchen sink.

"So," said Fieldbinder. "The reason I'm here. I was just next door, at Mr. Costigan's. Been there since early this morning. Trying to do some inventory work, following through, item-reference, et cetera." He looked at Slotnik. "You did know Costigan was a client."

"Sure, poor guy," Slotnik said, reaching for his coffee. "We helped him set up a little municipal bond shelter just last year. A good, tight little shelter. The man needed protection. Poor guy'll never get to enjoy any of the advantages, now."

"Right," said Fieldbinder. "Well, Alan put me on his estate."

"Really. Well we wondered who'd be doing it. We've had a look across, over the fence, to see if we saw anybody. Fred didn't know who Estates was going to put on it."

"Well, you're looking at him." Fieldbinder looked at Evelyn Slotnik and smiled. She smiled back.

Then her smile turned upside down and her hand went back to her collar. "Such an awful thing to happen to somebody," she said. "We were so upset. We were stunned, really, is what we were. So scary that something in a person's head can just . . . pop, like a balloon, at any minute, and you're gone. Veronica Frick two houses over told me he'd never had any sort of health problem before, at all, ever. It's just so scary." She snuggled in farther under Slotnik's arm.

"He was an old man, honey," Slotnik said, trying to keep Evelyn's snuggling from spilling the mug of coffee in his hand. "These things happen. How old was he, Monroe?"

"He was fifty-eight," Fieldbinder said.

"Oh."

"Neither of us could get over to the service," Evelyn said. "Donald was swamped at the office, and Scott was home sick with a sore throat. We sent flowers, though."

"Nice of you."

"Not at all," Slotnik said. "He was a good neighbor. Quiet, took care of his place, let the kids play ball in his yard. Sometimes when we were going out of town he'd offer to come over, take in the mail, water the plants. We liked him."

"Sounds like a nice man."

"He was," said Evelyn.

There was a moment of silence. Slotnik cleared his throat. "So then how's his estate?" he asked.

"Relatively trouble-free, although I'm just starting." Fieldbinder smiled and shook his head. "Not a problem at all, really. I'm only working on it today because I'm so behind in general, what with the house thing last week, and insurance people to deal with, fire department, red tape, et cetera."

"Hey, listen, damn sorry to hear about that, Monroe," Slotnik said. "That must have been a wrench. We didn't want to bring it up unless you did, right honey? We thought you'd be upset, tired of talking about it."

"It was just a house," Fieldbinder said. "All my important papers were at the office. And lawyers tend to be insured to the hilt, as you doubtless know." They all laughed. Fieldbinder looked at Evelyn. "I am sorry about my bird, though."

"You had a bird?" Slotnik said.

"Yes. A lovely one. I could feed her off my finger."

"Too bad," Slotnik said, scratching his neck.

"Yes."

"Yes."

There was more silence. Slotnik sipped coffee around Evelyn. Evelyn seemed to be looking at everything in the living room except Fieldbinder. The ducks on Slotnik's pajamas looked to be mallards.

"How are the kids?" Fieldbinder asked.

Evelyn cleared her throat. "The kids are fine. Steven has final exams right now, along with baseball, so he's busy. Scott's had a cold, but he's better now."

"They around?"

"Scott was up for breakfast, believe it or not," Slotnik said. "Scott?" he called. There was no answer. "He must have gone out back."

"Steve's still asleep," Evelyn said. "He's pitching this afternoon, Donald says."

"Damn right," Slotnik said. "When your dad's the coach, and you've got an arm like that kid's got on him, you get to pitch sometimes."

"Well, good," Fieldbinder said.

"Right."

"Right."

Slotnik put down his mug. "So you said you wanted to talk to us."

"Yes," Fieldbinder said. Evelyn was staring out the big living room window at the bright green front lawn.

Slotnik looked as if he would have glanced at his watch, had he been wearing one. "So?" he said.

"So you didn't know Mr. Costigan all that well, then, is the sense I get."

"We were neighbors. We knew him fairly well for a neighbor. We spoke over the fence. You know how it is."

"Sure," Fieldbinder said. He looked at his hands, in his lap. "How about the kids. Kids know him well?"

Slotnik's forehead became a puzzled forehead.

Evelyn cleared her throat again. "No," she said. "Well, not any better than we did. They played in his yard, sometimes, when things overflowed from ours. We agreed to make the fence only between the houses, not the yards. He was nice about that. He obviously liked children. The kids liked him, I know, because he gave really good Halloween treats. Giant Hershey bars, that they couldn't even eat all at once. He was nice, but he kept to himself."

"As a good neighbor should," Slotnik said.

"I don't think the kids knew him any better than we did."

"Especially Steve, I'm wondering about," Fieldbinder said.

Slotnik's forehead got worse. "Well, no, Monroe. What exactly seems to be the problem?"

Fieldbinder sniffed and reached down and popped his briefcase latches. He brought out a large photograph and handed it over the coffee table to Evelyn, all the time looking at Slotnik.

The photo was a color shot of a boy walking up the Slotniks' brick walk, toward the front door, with a backpack over his shoulder. The boy was about thirteen, healthy, rather big and strong for the age of his face. He had short, dull-blond hair. The photo looked to have been taken from a distance. There were some maple trees in the way of the shot, partly. Fieldbinder himself could make out maple-leaf shapes.

"Now as I recall that's Steve," he said. "Right?"

The Slotniks looked up from the photo. "Yes."

"What happened was I got it out of a room in Mr. Costigan's house," Fieldbinder said. He folded his hands in his lap. "Pretty clearly taken from over there, too, up high, with the maples out over the fence in the way." He gestured through a side window above Evelyn's head at some maple trees leaning over the fence, their new leaves looking extra green in the morning light. "Taken with a hell of a strong lens, too, as you can see. See the detail on Steve? Costigan had some really nice equipment."

"Okay," Slotnik said slowly. He made no move to give the photo back to Fieldbinder. "But I'm not sure I understand. We didn't know Costigan was a photographer, but so what? It's a good picture, you can see."

"Yes. It is," Fieldbinder said. He did something to a pant-leg.

"So are the literally hundreds of other pictures of Steve I found in this particular room in the guy's house."

The Slotniks looked at Fieldbinder.

"Which pictures themselves were not all that hard to find," Fieldbinder continued, "seeing as how this particular room in the house was wall-papered with them."

Slotnik put down his mug again.

"And I mean floor to ceiling, Don." Fieldbinder looked at Slotnik. Slotnik looked at Evelyn.

"Also in this room"—Fieldbinder cleared his throat—"this room on the second floor, with a window directly out of which I could see across the fence into a window in your home, a window with a 'Go Phillies!' pennant hanging in it, a window I'm going to assume, unless you tell me differently, is Steve's . . ." He looked at Slotnik, who said nothing. Fieldbinder sniffed. "Also in this room were" — he ticked off with his fingers—"who knows how many sketches, in charcoal and pencil, and some oils, really quite good, of someone who looks like . . . no, quite obviously *is* Steve. Some equally quite good pieces of sculpture, in varied media, I couldn't really tell, but again with just Steve as the subject, as far as I could see. Also some sort of video recorder set-up that's rigged rather ingeniously to play a continuing loop of a certain tape, a tape of some games of football in your yard, in Costigan's yard, of Steve raking some leaves, of Steve mowing the lawn, of Steve and Scott making a snowman, using what looked to me like a frozen sock for the thing's nose. Sound familiar?" Fieldbinder looked up at the Slotniks. "Also some . . . items, in a sort of very solid and expensive wooden box, that looks to me like a jewelry box, and is at any rate listed on Costigan's personal-assets sheet as an antique."

"Just what sort of items?"

"Now you said Costigan would take care of your house when you were away."

"Only sometimes," Evelyn said. "Usually Mrs. Frick . . ."

Slotnik ignored her. "What sort of items, Monroe?"

Fieldbinder made a bland face. "A few baseball cards. Some strands of hair, light hair, glued to an index card. A Popsicle stick, from an orange Popsicle. A couple of . . . Kleenex." He looked at

Evelyn. "There was a tee-shirt, a white tee-shirt, Fruit of the Loom. Very neatly pressed, folded, but not laundered. An unclean tee-shirt. And tagged, with a date, sometime in August of last year."

Evelyn twisted toward Slotnik. "When we were at the Cape."

"Can you remember Steve maybe ever losing some clothes?" Fieldbinder said.

"Oh, he's *always* losing things—they both are. You know how children are." Evelyn almost started to smile.

"No," Fieldbinder leaned forward in his chair, "the thing is, I really don't."

"What do you mean did Steve ever lose *some* clothes," Slotnik said.

"Well Don the thing is that the tee-shirt wasn't the only . . . Fruit of the Loom item in Costigan's box."

"What the hell does that mean?"

"Basically it means size twenty-eight briefs, Don." Fieldbinder looked at Evelyn, whose eyes were no longer quite focused. He took a tiny wrinkle out of the crease in his slacks with a thumbnail and refolded his hands in his lap. He looked back at Slotnik.

Slotnik stared into the air in front of him for a moment, trying to smooth his cowlick, which sprang right back up again. "I'm going to call the police," he said quietly.

Fieldbinder made a wry smile. "Well, now, Don, and have them do what?"

Slotnik looked at Fieldbinder.

"Maybe what we should do first, if you want my opinion," said Fieldbinder, "is have you two try to remember if there might have been any occasions when anything could have possibly happened." He looked at the Slotniks. "Anything even remotely bad."

Slotnik looked at the coffee table.

"Is Steve ever here alone? Without one of you around?"

"Neither of them, no, never without a sitter," Slotnik said firmly. "And if they're out, they're either with us, or at school, or with friends, or we know exactly where they are."

"That's what I figured." Fieldbinder bent over for a moment to reclose his briefcase. "Now but can either of you ever remember Costigan maybe doing or saying anything strange, having to do with

Steve, when you were around? Did he ever say anything to him? Did he ever do anything out of the ordinary? Did he ever maybe touch Steve, at all?''

"Never," Slotnik said.

There was silence.

"No, he did, once," Evelyn said quietly, looking out at the lawn. "Just once."

Slotnik turned uncomfortably to look at his wife under his arm. Fieldbinder looked at them blandly.

"It was so tiny I never thought to say anything to you, honey," Evelyn said. "I never thought to even think about it. It wasn't really anything."

"I think I'd better be the judge of that," Slotnik said.

Evelyn worked at closing the collar of her robe over her throat. She sniffed out at the lawn. "What happened was Steve and Scott and I were going out to the car. This was a long time ago, Scott was tiny, Steve was ten, I think. I think I was taking Steve somewhere, for something. The car was in the driveway, and Mr. Costigan was in his lawn on the other side of the drive. He'd been getting dandelions out of his lawn, I remember. He had a little wheelbarrow full of dandelions. Anyway, he was there." Evelyn took a deep breath, and her robe fell back open. "And we stopped, and I said hello, and we made some small talk. He was saying how hard it was to get the whole dandelions out, roots and all, how stubborn they were. I don't remember what else. And what he did . . ." Evelyn's eyes narrowed; she squinted at a memory. "What happened was that in the middle of the talking, for no reason, he just reached out a finger, very slowly, and touched Steve. With just one finger. He touched the front of Steve's shirt. On his chest. Very carefully."

"What do you mean, carefully? He touched our child carefully?" Slotnik looked down at Evelyn.

"It was like . . ." Evelyn looked at Fieldbinder. "It was like, sometimes when you're standing in front of a clean window, a very clean window, looking out, and the window is so clean it looks like it's not there. You know? And to make sure it's there, even though you know it's there, really, you'll reach out and just . . . touch the window, ever so slightly. Just barely touch it. That's what it was like. And Steve didn't do anything, I don't think he even noticed. I think he thought Mr. Costigan was just getting something off his shirt. But he wasn't, I know. It was strange, but it was so . . . tiny. I forgot all about it. I don't think I ever even put it in words to myself." She looked at Fieldbinder. "That was the only thing, just that one time, and it was so long ago."

"I see," said Fieldbinder.

The Slotniks didn't say anything.

"So you can maybe understand why I thought it was worth barging," Fieldbinder said. "I just thought you ought to know, at some point, and I figured now was as . . . well, better than some point." He made a small smile.

"Good of you," Slotnik said quietly.

"Listen," Fieldbinder said, "if you care to hear my advice, from having been next door, I think all you need to do is have a talk with Steve. Not to make a big fuss about anything, but simply to make sure nothing has ever happened, that might have upset him." He looked at Evelyn. "Which I'm sure hasn't. It just doesn't sound like that sort of thing. But of course naturally you'll want to just . . . talk to him."

"I'll go wake him up right now," Slotnik said. He rose. Fieldbinder and Evelyn rose. Fieldbinder picked up his raincoat and unfolded it, smoothing the wrinkles out.

"Probably a good idea, Don," he said. "Probably a good idea just to have a little talk. I personally think that's all you need to do. And Don, if you want to come over and have a look at . . . everything, I should be next door for about another hour."

"Not a chance in this world," Slotnik said. "We'd appreciate it if you'd have your crew just dispose of it. I don't want to see any of it." He attacked his cowlick. "If he's laid one hand on that child, I'll kill him."

A moment passed.

"Anyhow," Fieldbinder said, "I'm off. I hope I did the right thing, coming over. And I'm sorry if this upset you. I just thought you ought to know the story."

"Monroe," Slotnik said, "you're a good friend. We appreciate it.

You did the right thing. We appreciate it more than we can say."
He extended a sticky hand, which Fieldbinder shook, smelling syrup.
Slotnik whirled on his slippers and headed for the stairs.

Evelyn showed Fieldbinder to the door. She didn't say anything.

At the door Fieldbinder turned to her. "Listen," he said. He
looked up the staircase. "I'll understand if this isn't the right time."
He smiled warmly. "But I'd like to see you, and I'll just tell you
that I'll actually be next door all day. I've got to get it all finished
today, I'm so behind. But all day, is the thing. Although the crew's
coming at three. So I'm just telling you. Do what you want, of
course. But if you get a chance, feel like it, while they're at
baseball . . ."

Evelyn didn't say anything. She had opened the front door for
Fieldbinder. She was seeing something past him, in the lawn. Fieldbinder turned to look.

"Well there's Scott!" he said. "Hello, Scott! Remember me?"

Scott Slotnik was bouncing a tennis ball on the bricks of the
front walk, out by the street. The ball made a dull sound as it
bounced off the lawn clippings that lay on the walk. At Fieldbinder's
call, Scott looked up.

There was a silence, except for the chatter of a hedge trimmer
across the street. Evelyn stared at Scott, past Scott. Then she
seemed to give a start. "Scott!" she called sharply. "Please come
in here right now!"

Fieldbinder turned back to look at Evelyn. He smiled and put a
soft hand on the arm of her robe. "Hey," he said gently. "Come
on."

Evelyn looked at Fieldbinder's hand, there on her arm, for a
moment. Scott had begun coming toward the door. She looked
back out at him. "It's all right, sweetie," she called. She made a
smile. "Stay and play, if you want."

Scott looked at Fieldbinder and his mother and then at the ball
in his hand.

"Anyhow, the point is just know I'm here, is all; I'm there, all
day, till three," Fieldbinder was saying.

"Yes," Evelyn said. She went back in from the door, leaving it
open.

Fieldbinder moved down the rough brick walk toward Scott Slotnik.

Through the living room window, Evelyn watched Fieldbinder stop and smile and kneel down to say a few words to Scott Slotnik. Something he said made Scott smile shyly and nod. Fieldbinder laughed. Evelyn tried to smooth her morning hair back over her ears. Her sticky thumbs pulled at her hair.

/a/

9 September

A dream so completely frightening, disorienting, and ominous that Fieldbinder awoke streaming.
"Dr. J——— is in significant personal danger," he thought wryly.

Lang and I are in my office, in our respective chairs, the translation between us. We are both mysteriously and troublingly nude. It is noon; the shadow is moving. I look down and cover myself with a tea bag, but there is Lang in all his horror. Lang is drawing a picture of Lenore on the back of the final page of "Love." It is a stunning, lifelike drawing of an unclothed Lenore. I begin to have an erection behind my tea bag. Lang's pen is in the shape of a beer bottle; Lang sucks at the pen, periodically. Lenore is there on the page, on her back, a Vargas girl, a V. Lang puts his initials in the side of Lenore's long, curving leg: a deep, wicked W.D.L.

As the initials go down, hands and hair begin to protrude from the page; breasts swell, a tummy heaves, knees rise and part, feet stroke demurely at the edges of the page. Lang works his pen. Lenore emerges from the page and circles the room.

Fingernails click on the window. Outside the window is a young Mindy Metalman, very young, perhaps thirteen, with bright lipstick on her tiny bruised mouth. She holds hedge trimmers, points at the tea bag. I am sucked back into the shadow as it spreads like ink across the white wall. When I look away from the window, Lenore is kneeling, with the beer-bottle pen, signing Lang's rear end, signing her name with long slow curves, in violet ink, while her other hand finds what purchase it can on Lang's heroic front.

I scream an airless scream and begin explosively to urinate. The stream is upward, a fan of uncountably many lines, which lines are razor-thin and so hot that I am burned when I try to cross them. I am trapped behind my fan. Hot currents swirl on the office carpet, climbing to lap hollow white at Lenore's breasts as they tremble with her efforts. The tea bag bleeds into the hot spray. Tea is being made. "Tea symptosis," says Lang, laughing.

Lenore is drowning; Lang holds her head beneath the surface of the ocean of burnt-yellow tea with his rear end. She continues to sign. Mice boil in the hot currents, their tails wriggling. I am suffocating. It is Salada tea. On the tea bag is written a pithy "It takes a big man to laugh at himself, but it takes an even bigger man to laugh at that man."

Lang looks down at himself and begins ponderously to stir. I surrender myself to the horror. My diploma is washed from the wall and borne away in a rush of foam.

Fieldbinder awoke streaming, to find that he had actually wet the bed, but fortunately that the stained area was no bigger than a spot of ink, which he rubbed away with his handkerchief.

The thing is that they are at the Tissaws', and I am here. There is an unimaginable *thickness* about Cleveland after one has had a bad night, alone. One I am powerless even to hope to begin to describe. Really.

/b/

PARTIAL TRANSCRIPT OF RAP SESSION IN THE OFFICE OF DR. CURTIS JAY, PH.D., THURSDAY, 9 SEPTEMBER 1990.

PARTICIPANTS: DR. CURTIS JAY AND MS. LENORE
BEADSMAN, AGE 24, FILE NUMBER 770-01-4266.

DR. JAY: And so how does that make you feel?

MS. LENORE BEADSMAN: How does what make me feel?

JAY: The state of affairs we were just trying to articulate, in which your
grandmother's separation from and silence toward you paradoxically
evokes in you a feeling of greater closeness to and communication with
the rest of your family.

LENORE: Well, except there's the John thing, in Chicago or wherever.

JAY: Let's leave him out of the picture, for the nonce.

LENORE: For the what?

JAY: Go, go with your thoughts.

LENORE: What thoughts?

JAY: The thoughts we just characterized together.

LENORE: Well, I think in a certain way it's true. Clarice was clueless,
she really doesn't click with the whole Lenore thing, she never has,
but still I felt like when I went over there to tell her this troubling
family stuff, and then watched her and her own family go through that
whole little skit that in a way had to do with exactly what I needed
to talk to her about—I felt good, somehow. It felt secure. Is it dumb
to say it felt secure?

JAY: You felt connected.

LENORE: Connected and non-connected, too.

JAY: But all in the appropriate ways.

LENORE: Boy, you're really hot, today.

JAY: There's a ticklish, stimulating hint of breakthrough-odor.

LENORE: And then there's my other brother . . . that's the first time
I've actually talked to LaVache about anything important in a really
long time. He might have been flapped, but still. I just felt somehow
like we were really . . .

JAY: Communicating?

LENORE: I guess so.

JAY: And how long had it been since you two had had a meaningful
dialogue? Communicated?

LENORE: Oh, gee, quite a while.

JAY: I see. And how long, just to play a bit of a scent-hunch, here, had your great-grandmother been ensconced in the Shaker Heights Home?

LENORE: Umm, quite a while.

JAY: Would this make you uncomfortable?

LENORE: What is that? Is that a gas mask?

JAY: (*muffled*) Purely precautionary.

LENORE: Why do I pay money to somebody to make me less flakey when that person is flakier than I am?

JAY: Than I.

LENORE: Good thing I'm strapped in again.

JAY: And then of course you've implied that your brother had insights on the whole grandmother-disappearance problem.

LENORE: Not really what you'd call insights. He'd gotten a drawing, too, a different one, of some guy on a dune in the Desert, and he played some flap-games with it, and ended up telling me never to think about myself. It wasn't super helpful. And also it was pretty depressing to see that he's still got this schizophrenic thing about his leg, and that he probably personally accounts for about half the drug consumption in New England.

JAY: It's you I'm interested in, though.

LENORE: Well, sorry, but I tend to be concerned about my brother. Part of the me you're so interested in is brother-concern.

JAY: The Desert?

LENORE: Pardon?

JAY: You mentioned Desert, in the context of the drawing in question. Do you mean *the* Desert?

LENORE: Well, the sand was black, and LaVache mentioned sinister-ness.

JAY: So the G.O.D., then.

LENORE: Who knows.

JAY: But there's at least a possibility that the Great Ohio Desert bears on the whereabouts of the nursing home people.

LENORE: What's going on here?

JAY: Where?

LENORE: Don't look around, in your stupid mask. Are you trying to put words in my mouth?

JAY: This guy? Me?

LENORE: Why do I get the feeling people are trying to push me out into the Desert? Which for me has all these really far less than pleasant memories of when I was a kid, and Gramma would take me out wandering, and I'd have to hear her go on and on about Auden and Wittgenstein, who she thinks are like jointly God, and we'd fish at the Desert's edge, and look into the blackness . . .

JAY: A conspicuous hmmm, here.

LENORE: In your ear. And how come you're all trying to get me back out there? You, my brother, Rick's mentioned Desert, Vlad quotes Auden to me, that Gramma used to read in the sand . . .

JAY: A morsel for thought, if I may be so—

LENORE: And Mr. el creepo Bloemker was acting like some sort of Desert salesman with me before his girlfriend lost her dress and sprung a leak . . .

JAY: Excuse me?

LENORE: And then also out of the unwelcome blue comes this guy, who I unfortunately met, when I was a kid, and is married to my sister's old roommate, and it turns out his father more or less built the G.O.D., apparently. His father owns Industrial Desert Design. Dad was unbelievably interested in that. A lot more interested than in any stick-figure drawings, that's for—

JAY: What guy?

LENORE: Andrew Sealander Lang, who's doing obscure translation stuff at Frequent and Vigorous, whom Rick met in a bar in Amherst.

JAY: And you'd met him personally before.

LENORE: Why do you ask?

JAY: Why that face?

LENORE: What face?

JAY: You just got a dreamy, faraway expression on your face.

LENORE: I did not.

JAY: You're attracted to this man?

LENORE: Are you out of your mind? What's with you today? Is air getting through the air-hole in that thing?

JAY: I know an attraction-face when I see one. Psychologists' senses are keened to pick up on nonverbal signals.

LENORE: Keened?

JAY: Your pupils have dilated to the size of manhole covers.

LENORE: How lovely.

JAY: Does Rick know about this?

LENORE: About what?

JAY: Your infatuation with this Desert-and-translation person.

LENORE: You're really pissing me off.

JAY: It's written all over your face.

LENORE: Face must be getting pretty crowded. Manhole covers, dreamy expressions, writing . . .

JAY: Formal ejection warning.

LENORE: Boy, I'd think the one place where I could avoid getting pushed into places and having people pushed into me would be the place where I spend almost all my money for help with those very feelings of pushed-ness.

JAY: This guilt ploy is getting far less effective as time goes by.

LENORE: Maybe I ought to just skeedaddle, then.

JAY: A hugely important and also redolent question, Lenore. Why, when you feel valid human inclinations and attractions, purely understandable inclinations to pay a visit to a place that may or may not bear on the whereabouts of a loved one, attractions to someone your own age, who can perhaps—

LENORE: How do you know his age?

JAY: It's extractable from the *context*, you ninny. Cut the guano. Relax and let's try to make a stride or two.

LENORE: Maybe just a quick dash to the ladies' room, and then I could dash right on back—

JAY: Hush. If you feel a desire to go to the Desert, why don't you just go? What are you afraid of?

LENORE: You're blowing this way out of proportion, assuming there's anything to blow. Which come to think of it there isn't, because I'm not afraid of anything. I'm just not dying to go out there, is all. And it would be pointless. There's just no way twenty-six people, most of them incredibly old, and with walkers, and at least one needing things to be ninety-eight point six degrees all the time, are wandering around in the Desert in September. But what gets me is that it seems like everybody for some reason wants to *get* me out there. What I resent is just having no say in where I go or what I ostensibly want or—

JAY: I have one word for you.

LENORE: Goodbye?

JAY: Membrane. I say to you "membrane," Lenore.

LENORE: I think I'd prefer goodbye.

JAY: Think of our work together, Lenore. Our strides. Our progress. Don't you see that perceiving your own natural desires and inclinations and attractions as somehow being directed at and forced on you from outside, from *Outside*, is a truly classic instance of a malfunction in a hygiene-identity network? That it's exhaustively reducible to and explainable in terms of membrane-theory? That a flabby membrane is unhealthily permeable, lets the Self out to soil the Other-set and the Other-set in to soil the Self?

LENORE: I'm afraid I'm really uncomfortably in need of a shower.

JAY: And why, pray? I'll simply tell you straight out that in my perception it's because you are perceiving the above revelations, the above, yes, let's take a great stride forward and say the above exhaustive and deadly-accurate characterization and explanation of your whole trouble-set, as coming from *outside* you, as somehow *forced* upon you. When it's really coming from inside you, Lenore. It all is. Don't you feel it? Direct your attention to your Inside. Feel how clean it is. Forget I'm here altogether. Pretend I'm you.

LENORE: It's just impossible to take you seriously in that gas mask.

JAY: Were I to remove this now, my naïve young client and friend, the stench of breakthrough would blast me into unconsciousness. You would be truly and utterly alone.

LENORE: And what do you mean, pretend you're me? I thought the whole problem was supposed to be that that flabby old membrane wasn't keeping you on your side and me on my side. If I pretend you're me, what does that do to the membrane?

JAY: But don't you see, the pretending will come from *inside* you. A true pretending can only come off in the context of an intimate awareness of the real. For you to pretend I'm you, you must know I'm not; the membrane must be a strong, clean membrane. The strong, clean membrane chooses what to suck inside itself and lets all the rest bounce dirtily off. Only the secure can truly pretend, Lenore. The secure have membranes like strong, clean ova. Like ovums. These membranes withstand the onslaught of the countless Other-set, ceaselessly battering, the Others, their heads coated with filth, their underarms clotted with fungus, they batter, and the secure membrane/ovum waits patiently, strong, aloof, secure, and, yes, occasionally will let an Other in, will suck it in, on the membrane's terms, will suck it in like a sperm, will take it inside itself to renew, to create itself anew. Only a strong membrane can suck in a sperm, Lenore. Here, I know, pretend I'm a sperm.

LENORE: I don't care for the way this session is going one bit.

JAY: No, really. Be secure. Pretend I'm a sperm cell. Here. I take the string out of the . . . hood of my sweatshirt, affix it to my behind for a tail, like so . . .

LENORE: What in God's name are you doing?

JAY: Pretend, Lenore. Be an ovum. Be strong. Let me hypothetically batter at you. Batter batter. Surrender to the unreal of the real interior.

LENORE: Are you supposed to be a sperm, wriggling your sweatshirt-string like that?

JAY: I can feel the strength of your membrane, Lenore.

LENORE: A sperm in a gas mask?

JAY: Batter batter.

LENORE: I demand that you set my chair in motion.

JAY: Admit that your inclinations and attractions come from inside you.

LENORE: Look, quit wriggling that string all over the place.

JAY: Admit you're attracted to this young man. This translator. This blond Adonis who can offer you realms of Self-Other interaction you've never even dreamed of.

LENORE: How do you know he's blond?

JAY: The context is the fluid of the uterus. I'm swimming, to batter at you. Batter batter. Let someone inside your membrane.

LENORE: Is this a pass? Are you making a pass?

JAY: Don't misdirect so pathetically transparently. I speak . . . speak of this man who spreads your pupils from the inside, like the soft petals of some helpless flower. Who can show you perhaps how the strong membrane is permeated. Who can batter! Batter batter.

LENORE: What are you saying?

JAY: We're making gargantuan strides. The room is swirling with breakthrough-gases, in which, paradoxically, everything becomes strangely clear. Can't you feel it?

LENORE: I think you've flipped. I never signed up for sperm-therapy, buster, I'm telling you right—

JAY: Admit that your attraction to this Other comes from inside your Self. Strengthen the membrane. Let it be permeated as *you* desire it so!

LENORE: And how might I ask is Rick supposed to fit into all this? What about Rick?

JAY: Rick knows he must forever remain an Other to you. Rick knows the meaning of membrane. Rick is like a sperm without a tail. An immobilized sperm in the uterus of life. Why do you think Rick is so desperately unhappy? What do you think he means by the Screen Door of Union?

Lenore Beadsman pauses.

JAY: He means membrane! Rick is trapped behind his own membrane. He hasn't the equipment to get out.

LENORE: Hey, you're not supposed to talk about your other patients.

JAY: Why do you think he's so possessive? He wants you *in* him. He wants to trap you behind the membrane with him. He knows he can never validly permeate the membrane of an Other, so he desires to bring that Other into him, for all time. He's a sick man.

LENORE: Look, stop trying to swim around. You've made your point.

JAY: No, you've made *your* point. All distinctions are shattered. I am not here. I am the sperm inside you. Remember that you are half sperm, Lenore.

LENORE: Pardon?

JAY: Your father's sperm. It's part of you. Inseparable.

LENORE: What does my father have to do with all this?

JAY: Admit.

LENORE: Admit what?

JAY: That you want someone truly inside you. That your membrane is crying out.

LENORE: Jesus.

JAY: Listen. . . . Hear that? The faint cry of a membrane, isn't it? "Let me be an ovum, let—"

LENORE: He loves me.

JAY: He does? The Adonis? The valid Other?

LENORE: Rick, you dingwad. Rick loves me. He's said so.

JAY: Rick cannot give us what we need. Admit it.

LENORE: He loves me.

JAY: It's a sucking love, Lenore. An inherently unclean love. It's the love of a flabby, unclean membrane, sucking at an Other, to dirty. Dirt is on this membrane's mind. It wants to do you dirt.

Lenore Beadsman pauses.

JAY: Do you love him back? Does he batter validly at the membrane?

LENORE: Please, a shower.

JAY: Admit the source of your dispositions.

LENORE: Leave me alone. Start my chair.

JAY: Batter batter. We are helpless and inefficacious as parts of a system until we recognize the existence of the system. Batter batter. Hear the syrupy squelch of your membrane.

LENORE: Look, let me leave right now or I'll stop coming. I'm not kidding.

JAY: First admit it. Say it out loud. Bring it out. Your pupils don't lie. Make it real. Bring it into the network. Batter back. Take an Other inside.

LENORE: Shower. Please, a shower.

JAY: Admit everything. Do you want a gas mask too? Is that it? No problem at all. A permeated membrane is not a pretty smell.

LENORE: God.

JAY: What do we suppose Lenore would have to say to all this?

LENORE: Who?

/c/

"Are you all right?"

"Mmm-hmm."

"You look awfully pale."

". . . ."

"Would you like some of my oyster stew?"

"You know I hate oyster stew. They look like little mouths, floating in there."

"Surely you want more than just that tiny salad."

"Please don't tell me what I want, Rick. I've had more than enough of that already today."

"What does that mean?"

". . . ."

"Is that a Jay-reference?"

". . . ."

"Was it not a good appointment?"

"Don't want to talk about it."

"But if it's harmed you in some emotional way . . ."

"We made a deal that we wouldn't talk about Jay-appointments, remember?"

"You're so pale you're practically transparent."

"Well, you can touch my chest if you want, like in that stupid story."

"Pardon me?"

"That one story, the first one you had me read? Where the old man touches the little boy to make sure he's not a window?"

"You didn't care for that story? What was it called . . .?"

" 'Love.' "

"Yes, that's the one."

"I liked that other one, though. That 'Metamorphosis for the Eighties.' I thought it was a killer. The part when the people threw coins at the rock star on stage and they stuck in him and he died was maybe a little hokey, but overall it was deadly. I put a big asterisk on it for you."

". . . ."

"You don't want your stew anymore? I didn't mean it about the mouths. Eat up."

"But you didn't much care for the other one, then."

"Maybe I'm wrong, but I thought it sucked canal-water, big time."

". . . ."

"Oh no, did you really like it? Am I ignorantly stomping on a good thing, that you liked?"

"My tastes are for the moment on the back burner. I'd simply be interested to hear why you disliked it."

"I'm really not sure. It just seemed . . . it was like you said about all the other troubled collegiate stuff. It just seemed artificial. Like the kid who wrote it was trying too hard."

"I see."

"All that stuff about, 'And then context came in, and Fieldbaum looked bland.' "

"Fieldbinder."

"What?"

"Wasn't the protagonist's name Fieldbinder? In the story?"

"Right, Fieldbinder. But that stuff about context, though. Shouldn't a story *make* the context that makes people do certain things and have the things be appropriate or not appropriate? A story shouldn't just *mention* the exact context it's supposed to try really to create, right?"

". . . ."

"And the writing was just so . . . This one line I remember: 'He grinned wryly.' Grinned wryly? Who grins wryly? Nobody grins wryly, at all, except in stories. It wasn't real at all. It was like a story about a story. I put it on Mavis's desk with the ones about the proctologist and the snowblower."

". . . ."

"But I'll take it right back off if you liked it. You did like it, didn't you? This means my tastes aren't keened to the right pitch, doesn't it?"

"Not . . . not necessarily. I'm trying to remember where I got the thing. Must have been some kid, somewhere. Troubled. Trying to remember his cover letter . . ."

"Although it was well typed, I noticed."

". . . ."

"Let me just try one little smidgeon of your stew, here."

"Think he said it *was* almost like a story about a story. The narrative center being the wife's description of the occasion on which Costigan touched the son. . . . Almost a story about the way a story waits and waits but never dies, can always come back, even after ostensible characters have long since departed the real scene."

"Really not all that bad."

"What?"

"The broth is pretty good. Creamy. I guess it's just the oysters I don't like."

"I seem to remember he said he conceived it as a story of neighborhood obsession. About how sometimes neighbors can become obsessed with other neighbors, even children, and perhaps even peer into their bedrooms across the fence from their dens . . . but how it's usually impossible for the respective neighbors to know about such things, because each neighbor is shut away inside his own property, his house, surrounded by a fence. Locked away. Everything meaningful, both good-meaningful and bad-meaningful, kept private."

" . . . . "

"Except that ocasionally the Private leaked out, every once in a while, and became Incident. And that perceived Incident became Story. And that Story endured, in Mind, even behind and within the isolating membrane of house and property and fence that surrounded and isolated each individual suburb-resident."

"Membrane?"

"Sorry. Poor choice of word. I'm sure I'll hear it often enough this afternoon."

"You see Jay this afternoon?"

"I told you that yesterday. We discussed it yesterday."

" . . . . "

"Is there some reason why you'd like me not to see him today?"

" . . . . "

"And that, as I recall, some of the references in the story, the bird business, the burning house, the grinning-wryly business, had to do with a context created by a larger narrative system of which this piece was a part."

"Well you can imagine I found the bird stuff upsetting. Especially about its being dead. Which Vlad the Impaler now in effect is, at least as far as I'm concerned, at least for a while."

"He was on television last night, I'm told. Apparently Sykes's show airs every single evening."

"I know. Candy watched him last night. I guess he was really good. She said Sykes looked like he was in ecstasies."

"You didn't watch it?"

"Candy watched it at Mr. Allied's. He's got cable. We don't get cable, at the Tissaws'. Their house isn't hooked up. Mrs. Tissaw usually just watches Oral Roberts on a regular channel. Actually the whole East Corinth–cable story is pretty unhappy, because the cable company and Dad are still—"

"Where were you?"

"What?"

"Where were you last night?"

"Oh, God, what all did I do. I went for a walk for a while. Watched some of a softball game at the park. They were pitching fast. I like it when they pitch fast. I talked to Dad on the phone about the LaVache thing for what turned out to be a long time. And then I went to sleep early. I did read some more of the stories, though. I read—"

"Where was Lang, then, I wonder."

" . . . . "

"You're awfully pale."

"Why do you think I'd know where Lang was?"

"I was just thinking out loud."

"I heard a definite tone."

"You heard nothing but your own imagination."

"What's *that* supposed to mean?"

"What is wrong with you, Lenore? Darling I swear I meant nothing at all."

" . . . . "

"Are you sure you're all right?"

" . . . . "

"Was the Fieldbinder piece that awful? Is that it?"

"A story can't make you pale, or sick, Rick. That thing wasn't even good enough in my opinion to have any effect on me, good or bad, at all."

"Then what is it, Lenore?"

" . . . . "

"Shall we just go? Norman has been tending to come in here, a lot, for lunches, at about this time, so perhaps—"

"And now what's *that* supposed to mean?"

"My God, it meant nothing! I just thought you'd want to avoid seeing him, is all."

"How does he even get in here anymore?"

"Apparently he simply establishes himself on the sidewalk. Newspapers are laid down. Things are brought to him in huge industrial containers. It's not a pretty sight."

"I guess we should go, then. I don't want to have to try to get past him."

"The Bombardini Company vice presidents are deeply worried. They claim in all seriousness that Norman is trying to eat himself to death."

"Or everybody else to death."

"Surely you don't take those pathetic plans he was spinning seriously."

"Don't presume to tell me what I take seriously and don't take seriously, Rick."

"Good Lord, what is the matter with you?"

". . . ."

"Listen. . . . Listen to that."

". . . ."

"Hear it?"

"I do hear something. It's not thunder, is it?"

"Can't be. Sun's shining out past the shadow, see? I'm afraid I sense impending Norman."

"We better go. You better finish your mouths."

"Are you absolutely sure you're all right?"

". . . ."

/d/

At work, Candy Mandible was smoking and sipping a Tab and enjoying Judith Prietht's lunch break. Judith had been entering the too-much range. Today she had brought baggies full of sugar cookies in the shapes of cats and birds for Lenore and Candy. Judith was getting to be a real pain in the ass.

The console began beeping. Candy Started In and amused herself for a minute with a hoarse man wanting to know whether she

preferred rough banisters to smooth banisters. Then she handled
the next call.

"Frequent and Vigorous," she said.

"Who?" said a voice.

"Frequent and Vigorous Publishing, Inc., may I help you," Candy
said, rolling her eyes.

"Christ, I thought I'd never get through," the voice said. "Miss,
did you know your phones are all fouled up?"

"There've been rumors to that effect, ma'am. Can I help you
with something?" Candy took some Tab, around the mouthpiece.
She tried to place the voice on the phone. The voice sounded
vaguely familiar.

"To whom am I speaking, please," said the voice.

"This is Ms. Mandible, a Frequent and Vigorous operator," said
Candy Mandible.

"Ms. Mandible, I'm calling to see first whether you have a co-
worker there, a Ms. Lenore Beadsman," said the voice.

"Yes, we do," said Candy. "Can I take a message for you." She
reached for the Legitimate Call Log.

"And second to see whether you also have a new employee there,
a Mr. Lang," said the voice. "I think he's in the babyfood department, whatever that means."

"Ma'am whom shall I say is calling?" Candy said, opening the
Log.

"This is Mrs. Andrew Sealander Lang, of New York," said the
voice.

Candy looked at the console, the circuit buttons in their gelatins
of light.

"Hello?" the voice said.

"Yes, hello," said Candy.

"Is my husband there, is what I need to know."

"I believe he is with the firm at the present time, ma'am, yes,"
said Candy. "Shall I transfer you to his temporary office?"

"Does he have a direct number there?"

"All individual transfers are done through me at the switchboard,
ma'am. Please hold on." Candy looked at the switchboard directory,
got the number, Started In again, and transferred the call, just as
Judith Prietht slouched wearily back into the cubicle.

"What's happening, Candy?" Judith made a smile and changed her shoes for the slippers beneath her counter.

"Just fine," Candy said, still staring at the lights in the console, reaching again for her Tab.

/e/

PARTIAL TRANSCRIPT OF RAP-SESSION IN THE OFFICE OF DR. CURTIS JAY, PH.D., THURSDAY, 9 SEPTEMBER 1990. PARTICIPANTS: DR. CURTIS JAY AND MR. RICK VIGOROUS, AGE 42, FILE NUMBER 744-25-4291.

DR. JAY: So as I see it we have three major and not unrelated themes for discussion. Dream. You. Lenore.

MR. RICK VIGOROUS: Preferably the latter. What did you do to her in here, today? She looked simply awful at lunch.

DR. JAY: No pain, no gain. Enormous, enormous strides, today. Breakthrough positively looming on the emotional horizon. And of course there is the Lang issue.

RICK: The Lang issue?

JAY: The young man from your dream?

RICK: Why is he an issue outside the confines of the dream?

JAY: Who said he was?

RICK: You did.

JAY: Did I? I don't really recall explicitly saying that.

RICK: What an ass-pain you are.

Dr. Jay pauses.

RICK: I officially demand to know how and why Lang is an issue.

JAY: You said the Lang dream made you wake up screaming.

RICK: Streaming.

JAY: Watch me exercise self-control.

Rick Vigorous pauses.

JAY: Penis problems, still. Am I right?

RICK: Listen to this. I'm amazed. Last time I was here you said "penis shmenis."

JAY: But I sense intuitively that Lang has become for you the Other, no? The Other in reference to whom you choose to understand Self, in all its perceived inadequacy?

RICK: I don't know. What, did Lenore mention Lang to you?

JAY: Why did you bring this person back to Cleveland with you, if he upsets you so?

RICK: I really do not know. We met in our old fraternity bar. Things were strange. Affinities seemed to be jutting out everywhere. He simply seemed to fit in. To click.

JAY: So you brought him within your network.

RICK: I hate to sound like a mutual acquaintance of ours, but somehow I felt I had little choice. It was as though a context was created in which it would have been inappropriate not to bring him inside.

JAY: Inside?

RICK: Into the nexus of my professional and emotional life.

JAY: I see. And what about Lenore? Is Lenore "inside," to continue your use of a term positively dripping with Blentnerian connotations?

RICK: I hope that she will be someday.

JAY: A conspicuous hmmm. And you, Rick. Are you "inside," in the context of Lenore's network?

RICK: Don't be sadistic. You know I can never be that.

JAY: The Screen Door of Union, et cetera.

RICK: Make my ears stop rumbling.

Dr. Jay pauses.

Rick Vigorous pauses.

JAY: Rick, friend, has it never occurred to you that you might actually represent the genetic cutting edge?

RICK: The what?

JAY: I invite you to think about it. We as a species used to have tails, no? A full coat of thick body-hair? Prehensile toes? Far keener senses of taste, small, hearing, et cetera than we possess today? We eventually lost all these features. Tossed them aside. Why was this?

RICK: What are you trying to say?

JAY: Rick, we didn't need them. The context in which they had an appropriate function dissolved. They had no use.

RICK: What are you trying to say?

JAY: I suppose I am trying to bring into the focus of our emotional attention the following features of the contemporary society we both enjoy. Genetic engineering. Artificial insemination. Quantum leaps in the technology of sexual aids and implements and prostheses. Perhaps what most of us perceive as the centers of ourselves are simply no longer needed. And we both know that the absence of function, in nature, means death. There is nothing superfluous in nature. Perhaps you are the next wave, Rick. Have you ever thought of that, in the quiet times? Perhaps you are to this Lang what the first upright man was to the crouched, hunched, drooling simian. A sort of god. A prototype, seated on nature's right hand, for the nonce. A man for the future.

RICK: I think I'd prefer to be the drooling simian, thank you very much.

JAY: And why is that?

RICK: I'll bet you can puzzle it out.

JAY: It has to do with Lenore.

Rick Vigorous pauses.

JAY: Rick, I put a vital question to you in the gentlest and most diplomatic terms possible. Do you think you are truly what Lenore Beadsman wants? What she really needs?

RICK: We love each other.

JAY: You didn't answer my question. We both know that Lenore is a wonderful but not insignificantly troubled girl. Are you helping her? Are you concerned with her needs? Are you engaged in the sort of discriminating, mature love that focuses primary attention on the needs and interests of the beloved?

RICK: I definitely don't think Lang is what she needs.

JAY: Who said Lang is what Lenore needs? It's you we're discussing, here.

RICK: I think I'd rather discuss Lenore.

JAY: And the issues *are* separate, aren't they? And recognized as such. Discussing Lenore is different from discussing you.

RICK: There's something wrong with that?

JAY: I didn't say that, Rick. I was simply making an observation. You and Lenore are distinct. Your networks may overlap, but they are distinct. They are neither identical nor coextensive. They are distinct.

RICK: What about my dream? Now I'm both afraid to go to the bathroom and afraid to go to sleep. There's not too much left.

JAY: I personally think the dream is far too complicated to tackle in the short time remaining to us today. For what it's worth to you, I believe it represents a gigantic foot in the door of breakthrough. I might make a few off-the-cuff observations, if you wish. Shall I?

RICK: *(unintelligible).*

JAY: The dream strikes me as being simply chock full of networks. Inside-Outside relations. Inside is the office, outside is the shadow and the little girl, both threatening to enter, to suck you in. Lenore is inside the page, inside the drawing Lang creates with his bottle, but she transcends her context and comes quickly to emblazon her context on his *outside.* You are trapped behind, inside, the fan of urine, but the tea bag you use to try to cover your difference from the Other "bleeds out" into the hot liquid and stains, discolors, soils the already unclean out-of-control extension of Self that imprisons you. A tea bag in hot liquid strikes this psychologist as a perfect archetypal image for the disorienting and disrupting influence of a weak-membraned hygiene-identity network on the associations of distinct networks in relation to which it does, must, understand itself. So on and so on. Airless scream: air cannot get inside your lungs. Lenore "drowning": clean air in lungs displaced by the exponentially soiled element of soiling tea in soiling Self-extending liquid. Lang holds Lenore under the stained surface with his anus, the absolute archetypal locus of the unclean. There are of course the seemingly ever-present mice, in the putrid currents. Mice we've discussed at length already . . .

RICK: OK, that's enough. I might have known that—

JAY: But, see, it's not at all surprisingly Lenore who really fascinates me, in the context of the dream. Your unconscious conceiving of Lenore as somehow "rising off a page." The Lang drawing serving to place Lenore initially in the network he constructs, making her two-dimensional, non-real, existing and defined wholly within the border of a page, a page on the reverse of which is a story, a network very definitely of *your* construction, so that—

RICK: A story Lenore went out of her way to scoff at, at lunch, by the way.

JAY: I'm not equipped to discuss that; that's not my area. My area is the fact that Lang constructs a Lenore, constructs her the way we each of course construct, impose our frameworks of perception and understanding on, the persons who inhabit our individual networks. Yes,

Lang constructs a Lenore, and initially she is trapped and two-dimensional and unreal. . . . Ah, but then he puts marks, *initials*, his initials, on her, in her. Penetrates her carefully constructed network with his *Self*, his self, of which the initials are an elegantly transparent symbol and flag. So Lang in the dream is able to bring *himself* within the very Lenore-membrane he has constructed. He puts himself in her. And what happens, Rick?

RICK: Jesus.

JAY: What happens, my friend?

Rick Vigorous pauses.

JAY: Oh, she becomes real, Rick. She becomes free. She bursts out from behind the membrane of two-dimensionality the page represents and becomes real. Hair, hands, breasts, feet tumesce and burst up and out from the flattening, constricting network of membrane. She rises and circles the room. Was this circling a walking circling, Rick, or a floating circling?

RICK: It wasn't clear.

JAY: Well, no matter. She escapes, Rick. She is free, real. That is to say, she is no longer merely inside a network, she *is* a network. Reality and identity rear their Siamese heads at the junction of Network. And what is the newly three-dimensional Lenore doing? She is *signing* the Other, putting herself on, in, the Other who set her free through membrane-permeation. She puts herself inside a network.

RICK: Lang's network.

JAY: The network that set her free, Rick. The network that made her real. Only as real is she able to bring herself truly inside an Other. A clean thing is necessarily a reciprocal thing, Rick. Lenore kneels, with overtones perhaps not so much sexual as they are religious, I think, and puts herself on, in. She is valid, Rick. You are watching Lang and Lenore give birth to validity.

RICK: But where am I in all this? Am I chopped liver in the validity-scheme?

JAY: You are *watching*, Rick. You are the watcher, the observer, looking on from a spatial-dash-emotional elsewhere. You are intrinsically Outside, here. You cannot enter the networks. Why not?

RICK: Jesus.

JAY: And what is the last recourse of an inefficacious hygiene network unable validly to interact with the networks of the Other-set? You soil, Rick. You soil. You enter the networks by dirtying. The childish loss of bladder control, the fan, the swirling currents. The uncleanness made all the more unclean by the introduction of the contents of the tea bag, the shield and symbol within the dream of the locus of your difference and inability validly to enter, its introduction into the hot unclean liquid that represents your only interaction-vehicle. From Outside, you can influence only by soiling, dirtying, disrupting the hygiene networks of those who are valid.

RICK: You're being cruel, Jay. Go back to blatant bullshit. I vastly prefer blatant bullshit to overt cruelty.

JAY: You know, Olaf Blentner once said to me, over tea, that when reality is unpleasant, realists tend to be unpopular. Rick, as a last resort you try to soil. You try to drown and negate the valid Lenore by dirtying. But it does not work. It cannot. Even from below the currents of your filth and difference, Lenore's hand, with the violet pen, emerges to carry on the valid membrane-interaction. You are truly Outside, here, Rick. You cannot meaningfully influence. The only recourse of the defective hygiene network is the unclean, and it is impotent in the face of the real, the true.

RICK: Lenore has spoken to you of Lang, hasn't she?

JAY: Rick, you and your dreaming unconscious have spoken to me of Lang far more eloquently than poor Lenore ever did, or even could. You have, I think, truly perceived a valid need in an Other. You are striding, in my opinion.

Rick Vigorous pauses.

JAY: And why are you and Lang naked in the dream, Rick? Why is the validating pen in the shape of a beer bottle, with all of that image's attendant phallic and urological overtones?

RICK: And then why, in this context, does Lenore grasp Lang's member as she signs? Is the member supposed to be the symbol of membrane-penetration?

JAY: The symbol, Rick? The symbol?

RICK: More than the symbol?

JAY: I am being knocked backward by the force of breakthrough-smell.

RICK: Sit back up, you ass. This is my life you're fucking with.

JAY: What an interesting choice of verb.

RICK: So when I'd come to you with these clearly profoundly sexual dreams and you'd say that they were just hygiene-dreams, you weren't, under your analysis, really disagreeing with me, were you? The hygiene-fixated is the sexually fixated.

Dr. Jay pauses.

RICK: Don't just smile at me, damn you. And the hygiene-identity membrane is you're implying the what? What is it?

JAY: What might the membrane be, here, Rick? Let's think together. What membrane might Lenore have needed to have permeated in order to feel real, connected? Valid? Transcending in and for her reality the mere reference and emotional attention of the Other, of you? What membrane does the thinking student and friend of the center of your existence conclude that Lenore needed to have penetrated for her?

RICK: What do you mean needed to have penetrated? What does that mean? What has she told you?

JAY: Was Lenore a virgin when she became part of your intrinsically inefficacious network, Rick?

RICK: My God.

JAY: No symbol is merely a symbol, Rick. A symbol is valid and appropriate because its reference is real. You should know that, being a man of letters yourself.

RICK: Lang has had her.

JAY: Would that make you uncomfortable in this context?

RICK: Oh my ears! God!

JAY: Would you like to try some gum?

RICK: I'll kill him. I'll kill her.

JAY: That's right, Rick. Perform the ultimate soiling. Blacken, erase, discipline and negate the valid network that of necessity finds its validity-reference outside your own system.

RICK: My life is over. It's all over.

JAY: Please see that I have here said nothing to you about Lenore Beadsman's private affairs. That is not my place. Whatever interactions she might choose to engage in with a virile blond bestower of validity, close to her own age and socio-economic background, are no matter for my tale-telling relationship with you. Let your dreams speak, Rick. That's what they're for.

RICK: How do you know his age? That he's blond and virile, with a socio-economic background?

JAY: I'm simply going to have to put this gas mask on. Also please note that our time is nearly up.

RICK: Wear whatever you want. But I'm not leaving until I'm good and ready.

JAY: (*muffled*) What a task lies before us, my old friend. What a horrible, wonderful opportunity for the exercise of strength. The vital question: Are we mature? Do we love truly? Do we love an as yet two-dimensional membrane enough to afford that membrane entry into validity, reality, three-dimensionality, to afford it an escape from the very flattening context exclusively within which the original love can be exercised and pseudo-reciprocated? Do we, recognizing our inability to enter and fertilize and permeate and validate a membrane, an Other, let that Other out, back outside, to a clean, odor-free place where she can find fullness, fulfillment, realness?

RICK: I suddenly take it all back. This is utter tripe. I reject everything you've said. Your supposed to be helping me, you shit. Your function here is to help me. All this Blentnerian crapola boils down to the fact that you want me to sit idly by and watch the object of my adoration and the complete reference and telos of every action of my whole life go off and get balled until she bleeds by some horny, silky-smooth, lecherous yuppie, one who just happens to have a large organ where I do not.

JAY: But precisely my point has just been borne out, Rick. Listen to what you just said. The *object* of your so-and-so. The *reference* of your so-and-so. An object and reference are intrinsically and eternally Other, Rick. See? And so she must remain for you. The question: have we the wherewithal to allow that Other to be a Self?

RICK: Shall I simply eat her? That's what Norman Bombardini apparently proposes to do. Shall I consume her? Then the Other will certainly become Self.

Dr. Jay pauses.

RICK: Lang wears a type of shoe toward which Lenore feels a rabid hatred.

JAY: Lenore Beadsman's foot- and shoe-fixations occur and exist within a disordered hygiene-network thoroughly infected with membrane ambiguity. Surely you can see that.

RICK: This is shit. I cannot believe I'm listening to this.

Dr. Jay pauses.

RICK: Where is this Olaf Blentner? I'll talk to him directly. Spit in his eye. How'll he like those apples?

JAY: Olaf Blentner is no more. Professor Blentner has returned to the soil.

RICK: How appropriately ironic. Hopefully interred in a cow pasture, laced with bullshit. Dust to dust.

JAY: Anger is absolutely appropriate and natural, here, Rick. Shall I get out the Nerf clubs, and we'll go a few rounds? I'm here to help as best I can, within the limits imposed by the reality of the situation we find ourselves in.

RICK: Shut up. Where are these so-called Heidelberg Hygiene Lectures? Let me read them. I'll write and publish a review of them so scathing your eyes will bleed.

JAY: I'm afraid they're on loan to another client and friend.

RICK: Not Lenore.

JAY: Rick, I'm afraid our time looks to be truly up. I have other longtime clients and friends waiting. Shall I start your chair?

RICK: You bastard.

JAY: Come see me again just as soon as possible. Tell Mrs. Schorr you're to be given the very next available appointment.

RICK: Jay, convince Lenore that I am what she needs. Help me bring her into me. Then nothing will matter. I'll pay absolutely anything.

JAY: You insult my integrity. You also cast doubt on the very emotion you profess to believe motivates all your actions. I'll dismiss this as coming from the understandable emotional strain of the moment.

RICK: Oh, God.

JAY: Goodbye, Rick. Think over what we've seen together today. Call me anytime. I am truly here for you. Here goes the chair. Goodbye.

Rick Vigorous pauses.

JAY: Goodbye.

RICK: *(unintelligible).*

DOOR: Click.
JAY: (unmuffled) Wow.

/f/

9 September. 9 September.

Lenore Beadsman is fucking Andrew Sealander ("Wang-Dang")
Lang. It is. In a matter of moments this boy, with a grin, perhaps
a brief nail-polishing brush of his hand against his shirt, has taken
something I can never have. My object and reference sits outside,
punctured and validated by the extension of another. And

9 September

Idea for Fieldbinder Collection

*Fieldbinder ruminates in presence of pathetic and sadistic psychologist
Dr. J＿＿ on the comparative merits of the word "fuck."*

*"We beg your pardon?" said Dr. J＿＿, curling his harelip in incre-
dulity.*

*Fieldbinder smiled coolly. "The word 'fuck,' Dr. J＿＿. Has it never
occurred to you that the word, far from being harsh or ugly, is in truth
a strangely lovely word? An appropriate word? I'll not say onomatopoetic,
but rather lovely and appropriate. Perhaps even musical."*

*Dr. J＿＿ wriggled his hideous body in his chair. Fieldbinder smiled
coolly, continuing, "The word chosen to designate the act—the supreme
act of a distinctively human life, the act in reference to the pleasure and
meaning of which I naturally understand myself, being as you once
remarked an almost exclusively sexual entity—the word chosen to designate the act must also be extremely important, no?"*

*"God, what a man he is," whispered the doctor, barely audibly, roll-
ing his walleyes until the action hurt the styes which crusted his
eyelids.*

*"No, really," smiled Fieldbinder. "Think of the sound, 'fuck.' 'Fuck.'
A good sound. A solid sound. The sound of a heavy coin rattling in a*

thick porcelain cup. The sound of a drop of clear cold water falling into a still pond from a great height. Roll the word on your tongue for a while, Dr. J_____."

There was a silence while the doctor rolled the word silently on his cold gray tongue. Across the ambiguously lit room, Fieldbinder obliterated a tiny wrinkle from his impeccable slacks.

"I can recall being a student in college," Fieldbinder ruminated after a time. "I can recall even then a deep dissatisfaction with the words used by my peers to designate the act. In college, women were locutionally reduced to earth, or impediment. 'Have you blasted her?' 'Drill her yet?' 'I pounded hell out of her last night.' None of these are right, Dr. J_____, is this not transparently clear? None of these words are adequate to capture not only the reference but the sense of an act in which two distinct selves interpenetrate, not only physically, but also of course emotionally. I simply must say, as crass as we are conditioned by a troubled society to regard the word, I am a firm believer in the comparative merits of the word 'fuck.' " Fieldbinder looked up and smiled coolly. "Have I offended you?"

"No," hissed Dr. J_____, playing maniacally with the controls of his mechanical chair, making it bounce up and down suggestively, as drool coated the doctor's pathetically weak chin.

Fieldbinder smiled coolly and speculatively stroked his own generous jaw, lingering over the deep cleft that somehow through physical processes obscure caught and reflected light in such a way as to blind anyone who tried to look directly into Fieldbinder's deep green eyes
deep blue eyes, the color of cold crystal, with tiny fluffy white diamonds frozen in irises of ice.

Fieldbinder grinned wryly. "The word has a music, in my opinion, is all."

I just

"And your house?" Dr. J_____ lispingly hissed. "Are we not deeply upset at the destruction of your house, at the death of your phenomenal pet in its iron cage, at the disastrous fire and the plunge into disorientation and chaos which such an event must symbolize and entail?" J_____ played with himself covertly under his note pad.

Fieldbinder smiled coolly. "Doctor, I believe I have progressed to the point where I can honestly say that the event did not significantly 'upset' me—with all the ramifications and meanings implicit in your choice of the word. Attachment to things, to places, to other living beings requires in my view expenditures of energy and attention far in excess of the value of the things thus brought into the relation of attachment. Does this seem unreasonable? The attempt to have the order of one's life depend on things and persons outside that life is a silly thing, a thing perhaps appropriate only for those weaker, less successful, less fortunate, less advanced than I."

"We are not sure what you mean," bleated Dr. J____, lovingly stroking the controls of his mechanical chair.

"Think of it this way, doctor," said Fieldbinder patiently, smiling coolly. "Think of the Self as at the node of a fan-shaped network of emotions, dispositions, extensions of that feeling and thinking Self. Each line in the protruding network-fan may of course have an external reference and attachment. A house, a woman, a bird, a woman. But it need not be so. The line that seeks purchase in and attachment to an exterior Other is necessarily buttressed, supported, held; it thus becomes small, weak, flabby, reliant on Other. Were the exterior reference and attachment to disappear, unlikely as that obviously sounds in my own case, the atrophied line would crumble weakly, might also disappear. The Self would be smaller than before. And even a Self as prodigious as myself must look upon diminution with disfavor." Fieldbinder grinned wryly, removed a molecule of lint from his impeccable slacks. "Better to have the lines of the fan stand on their own: self-sufficient, rigid, hard, jutting out into space. Should someone find herself attracted to one of the lines, she could of course fall upon it with all the ravenousness that would be only natural. But she shall not be the reference. Only the ephemeral night insect, drawn to a light that is intrinsically inaccessible. She may be consumed in the line's light, but still the line stands, juts out, rigidly, far into the space exterior to the Self."

"We are afraid we are inequipped to understand such a thing," hissed J____. "Please allow me to consult and masturbate over the writings of my teacher."

"No real need for that, doctor." Fieldbinder held up a stop-palm and smiled coolly. "I think it is in my power to put the insight in terms you

can readily understand. Have you by any chance ever watched an animated television program called 'The Road Runner'?"

"I watch the cartoon ever week; I am a rabid fan." Drool cascaded
over J_____'s chin as he wriggled in his chair, his feet dangling far above
the burnt-yellow office carpet.

"I somehow guessed as much," smiled Fieldbinder. "So too is my latest
mistress, when she is not busy working as an incredibly successful recorder of messages for cash registers in high-quality supermarkets. I have
on occasion taken a Saturday morning off and watched the program
with her. Has it occurred to you that 'The Road Runner' is what might
aptly be termed an existential program? That it comments not uninter-
estingly on the very attitudes that would be implicit in a person's feeling 'upset' over a catastrophic fire in his home? I see you are puzzled,"
Fieldbinder said, noticing Dr. J_____ frantically scratching his head, a
plume of dandruff shooting up into the air of the office only to reset-
tle on the obscene bald spot in the middle of the doctor's skull-shaped
head.

Fieldbinder smiled and continued, "I invite you to realize that this
program does nothing other than present us with a protagonist, a coyote,
functioning within a system interestingly characterized as a malevolent
Nature, a protagonist who endlessly, tirelessly, disastrously pursues a
thing, a telos—the bird in the title role—a thing and goal far, far less
valuable than the effort and resources the protagonist puts into its pursuit."
Fieldbinder grinned wryly. "The thing pursued—a skinny meatless bird—
is far less valuable than the energy and attention and economic resources
expended by the coyote on the process of pursuit. Just as an attachment
radiating from the Self outward is worth far less than the price the establishment of such an attachment inevitably exacts."

Dr. J_____ inflated an anatomically correct doll and began to fondle
it as it stared blankly. Fieldbinder smiled patiently.

"A question, doctor," he said. "Why doesn't the coyote take the money
he spends on bird costumes and catapaults and radioactive road runner
food pellets and explosive missiles and simply go eat Chinese?" He smiled
coolly. "Why doesn't the coyote simply go eat Chinese food?" Fieldbinder's
face assumed a cool, bland, wry expression as he attended to his impeccable
slacks.

Dr. J_____ snarled and

/g/

"Rick? Am I interrupting?"

". . . ."

"I can come back."

"What is it."

"It's just about this kid-putting-himself-through-prep-school submission. Is the *Physicians' Desk Reference* a real book, or is it just a made-up name?"

"The *P.D.R.* is real."

". . . ."

"It numbers among its features a cataloguing, chemical breakdown, manufacturer, dosage, and contraindications for almost every known form of prescription medication available in the United States, in a given year."

"Oh."

"People seriously interested in drugs and things medical, but particularly drugs, swear by it."

"Even kids?"

"Especially kids."

"How come you know all this?"

"I knew a child who swore by his copy of the *P.D.R.* Who used to keep it hidden in his toychest, under his old football pads and helmet."

"Your son?"

". . . ."

"It's pretty late, you know. The lake's all spoiled mayonnaise now, see?"

". . . ."

"Look, I'm sorry I was testy at lunch. Dr. Jay had just got done being incredibly weird and obnoxious. I'm seriously considering not seeing him anymore. I think we need to talk about it."

"Do we."

"Anyway, I'm sorry."

"Not a problem at all. Not a problem, at all."

"Are you going to work much more? Is that Norslan stuff?"

"No. Yes."

"Is Andy still around?"

"I'm afraid I don't know, Lenore."

"You should have heard what he said to Candy this afternoon, at Mr. Bombardini's meeting. You want to hear about it?"

"Not particularly."

"Are you going to work much more?"

"I haven't picked up my *Plain Dealer* yet. I believe I'll drop down and pick it up and catch up on things, for a bit."

"You don't feel like going to dinner, then?"

". . . ."

"Um, maybe I'll just stay out at Mavis's desk and do some more submissions, and wait until you maybe want to go."

". . . ."

"Are you OK?"

"Come closer. I can't see you in this light."

"Look, I'm sorry I said that that Fieldbinder story you obviously liked sucked canal-water. It was one an eminent friend sent you, right? It all became clear to me this afternoon. Let's consider it one of the things that keened my pitch. I took it off the rejection pile. I asterisked it."

"Not a problem at all."

"So should I wait for you, for dinner?"

"Do whatever you feel valid and three-dimensional doing, Lenore."

"Pardon me?"

"In answer to your question, the *Physicians' Desk Reference* is very real. It has transcended its context, one might say."

"Are you sure you're OK? Was Jay a total shit to you too?"

"Just feel a bit . . . tired and small tonight. A little coyote-ish."

"Coyote-ish?"

". . . ."

/h/

Nearly six, the sun low and the shadow full and the watery lights lit high overhead in the lobby ceiling, Judith Prietht was closing up shop and getting ready to shut down the console for the night, the Bombardini Company getting more than enough legitimate calls during business hours. Into her shopping bag went the limp-necked sweater she had almost finished knitting; off went her slippers and on went her street shoes; now off when her console (Position Release and Position Busy pushed together shut down a Centrex 28 equipped with a special Shutdown feature, which the Frequent and Vigorous console wasn't, and could only be put to rest by removing the console cable itself from its jack in the back with a ratchet wrench, an option exercised on more than one occasion by Vern Raring in the really empty, quiet part of the night); off went her lamp, leaving the Frequent and Vigorous half of the switchboard cubicle in a softer kind of light; on went her hair net; in went a Certs. Out she went, blowing a not-returned kiss to Candy Mandible, home to feed her cat.

Candy sat smoking again, waiting for Vern Raring to come in at six, trying not to look at the little clock over the console while she told the latest Lang story to Walinda Peahen, who sat completing time sheets for submission to Payroll the next morning, Friday. Walinda was not in a good mood, having been kept overtime in her other job at Frequent Leisure Suit today, but Candy Mandible was the kind of woman who tended to ignore moods not caused directly by her; and since Walinda Peahen was the kind of woman whose bad moods tended to be made worse by people around her behaving as if she were in a bad mood, she and Candy actually got on fairly well, and it was Candy who had originally gotten Lenore her job, this fact now being the only really sore point in Candy-Walinda relations.

"Be needin' to hire somebody else now that the girl finally got promoted by her squeeze," Walinda had said.

"Only a temporary person, though," Candy said. "Because she's only going to be helping Mr. Vigorous temporarily, while he's incredibly busy with the Stonecipheco account."

"Huh," said Walinda. She turned eyes thick with shadow on Candy. "Girl what you mean Stonecipheco? Vigorous told me it was a big new Norslan account they got."

"Andy Lang told me that's what Mr. Vigorous is supposed to tell people," Candy said, turning slightly to avoid blowing smoke in

Walinda's face. "But it's really not. It's really Stonecipheco baby food."

"And that crap be *nasty?*" said Walinda. "On sale once, and I give it to my child, and he like to die. Lenore be makin' some foul-ass food, for all her money."

"Lenore doesn't make the food, Walinda, you know that." Candy sighed. "And you know she doesn't get any money from it. And just please remember to only hire somebody temporary, is all."

Walinda didn't say anything, and Candy launched into the Lang story.

"It was a scream," she said. "I died. I laughed so hard that I died."

Walinda worked the adding machine and didn't say anything.

"I know you couldn't come," Candy continued, "but you know today Mr. Bombardini was having a meeting for everybody in both firms in the Building? You got the memo about that, right?"

"I got it. And I heard y'all just had to hear the fat man talk about his Building."

"Well it was just really bizarre, is all I can say. He was on this platform, with these like eight incredible *hunks* in loincloths holding him up in the air, and he was going on and on about how we all needed to begin to reconcile ourselves to having less space in the Building, because there was going to be a steadily decreasing amount of space for us, and then he stopped even mentioning the Building at all and started talking about there like being less space for us in general, like the world was getting small or something, and he had this weird fiendish light in his eyes, and plus it looked like he'd gained about a thousand pounds or so, and he kept looking at Lenore like he wanted to eat her, and kept dropping all these hints about how there could be some space for some of us if we came around and played our cards right. Bombardini's totally infatuated with Lenore, ever since his wife left him for a yogurt salesman. He sends her flowers almost every day."

"Maybe she can get us a bigger cubicle in here, then," Walinda said thoughtfully, adding up hours.

"But anyway the point is that it was supposed to be an incredibly serious meeting, and it was really a tense scene, and deadly quiet, 'cause everybody's scared to death of Mr. Bombardini," Candy said, blowing a ring and putting a red-nailed finger through it. "So it was deadly quiet, and Bombardini was going on and on, and this Andy Lang guy was sitting right in front of Lenore and me, and he all of a sudden starts turning around in his chair, really slowly, and looks all intensely at us, like he's got something really important to say, and we lean forward, and he leans back to us, and he whispers to us, real loud, 'I have an *erection*.'" Candy began to laugh, with big breaths, making Walinda laugh too. "And I died, and started laughing, and it was even worse because it was such a deadly quiet and serious situation, and Lenore started laughing too, and we couldn't stop. And then but Lang turned back around innocent as can be and started listening to Mr. Bombardini again, and there we were dying, laughing like hell. It was . . . awful." Candy was laughing so hard that smoking became impossible. She dropped her cigarette in an old can of Tab, where it hissed and fizzed and died.

Walinda chuckled. "Ooh child. What'd Lenore's little man think of that, I wonder. Was he sittin' in her lap at the time?"

"Mr. Vigorous wasn't there," said Candy. "He apparently had some kind of appointment. I think you two were the only ones not there, of the day people."

Walinda wet her finger and turned a time sheet. Candy started to get her things together in preparation for Vern's arrival. Into her purse went her pack of Djarum; on went her shoes . . .

"Excuse me," said a voice in front of the switchboard counter. "I'm looking for Mr. Lang."

Walinda looked up briefly and narrowed her eyes and went back to her adding machine. Candy straightened up from putting on her shoes and looked into the eyes of Mindy Metalman Lang.

"I'm Mrs. Lang," the woman said coolly. "I'm here looking for Mr. Lang. My husband. I was told by someone on the phone that he works here, even though the number they said was his when they put me through to him didn't answer after thirty rings."

Candy didn't answer right away. She was busy staring at what she, Candice Eunice Mandible, would very probably be, had she not had the ever so slightest bit of an overbite, and had she had perhaps ten more judiciously distributed pounds, and eyes more like wings, and had she been rich per se. She saw perfection; she smelled White Shoulders; she assumed the fur jacket was sable. This was an enormously beautiful woman, here, and Candy stared, and also unconsciously began smoothing the tight old violet cotton dress she had on.

Mindy was staring back, but not really at Candy so much as at Candy's dress. Her eyes faded a bit, as if she were trying to latch onto an elusive memory. Her eyes were different from Candy's, too. Very. Where Candy's were light brown and almost perfectly round, giving her face almost too much symmetry, making it an almost triangular face when it would have been nicer and more comforting as a rounder, more vague-at-the-edges face, Mindy's eyes were so dark they were almost black, and they seemed to spread out far more across the upper ridges of her cheeks, and back at the sides, like the wings of a dark sort of fluttery bird: large, delicate, full of a kind of motion even when still. Really nice eyes. A face very much like Candy's, but vaguer at the edges, and so really better. Candy smoothed at her dress some more.

"Girl what you doin', employee addresses in the directory," Walinda said to Candy, and she pushed the directory across the white counter until it hit Candy's hand. "Wrote his address down at the back myself," Walinda said.

Candy didn't have to look at the directory. "Mr. Lang's temporarily staying in a building in East Corinth, which is a suburb south of here." She smiled at Mindy. "Actually the same building, or house is more like it, as mine, which is how come I know, although it's a rooming house, so still like a building; it's not like he's living in my house." She laughed breathily.

"I see," Mindy said with a bit of a smile, nodding. "Perhaps then you could just jot down the address for me."

Candy reached for a pad and pen and jotted.

"There was, too, the office number, which the operator tried before," said Mindy. "Perhaps you could try him again for me. What . . . department is he in?" She looked around her at the marble lobby and the soft red chairs for lobby-dwellers and the tiny veins of the last bit of sunset moving together in the blackness of the walls.

"Translation," Candy told her, not looking up.

"Translation?"

"Baby food," Walinda Peahen said, flashing hostile green-shadowed eyes at Mindy's fur jacket and then returning to tax forms.

"Baby food?"

"Nix," Candy murmured into Walinda's ear. She stood up and pushed the Tissaws' address across the counter to Mindy.

"And I'd ring his office for you, but I happen to know he's not there," Candy smiled. "He left the office after a Building-wide meeting, about three this afternoon. I know more or less where he'll be tonight, though."

"Do you."

"He's going to be in a bar called Gilligan's Isle with an old friend of his, watching religious television."

Mindy was putting Lang's address into a really nice Étienne Aigner purse. She snapped it closed and looked up. "Religious television? Andy?"

"One of the . . . The show features a bird who belongs to a friend of mine, and of Mr. Lang's," said Candy. "We're all going to try to watch the bird tonight."

"A bird? Andy's going to watch a bird on religious television?"

"Gilligan's Isle is just right across Erieview Plaza from here," Candy said, pointing in the correct direction out through the revolving door of the lobby. "It's pretty easy to find. Has big colored statues in it."

Mindy was staring at the violet dress again. She looked up into Candy's round eyes. "Have we met before?" she said.

"No we haven't, I don't think." Candy shook her head and then cocked it. "Why?"

"I'm not sure. I don't mean to be impolite, but I know I've seen that dress before."

"This dress?" Candy looked down at herself. "This is an incredibly ancient dress. It used to belong to a friend of mine, the person who also owns the bird I just mentioned. Do you know Lenore Beadsman?"

The console began to beep. "Wait a minute," Candy was saying to Mindy. "You mentioned Lenore on the phone when I talked to you." Mindy just looked at her. Walinda was making no move toward the console. Candy bent to the call. A rapid, in-house flash. "Operator," she said.

Mindy had suddenly bent over the top of the cubicle counter and was looking down at the equipment. "That's a Centrex," she said to Walinda. "Is that a Centrex?"

Walinda looked up and narrowed her eyes again. "Yeah, it is."

"In school, in Massachusetts, my roommate worked as a student operator, for the college, and sometimes I'd read at the switchboard at night to keep her company. They had a Centrex."

"Twenty-eight?"

"I really have no idea."

"Mmmm."

Candy released and straightened up. "Well that was just Mr. Lang's supervisor, on the phone, Mrs. Lang. He's coming down for his newspaper, the supervisor." Candy gestured over at a well-perused issue of that day's *Plain Dealer* that lay on top of the cubicle typewriter's gray plastic dustcover. "If you'll wait here a second, he could probably answer your questions a lot better than I could."

Mindy continued to look down at the console. Then she smiled up at Candy. "I was freshman roommates at Holyoke with Lenore Beadsman's sister," she said in a low voice.

Candy's jaw dropped. "God, is this Clarice's dress?" she said. "Lenore sure didn't tell me. And well I had no idea you knew Lenore's *family*." Through the doors came Vern Raring, at 6:05. "Listen, here's my relief, so to speak," Candy said. "Let's just go have a seat out in the lobby, here, and we can—"

"But Lenore and I have met too," said Mindy, as if she had decided something, smiling for Candy a truly beautiful smile.

"No *kidding*. Well I had no idea Lenore knew Andy's wife." Candy clapped her hands once and smiled back into the wings of Mindy Metalman's eyes. "Listen," Candy said. "I really just love your jacket. Can I maybe touch it?"

"I suppose so."

Candy was stroking Mindy's sleeve when she looked past Mindy at the elevators in the northeast corner and saw Rick Vigorous and Lenore emerge.

"Well here's Lenore and Mr. Vigorous both, now," she said. Vern Raring entered the cubicle and gave Walinda Peahen a big kiss on the cheek, and she pretended to swat him, both of them laughing.

Mindy turned way around, so that her sleeve was all of a sudden out of Candy's reach. Candy's hand hit the counter. Mindy looked into the orange and black.

"Mr. Vigorous?"

17   1990

/a/

10 September

"You hurt me, Andy," says Lenore. "You hurt me inside."
"Well sugar that's love," says W.D.L.

So look, very closely. If one looks, very closely, into the bowl of the toilet, one sees the water inside is in fact not still, but pulses in its thick porcelain cup; rises and falls, ever so slightly, influenced by the ponderous suck and slap of subterranean tides unimagined by any but the devoutest morning pilgrim.

/b/

" 'Down the Laughing Brook came Billy Mink. He was feeling very good that morning, was Billy Mink, pleased with the world in general and with himself in particular.' "

"Roughage," said Concarnadine Beadsman.

" 'When he reached the Smiling Pool he swam out to the Big Rock. Little Joe Otter was already there, and not far away, lazily floating, with his head and back out of the water, was Jerry Muskrat.

" ' "Hello, Billy Mink!" cried Little Joe Otter.

" ' "Hello yourself," replied Billy Mink with a grin.' "

"And this one is called what again?" asked Mr. Bloemker from across Concarnadine's bed, doing something to his eye with a finger under his glasses.

"It's called 'Billy Mink Goes Dinnerless,' " Lenore said without looking up from the book. "Can we please just do it, here? I sense Concarnadine really liking this one."

"By all means."

"Roughage."

" ' "Where are you going?" asked Little Joe Otter.

" ' "Nowhere in particular," replied Billy Mink.

" ' "Let's go fishing down to the Big River," said Little Joe Otter.

" ' "Let's!" cried Billy Mink, diving from the highest point on the Big Rock.' "

"Her face is healing well in the moisture, don't you think?" said Mr. Bloemker.

Concarnadine actually didn't look all that good. There were sores, and there were bandages. A translucent white bandage stretched tight from just above Concarnadine's left eye up into her forehead; one of her tiny pale eyebrows was lost in the bandage that seemed to be growing into the skin.

"I think it was a splendid idea, having the humidifier brought in," Mr. Bloemker said, looking at his thumb. "We're just beginning to lose the heat and moisture that was in such generous attendance all season, as I'm sure you're aware. Concarnadine had such trouble last year, and if I recall correctly it was at just this time. As do so many of the J-ward residents. In any event, a splendid idea, Ms. Beadsman."

"Roughage."

" 'So off they started across the Green Meadows towards the Big River. Halfway there, they met Reddy Fox.' "

The red sores looked soft and bright in the light of the morning that spilled into Concarnadine's wall of windows from the central courtyard full of colored water. They looked wet. No running, though. The bandage that Lenore particularly objected to covered a whole big patch like that, right above Concarnadine's eyebrow. Lenore thought of the adhesive sticking to the soft of a sore. She thought of the bandage getting taken off.

"How often do you guys change that bandage?" she said.

"I'm afraid I don't know, precisely. I would imagine daily."

"There's no way you guys—"

"Roughage."

"—*rip* the thing off, right? You always wet it and peel it off carefully?"

"Of that I'm sure. We do not rip here."

Lenore looked into Concarnadine's eyes. Concarnadine smiled.

" ' "Hello Reddy! Come on with us to the Big River, fishing," called Billy Mink.

" 'Now Reddy Fox is no fisherman, though he likes fish to eat well enough. He remembered the last time he went fishing and how Billy Mink had laughed at him when he fell into the Smiling Pool. He was just about to say "No" when he changed his mind.

" ' "All right, I'll go," said Reddy Fox.

" 'Now Billy Mink and Little Joe Otter are famous fishermen and can swim even faster than the fish themselves. But Reddy Fox is a poor swimmer and must depend upon his wits. When they reached the bank of the Big River they very carefully crawled down to a sandy beach. There, just a little way out from shore, a school of little striped perch were at play. Billy Mink and Little Joe Otter prepared to dive in and each grab a fish, but Reddy Fox knew that he could not swim well enough for that.' "

"Roughage roughage roughage roughage."

Lenore remembered how last fall Mr. Bloemker had shown her a lot of other people in the Home with Concarnadine's particular condition. Mr. Bloemker had called the condition geriatric acne. He had had a theory. He said that both kinds of acne had to do with the skin not doing what it was supposed to do. He had said, "Someone disposed to see it this way might say that the skin is designed to keep what is properly inside the body inside the body and what is outside the body from getting in," and then that, "whereas in the case of young people we might say that they are so full of interior life and energy and whatnot that said life and bits of its interior may actually protrude from the envelope of the skin, forced outward, in the case of the residents here we might say that the assault here works in the reverse direction, that the residents' energies and attentions have collapsed on their still centers to such an extent that there is no longer sufficient interior life and energy to keep what is outside from puncturing the envelope and impinging

on the steadily receding interior," and so on. "Not infection rising
from within, but injury punched into the tired envelope from without," "the skin no longer a viable boundary," and so on. He had
not said membrane, to Lenore's knowledge.

"Except it only happens in the fall, when it gets drier," Lenore
had said. "Next fall we'll get Concarnadine a humidifier."

" 'But Billy Mink jeered at Reddy Fox.

" ' "Pooh! You're no fisherman, Reddy Fox! If I couldn't catch
fish when they are chased right into my hands I'd never go fishing."

" 'Reddy Fox pretended to be indignant.

" ' "I tell you what, Billy Mink," said he, "if I don't catch more
fish than you do to-day I'll bring you the plumpest chicken in Farmer
Brown's dooryard, but if I do catch more fish than you do you will
give me the biggest one you catch. Do you agree?"

" 'Now Billy Mink is very fond of plump chicken—' "

"Roughage."

" '—and here was a chance to get one without danger of meeting
Bowser the Hound, who guards Farmer Brown's chickens. So Billy
Mink agreed to give Reddy Fox the biggest fish he caught that day
if Reddy could show more fish than he could at the end of the day.
All the time he chuckled to himself, for you know Billy Mink is a
famous fisherman—' "

"Roughage."

" '—and he knows that Reddy Fox is a poor swimmer and does
not like the water.' "

Concarnadine Beadsman, Mrs. Stonecipher Beadsman, Jr., had
been in residence at the Shaker Heights Nursing Home even before
the Home had been bought by Stonecipheco Baby Food Products.
Concarnadine Beadsman had unfortunately gone senile while still
in her fifties. She had giggled in the rain at the funeral of her
husband, after the accident involving the Jell-O alternative. She
had moaned in the car on the way to the main Beadsman home in
Shaker Heights, to which she was moved from her own home in
Chagrin Falls after the death of her husband. Then, for a few years
in Shaker Heights, her days had been filled with trips to the mailbox:
two hours' walk to the box at the end of the block; the meat of the
day spent peering into the black mouth of the box as the slot was
held open first with one hand and then the other, the day punctuated

neatly by the mailman coming at four and unlocking the bottom of the box and mail heaving out all over—an end-of-the-day release with which Concarnadine often unfortunately found herself in involuntary empathy—followed by a thirty-second drive back to the house with a family-member who drove low in the seat and wore sunglasses. . . . Then just rest, relaxation, unlimited Lawrence Welk, a plethora of mail-watching options, function-labels for things. As far as Lenore could tell—and she did try—Concarnadine was really happy.

" 'By and by they came to another sandy beach like the first one. They could see another school of foolish young fish at play. As before, Reddy Fox remained on shore while the others swam out and drove the fish in. As before, Reddy caught half a dozen, while Billy Mink and Little Joe Otter each caught one this time. Reddy had five and then pretended to be so tickled over catching one, the smallest of the lot, that Billy Mink didn't suspect a trick.' "

Mr. Bloemker sighed to himself and jiggled a shoe.

Lenore looked at him. "You know, you're really more than welcome to go. I'm sure you must be busy."

"Roughage."

"I have been instructed to wait for the owners of the facility, or of course for a representative," said Mr. Bloemker. "I can just as well wait here. I hope to have a chance for an additional chat, once this delightful piece is through."

"My father's coming down here?"

"It is not impossible."

"I think he's too busy gearing up for getting all pissed off about Kopek Spasova doing Gerber ads in Erieview tonight."

"Nevertheless."

"Roughage."

"Is it Karl Rummage who's coming? Do they maybe want to have you look up patients' ages for them again?"

"For your information, I have been led to understand that the relevant unavailable facility-connected individuals will apparently be back with us very soon."

"You said the exact same thing a couple days ago, and I called Dad, and nada."

"But this time I have been led to the above understanding by persons connected with the ownership of the facility."

"Roughage."

"Mr. Rummage?"

"A young person in Chemistry, at Stonecipheco Baby Foods."

"Obstat?"

"That sounds right."

"Dad swore up and down that he'd call me the minute he had anything about Lenore. He said he's about ready to call the police if she and everything else missing don't turn up, or at least drop a line."

Mr. Bloemker didn't say anything. He scratched at his beard.

"Anyway," Lenore said, "the point is that he sure didn't call this morning. So I don't believe it."

Bloemker looked at his shoe and shrugged.

"And Rick and I supposedly have alternate Lenore-finding plans. Largely and weirdly Rick-inspired, but still."

"As you wish. I will of course pass on any and all relevant information, as per our agreement."

"You and Brenda are too kind."

"Roughage."

" 'For the rest of the day the fishing was poor. Just as Old Mother West Wind started from the Green Meadows to take her children, the Merry Little Breezes, to their home behind the Purple Hills, the three little fishermen started to count up their catch. Then Reddy brought out all the fish that he had hidden. When they saw the pile of fish Reddy Fox had, Billy Mink and Little Joe Otter were so surprised that their eyes popped out and their jaws dropped.' "

"Roughage." Concarnadine's jaw dropped, too. Her legs were straight out before her as she sat up in bed; her feet, in wool socks, pointed in different directions. Her shins, visible between the flaps of her robe, were spotted.

" 'Reddy walked over to the big pickerel and, picking it up, carried it over to his pile. "What are you doing with my fish?" shouted Billy Mink angrily.

" ' "It isn't yours, it's mine!" retorted Reddy Fox.' "

"Roughage."

" 'Billy Mink fairly danced up and down he was so angry. "It's not yours!" he shrieked. "It's mine, for I caught it!"

" ' "And you agreed that your biggest fish should be mine if I caught more fish than you did. I've caught four times as many, so the pickerel is mine," retorted Reddy, winking at Little Joe Otter.' "

"Roughage roughage roughage *roughage*," said Concarnadine Beadsman.

"What's with this roughage stuff?" Lenore said. "How come she keeps saying 'roughage'?"

"We have noted that as the autumn begins to cut into the heat that infallibly and understandably drove so many of the J-ward residents into themselves, the residents begin as it were to come around, to begin to rediscover the rewards of communication," Mr. Bloemker said. "Recall that Concarnadine said absolutely nothing all summer. Now we hear words for the sake of words. Explanation? A nurse probably remarked that it would be good for Concarnadine to eat her salad, for the roughage it contained, and Concarnadine fastened on the word, more than likely. Of course you know that here at the Shaker Heights facility we like to encourage regularity through the consumption of fiber, not through harsh chemicals."

"Roughage."

"Except she probably doesn't have any idea what the word stands for," Lenore said.

"Doubtless. Although Lenore did have 'roughage' in the J-ward lexicons. Shall I hunt around for one?"

"And why that word to get fixated on?" Lenore said. "Concarnadine never used to care what she ate. She even ate Stonecipheco stuff, a lot of the time, when it was around the house. She was a weird eater. One time I was little, and we went over for Christmas, and Gramma C. and Grandaddy had had a fight, and Gramma C. didn't eat all day; she just stayed in the basement, throwing darts at a poster of Jayne Mansfield."

Concarnadine Beadsman smiled.

Mr. Bloemker leaned over the bed toward Lenore. His eyes had a way of attracting sunlight and turning weird colors behind his glasses.

"Ms. Beadsman, may I bounce a theory off you, bearing on matters we've previously discussed?"

"Let me finish this story. You can tell by her smile she likes it."

"Roughage."

"Merely this. Has it not occurred to you that a sense of shall we say social history is strongest among the *young*, not the old?"

" 'Then Billy Mink did a very foolish thing; he lost his temper completely. He called Reddy Fox bad names. But he did not dare try to take the big pickerel away from Reddy, for Reddy is much bigger than he. Finally he worked himself into such a rage that he ran off, leaving his pile of fish behind.' "

"That as people age, accumulate more and more private experience, their sense of history tightens, narrows, becomes more personal? So that to the extent that they remember events of social importance, they remember only for example 'where they were' when such-and-such occurred. Et cetera et cetera. Objective events and data become naturally more and more subjectively colored. Does this account seem reasonable?"

" 'Reddy Fox and Little Joe Otter took care not to touch Billy Mink's fish, but Reddy divided his big pile with Little Joe Otter. Then they, too, started for home, Reddy carrying the big pickerel.' "

"Roughage."

"Any thoughts on this? I am of course extrapolating on some of the issues we tackled when last we met face to face. Of course I feel the insight holds particularly true of Midwesterners, who stand in such an ambiguous geographical and cultural relation to certain other less occluded parts of the country that the very objective events and states of affairs that are proper objects of a social awareness must pass in transit to the awarenesses of the residents here through the filters both of subjectively colored memory and geographical ambivalence. Hence perhaps the extreme complication we can see all around us at the Shaker Heights facility."

Behind Concarnadine's lovely red lip and the bottom row of her even teeth Lenore could see a clear lake of saliva accumulating, growing, lapping with each breath at the backs of the teeth and beginning to shine at the corners of Concarnadine's mouth as her jaw still hung low.

" 'Late that night, when he had recovered his temper, Billy Mink began to grow hungry. The more he thought of his fish, the hungrier he grew.' "

"Any thoughts at all, then?"

"Not really."

"Roughagegegege."

"Oh, dear."

"She just got too much saliva in her mouth, is all." Lenore reached for some Kleenex from the bedside table. "Just a little too much saliva."

"Happens to the best of us."

"Mr. Blumker?" At the doorway was Neil Obstat, Jr., knocking faintly at the thin pretend-wood paneling, staring at Lenore, who was bent over a smiling beautiful gray-haired figure in a cotton bathrobe and wool socks, with a handful of sopped Kleenex. "Hello," he said. "Hi, Lenore."

"Hi."

"How are you today?"

"Roughage," said Concarnadine, wiggling her toes.

"You can swallow, you know, Gramma C. You can just swallow your saliva, you know."

"How's your Mom, there?" said Obstat.

"Perhaps we'll just step outside and let you finish reading to Concarnadine," Mr. Bloemker said, his finger tracing the outline of his beard.

Lenore put the wet Kleenex in Mr. Bloemker's outstretched hand and bent to the book again. She heard the tissues drop into Concarnadine's metal wastebasket with a heavy sound as Mr. Bloemker went for the door where Obstat was standing.

"Mr. Blumker I'm Neil Obstat, Jr., of Stonecipheco Baby Food Products," Lenore heard Obstat say. She could tell he was still looking at her from the back.

"Bloemker, actually . . . ," Lenore heard. "Just step out a bit . . . hall." There were sounds.

" 'Finally he could stand it no longer and started for the Big River to see what had become of his fish.' "

Lenore could remember that at Shaker School one time Neil Obstat had been given a wedgie in the boys' locker room by Ed Creamer and Jesus Geralamo and the whole sinister crew, and had been left by Creamer hanging by his underwear from a coat-hook in the hall outside the locker rooms, in full view of Lenore and

Karen Daughenbaugh and Karen Baum and all the rest of the girls in seventh-hour P.E. who were on the way to the bus, and that a janitor had had to lift Obstat down, and that Karen Baum had said she'd been able to see just about Neil Obstat's whole butt.

" 'He reached the strip of beach where he had so foolishly left them just in time to see the last striped perch disappear down the long throat of Mr. Night Heron.' "

"Roughage." Concarnadine was foraging for something in her mouth with a finger. Lenore looked back down at the book.

"Membrane, Concarnadine," Lenore said, trying to make her voice deep. "I say to you 'membrane.' "

"Roughage."

LaVache Beadsman had said, years ago, that Lenore hated Concarnadine because Concarnadine looked like her. True, Concarnadine's hair was long and full and curled down all over the shoulders of her pink bathrobe, where Lenore's was of course shorter and brown and hung in two large curls to meet in points below her chin. But Concarnadine's actual face was Lenore's face, too, more or less, the less being a dust of wrinkles at the corners of Concarnadine's eyes and two deep smile-furrows from the corners of her mouth down into her jaw.

"Lenore hates Concarnadine because Concarnadine looks like her," LaVache had said to John, in the east wing, while Lenore read by the window and listened. "Lenore identifies with her in some deep and scary way."

"Then are we invited to extend the same reasoning to your relationship with Dad?" John had said with a laugh. "Since we all know that you're basically just Dad's image in a tiny little mirror."

LaVache had moved in, brandishing the leg. And Lenore had watched Miss Malig, current in her fingers, iodine in her eyes, descend, restore order.

"Oh, Lenore."

Lenore looked up from the book. "Pardon?"

"Roughage roughage." The bathrobe was now up over her knees, knees that looked to be covered with the kind of gray skin usually found at the backs of elbows.

Obstat's voice was in the hall. Lenore could hear the wet sound of Mr. Bloemker doing something to his own face. Protruding from the edge of the frame of the door, she could see, was the bottom of Mr. Bloemker's brown sportcoat. The floor of the doorway looked dusted with a faint black that trailed out into the hall. Lenore wished Concarnadine's room were cleaner.

" 'And this is how it happened that Billy Mink went dinnerless to bed. But he had learned three things, had Billy, and he never forgot them—that wit is often better than skill; that it is not only mean but is very foolish to sneer at another; and that to lose one's temper is the most foolish thing in the world.' "

Lenore watched steam chug out of Concarnadine's humidifier and turn pale yellow in the light of the glass wall. The steam made her think of another room.

"What should we do, Gramma C.?"

Concarnadine smiled beautifully and plucked at the papery skin on the backs of her hands. Lenore watched her roll her head back and forth at the ceiling, for joy.

/c/

10 September

Shall we begin, then. Calves. Posture. Scent. Sounds amid fields of light.

One. Calves. Shall we discuss the persistent habit the light of the sun had of reflecting off Mindy Metalman's calves. Thus then the calves themselves. An erotic surface being neither dull nor hard. A dull surface equalling no reflection; a hard surface equalling a vulgar, glinting spangle.

But a reflection from soft, smooth—perfectly shaved smooth—perfectly clean suburban skin. Light off the shins of her calves as said calves projected their curves from chairs, or scissored the air above clogs that made solid sounds in the sidewalk . . . or yes go ahead hung over the edge of the country club pool, pressing, so that the flesh of the calf behind swelled out and made the reflection two ovals of light.

I pull a new red-eyed Vance Vigorous from the pool, and as we enter into corn-dog negotiations there is Mindy Metalman, in a deck chair, sipping something cold through a straw, and there is the light of the Scarsdale sun, reflecting from her smooth shins, and I am elsewhere as Vance shrinks on the deck.

Heavy of necktie, I rise from the plume over baby Vance's crib to see Mindy Metalman, and yes perhaps two or three incidental neighborhood children around her, for decoration, doing her Circe dance around Rex Metalman's sprinkler. And yes there is the light, reflected from her legs through the water, and the light comes out and breaks the mist of the sprinkler into color, and the mist and the light settle into the wet grass and the light remains and affects the air around it; I see it even much later as I sip something from my den window and watch Rex on his knees in the trampled, sprinkled, misted lawn, straightening each precious bent blade with tweezers. And in the breeze of late afternoon my own chaotic blades vibrate in sympathy.

From my den window, here, is to be seen Mindy Metalman, at her own window, seated on her desk, legs up and calves demurely thrust curving over the sill of the open pane, shaving in the sun. She sees me across the fence and laughs. Fresh air does absolutely everything good, doesn't it? And here the blade moves down, too slowly by far to be taken seriously by me, for whom the whole process is a rite entirely other, but at any rate each furrow of foam in the curving field is replaced by an expanse of soft shaved gold, in the light.

Calves, light, legs, light, everything will be all right.

Two. Posture. Am invited by Rex Metalman to a cotillion for his daughter, Melinda Susan Metalman. (Was it a real cotillion? Why can't I remember?) Am invited by Rex Metalman to some Puberty-Rite function for his daughter.

Said function consisting of row after row, group after group, whole nations of tired, nervous, bad-postured girls in immoderate pink gowns. Thin, heads thrust out, hands resting on one another's shoulders, lips moving just inside one another's ears. I squint a bit over my third or fourth something and am in a tinkling, frosted swamp, a cold pond of candy flamingos, flowers of snow, slowly hardening under a varied crystal sun. Then the girls change and become for a while vaguely reptilian, heads out like turtles, vaguely amphibian, seeming ever to scan for threat or reward—pimples to be seen at some of the corners of some of the mouths.

Yes and of course the key here is except for Mindy Metalman, who was in a white gown, with a carnation of pink sugar, and her hair pulled up in a tight bun, but with a burst of a black curl here, and there, and here, hinting at the dark nova the hair could become at any time, should someone outside my influence wish it.

And Melinda Metalman standing straight, with a straight spine, but for the swan's curve of her neck and the bit of the hip-shot pelvis with which she pummeled the unwary, a solid, straight, juicy girl, her gown just low enough to afford the thinking man imaginative access to the systems that must have lain just within, revolving broad and silent about their still red point. And, and this posture—what was it about a head, with its dark, spreading, fluttery eyes, about a head placed so easily atop a simple vertical line? Perhaps just the contrast with the rest of the wildlife in that cold frosted marsh, perhaps merely the fact that the head was easy and content to let things come, that it did not jut out to snap at them. Sounds of snapping were all around me, and I loathed them, and I loathed too and still do loathe any and all heads which jut.

But dancing was of course out of the question, and this girl in the throes of Rite of course either danced or installed herself in a social orbit around the hors d'oeuvre bar, and I will never ever again approach a female at an hors d'oeuvre bar.

And yes too following me about the perimeter of the room as I circled, joined at the soft parts of our bones, was as always the deeply chilling presence of Veronica Vigorous, and so yes anything at all was rendered impossible, assuming that it wouldn't have been, which it would have, and so here I was tiny and icy and tired. But I can remember in the cold bath of the chandelier that vertical line, and the hair, and the eyes that were wings in a head to which jutting was clearly a thing unfamiliar, to be laughed at with the toss of a tiny star-burst curl.

She said Mr. Vigorous what a terribly wonderful surprise seeing you here of all places after all these years, do you remember who I am, and there with her was Mandible, and there in the cubicle the northern regions of the dark planet of Walinda Peahen's hair, and there was Raring, setting up his magnetic chessboard, he plays chess with himself all night, and there was Lenore, she had wanted to bolt back into the elevator when we stepped into the lobby, she had seen, I could feel, and Mandible was petting the arm of Mindy's coat as if it were an Airedale, and there she was, and the day had been such that when she said Mr. Vigorous what a terribly wonderful surprise to see you I felt deep beneath all our feet a heavy liquid clicking, as if the gears and cogs of some ponderous subterranean device had all moved into positions of affinity within their baths of lubricant, and she was saying Lenore do you remember me, I certainly remember you, I will bet you remember my husband, at whom you threw a shoe, how is Clarice, and as I rode the rhythm of the device I heard from above talk of parlors and tanning accidents, and uncountably many words from her about husbands, and lawns, and schools, and some dress or other, and careers, and marriage therapy, and Lenore was monosyllabic throughout, and then the tangent involving the type of switchboard equipment we used, and temporary things, and the whole Peahen planet dawned over the cubicle horizon, and cogs bit into one another, and eyes were rolled, and there was talk of Lenore's bird, our bird, all in the context of the husband being in some bar with a self-flagellating bartender, and the Desert was mentioned, suddenly, and Lenore's nostrils abruptly flared as she pulled away, and a long look passed that did something to the air between them, and over it all and muffling it all was the sound of hoofs on the marble lobby floor, the Scarsdale Express, bearing down, cold sparks at the wheels, pulled by the marvelous set of horses that whip themselves: Calves, Posture, Scent and Sounds, and all the suns went down.

Three. A scent came off her. Turn just right and it would go through me and leave a tiny hole in which the wind whistled, when I turned just right.

I was behind her in the car, on occasion, when Rex would drive into the city and she to school and me to work. When I rode in the back she would be in front, on the passenger side. She would not wear a seatbelt, and Rex would say You are riding in the Death Seat Melinda, the seat you are in is called the Death Seat you know, and I would be directly behind her, in the Rear Death Seat, with my feet not touching the floor except at the hump in the middle.

And now in the passenger window beside her were reflected at an angle the images of the oncoming cars and trucks, and there was her image, there, too, waiting; and the cars and trucks bore down in the window and emptied head-on into her reflection, were swallowed and exploded, and out the back of her reflection into my sleepy puffy face came fragments of light, the street made pale, and a wash of scent.

Yes the scent really came off her head, not off images exploding into light in glass; I am not a complete shitty fool. It was just a scent: clean, rich, vaguely fleshy. Imagine something blown dry on a line in a soft wind. Much should not be made of what is only a horse with cold hoofs.

Or once finding myself behind her and a friend on a city street. I was eating a pretzel for lunch, big and soft as my own face, a monstrously salty pretzel, and soon the pretzel man's partner some blocks down would cheerfully sell me a Pepsi, but here were the solid, very solid sounds of her boots on the pavement, like a pump in the roots of a deep well, and here was the dark, thick hair, hanging almost all the way down her back, and having things done to it by the wind, and of course hair equals scent, and I was riddled, and salt poured from me like sand, and Mrs. Lot stood stock still in her beret in the middle of gridlock, transfixed by a red light.

Too much cannot be made of a scent.

Four. Sounds and a Lonely Little Thing.

Veronica and Vance were somewhere, away. For Veronica and me it had been a matter of *years*, so you can imagine. And it was August, and I had my usual Rex-Metalman-world-of-pollen Scarsdale allergies, and was into my second week of being wired on antihistamines, salivaless and bumping into walls . . .

And it was nighttime, and I was in my den, and because it was nighttime the light was on, and over across the fence Mindy Metalman's light was on, in her room, and her window was open, but the shades were drawn. Antihistamines make me dream. My light was on, and, it being August, insects wanted in. I established for my purposes levels of insects, levels of entry, each corresponding to a field of light. The lit den made the insects tap and bounce on the windowscreen, wanting in. And a few would get in, that was OK, but then I would hear tiny dry sounds of impact and I would look up and there would be the insects, bouncing off the frosted glass shell around the light fixture: let us in let us in. And unscrew the shell, and then there you would be as before, but with the insects now bouncing off the hot thin skin of the lightbulb itself, let us in, banging with blunt heads and burnt wings, let us in. All right, but where did they want to go? Because break the lightbulb open with, say, the tiny screwdriver you use to fix the keys of your typewriter, break open the skin of the bulb to let them in, and either the light they want is killed and the game is over, or else they simply orbit the unenterable filament until they are fried dry and fall away.

So I stood on tiptoe on my desk, with my screwdriver, and bits of glass in my hair, and a dry mouth, in the dark, wishing for a Flit gun, or else to know where the appropriate place to want in *was*, then; and I heard sounds, from across the fence.

And they came from Mindy Metalman's room. Behind the white shade there were shadows. And, too, there were the sounds . . . like the scent, tiny but penetrating . . . of a passion, not a person, being yielded to. And I got down on fours on the desk amid papers and glass and allergy capsules and looked out and saw in the Metalmans' driveway a strange, deep-red Mustang with big rear tires, and the shade with its shadow dance, and behind and above the car and the house the slow, liquid pulse of a distant aerial tower's red light that matched the spasms of my own drugged heart and so became my falling star. And there were the sounds of Mindy Metalman, in another world, the world of the liquid pulse; and the thought of someone unknown to me sharing the world with her, the thought that some actual person with big rear tires was with her, *now*, all this sent me off the desk and into the bathroom to climb atop the laundry hamper and brush away hot insects and listen at the light- bulb. For my dry dull head full of pollen thought that if we could just catch something the *same*, here, the insects and I could all kick off our shoes and have a beer.

I have said to her, no I will not be going to any gymnastic baby- food spectaculars with you.

And when she says why not I say ask Lang.

I say by all means, take the morning off. Go roll about. Be three- dimensional. Sign bottoms.

And she says I am going to go read to my grandmother.

And I say go, ask valid young Lang whom to take to Erieview, he's in the next room.

And she stands there in her sneakers and says don't push at me.

Darling darling darling, tell me about the reversal I say.

How something or other to have her down below, in my network, all over again. In the cubicle. The lobby will resound, glow. I have bought breath mints.

Lenore what does it mean to feel that you must either kill or die. Does that make us an insect, in a field of light that can be only desired, or else extinguished?

Between yesterday and me lies a whole field of it.

The mints make it cold when I suck at the air. A suck at the air equals a sigh. Dinner, with Mindy Metalman? Oh yes oh no.

The burnt house stands delicate and everything is still arranged but now everything is black and hollow and featherlight and near dust and squeaks in the wind. The toilet is untouched, and pulses quietly as the wind blows through hollow ribs, all around it.

One, Two, Three, Four: that's utter tripe, says his Lenore.

/d/

"I know what I know, is all."

"What does that mean, 'I know what I know'?"

"I know the whole story."

"Well if I don't know the story I obviously don't know if you know the story."

"The Andy story."

"What, like his historical story, the story of his life, or what he's been doing here, or what?"

"You are so funny."

"Why am I funny?"

"This isn't the same material, you know."

"It's close. It's the same color."

"But it's not the same texture. I want that thin cotton texture, that fadedness and thinness, that it-could-give-way-at-any-second quality."

"Well maybe you should know that this particular dress is like ten years old, is why it's so thin. I don't know why you're so fixated on this dress."

"I'd buy it from you, but if it barely fits you like that there is simply no way it could fit me."

"Who says I'd sell it?"

"So what we need is this color in a lighter, more cottony material."

"Anyway, it's Lenore's. I couldn't sell Lenore's dress. I'd have to buy it from her, which I'll probably do anyway given the Nick thing, but then I wouldn't want to sell it. See?"

"Relax. It wouldn't fit me anyway."

" . . . "

"I am having lunch in the cafeteria of something called Mooradian's Department Store, Cleveland, Ohio. Alan and Muffin would just die."

"This is a really good store. Don't underrate this store."

"Not mad about its fabric selection one bit."

"I'll give you the names of some other stores, but I can't go with you, I don't think. Walinda embolisms if I go over an hour for lunch."

"She is not my very favorite person."

"She's just hard to get to know. You get to know her, everything's OK. She just didn't like your jacket, probably. She tends not to like people who have a lot of money. Which you pretty obviously do."

" . . . "

"Have money, I mean."

" . . . "

"Which if you'll excuse me makes me sort of wonder why you're even considering working even as a temporary at the Frequent and Vigorous board. Which don't get me wrong is not a horrible job or anything, I'm not talking down my job, but it just isn't too exciting, and right now it's especially hectic and a pain because of line trouble, and you might or might not know it only pays four an hour, which is a pretty un-princely sum."

"Money isn't even an issue. I'm on vacation. I have unlimited vacation time, nearly, in my career. Retail food prices aren't expected to change in the next few weeks."

"What a job. I couldn't believe it. I can't believe you do that."

". . . ."

"Hey, do it again."

"Not here, Candy."

"Come on. It's noisy, no one'll hear. Please."

"Honestly."

"Please."

"Total: seventeen-fifty. Cash: twenty dollars. Change due: two-fifty."

"That's just too super."

"It gets less super as time goes on, believe me."

"But so you'd only work at F and V to be near Andy."

"Maybe in a way."

"What way is that, if you don't mind my asking? And why do you want another version of this dress? I don't get it."

"You are an inquisitive little thing."

"You and I look enough alike as it is. Why do you want my dress?"

"That was the point, a minute ago. As you pointed out, it's Lenore's dress, not your dress."

"All right, this is technically Lenore's dress, if you want to get technical. And this is the dress she wore the time you met her."

And the time Andy met her."

"Right."

"Right."

"So what?"

"I know what I know."

"How about letting *me* know a little of what you know, then?"

"Look, I know all about Andy and Lenore Beadsman. I know you're her friend, and you can go ahead and tell her I know all about it."

"What do you know?"

"Everything."

"I mean what is there *to* know?"

"Listen, I know you two are friends, but if I'm going to be honest with you you can at least not insult my intelligence."

"I'm not insulting anything, Mindy."

"See, I can not only see what's going on, but I have the advantage that I can also see *why* it's going on."

"Hey, Lenore doesn't even like Andy very much, to tell the truth."

"Frankly Lenore does not interest me. My husband, *he* interests me. And I can see why he's doing what he's doing."

"What's he doing?"

"Don't you see why? Yes we've had a bad period, but you know all relationships go through bad periods. There are bad times in all relationships. But yes this was a bad period. And now Andy sees your little friend Lenore, in the middle of this admittedly bad period, and suddenly he feels he's able to go back to a branch in the tree of his life, the branch nine years ago, when he met me and fell in love with me and started a relationship with me, but also, see, the exact same branch he met Lenore at, sitting in her little violet dress and being antisocial and throwing shoes at people, and so suddenly Andy feels as if maybe he can go back and just take a different path from the same branch, to—"

"She threw shoes?"

"Andy sees in this Lenore person a chance to change the past. Andy is always trying to change what he can't change. He's a silly. And remember there are two sides to every coin."

". . . ."

"Always lots of branches in the same relationship-tree."

"I don't think this branch stuff is right, Mindy."

"You've made that perfectly clear."

"Lenore is pretty heavily involved with Mr. Vigorous, is the thing."

"Ah, Mr. Vigorous."

"Who was really your neighbor, in New York City, when he was married?"

"In Scarsdale he was, yes."

"This whole thing is making me feel a little eerie."

"Branches and trees, darling."

"But they're involved, Mindy. They have been for like a year and a half. Really involved."

"Andy sometimes likes to hurt, too, when he's not himself."

"But I mean they're really close. Lenore more or less lives over there with him a lot of the time. Mr. Vigorous is incredibly jealous."

"Poor thing."

"He even bought the bird for Lenore that's on 'The Partners With God Club' right now."

" 'The Partners With God Club'? On the evangelist network?"

"Didn't you even see it when you went over to Gilligan's Isle to see Andy?"

"I only saw him. I was only there to say hello, it turned out. I was only there a moment or two."

"What did he say?"

"He said, I remember this, he said, 'Guess how much shit I want out of you right now, Melinda-Sue.' He says that sometimes."

"Sheesh."

"He calls me Melinda Sue."

". . . ."

"But you say her bird is on the show?"

"Her bird more or less *is* the show right now. The bird, Vlad the Impaler, except on the show he's got some weird Italian name that Reverend Sykes said Vlad the Impaler chose in a moment of ecstasy . . ."

"Hart Lee Sykes?"

"Yes. Vlad the Impaler is a cockatiel who can sort of talk, or at least repeat things so convincingly it's apt to seem like he's talking, and the Reverend gets him to ask people in pathetic-Christian-TV-viewer-land to send money, and they do. Our landlady is with him in Atlanta, and our landlord says she says the money is supposedly tidal-waving in, right now."

"I'll have to watch this."

"It's on every night on cable at eight, on I think like channel ninety, one of those cable channels."

"Hmmm."

"Except now Rick's being all spastic and weird about the bird, Lenore says. He has the receipt from Fuss 'n' Feathers pet shop, which if you do any time at the F and V board you'll get to know really well, because our lines are like super fouled up and we get a lot of their calls, but anyway he has the receipt, and he says because

Lenore didn't give him this certain gift at Christmas, Vlad the Impaler is legally and emotionally his. That's what Lenore says he says."

" . . . . "

"And maybe he's really trying to get ahold of the royalties, because Vlad is apparently raking in a lot of royalties, from the tidal wave of money, but that just wouldn't be like Rick. Rick is intensely weird, but he's not weird about money. Money just isn't very important to him."

"But he legally owns the bird because Lenore didn't give him something?"

"Yes."

"What?"

"I really shouldn't say."

"I'll pay for lunch. Including dessert."

"A spanking. Rick supposedly wanted a spanking."

"A spanking?"

"That's really all I should say."

"And he owns the bird, on the show."

"Kind of hard to take a man seriously who wants a spanking for Christmas."

"That doesn't match my memory. My memory is of a nice man in a beret who spent a lot of time at his den window and helped get Daddy out of the lawn, sometimes. I guess we'll see."

"Your Daddy was in the lawn?"

" . . . . "

"I think you've misjudged Lenore."

"So I gather."

"I think you've misjudged Andy, too, if you excuse my saying so. I don't think you can expect to get him back by pretending to be a different violet branch of the same tree."

"Shall we go?"

"Here's the check, thanks a lot, Mooradian's tends to get a little expensive."

"God, you're not kidding. This bill is obscene."

"I think you and Andy just need to sit down and rap. You should try to go out of your way to see him tonight, straighten things out."

"Tonight Andrew S. Lang is taking Lenore Beadsman to some gymnastics show."

"No."

"The symbolism of which doesn't escape me, rest assured."

"I think there's been some kind of mistake. I think you maybe misheard him."

"We'll see."

/e/

"This is suck!" said a small oriental man ahead of Lenore in the line.

He turned to her and said it again. "This is suck!"

With him was another man and two women, all in leatherish jackets. They were all nodding, agreeing that it was suck. Lenore thought they were maybe Vietnamese. She knew Vietnamese people tend to have really high cheekbones. Lenore's junior roommate at Oberlin had been a Vietnamese woman.

"Pardon me?" Lenore said to the man.

The man took his hands out of his jacket pockets. "This is suck, that we must wait like this. We have been this line for a *long* time."

"Pretty decent little old crowd, all right," said Wang-Dang Lang. He jingled his car keys.

Lenore turned from the man and looked behind her in line. There she could see two girls, from maybe about high school, with short hair Lenore could tell was a very strange color, even between the lights of the Building and the marquee. They both had on big winter coats that looked like some shiny quilts sewn together. Whatever they were talking about they couldn't believe.

"I just *could not* believe it," said one of the girls, who, Lenore saw, had paper clips hanging from her ears.

"What an asshole," said the other girl.

"No, I mean I could *not* believe it. When he said it to me, I just totally freaked out. I totally freaked. I was like:" the girl gestured.

"What a gleet."

It was cold for September, tonight. Lenore had on her gray cloth coat. Lang had on a sheepskin jacket with some false wool fluff around the collar. They were now near the ticket window, after about half an hour.

"Very nice of you to take me, Andy," Lenore said. "On such short notice, what with Mindy in town, work, et cetera."

Lang smiled down at her and played with his keys.

"Rick just pretty clearly didn't feel like going," Lenore went on, "and he more or less told me to ask you to go."

"Well shoot, that makes it a bit like an order, then."

"Candy has to work tonight over at Allied, is the thing."

"I don't look at it like a job, Lenore," Lang said. "I'm looking forward to it."

"Kopek Spasova's really supposed to be great."

"And your Daddy told you to go?"

"Dad doesn't tell me to do anything. He said he'd appreciate it, is all. If I didn't want to go, I wouldn't go."

Lang grinned. "You sure about that, now."

"Of course I'm sure. If I thought this was going to be suck, to coin a phrase, I wouldn't do it."

"My own personal Daddy tells me to do something, I as a rule do it."

Lenore looked at him. Her breath went up toward him a little before it disappeared. "Except he told you not to marry Mindy Metalman, you said in the car."

Lang laughed. "OK, usually I do what he says." He looked serious. "Sometimes me and Daddy just take a while to see eye to eye."

Erieview Plaza was all lit up. A marquee had been set up in front of the Erieview Tower lobby, by the ticket window. On the marquee a little electric girl was pulsing around a bar, connected to it by her feet. Beside her throbbed the bright-white perimeter of a baby, with a spoon in its hand. Yellow light from the windows of the Bombardini Building across the Plaza illuminated the rear of the line for the tower lobby.

"So let me get this totally straight, for the record and all," said Lang, watching his own breath. "You're just here 'cause you want to be. *In toto.*"

"I like gymnastics. I was totally glued to the TV for the World Championships, last month."

"But what I understand, this little girl's helping these Gerbers launch a kind of a Tet Offensive against your Daddy's company. That's what Neil said."

"That's beside the point. I'm not Dad, or Dad's company."

"So what're we doing here, then? I can think of a thousand funner places for us to be."

"You're no joke, brother," the Vietnamese man in front of them said as his group got to the ticket window. He and one of the women began to talk very fast at the man behind the window.

"Good God, that's Mr. Beeberling, selling tickets," said Lenore. Lang looked briefly at the ticket window before returning to scanning the line.

"He's really Bob Gerber's right hand man," Lenore said. "He's the one who supposedly came up with this ingredient in Gerber baby food that's supposed to help babies chew."

"Instead of singing like birds?"

"What's that supposed to mean?"

There was definitely some sort of controversy at the window. The Vietnamese man was jabbing his finger toward the doors to the Erieview lobby. Mr. Beeberling was being told that he was suck.

"Look here," Lang said, leaning way over to make himself heard in Lenore's ear above the din around the window. The side of his jaw was smooth and smelled sweet, even in the cold air.

"Look here," he said. "If we just go on back right now, 'Dallas' is on. We can watch 'Dallas.' It's a show that kicks ass. I just got a new TV, a big sucker. I got wine. We'll have more fun than a whole barrel full of prehensile-toed little tumblers." He stopped and looked at Lenore. "Of course I guess that's assuming you're only doing what you want to do, not what your Daddy or anybody else tells you to do."

"Hey, look . . .," Lenore was saying up to Lang when they were pushed by the force of the line behind them into the glass of the ticket window. Lang lost his cowboy hat. Lenore dropped her purse, and lottery tickets spilled out and went everywhere. She bent and started picking them up. Some blew away.

"Hold your horses God damn it!" Lang shouted back at the line. The two girls, orange and pink hair in the light of the marquee, gestured.

"Hi Mr. Beeberling," Lenore said, stuffing the last of the bright tickets into her purse. "Two, I guess, please."

"Lenore," said Mr. Beeberling. "Lenore Beadsman."

"Andrew Sealander Lang, here," Lang said absently, looking around for his hat.

"Two coming up," smiled Mr. Beeberling. He opened a drawer and began to rummage. He was wearing a porkpie hat that said GERBER'S across the brim. "Just missed Foamwhistle and your Jars guy, Goggins, you know," he said. "Just came through."

"Blanchard, or Sigurd?" said Lang.

Lenore turned and stared at Lang.

"Well now here we go," said Mr. Beeberling. He pushed back his hat and smiled. "That'll be four hundred dollars, please."

"Pardon?"

"Special Stonecipheco rate," Mr. Beeberling said. "If you're going to scout us out, you can at least help to defray costs."

"But except I'm not here for Stonecipheco," Lenore said as Lang fought off another surge of the line behind them. "I'm just here because I really like Kopek Spasova."

"Well certainly," said Mr. Beeberling. "So you can be thoroughly entertained, and help defray, all at once." He gestured back at the long line and the circle of pale breath that wove into itself and vanished above it. "You see what the fray is like. Surely you want to help defray."

"There's just no way you can tell me two tickets can cost four hundred dollars," Lenore said.

"Well, these're really big tickets, as you can see for yourself," Mr. Beeberling said, holding up two large black tickets behind the window and sizing them up suggestively with a thumb and forefinger.

"You dung beetle," Lang said to Beeberling, who smiled and made a little bow.

"I don't have near that much on me," said Lenore.

"What an *arse!*" the two girls were yelling in unison at Lang's back.

"Lenore, let's just git. Who needs this, if we're just doin' what we want?"

"Mr. Beeberling I'm *not* here for Stonecipheco."

Mr. Beeberling grinned and scratched his head under his hat. The electronic image of Kopek Spasova kept lightening and darkening sections of the street.

"This *is* suck, isn't it," said Lenore.

"You can't get pushed around like this, Lenore. Screw him. Let's git." Lang twirled his car keys on a bandaged finger.

"Shit on a twig."

/f/

"I think you should. I hope you shall."

"Should I, Rick? Oops, may I call you Rick?"

"Of course. We're both adults, now. Call me anything."

"Should I, Rick?"

"As I see it, you would be doing everyone a favor. We need the help. We're marginally frantic right now, though of course not unpleasantly so. It would be an enjoyable, brief taste of college memories for you, apparently. And I—thank you, waiter."

"Sure thing."

"We need some more vino."

"More wine, please."

"Right away sir."

"I should like to be able to see you around, every day, working. It would be nice. And you would of course have the opportunity to spend time around . . . those Frequent and Vigorous personnel whom you wished to be near."

"Who*ever* I wanted to be near?"

"What does that mean?"

"Hey, this is yummy."

"The eclairs are good here, I've found. Lenore and I sampled the eclairs here, not too far back, with Norman Bombardini, our Building-mate, and—"

"It's really good."

"I think you should. I *so* hope you will, Mindy. May I call you Mindy?"

"You silly."

"Mindy, it would simply be fun. That's all I'm saying. And how long could it be?"

"Good question."

"What?"

"Can I have some more of that vino?"

". . . ."

"And then but what will Lenore think?"

". . . ."

"Rick, what about Lenore?"

"What about Lenore?"

"How will she feel about me taking her place at the switchboard, however temporarily? I saw that she still has a lot of her personal items scattered around in there. How will she feel about me being in the middle of her personal items?"

"Her items can be moved with minimal trouble."

"That's not exactly what I mean, Rick."

"Perhaps if you were a bit more explicit, then."

"Let's just say it has to do with my husband and your fiancée."

"Lenore is not quite exactly my fiancée."

"And Andy might not be my husband much longer."

"What?"

"Did you know he was taking Lenore to see gymnastics tonight? The symbolism of which doesn't escape me, rest assured."

"Here the answer is that I told Lenore to ask Lang to go to this function with her, I'm afraid. We had a tiff this morning and I told her to. I was being juvenile."

"But Andy told me last night he was taking her. He told me he didn't want any . . . any flak from me about it. That was last night, not this morning."

"More wine?"

"Rick, can I ask do you really own that fabulous bird who's lighting up religious television?"

"If you're referring to Vlad the Impaler, he is Lenore's cockatiel."

"That's not what I heard, emotionally speaking."

"What did Lenore say to you?"

"Rick, should I be straight with you?"

"You can certainly be straight about anything Lenore told you."

"I find you very attractive. I'm sorry if that offends you, but I always have, really, in a way, ever since I was little, and you and Daddy would walk around the lawn in tennis clothes, looking for weeds and drinking things that I'd get to drink the last bits of out in the kitchen."

". . . ."

"I remember how wet the glasses got in the summer, the water ran down the sides. I remember that. And you were out there in tennis clothes. It was like a childhood crush."

". . . restroom, very briefly, if you'll perhaps excuse me for just a second, I'll be . . ."

"And all it would take is one word from Lenore, or you, to CBN, to get me in the door as a voice on 'The Partners With God Club.' Rick, you could be an absolutely tremendous help to me."

"What about Andy? What would he think?"

"What about Andy? What about *Lenore*?"

"I'm afraid I don't understand what's going on."

"Look. I'm a professional voice. I'm the best young corporate voice on the market today. Listen to this. This is CBN. This is 'The Partners With God Club,' with your host, Father Hart Lee Sykes, and his bird Vlad. Stay tuned, please."

"That really is awfully good."

"Damn right it's awfully good. I'm a professional."

"But the bird's stage name is Ugolino, not Vlad."

"Ugolino?"

"Yes. Sykes claims Vlad the Impaler revealed his own stage name on the plane to Atlanta, amid a divinely induced aura of glazed blue light. Sykes claims Ugolino is some Biblical character or other. He's still trying to pin down the reference."

"And his bird, Ugolino. Please stay tuned."

"No argument about quality from this end, Mindy."

"You could call the Christian people tomorrow."

"Lenore and I have an uncancellable appointment during the day tomorrow."

"An appointment?"

"You might say we are going to the dentist."

"You're going to the Ohio Desert, mister. I know all about it. Andy told me all about it. He's going, too."

"No he isn't. That is not possible. Just Lenore and I are going. That's a fact."

"Relax. So maybe he's going on his own. Maybe he's going with that creepy guy from the baby food company who helped him with the Desert a long time ago. All I know is he said he was going to wander and commune."

"Just Lenore and I are going with each other, though."

"Whatever you say."

". . . ."

"So OK. I'll fill in for a while."

"Good. Good. Fine."

"It'll be fun, and like you said I'll be able to be around whoever I want to be near."

"Yes."

"Except there's still the matter of training."

"Not a problem at all."

"I'll need to be trained. Although I think you'll find I can remember whatever you want me to remember. I have a great memory."

"Well certainly. Ms. Peahen . . . gave me some introductory material for you, which I as a matter of fact have right here . . . somewhere. Walinda is willing to install you temporarily at my say-so."

"Train me."

"Just listen to this: 'A Phase III Centrex 28 console with a number 5 Crossbar has features which greatly aid the console operator in the efficient performance of his or her duties.' "

"That isn't what I meant, Rick."

"Excuse me?"

"I have an idea. Let's go discuss training. I'm staying right over at the Marriott."

". . . ."

"It'll be fun and instructive. Trust me. Check please!"

"Not entirely sure I even . . ."

"And but what are those reflections in the street, Rick? Look there, by the corner. The street lights up, and then it doesn't. What's going on?"

"Neon. Gymnastic neon, I think."

"Neon. Isn't that pretty. Off, on. One, two."

"You don't find it a bit troubling?"

"Not one tiny bit."

/g/

"I don't know," Lang said. "I just don't know what's with these freakin' locks."

"You have to jiggle the key sometimes. Sometimes Candy and I have to jiggle it."

"You're telling me," Lang muttered. He got the door open.

Misty Schwartz's second-floor apartment looked a lot like Lenore's room, except it was a bit smaller, and had only one west window, and was definitely much tidier. Lenore looked around, then up at the ceiling that was her floor upstairs.

"You must be very neat," she said.

Lang was hanging up their coats. "I was a boy, and I'd make my bed, and here'd come my Daddy with a Kennedy half-dollar, and he'd flip it onto the bed, and if the thing didn't just bounce right back up onto my Daddy's thumb with the Kennedy head back on top I had to make the sucker up all over again."

"Geez."

"Look, you maybe want a can of wine?" Lang said, making motions toward the door of the apartment. "I got some wine downstairs, in the Fridgidaire. It's next to your soda water, you might have seen."

"A *can* of wine?"

"They were on sale."

"Think I'll pass," Lenore said. She smoothed out her dress from the hairy ride on the Inner Belt in Lang's new Trans Am. A plane came in very low now, and for a moment everything seemed to slow way down, in the noise. Lang stood by the door, looking at her. Lenore could see the way the bright light from Misty's overhead fixture hit off Lang's eyes, hitting and breaking up like there were chips of mint in his eyes. Lenore felt the back of her neck with her hand.

As Lang smiled and turned to go she said, "Look, why not. I'll try a can, or some of your can, whatever. Why not try some wine," she said.

"Well that's just fine," said Lang. "You can warm up that old TV, if you want." He went out and left the door open.

That old TV was a huge white sail of a screen that curved predator-like over a squat mahogany box. Inside the box a projector pointed like a gun at the screen's breadbasket. Lenore hit a red button on the box, and an enormous head filled the screen, and there was volume. She hastily turned the thing off, and the screen drizzled and was blank again. The head had been someone from "Dallas," though, Lenore was pretty sure.

When someone has the same general kind of room you do, it's usually very interesting to see what they've done with it. In Misty Schwartz's case it wasn't quite as interesting as it might have been. Lenore didn't know Misty very well; there had been some unpleas-antness over a phone bill, on the Tissaws' central kitchen phone, a few months ago, and Lenore had since been down to Misty's place only once or twice, when she had to borrow necessities. Candy Mandible, who had borne the brunt of the phone bill unpleasant-ness, had said that the only reason Misty Schwartz wasn't a lesbian was that she had never seen her own face in the mirror. Lenore thought that made no sense at all.

Which didn't keep her from really not caring too much for Misty's apartment, though: a room in which lines of steel and a certain kind of grainy white burlap fabric predominated. There was a chair made of white burlap cushions collected and given shape in a frame of polished metal bars. A clear glass table with the same kind of metal frame. At right angles a small couch of the same material as the chair. On the wall a painting of a plain pale orange square against a white background; also a picture of Misty Schwartz and some man on a black statue of a sperm whale, the kind of whale with those jaws. The man was down lying in the jaws, with his arm back over his forehead like Pauline in Peril, and Misty was riding on the thing's back, pretending to give it the whip, her mouth and eyes open wide. The photo was right flush up next to the painting. That was it for the walls, except for the television screen, which was pretty clearly a Lang addition.

Lenore looked for evidence of Lang. By the bed—a bed tightly made; Lenore thought about trying the thing with the half-dollar and decided against it—was a duffel bag, stuffed full and with some of its contents vomited out onto the floor around it, which fact was partially hidden by a carefully folded blanket Lang had placed over most of the scene, as if he had been in a hurry. On the bed were some new shirts and white socks, all still in their store plastic. But that was all. On the whole it just didn't seem like a Lang sort of room, to Lenore, at all.

"This just doesn't seem like your kind of room," Lenore said to Lang when he came back with his hands full of cans and glasses. She watched him put everything down carefully on the glass table.

"Well it's a inexpensive room, and no bugs, and the neighbors are tough to beat." Lang grinned.

"I just mean decor-wise. I just can't picture you really living in a room with Swedish furniture and paintings of squares."

Lang hunkered down on the couch and looked for a second over at the blank white television screen. "And so what kind of decor do you picture me in the middle of?" He closed his eyes and popped the top off a can of wine.

Lenore ran her hand along the mantle of Misty's cold fireplace. "Oh, I don't know." She smiled to herself. "Smoky leather. Leather chairs. A leopardy rug, with maybe a snarling bear's head on it. Lascivious calendars and posters . . ." She turned. "Maybe some expensive stereo stuff with its control-knobs all gleamy in an over-head light whose brightness you can adjust by turning a dial . . ."

Lang laughed and hit his knee with his fist. "Undamncanny. You just largely described my old college room."

"Did I."

"Forgot the animal heads on the walls, though." Lang manipulated his eyebrows at her.

Lenore laughed. "The animal heads," she said. "How could I."

"And the mirrors on the ceiling . . ." Lang looked down and came back up holding a big glass. "A little vino?"

Lenore came over to the couch.

"Couldn't find any damn wine glasses, so I used these. I hope it's OK to just take glasses, if we wash them out after." They were Road Runner glasses that Candy Mandible had gotten in some sort of fast-food restaurant promotion.

Lenore took a glass of wine. "It's OK. They're Candy's. She's pretty generous with her stuff. As I'm sure you know." She sat down in the white chair, carefully pulling the back of her dress down so the skin of her legs wasn't touching the burlap cushion. She crossed her legs.

"I figured they were either hers or yours, or poor old Misty Schwartz's," said Lang. "And I didn't think that poor girl needs any glasses about now." He leaned back on the couch. "Sent her a card, by the way, in the hospital, saying who I was, about the room, saying I hoped she got better and all."

"That was pretty nice of you," Lenore said, picking the glass up from the table. The wine was yellow and sweet and so cold it hurt Lenore's teeth. She put her glass back on the table and got a bit of a tooth-shiver from the sound of glass on glass, on top of the cold of the wine.

"Nah," said Lang, crossing his leg over so his ankle was on his knee and holding onto the ankle with one big hand. Lenore looked at his shoe and his hairy ankle.

"Nah," said Lang. "Just polite, is all. Melinda Sue had a similar thing happen to her, except I guess not as bad. Woman was still slathered to hell in Noxzema for a week."

"Sounds horrible."

"Should tell your sister to watch out, not get burnt."

"Will do."

"You like the wine?" Lang held his glass up toward the light fixture and tried to look at the wine around a cartoon of the coyote, who was wincing and holding a tiny umbrella over his head, apparently about to get clobbered by a boulder.

"It sure is cold," Lenore said.

"Uh-huh," said Lang. He looked over at the white screen again. "Should I just assume you don't want to watch 'Dallas,' then?"

"I turned it on for a second," Lenore said. "It's really not my show, which doesn't mean it's a bad show or anything. If you want to watch it, go ahead; I'll watch just about anything, at least for a while."

"Nah," said Lang. He took off his sportcoat and got up and hung it up. Lenore touched the sides of her hair. She could feel lines of heat going into her arms and legs, from the wine. She held her glass up to the light. On her glass the Road Runner was running, his legs were just a blur, and the curving road behind him looked used and limp and rubbery against the brown hills of some desert. There were cacti.

"Can I maybe ask where all those lottery tickets come from, that are in your purse?" Lang said, sitting down again, now on the edge of the couch closest to Lenore's chair, so they could see each other in the glass of the table when they looked down. He looked down at her. "Who's the lottery-playing demon around here?"

Lenore laughed. "Candy and I play a lot. I mean a *lot*." She smoothed hair out of her eyes, and Lang watched her do it. "We play a lot. We have all these systems, using our birthdays and the letters in our names and stuff. Ohio has a really good lottery."

Lang drank. "Ever win at all?"

"We will," Lenore said. She laughed. "We started playing in college, just for fun, and I was a philosophy major, and for a joke we hit on this sort of syllogism, ostensibly proving we'd win—"

"Syllogism?"

"Yeah," Lenore said. "Like a tiny little argument." She smiled over at Lang and held up fingers. "One. Obviously somebody has to win the lottery. Two. I am somebody. Three. Therefore obviously I have to win the lottery."

"Shit on fire."

Lenore laughed.

"So why does that seem like it works, when it doesn't, since you haven't won?"

"It's called an E-screech equivocation. My brother disproved it to me that same year when I made him mad about something. It's sort of a math thing." Lenore laughed again. "The whole thing's probably silly, but Candy and I still get a kick out of it."

Lang played with the hairs on his ankle. "You were a phi-los-ophy major, then." He drew out the word "philosophy."

"Philosophy and then Spanish, too," said Lenore, nodding. "I was a double major in school."

"I personally majored in ec-o-nomics," Lang said, doing it again.

Lenore ignored him. "I took an economics class one time," she said. "Dad wanted me to major in it, for a while."

"But you said no sir."

"I just didn't do it, is all. I didn't say anything."

"I admire that," Lang said, pouring more wine for both of them and crushing the empty can in his hand. He threw it in the wastebasket from clear across the room. "Yes I do," he said.

"Admire what?"

"Except I have trouble picturing you as a phi-los-opher," he said. "I remember seeing you in Melinda-Sue's room that one time, so long ago, and thinking to myself: artist. I remember thinking artist to myself, that time."

The wine was warmer now. Lenore fought off a cough. "Well I'm sure not an artist, although Clarice has what you could call a sort of artsy talent. And I wasn't ever a philosopher, I was just a student." She looked into the table. "But how come you can't picture it?"

"I dunno," Lang said, throwing an arm back along the top of the couch, holding its steel bar in his hand and stroking it with his fingers. Lenore's neck felt even tighter at the back. She felt like she could see Lang from all different angles all of a sudden: his profile next to her, his reflection down in the glass table, his other side in the window out past the couch and the television screen. He was all over, it seemed.

Lang was saying: "Just have this picture from school of all these phi-los-ophy guys in beards and glasses and sandals with socks in them, saying all this wise shit all the time." He grinned.

"That's just so *wrong*," Lenore said, leaning forward in the chair. "The ones I know are about the least wise-seeming people you could imagine. At least the really good ones don't act like they think they're wise or anything. They're really just like physicists, or math —"

"You care for a peanut?" Lang said suddenly.

"No thank you," said Lenore. "You go ahead, though."

"Nah. Little suckers get back in my teeth."

"Mine too. I hate it when peanuts do that."

"So go ahead with what you were saying, I'm sorry."

Lenore smiled and shook her head. "It wasn't important. I was just going to say that they're like mathematicians, really, except they play their games with words, instead of numbers, and so things are even harder. At least that's the way it got to seem to me. By the end of school I didn't like it much anymore."

Lang put some wine in his mouth and played with it. There was silence for a bit. Through Misty's wood floor Lenore could hear faint sounds from the television in the Tissaws' living room.

Then Lang said, "You're weird about words, aren't you." He looked at Lenore. "Are you weird about words?"

"What do you mean?"

"You just seem weird about them. Or like you think they're weird."

"In what way?"

Lang felt his upper lip absently with a finger while he looked into the glass table. "Like you take them awful seriously," he said. "Like they were a big sharp tool, or like a chainsaw, that could cut you up as easy as some tree. Something like that." He looked up at her. "Is that from your education, in terms of college and your major and such?"

"I don't think so," said Lenore. She shrugged her shoulders. "I think I just tend to be sort of quiet. I don't think words are like chainsaws, that's for sure."

"So was that really all just bullshit, what I said?"

Lenore recrossed her legs and played with the wine in her glass. She looked down into her purse, with the tickets, next to her chair. "I think it's just that my family tends to be kind of weird, and very . . . *verbal*." She looked into the table and sipped. "And it's hard sometimes not being an especially verbal person in a family that tends to see life as more or less a verbal phenomenon."

"Sure enough." Lang smiled. He looked at Lenore's legs. "And now can I ask you how come you wear those Converse sneakers all over? Your legs are just way too nice to be doing that all the time. How come you do that?"

Lenore shifted in her chair and looked up at Lang to make him stop looking at her legs. "They're comfortable, is all, really," she said. "Everybody likes different kinds of shoes, I guess."

"Takes all kinds of shoes to make up a world, am I right?" Lang laughed and drank.

Lenore smiled. "My family really is funny about wordy things, though. I think you're right about that. My great-grandmother especially, and she sort of dominated the family for a while."

"And your Daddy and your housekeeper-lady, too," said Lang, nodding.

Lenore looked up sharply. "How come you know about them?"

Lang shrugged and then grinned at her. "Think R.V. mentioned something or other."

"Rick did?"

"But funny how?" Lang said. "I mean it's not too unusual just to get people who like to talk. World is full of dedicated and excellent talkers. My mother used to get talking, and my Daddy'd say only way to really get her to hush was to hit her with something blunt."

"Well but see, it wasn't just talking a lot," Lenore said, smoothing her hair. "Although everybody sure did. But it was as you said, the *importance* they attached to everything they said. They made just a huge deal out of what got said." Lenore felt the rim of her glass for a second. She smiled. "Like to take an example I was just remembering this morning, my little brother Stoney had this stage of his childhood where he called everything *brands* of things. He'd say, 'What brand of dog is that?' or 'That's the brand of sunset where the sun makes the clouds all fiery,' or 'That brand of tree has edible leaves,' et cetera." She looked over at Lang, who was looking at her in the table. He looked up at her. Lenore cleared her throat. "Which obviously, you know, wasn't all that big a deal," she continued, "although it was kind of irritating, but still understandable, because Stoney watched television like *all* the time, back then." Lenore recrossed her legs; Lang was still looking at her. "But my family was just having a complete spasm about it, after a while, and one time they even arranged to have Stoney out of the house so we could all supposedly sit down in the living room for like a summit meeting about how to get him to start saying 'kind' instead of 'brand,' or whatever. It was a huge family deal, although my father I remember kept talking on the phone during the meeting, or going to get stuff to eat, or even reading, and not paying attention, because my great-grandmother was running the meeting, and they don't get along too well. At least they didn't."

"Now is this your Amherst brother you're talking about?" said Lang. "LaVache, the one at Amherst now?"

"Yes. LaVache is Stonecipher's middle name. Stonecipher's his real name."

"Then so how'd they break the little guy of the habit? He didn't say 'brand' at dinner, at all, that one time—at least not to his leg, which was about all he was talking to."

"I think it just stopped," Lenore said. "I think it just petered out. Unless Miss Malig started hitting him with blunt things on the sly." She laughed. "I guess anything's possible."

"Miss Malig, your nanny, with legs like churns and all?"

At this, Lenore stayed looking into the table for some time, while Lang watched the side of her face. Finally she said, "Look, how do you know all this stuff, Andy?" She put her glass down in its circle of moisture on the table and looked calmly at Lang. "Are you trying to freak me out? Is that it? I think I need to know what exactly Rick told you."

Lang shook his head seriously. "Freaking you out never even crossed my mind," he said. He popped the tab on another can of wine. "This was just on the plane, coming on out here, while you were sleeping your pretty head off. We didn't have nobody to talk to except us." He tossed off some wine and smiled. "R.V. I remember was telling me about how he was going to promote you up from the phone board up to reader and weeder, and how you'd really get fulfilled by that."

"Rick told you then that he was going to do that? That's like two days before he told me he was going to do that."

"But are you getting fulfilled? Is it rewarding like he said?"

Lenore looked for sarcasm in Lang's face. She could never tell whether Lang was being sarcastic or not. Her neck really hurt, now. "It's at least rewarding to the tune of ten smackers an hour," she said slowly. "And some of the stories are really good."

"R.V. says you really get into stories. He says you understand yourself as a literary sensibility."

"He said that?"

"He did."

Lenore looked back into the table. "Well I do like stories. And Rick likes them too. I think that's one reason we seem to get along so well. Except what Rick really likes to do is tell them. Sometimes when we're together he'll just tell me stories, the whole time. From what gets submitted to him."

Lang put his shoe out onto the glass tabletop, twisted it back and forth. "He does like to spin, doesn't he," he said absently. He paused

THE BROOM OF THE SYSTEM 401

and looked over at Lenore. Lenore looked down at her shoe. Lang cleared his throat. "I probably shouldn't do this, but I've been wanting to ask you about this one whopper R.V. told me about your brother, with his leg: how the little sucker lost his leg when your mother fell off the side of your house trying to get away from her bridge coach and break into your nursery. Or some such. Now just how much of that is true, and how much was my own personal leg getting pulled, on that plane?"

A lot of little lines seemed to come out of the lines of heat in Lenore's body. She stared at Lang's shoe on the table. She closed her eyes and felt her neck. Lang watched her. "Let me get this straight," she said finally. "Rick told you personal stuff about my family? On the plane? While I was right there, asleep?"

"Was that a mistake, telling you what he told me? Lenore, hurt me with something hot if I just screwed up in any way. Just forget I said anything."

Lenore kept looking at the glass table, and Lang's shoe, and Lang's shoe's reflection, and Lang's reflection. "He told you all that while I was asleep," she said. In the table it looked as though Lang was looking away from her, because the real Lang was looking at her. When he finally looked down at the table, Lenore stared at him.

"Well he said you were his fiancée," Lang said, "and how he was just passionately and totally interested in everything about his fiancée. It all seemed real innocent to me. Not to mention just articulate as *hell*."

Lenore had looked up. "He told you I was his *fiancée*? As in soon-to-be-married fiancée?"

"Oh *shit*." Lang hit his forehead with the heel of his palm. "Oh shit, did I just do it again? Oh Lord. Just forget what I said. Just forget I said anything."

"Rick said we were engaged? He just said that to you, unsolicited, out of the blue?"

"He probably just didn't mean it the way he said it."

"Shit on a *twig*."

"Now Lenore I sure don't want to come between two people who—"

"What the hell did he say there even was to come between?"

"Jesus H.," Lang said, massaging his jaw. His reflection in the glass looked away from Lenore. Then it looked down, and seemed actually almost to wink, in the glass, all of a sudden. Lenore looked up, but the real Lang was looking at his hands.

"Jesus H. Christ," he was saying to himself. He drank some wine. Lenore smoothed her hair back with hot fingers.

"Look," said Lang. "I'm just real sorry. How about if I just tell you everything, everything that's been making me feel all terribly guilty around you, and then we can just go ahead and—"

"Why on earth should you feel guilty because of Rick?" Lenore said tiredly, massaging her neck with her eyes closed again. "That he told you stuff is no reason for you to feel bad, Andy. I'm not mad at you about it."

"Except there's a few sort of sizable items R.V. doesn't feel inclined to tell, it looks like," said Lang. He took a very deep breath and looked at his hands again. "Like I'm not in actual fact translating any herbicide or pesticide crap into idiomatic Greek for you." He looked at her. "Like I'm really working on a pamphlet for your own personal Daddy's company, and its wild-ass new food that makes kids supposedly talk, like your bird can do."

Lenore looked into the table. There was silence. "You're really working for Stonecipheco," she said.

Lang didn't say anything.

"Which means Rick is, too. And Rick didn't tell me."

"I'm afraid that's right. Except like I say I'm sure there was a good reason for his not."

Lenore slowly reached for the open can and poured some more wine into her Road Runner glass. She hunched forward in the white burlap chair until her face was right over the table. She could see some of Lang in the top of her wine, erratic and shimmery, with mint eyes, in the yellow.

"And for his more or less ordering me not to tell you, either," Lang was saying. He looked at the side of Lenore's face. "The thing is, Lenore, he more or less ordered me not to tell you, which is why I didn't tell you."

Lenore shook the glass a little, rattled the bottom against the tabletop. The wine in the glass sloshed; Lang was broken into pieces that didn't fit.

"Which means I'm afraid I need to ask you maybe to promise not to tell R.V. I told you, for fear of my job and all," he said.

"Just like you yourself apparently promised Rick not to tell."

Lang took his shoe off the table and leaned forward too, so his head was alongside Lenore's, a big curl of her hair hanging in the air between them. Lang looked at the curl. "I guess that promise has to get chalked up to what you might call strategic misrepresentation," he said, very quietly.

"Strategic misrepresentation."

"Yes. 'Cause I made it before I ever got exposed to your good qualities and began to care about you as a person." Lang set his glass of wine down and slowly took hold of some of Lenore's curl and twisted it this way and that, all very gently.

"I see."

"Not entirely sure you do, here, Lenore."

"Oh, I think I do," Lenore said, getting up and gently getting her hair out of the reach of Lang's fingers. She walked over to the window and looked out at the houses across the Tissaws' dark street. All the houses seemed to have their lights on.

"Well then maybe I should ask what do you think," Lang said from back at the couch, where Lenore could see in the window he'd recrossed his legs and picked up his wine again. "What do you think about it, then," he said.

"I don't know," Lenore said after a minute, breathing on the cold window. She watched how what she said made it hard to see out. "I don't know what to think, old Wang-Dang Lang. Tell me what to think, please, and then I'll think that way about it."

"Well now that's no way to talk, Lenore."

Lenore didn't say anything.

"And you should call me Andy," said Lang. "You shouldn't call me anything but Andy, I don't think."

"There, that's what we need," Lenore said, nodding, with her eyes closed. "We need it explicit. We need this control thing made explicit. No more games. People tell me what to do and think and say and call them, and I do it. It'll all be simple. Then everybody can stop whispering when I'm asleep, and hiring each other behind my back, and wearing gas masks. They can just start making sense."

Lenore turned around. "So let's really do it, OK? How are you supposed to be mixed up with my great-grandmother?"

"Now let's just hold up here a second, Lenore," said Lang. He put down his glass and came over to within a few feet of where Lenore was standing, at the window. On one side of them was the television screen; behind Lang was the way to the door. "Whoa there," Lang was saying. "I don't know anything about any great-grandmother mix-ups. And all I got to do with your family is basically you." He shook his head. "Far as I know there's nobody sneaking around about you and me."

Lenore looked at the floor and put one of her curls behind her ear and crossed her arms. Lang was between her and the door. Her eyes began to get big and hot, and she felt as if there was wood in her voice box. She looked at Lang, who had his thumbs hooked into the pockets of his pants.

"Then how come I feel like the whole universe is playing pimp for me with you?" she said quietly. She thought she felt herself beginning to cry.

Lang looked at her. "Hey now please don't cry," he said.

"When I didn't ask for it at *all?*" Lenore said. "When I didn't even *like* you? I didn't *want* you." She looked past Lang at the door and began to sob, felt her shoulders curl down over her chest.

Then there was Lang, and her face was in Lang's shirt, and a Kleenex got pressed into her hand from out of nowhere, and the wood in her throat seemed to break apart and go in all different directions, hurting.

Lang was making a soft rhythmic sound with his mouth into Lenore's hair.

"I *hated* you," Lenore said into his shirt, talking to his chest. "You came in that time, and terrorized us, and were drunk, and that guy's stupid bottom, and Sue Shaw was so *scared.*"

"It's OK," Lang was saying softly. "It's OK. We were all just kids. We were just kids. That's all it was."

"And I say I don't want you, that I'm mad, and have a right to be, and everybody just winks, and nudges, and gets a tone, and pushes, pushes, pushes." Lang's shirt was getting wet. "I've just felt so *dirty.* So out of control."

Lang pushed her away a bit and dried her eyes with his sleeve.

Lenore looked into his eyes for a second and thought for no reason of mint, lima beans, tired grass. His eyes were totally unbloodshot. "Lenore," he was saying, "it's OK. Just believe I don't want to push you, OK? Just believe it," he said, "OK? You can believe that, 'cause it's true. I wouldn't do anything to hurt you, one bit." He rubbed at his perfect eye and Lenore went back to smelling his chest. It was true that even while she was crying she had been able to feel him through his clothes, and her clothes.

"Lenore?" Lang said after he'd let her breathe into his shirt for a while. "Hey, Lenore?" He bent and cupped his hands around her ear and made as if he were talking into a bullhorn. *"Lenore Beadsman."*

Lenore laughed a convulsive laugh and brought the Kleenex up to her face. It was hot, and wet, and little bits of it were all over her hand.

"I'll just say it, Lenore," Lang said. "I sure don't want to control you at all. Believe that. But I'll just go ahead and say that I think the one's maybe trying to do more controlling than's good for anybody is old R.V."

For no reason Lenore looked up past Lang at Misty's ceiling, her own floor.

"Lenore," said Lang. He stroked the white sleeve of Lenore's dress with a big warm hand, and through Lenore's body from the hand went heat.

"Lenore," he said quietly, "R.V. sat there in that plane, with his little feet dangling and all, sweating like a freaking pig"—he put his hand through his hair—"and just flat out told me you were *his*, and said I had to promise not to even try to take you away from him." He looked down at her. "I just thought you should know that."

Lenore took Lang's hand from her sleeve and held it while her eyes dried. She could smell herself.

"Like you were his car, or a TV," Lang was saying, shaking his head. "He wanted me to promise to like respect his ownership of you, or some such."

His arm brought Lenore into his chest again. She felt something pressing against her stomach, and didn't even think what it was until later.

"How does he think something like that's going to make us feel?" Lang was saying into her hair. "Where's what's fair in that?"

/h/

"Just sorry, is all."

". . . ."

"If such is appropriate."

". . . ."

"Which I rather think it is."

"Ricky that's silly, don't be sorry. There's no need to be sorry."

". . . ."

"The situation, the way it turns out we are, sorry doesn't enter into it at all."

"As it were."

"What?"

". . . ."

"You're probably just all tense and worried, Rick. Being tense and worried is world-famous for doing this."

"Look, even if I weren't tense and worried, you wouldn't have been able to tell. Is that not clear?"

"You're probably just tense and worried about your fiancée being in the arms of my husband right now. God knows I'm not exactly thrilled myself."

"Not after tomorrow I'm not upset. Tomorrow is the end."

"End of what?"

"Tomorrow Lenore and I are going to melt into the blackness, united in discipline and negation."

"Discipline?"

". . . ."

"Negation?"

"All so to speak."

"You're just going to go out and buy admission tickets to Andy's desert and look for Lenore's grandmother climbing some dune. I know all about what you're supposed to do tomorrow."

"Why on earth does Lenore tell you things like this?"

". . . ."

"Lenore never tells me anything, really."

"Rick, I don't know how long I'll be around, I mean I'm pretty sure I'll have to go to Atlanta at some point in time, if you know what I mean, but while I'm here I think you'll find I can do all kinds of things she can't. Or won't."

"I think it is always can't. It now occurs to me that there has probably never been a bona fide won't."

"You know Andy's had your ex-wife, too, don't you? I'm almost positive. I've seen him coming out of your house."

"She is a good person, it occurs to me."

"Who?"

"Do you think of yourself as a good person, Mindy? When you think of yourself, do you think of yourself as good?"

"Well of course, silly. Where are you if you don't think of yourself as good?"

". . . ."

"Then you can't even like yourself, and then where are you?"

". . . ."

"This is the Christian Broadcasting Network. Stay tuned for the Reverend Hart Lee Sykes, please."

"What about my son?"

"What?"

"Vance, my son."

"I think Andy's pretty much left Vance alone. I don't think you have to worry about Vance."

"I mean have you seen him. Does he come home, ever. Do you see him around the neighborhood."

"Remember when Vance would be out kicking footballs all day long? Honestly, I never could see how anybody could just kick a ball for hours and hours, over and over. And remember Daddy would spend the whole time looking out the window, making sure the ball never hit our lawn, and if it did he'd run out with a screwdriver and let all the air out of the ball?"

". . . ."

"I haven't seen Vance for years, Rick. I don't think I've seen Vance since I got out of school. Where is he now?"

"He's in the city. He's at Fordham. At least I certainly pay tuition to Fordham."

"I haven't seen him."

"Nor have I."

"I'm sorry."

"Certainly not your fault."

" . . . "

" . . . "

"Look, you can take it off, you know."

"Excuse me?"

"Your beret. You can take it off, you know. I like a spot. Daddy has a simply humongous spot, now."

"Great."

"Anyway, don't be sorry, is what I want to say."

"Thank you, Mindy."

"But roll over."

"What?"

"You heard me. I think I can help you out if you'll roll over."

"What?"

"Trust me."

"What are you doing?"

"This is . . . going to hurt me more than it hurts you. Is that what I should say, Rick?"

"Good Lord. What on earth have you been told?"

"Daddy used to say I knew . . . everything from the . . . beginning . . . of time. A . . . witch in a tartan skirt, is . . . what he said."

"Jesus."

/i/

"Now this is definitely cuddling," Lenore said. "Am I right? I think I know cuddling when I see it, and this is it."

Lang laughed.

Lenore and Wang-Dang Lang were on Lang's bed, on their sides, facing each other, amid shirts and socks in their plastic wrappers. Lenore had on her bra and panties and socks; Lang had on just his chinos and belt. Lenore's legs were together, and Lang had one of his legs thrown over her hip. Lang was looking at Lenore's breasts, in her bra. Being on her side was pressing them together, and they were pushing partway over the bra, which Lang obviously liked. He looked at Lenore, and touched her. He rubbed the back of her neck for her. And from time to time he would trace lines on her body with his finger. He would trace a line down the center of her lips, her chin, her throat, and down the line where her breasts pressed together, and over the bottom of the bra, and onto her stomach, where his hand would spread out and cover her, making Lenore need to blink, every time. He would also shift a bit and trace the line where her legs pressed together, from the bottom of her panties to the tops of her knees. He would press his finger deep into the line between her legs, and Lenore knew her legs felt soft and hot to him, from being pressed together. Lang had an erection in his slacks, Lenore could tell.

As for doing anything much more than they were doing, though, Lenore had said she needed time to think it over carefully, and to think about absolutely everything having to do with Rick, before anything like that could even be possible.

"I couldn't have intercourse with you without coming to an understanding with Rick first," she'd said. "Not the way things are now. I have to talk with him. That's just the way I feel."

Lang had traced a line. "I don't think I agree that we owe R.V. anything, but I'll respect your decision for now."

"Thank you."

Lang laughed. "You're welcome." He was very smooth: Lenore ran her hand over his arm and part of his back. It was really smooth. His chest had a fine covering of yellow hairs that were hard to see in the bright line of the overhead fixture. There was more hair on his stomach, in a line.

"And you shouldn't say 'intercourse.' You should say something else. 'Intercourse' sounds like you saw it in a manual."

"I'm sorry."

"Well don't be sorry," Lang laughed, touching Lenore's lip with his lip. "I was just making a point is all. Intercourse is what people have when they're married, and about maybe sixty, and they've been married for years, and have kids and all."

"What would we be having, then, do you think?"

"Something very much else, believe you me. You just trust me and you'll see."

Lenore had been tracing a line of her own, from the point on Lang's forehead where his eyebrows almost met, down his nose and into the furrow of his upper lip. When she got to his lip she stopped and looked at him and took her hand away.

"Hey," she said. "What happened to the way you talk all of a sudden? Why aren't you talking the way you usually do? Why aren't you saying stuff like, 'Well strap me to the hind end of a sow and sell me to Oscar Mayer'?"

Lang laughed at Lenore's imitation of his voice. He ran his hand over the flank of her hip and smiled. "I guess I don't know," he said softly. "I guess I just don't feel like it about now. I guess maybe we all talk differently with different people. The good old boy stuff is what I grew up on, and then at school I was from Texas and so everybody expected this sort of talking, and so it kind of became my thing, at school. At school you more or less got to have a thing."

"So I hear."

"Without a thing there, believe me, you're nothing," Lang said. His finger was in the hot part of her legs again.

"What about Biff Diggerence?" Lenore said. "What was his thing? No, let me guess: I'll bet his thing was burping." She made a face.

Lang took his hand out of her legs to scratch along his jaw. "That's kind of a tender subject, Lenore," he said. "Old Biff got screwed up at school. School messed him up. He got weird."

"What's he doing now?"

"I do not know. I think he's back in Pennsylvania or wherever. He got real screwed up, at school."

"Screwed up how? Did he maybe get tetanus from making people sign his bottom, or what?"

"Now that's not very kind, Lenore," Lang said. He sat up and bent to get his glass of warm wine by the bed. Lenore looked at his back while he drank. "He just got real screwed up," he said. "Basically he just started stayin' in his room all the time. And I mean all the time. Never seein' anybody, never talkin' to anybody. Just locked up in his room, with the door locked."

"Well that doesn't sound all that awful," Lenore said. "Lots of people keep to themselves. Lots of people stay in their rooms a lot. I stayed in my room a lot at school."

Lang turned around to her and shook his head. "Yeah," he said. "But when it gets to the point where you're like pissin' in empty beer cans so you don't have to go out of your room to the bathroom just down the damn hall, then that's gettin' to be bad news, in my opinion."

"No argument on this end."

"He got creepy. He got weird."

"Maybe he pounded too many walls with his head."

Lang grinned down at Lenore. "Except what you don't know is he started a real tradition with that. Everybody started doin' it. He got to be a sort of legend, by our senior year. I don't think folks even knew he was the one who stayed up in his room all the time. I think they thought he was somebody else."

Lenore thought of big Biff Diggerence, all alone in a room. Moving around from time to time. Going to the bathroom in beer cans. She remembered his bottom, and his playing with Sue Shaw's hair while she cried.

"He didn't marry Sue Shaw, did he?"

"That girl?" Lang said. "Good Lord no. Least I don't think so. Unless you know something I don't."

Later they had switched. Lang lay where Lenore had been and she moved over into his spot. Lang had shoved his duffel bag under the bed and had put the shirts and socks in a drawer that still had some of Misty Schwartz's clothes in it. The big television was now on, with the volume low. Out of the corner of her eye, Lenore could see enormous heads on the screen, flashing back and forth, talking about the news. There were shots of gymnastics, but Lenore didn't really watch.

Lang told Lenore that he had been unhappy. He told her that he had felt trapped and constricted and claustrophobic for quite a while now. That he had been an accountant lately and hated it with a righteous fire. About his wife's voice being all around him. Lenore told Lang a little bit more about LaVache, and about Clarice and Alvin Spaniard and their troubles, and family theater.

Lang told Lenore that what he really wanted to do, he was pretty sure, was to go back to work for Industrial Desert Design, Dallas.

He told her about the Great Ohio Desert, and about Neil Obstat, Jr., and Ed Roy Yancey, Jr., and about the Corfu Desert. He told her what had happened was that his father had said that if Andy married a Jewish lady, he wouldn't let him into the company. His father had been dumb and stubborn, and so had Lang, and so Lang had been an accountant for the past few years.

"And it wasn't even like she was really Jewish, even," Lang said. "She never goes to church. And God knows her Daddy don't go to any Jewish churches. Her Daddy's this insane pantheist fucker who worships his lawn." Lang told Lenore some items of interest concerning Rex Metalman, and his lawn, and Scarsdale, and Rick's ex-wife, Veronica. Then he kissed her for a long time.

They probably kissed for about five solid minutes. Lang was an unbelievably gentle kisser. Lenore wouldn't have believed it. Rick's kisses had always been really intense. Rick had said they mirrored and were informed by the intensity of his passion and commitment toward her.

While Lang traced lines everywhere with his finger, Lenore told him about her brother in Chicago, about a strange dream she'd had last night in which she dreamed that her mother dreamed where her brother was, and the dream made him be in that place, someplace with bright lights and people you could just tell were kind.

Lang said he felt really strongly that everything was going to be all right. He felt John was going to be OK, and he now knew for sure, personally speaking, that he was going to get a divorce from Mindy. Then he told Lenore a story about his own brother, his half-brother, who had been much older than he, his father's son by his first marriage, and about how this brother had unfortunately been killed in the conflict in Vietnam, in the Marines.

What had happened was that Lang's brother had been trained, along with all the other Marines at a certain training fort in Virginia, to throw grenades into enemy buildings and then wait just out by the door while the grenade exploded inside and put everybody out of commission, and then to come in and finish people off. And how, in Vietnam, Lang's brother had been fresh off the plane, and had tried to pull the grenade maneuver on a hut in a small village, apparently an enemy hut of some kind, but anyway that the walls of the hut had, not surprisingly, been made of grass and straw and dried water-buffalo droppings, and so the grenade's explosion not surprisingly tore right through the soft wall of the hut, and killed Lang's brother where he stood, waiting to finish people off. Lang said he had hardly known his brother at all. He said that the Marines had revised the fort's training after a lot of other Marines educated in Virginia had died this way. This was apparently early in the Vietnam conflict.

Lenore told Lang about the situation involving Lenore Beadsman, her great-grandmother. It turned out that Lang knew a lot already, from Neil Obstat, Jr.

"He's got your picture in his wallet, you know," Lang said. "Neil does."

"I've always found him a little on the creepy side," said Lenore. "He used to follow me around in school, when we went to school together, but never say anything." At this point Lang kissed the part of Lenore's throat right under her chin, and Lenore held his head there with her hand. "I didn't like him because I thought his head looked like a skull, I'm afraid. I know that's really shallow." She massaged the back of Lang's head while he kissed her throat. "And one time some bigger kids hung him from a hook by his underpants in P.E., and I saw him there, and I remember I felt like I was seeing somebody dead, because his head was all skully, and his eyes were closed, and we could see pretty much his whole bottom."

Lang said that in reality Neil Obstat wasn't a bad guy at all. He said that he and Neil were thinking about taking the day off tomorrow, seeing how it was Saturday, and going off somewhere. He said Lenore was more than welcome to come along, that he'd keep Obstat from being at all creepy. Lenore laughed. Then she told Lang that she was supposed to go out to the Great Ohio Desert with Rick Vigorous tomorrow, that they had made the plans already, and that the plans were pretty unchangeable. Lang was not too pleased.

"It's just that about a million people seem to think Lenore's out there," Lenore said. "As they keep making incredibly clear." Here Lang tried gently to lift her knee up with his hand, but stopped when she resisted.

"Also Rick really wants to go for some reason," Lenore said. "Today he was completely unsubtle about it. He almost yelled. And

my brother, my father, Mr. Bloemker at the nursing home . . .
everybody looks to be made weirdly happy if I just go out and
look for Lenore on a dune for a day." She had put her hand on Lang's
cheek. "I'm too tired and pissed off to argue with them anymore,"
she said. "And I guess now I need the chance to talk things over
with Rick."

"Please just don't be too hard on him, Lenore," Lang said. He
ran his thumb all the way along Lenore's leg, making her blink
again.

Lang said he sensed everything was going to be all right with
respect to Lenore's great-grandmother, too. He said he just felt it.
But he said he didn't think Lenore should go to the G.O.D.

"Nobody ever finds anybody in a place like that," he said. "People
don't go to a place like that to look for other people. That's the
opposite of the whole concept that's behind the thing."

"I think I ought to grab the opportunity to talk to Rick in private,
though, anyway," Lenore said.

"Uh-huh," Lang said.

Faint music was coming from the television screen now. Heads
kept replacing one another on the screen. Lang had a finger just
under the elastic band of Lenore's panties, on her hip. Lang said
the curve of Lenore's particular hip drove him right straight wild.
He kissed her throat again.

Lang said grandmothers made him awfully sad. He said grandmothers were in his opinion basically sad things, especially the really
old ones, who had all kinds of sad troubles. He told Lenore he
remembered his father's mother in a nursing home in Texas in the
1960s. He said his grandfather had died and his father and mother
had taken the grandmother in, for a time, but that things just hadn't
worked out, even with a sort of nurse hired to come in during the
day to look after the grandmother, and that Lang's father and grandmother had sat down and had a talk and Lang's father had told her
she was going to get moved to a nursing home.

"She was just real decrepit, I remember," Lang said. "I remember
she didn't move good at all, and her eyes they got milkier and
milkier as time went by. She didn't kick up at the idea of going to
the nursing home. I remember she nodded when my Daddy told
her. You could tell she knew things just weren't working out.

"And the thing was we'd visit her in that nursing home every Saturday," Lang said. "We made it like a routine. My Daddy tried real hard to be a good son. And the place wasn't but over in Fort Worth, so we'd all just pile in the car and go see her. Always my Daddy, goddamn near always me. Sometimes my mother and my brother. We'd pile in, and drive over, and we'd come through this gate of the place and have to go up this long, real windy gravel road to the place. This was a real nice place, too. It was real expensive. I can't say anything against the care she must of got."

Lenore nodded, and Lang touched her lip.

"So we'd just wind on up that road, and I remember how it always looked all sinister up at the actual home itself, which was at the top of a kind of hill, 'cause my Daddy always had tinted glass in his cars, so when I'd look up at the place through the windshield I'd see all this shit through tinted glass, and it'd look dark as hell, and like it was going to rain and storm and all. It always looked weird," Lang said. "And we could always see her, as we were coming up that road, 'cause she was always waiting for us on the porch of the place, every time. Place had a real nice porch, raised up. We'd see her as we drove up, see her from far away, 'cause she had this bright-white hair you could see for miles, and a wheelchair. But and anyway she'd be out there, and we'd come up and pile out, and up we'd go to visit. She was always real glad to see us. It was good to see her, too, but also of course kind of an obligation, you couldn't deny the fact. I remember I bitched about it, some Saturdays. Had other shit to do. I was like eight." Lang took his hand off Lenore's hip and brushed it softly back and forth over her breasts. "But you know we'd visit and all, and she'd fill us in on what she was doing. Which didn't take much time, 'cause I remember what she was always doing was just making pot holders, for my mother. She made about one pot holder a month, was all. Her hands always moved like it was real cold."

Lang cleared his throat. "But then after some time went on like that, on one particular Saturday we didn't go. We couldn't go that time. My Daddy had some emergency, I had shit to do, so on. So we didn't go that Saturday. And the next day I remember we couldn't go that day either. There was just no two ways about it. But Monday we did go, to make up the visit, like surprise her with a visit, to make it up, which seemed fair and all. We all went ahead and piled in that Monday after I got off school. We went, and as we pull up that long drive up the hill we're confused, 'cause we can *see* her, hair all white and wheelchair shining, there on the porch, with everything looking all dark and nasty around her in the tinted glass. And my Daddy goes 'What the hell?' 'cause here it was Monday, not Saturday. And it was cool out, you know. It was like November, and things could get cool. But and so she's sitting there anyway on the porch, in her chair, in blankets, so on.

"And we get up there and get out of the car and go on up to the porch, and she's glad as hell to see us, like I said her eyes were milky but the milk seemed like it went out of them when she was real happy. She was clapping her hands real slow and soft, and smiling, and trying to hurry to pull pot holders and shit out of the blankets in her lap to show my mother, and grabbing at us and all, and my Daddy says something like 'Momma it's Monday, it's not Saturday, we couldn't come Saturday so we come today instead to be fair, now you tell me how'd you know to be out here waiting for us today, we didn't tell anybody we was coming,' so on. And she looks at my Daddy I remember like she don't understand, for a time, and then she smiles, real nice, and shrugs, and looks around at us and says well she waits for us every day. Then she nods. Every day, see. She says it like she thought we knew how she waited for us to maybe visit every goddamned day."

Lenore watched Lang.

"Turned out she didn't know Saturday from Adam anymore," Lang said. "She didn't know we had this shit down to a routine." He looked out past Lenore. "Or else maybe she did know, but she waited anyway, thinkin' maybe she'd get lucky and we'd want to see her even on some day when we didn't have to. Even when it got real cool out on the porch of the place she'd wait, it turned out. She just kept looking at my Daddy like she didn't see what the problem was, this was just her life, now, here, didn't we know it? While all the while we just stood around feeling terrible. I remember I felt like shit after that. I was big-time sad." Lang rubbed at an eye. "She died after that, too, 'fore I got much older."

Lenore watched Lang rub one eye. She thought about his grandmother. Lang stopped rubbing his eye and looked at her. Lenore found her throat aching again. She began to cry, just a little bit.

"Now I didn't mean to make *you* sad," Lang said. He smiled kindly. "That's my sad, it's not your sad."

He began kissing at Lenore's eyes, to get the tears. He did it so gently that Lenore put her arms around his neck. After a minute Lang rolled her toward him and began with one hand to try to unhook the fastener on her bra. Lenore let him, and kept her arms around his neck. Lang played with Lenore's breasts while she cried and held onto him and thought of a sky in Texas, in November, through tinted glass.

/a/

"Good morning, Patrice."

"Good morning. How are you this morning?"

"I'm just fine thank you. The nurse tells me you have something for me."

"Yes."

"Can I ask what it is?"

"Three men go camping in the woods. One of the men starts out doing all the cooking, but the three men make an arrangement where, if either of the other two complain about the man's cooking, the complainer will automatically take over the cooking."

"I'm not sure I understand, Patrice."

"The cook cooks and cooks, and the other two campers smile and say it's very good, and they all continue to camp. And by and by the cook gets tired of cooking, and wishes someone would complain and so have to take over for him, but there are still no complaints. So the cook begins overcooking things on purpose, or burning them, or hardly cooking them and having them be raw. But the other two campers still eat it all and manage to smile. Soon the cook begins putting soap in the coffee, sprinkling dirt on everything he cooks, but still the other two go out of their way not to complain."

"Is this a joke? This is a joke, Patrice, I can tell."

"So finally the cook gets angry, he's so very tired of cooking, and he goes deep into the woods and finds a pile of moose droppings, and he takes them back to camp and roasts them, and serves them for dinner, along with soapy coffee. And the other two campers dig in, and the cook smiles at them expectantly, and they're eating very slowly, and also looking at each other, with faces. Finally one of them puts down his fork and says to the cook, 'Hey, Joe, I'm afraid I've got to tell you that these things taste like moose droppings. *Good, though.*' "

"Ha-ha."

"Ha-ha."

"Patrice, that was splendid, that joke. Where did you hear that? Did you make that joke up?"

"My son told it to me."

"Well isn't that just good, Patrice."

"Yes."

"When exactly did he tell that joke to you?"

"I think a joke like that ought to be worth some breathing, don't you?"

"I certainly do."

"I sure think so."

/b/

11 September

The End Is a Night Fire.

It is another May night, because May never ever ends. Here is a street that should be dark. In a gust of light the cement of the street can be seen to be new and rough. Some of the homes do not yet have lawns. All the trees are young and thin and supported by networks of ropes and stakes. They flicker and whip in the wind of light.

The wind is a wind of hot sparks. The sparks rise and whirl and die in the shrouds of light they make. At the end of the street sighs a burning home. The home looks the same as every other home on the street. It is on fire. Fire comes out of every opening in the home and rises. As the fire makes more openings in the home and rises from them, the home sighs and settles. The heat of the fire makes the fence in the lawn glow red, and the fence cooks the lawn around it.

The home begins to fold into its fire. Fire comes out of all the openings. It sounds like paper crinkling. It tightens the skin of your face. The fire cannot be controlled, and the home draws in all the air on the street and with a sigh folds down into itself. It takes forever. Everything falls into itself, slow as feathers.

Out the door of the home flies a bird with its tailfeathers on fire. It rises into the sky in circles. It spirals up and up into the sky until its light melts into a sparkle of stars. Down to the lawn floats a corkscrew pattern of burnt feathers.

Feet run over the lawn, through the flaming feathers. Fieldbinder and Evelyn Slotnik, hand in hand, run into the night, their hair on fire. In the light of their own hair they are wind. They make glowing cuts in the black square blocks of the suburbs as they run the tiny miles to the Slotniks' pool. Fences blush and fall away. An airplane is flying low overhead. The passengers look down and see it all. They see one shining pond of fire soaking out into the lawns and making shrouds of needled light that float up toward them, disappear when they touch. They see two surprised points of orange fire moving too fast through black backyards and waffled fences, making for a kidney of clean new blue water that lies ahead in a line lit up from below. It is captured forever on quality film.

/c/

One of the oars fell into the water and Neil Obstat, Jr., lunged for it, knocking over his can of beer so that beer fizzed on his pantleg. He struggled to get the heavy oar back in its lock.

"God damn it," he said.

"Just keep the fucker still, Neil," said Wang-Dang Lang.

"Shit," said Obstat. Some people trying to fish over in the next rowboat were mad at the commotion and were giving Obstat the finger.

Lang was in the bow of the boat he and Obstat had rented at the Great Ohio Desert Fish License and Boat Rental Center for what Lang thought was a truly criminal amount of money.

"This whole thing's just gettin' too goddamn commercialized," he'd said to Obstat. Obstat had shrugged and hefted the beer.

Lang had some binoculars through which he was watching Lenore Beadsman and Rick Vigorous wandering along the lake's edge through one of the really blasted and forbidding parts of the Desert. Despite the weekend crowds, Lenore was easy to see in her bright white dress, and of course there was too the matter of Rick Vigorous's beret. Lang and Obstat were way out in the lake. Obstat was supposed to be rowing the boat so that they stayed just even with Lenore and Rick.

"What do you see?" Obstat had asked from the oars.

When Rick and Lenore were turned the right way, Lang could see their faces, but he couldn't yet make out what they were saying. They weren't talking much. Lenore was moving pretty easily through the deep sand, but Lang could see Rick Vigorous having trouble and sometimes needing to trot to keep up. Lenore kept making him look at his watch, as if time were an issue. It was still only midmorning, but it was hot for September. Crowds wove in and out around Lenore and Rick. Someone on the rim was hawking black tee-shirts in a voice Lang could hear clear out on the water.

Lang held the binoculars in one hand. His other hand hurt like hell today, from twirling his car keys on his injured finger last night. He thought his bird-bite might be getting infected.

"Fucking bird," he said.

Obstat was grunting at the oars. He kept clunking them against the sides of the boat. Lang and Obstat were positively mowing over people's fishing lines, and the people in the other boats were getting really pissed off, but Lang told Obstat not to pay them any mind.

"Just remember I get a gander or two at those unearthly legs, climbing dunes," Obstat gasped as he pulled.

"They'll start sayin' important shit any minute now," Lang said.

/d/

"I absolutely insist that you invite me to relate a story."

"My shoes are full of this goddamned sand."

"Lenore . . ."

"Hey! Watch where you're going for Christ's sake!"

"Dear. Excuse us, please."

"For crying out loud."

"Terribly sorry."

"Hell of a place for a picnic."

"If you want my opinion, Lenore, they should either obliterate this place or enlarge it. The touristiness of the whole thing is negating whatever marginal attractions this place had to offer."

"People aren't smelling too terrific in this sun, either, I notice."

"Forget smells. You're here to concentrate on potential grandmother-signs."

"What kind of signs, Rick? I should look for Lenore neither climbing up nor sliding down a dune, all because of a game my brother made up when he was flapped? This has got to be a waste of time. I don't understand your obsession with this. With getting me out here today."

"Apparently Lang and his anus-eyed Sancho Panza are about, too. Lurking, et cetera."

"How do you know where Andy and Obstat are supposed to be?"

"I know what I know."

"Look, Rick, speaking of knowing, I think we maybe ought to just talk, right here, at some length."

"I implore you first to implore me for a story."

"What's with this story stuff?"

". . . ."

"Look, you might have forgotten I *have* to read the things now. They're work now. When I'm not working, I'd rather not do a work-related thing."

"You won't be called on to evaluate, merely to enjoy. To be caught up, engaged, and entertained. You should find this entertaining and engaging."

"Rick, the thing is we really need to talk. You're dealing with an upset person, here. We really need to have a long talk."

"I'm almost convinced the issues here can be treated and perhaps even resolved in the context of the story I have in mind."

"I really doubt it."

"Just keep your eyes peeled for things covertly elderly, and I'll take it from here."

"So you're deciding how the talk I want to have is going to be. That's just super."

"This story concerns a man who is presented as the most phenomenally successful theoretical dentist of the twentieth century."

"Theoretical dentist?"

"A scientist specializing in dental theory and in high-level abstract reasoning from empirical cases involving anything at all dental."

"Wonderful."

"Do you recall that sweetener that was positively omnipresent for a while? SupraSweet? The one that was abruptly yanked from the supermarket shelves when they discovered that it made certain women give birth to children with antennae, and fangs like vampires?"

"Do I ever."

"Here the theoretical dentist in question is presented as the man who cracked the antennae-and-fang problem, working as it were from the dental end and tracing matters back to the ubiquitous and malignant sweetener."

"Jesus, Rick, look at this crowd. How are we supposed to get through all this?"

"They're just waiting for the shuttle to the interior wastes. It'll be here soon—see the dust cloud? Perhaps we might just wait over here, under this statue, in this bit of shade . . ."

"I remember this statue all right. I can't stand this statue. It's like Zusatz was trying to set himself up as god of the Desert or something. Sheesh."

"So the man in question is a theoretical dentist of consummate skill."

"Uh-huh."

"And in his spare time he is also a thoroughly competent and experienced Scoutmaster.

" . . . . "

"For the Boy Scouts of America."

"Got it."

"Having been himself in his youth a phenomenal Scout: a Tenderfoot at nine, a First Class Scout at eleven, a Star, Life, then finally an Eagle Scout at the amazing age of fourteen. Amazing for his era, anyhow. We may note for example that before my son, Vance, quit the Scouts he had been a Life Scout, the penultimate kind of Scout, at the age of twelve."

"How nice for him."

"But the point is that the theoretical dentist had been an exemplary Scout, and one so committed to Scouting in general that when he exited the Scouts because of his age he turned right around and became a Scoutmaster, while still training in theoretical dentistry. This was twenty years ago, fixing the dentist's present age somewhere in his forties."

". . . ."

"And one summer day the dentist is leading his troop of Scouts through some orientation and compass exercises in the dense and desolate interior regions of the coniferous forests that as you may or may not know cover vast portions of the state of Indiana. The whole story takes place in Indiana."

". . . ."

"And the dentist is effortlessly leading the Scouts through the forest, preparing them for woodsman merit-badge tests, and now in the densest and most desolate interior section the dentist and his Scouts come on an exhausted and haggard-looking man, dressed exclusively in flannel, with many days' growth of beard, and bright-red eyes, and white pine-pitch residue smeared around his mouth, who right away moans and faints in the arms of a Star Scout; and with him is an also haggard-looking but still achingly lovely woman, with her dress in a noticeable state of disarray, who immediately falls weeping on the neck of the theoretical dentist, crying that she has been saved. The woman tells the dentist that she and her unconscious companion, who is also it turns out her psychologist, had been lost in the desolate interior coniferous region for days, that the psychologist's magnetic clipboard-and-pen set had ruined their compass, and that they had been wandering for days, losing hope steadily, sustaining themselves only by eating the truly nauseating white remains of the pine pitch that crusted the bark of the trees all around. The woman tells the dentist all this as they stare deeply into each other's eyes, and as all around them the badge-happy Scouts are running here and there, positively radiating Competence In The Wild, raising and striking tents, building elaborate multi-tiered fires, detoxifying water with Halazone pellets, and administering to the still swooned psychologist every form of first aid you could possibly imagine. And now, if I may import a bit of context to save time, it is made clear that the woman and the psychologist have been out in the Indiana forests for ostensibly therapeutic reasons, that the woman suffers from a nearly debilitating neurosis under the rules of which she needs constant and prodigious sexual attention and activity, in order to stave off feelings of raving paranoia and loss of three-dimensionality."

"Let's go. Here's the bus. The crowd's mostly getting on. Let's get out of this shadow."

"Did you get all that?"

"Dentist, Scoutmaster, merit badge, rescue, woman with dimension problems. Check. But I'd really rather be talking, Rick."

"Listen, Lenore, shall we get on the bus? Just on a lark? What do you say?"

"Are you kidding? Do you know what the crowds'll be like in the interior? It's Saturday, you might have forgotten. Let's just stay along the good old lake, here."

"Why this fixation on the proximity of the lake?"

". . . ."

"At any rate, we are informed that the now still unconscious psychologist had in therapy sessions professed to see the achingly lovely woman's psychological troubles as stemming from the continual sexual advances and erotic situations that necessarily confront the woman as she goes about her life in the collective societal environment of Indianapolis, where she lives, so that the problem is conceived of as, a, due to the constant erotic battering at the woman's sexual identity from without by other members of Indianapolis's society, which societal unit the psychologist clearly loathes, but and b, due to the woman's own failure to develop a sufficiently strong sense of self and interior worth to allow her to be discriminating about which of the constant stream of advances to respond to and allow to have any bearing whatsoever on said interior self and sense of worth."

"My nose is going to get sunburned. I can feel the sunburn starting."

"I suppose you want me to ask about the gymnastics. I read a rather cutting review in the *Dealer*."

"Look, if you want to talk, like as in have a conversation, good, because we really need to. Let's just hunker right down here in the sand and—"

"No, no, wait. Not yet. We're still dangling."

"Beg pardon?"

"To return, the context gives us to understand that the psychologist is actually at best warped and at worst simply evil, and that though he had lured the achingly lovely but troubled woman out deep into the coniferous interior Indiana wastes ostensibly to rap, one on one, about her sense of self and the strength thereof, ostensibly away from all the disturbing exterior erotic assaults the woman suffers in collective society, actually the psychologist really just wanted to seduce the poor woman, which seduction is immediately attempted, in a positively oafish way, the minute the two have hiked out of earshot of civilization, and but which seduction, however oafish, the poor insecure ambiguously dimensional woman is in no shape to resist, and thus the better part of two days were spent by the psychologist and the woman rutting like crazed weasels on the bed of soft pine needles that covers the coniferous wastes, and actually it was in the throes of one such rutting-session that the psychologist's magnetic clipboard came into contact with and potentially disastrously damaged the woman's compass, which was the hikers' only means of orientation."

" . . . . "

"The disaster being only potential, of course, because of the timely intervention, after a tense, pine-pitch-eating week or so, of the theoretical dentist and his troop of Scouts, which intervention and rescue prompts a gush of narrative and explanation and context from the woman, who clearly flips for the dentist at first sight, even though he has a slight hair-loss problem, but anyway the gushing and flipping, not to mention the initial aching loveliness, prompts a reciprocal rush of emotion in the dentist, who is a widower; and so in a dubious but not entirely inappropriate passage we are informed that a certain nascent love-plant sends up a fragile and vulnerable green shoot or two through the desolate coniferous soil between the woman and the dentist, while, all about them and the love-shoot, Scouts mill, and accomplish difficult merit-badge-related tasks, and chart elaborate return-courses that involve steering by the lights of esoteric nebulae, and propose to drag the very worse-for-wear psychologist back to civilization on a gurney sled of branches and pitch and woven pine needles."

"Rick, is this supposed to be a sign?"

"Just wait for the climax."

"No, Rick, here. See? Footprints, but around every print four holes, like from an old person's walker sinking in the sand. Is this supposed to be somebody walking, with a walker?"

"I think not. I think this person here was simply steering a course through a field of sun umbrellas. This place is after all positively littered with sun umbrellas. These holes don't work for me as walker tracks. Besides, we're duneless, here, you might have noticed."

"I guess you're right. . . ."

"Anyway, to make something long attractively shorter, the theoretical dentist and the achingly lovely woman get married. They fall madly, uncontrollably in love, and decide to unite forever, and the woman tells the dentist about her whole neurosis-set, and the dentist is incredibly compassionate, and says he doesn't care, and he goes and has a long talk with the eventually physically recovered psychologist, and forgives him for taking advantage of a completely helpless patient, and purely out of compassion and goodness asks him to be the best man at the impending wedding, the wedding is impending, and the psychologist is understandably relieved at the dentist's discretion, but he's also still wildly infatuated with the achingly lovely woman, and so even during the wedding—which is attended by, among others, the dentist's brother, the woman's whole huge Indianapolis clan, and by everyone who's anyone in the field of theoretical dentistry—the psychologist is covertly smirking and chuckling and checking out the woman's body under her wedding dress."

"I'm tired."

"Which checking out is at this point futile, though, because although the woman still has the pathological need for sexual attention and activity in order to stave off violent neurotic upheavals, said need is let's just say being more than adequately fulfilled by the theoretical dentist, in whom the lovely woman has reawakened a surge of passion and an urge for intimacy the dentist has not felt since his youth, when he was fresh out of the Scouts. And here a long section is devoted to graphic descriptions of the implications of all these reawakened surges and fulfilled needs, some of the most vivid of which involve certain dental apparati being put to uses which—although emotionally innocent, and so of course ultimately OK—are far in excess of the average dentist's wildest fantasies. If you get my drift."

"Maybe the drift should be sped up. I really want to talk to you."

"I sense that, Lenore, believe me. Let's do it within the context provided."

"So at least get on with it, then."

"And so the theoretical dentist and the achingly lovely woman are married, and truly staggering levels of intimacy are being attained, and neither partner rejects anything the other wants to do as undesirable or sick, and the woman is unbelievably happy, because she is wildly in love with this admittedly older but still very impressive theoretical dentist, and because her pathological needs are being satisfied within an emotionally and socially acceptable framework. And the theoretical dentist is unbelievably happy, too, because of his fierce and complete love for the achingly lovely woman, and because satisfying her prodigious needs is not exactly torture for him, either. So things are simply wonderful."

". . . ."

"Until, that is, the theoretical dentist is the victim of a hideous auto accident, in which he was not at fault, and is catastrophically injured, being as a result of the accident now deaf, dumb, blind, and nearly completely paralyzed and insensate, again through absolutely no fault of his own."

"Another one of these real happy stories, I see."

"And now the theoretical dentist lies in the hospital bed that will be his home for the rest of his life, and the lovely woman is of course frantic with grief and love for her husband, and the dentist is lying there, in complete blackness, numb blackness, paralyzed, almost wholly insensate. But not, and now I repeat *not*, entirely incommunicado."

"You can tell my socks are going to be all black and nasty from this rotten sand, Rick. This is that cheap kind of sand. Shit on fire."

"Yes, not incommunicado, as I'm sure you see would be a very significant and precious thing for someone otherwise plunged completely into numb silent blackness. Not incommunicado because exactly one area of the dentist's devastated body actually retains some feeling and power of movement, namely the central portion of his upper lip. And also because the dentist, having been as we know a consummate Scout, knew and knows Morse code, inside and out."

"Morse code? Lips?"

"Communications *to* the dentist are effected simply by tapping the relevant message out in Morse code on the dentist's upper lip. Messages *from* the dentist are possible provided that one is willing patiently to tap each letter of the Morse code alphabet onto the lip and wait for a signal from the dentist—a heart-tweakingly feeble and tiny movement of the upper lip—when the right letter has been reached. Needless to say, communications from the shattered dentist are incredibly slow and difficult to receive."

". . . ."

"But see that communications *to* the dentist are comparatively easy. And now the Midwestern theoretical dentistry community, out of sheer respect for the broken and insensate dentist, and a desire to get his input, however understandably slight, on certain vexing high-level dental problems, seeks to engage someone in the Indianapolis area with a working knowledge of Morse code, to tap some of the current and pertinent developments in the dentist's professional world onto his lip. Meanwhile the achingly lovely woman has undergone an intensive course in Morse code, so that she can communicate on a personal level with the broken dentist, and she visits him every day, relating items of interest, comforting the dentist in his numb black silence, tapping onto his upper lip how very much she loves him, et cetera, and also reading fiction to him, via Morse code, because the dentist has been a fanatical fiction reader, when sighted and whole. Specifically she begins tapping onto the theoretical dentist's lip Frank Norris's stunning novel *McTeague*, which the dentist had been reading just before his hideous mishap, and which she had picked up and seen on the very first page concerned the adventures of a dentist, and which indeed, you can tell from her husband's lip movements, he enjoys having Morse-coded onto him."

"   . . . ."

"But and meanwhile the psychologist, having seen the news of the hideous auto accident, and having begun to scan the journals of theoretical dentistry for further news of the brilliant dentist's physical and professional condition, sees in said journals the appeal for an Indianapolis Morse code tapper with some dental savvy, and he immediately comes forward to volunteer his services, although in reality we're informed that his sole exposure to Morse code had been when he sent away for a Lone Ranger decoder ring as a boy, which ring turned out to be simply a Morse code key, which the boy was to use to decode disappointingly dull ads for Ralston that were transmitted in a supposedly mysterious code at the end of every episode of 'The Lone Ranger,' in Indianapolis."

"Lone Ranger rings? Ralston?"

"He also passes himself off as having a keen amateur interest in the whole theoretical dentistry scene, et cetera. Of course the psychologist's true motive is to insinuate himself back into the arms and lap of the achingly lovely, but also as he and we can anticipate given the situation and context increasingly troubled, woman. So the psychologist appears in the dentist's hospital room with armloads of cutting-edge-theoretical-dentistry literature, and he and the woman reestablish an acquaintance, because the woman is almost always in the room tapping *McTeague* onto the dentist's lip when the psychologist arrives."

"Here's the curve of the lake. We're getting near the end of the trail."

"And the psychologist begins ostensibly tapping important cutting-edge dental theory onto the dentist's lip, while the woman stands there at the door, her eyes shining with gratitude at the psychologist. But in reality the psychologist is simply tapping random and meaningless taps onto the lip, he doesn't give a damn what he's tapping, and the paralyzed, deaf-dumb-and-blind dentist gets enormously confused, there in the numb black, and he begins trying to move his upper lip, to communicate his confusion to his wife, to ask what the problem is, what's this gobbledygook being tapped onto his lip, but the psychologist is meanwhile engaging the woman in clever conversation, and mild flirtation, and the woman has been without the erotic attention and activity she involuntarily craves so desperately for an ominously long time, now, and so she's distracted, and beginning to be torn, but at any rate she's distracted, and since the relevant signal-movement of the theoretical dentist's lip is such a truly pathetically tiny movement, she doesn't ever see it, and so the wildly disoriented and frightened paralyzed dentist continues to have gibberish tapped onto his lip for hours each day, until one day the psychologist taps and repeats one particular Morse code message that he went to the trouble especially to learn, the message being to the effect that he was going to ball the paralyzed dentist's achingly lovely wife until she bled, that he was going to take her away from the dentist and leave the dentist all alone in his numb lonely blackness, and that there was nothing the pathetic, paralyzed, helpless dentist could do about it; he was as inefficacious as he was inadequate."

"Jesus, Rick, what is this?"

"I promise we'll be able to relate to it. Let's just bear with. On receipt of this Morse code message, the dentist in his hospital bed is flung into a state of such depression and despair that he stops moving his lip, however pathetically tinily, to signal his wife, even when she taps 'I love you' onto the lip. And the lovely wife perceives this sudden absence of lip movement as a sign of further physical deterioration in the dentist, and so she too is thrown into despair, which despair further aggravates her emotional condition vis à vis the sex-and-dimensionality neurosis, and she begins to offer less and less resistance to the malevolent blond psychologist's frequent and oafish sexual advances, many of them made right there in the dentist's hospital room, while the dentist lies right there, helpless and insensate."

"Blond? A blond psychologist?"

"Affirmative."

"Why is this story beginning to give me the creeps?"

"It means you're beginning really to relate. You're being intuitive about it."

"What does being intuitive have to do with it?"

"Here's the end of the trail. Shall we strike off into the interior? I sense that whatever it is we're looking for is best looked for in the interior. In the heart of the Desert, Lenore. What do you say?"

"Let's just go back the way we came. My nose hurts. This is clearly a waste of time. At least this way I get to look at the lake."

"Christ, the lake, again. The lake is just a bunch of people fishing for black fish. Who cares about the lake?"

"Rick, why are you sweating like this? It's hot, but it's not that hot. Are you OK?"

". . . ."

"Rick, are you all right I said."

"Maybe just the effects of trying to relate a difficult and emotionally intricate story in the face of your complete insensitivity you bitch!"

"What?"

"I'm sorry."

"What did you say to me?"

"Please, forget I said anything. Let's just walk back along the lake."

"We really need to talk, buster, and I mean now."

"Just trust me."

"What the hell are we even doing out here? Andy was right."

"Have I not earned some trust?"

/e/

"I don't like this at all," Lang was saying. He squatted on his hams in the bow, resting his elbows on his knees and looking through the binoculars. "Not one little red bit, good buddy."

Obstat took two Pop Tarts out of their wrapper and tossed the wrapper into the lake. "At least they've stopped for a second," he said with his mouth full. "My arms are fucking numb, Wanger."

"Something's up," said Lang. "The little dung beetle's up to something."

"What's he doing?"

"It's not so much what he's doing." Lang shifted up into a seat. "It's the way Lenore's looking, here."

"How's that dress doing in all this heat, is what I want to know," Obstat said eagerly. "She got that little V of sweat at the chest yet? I love that little V."

"Fuck off," Lang said.

"Hey now Wanger, you said I could look at the legs, and the V too if there was one!"

"Stop whining goddammit Neil," Lang said angrily. He looked at Obstat, who was looking at him as he chewed. Lang rolled his eyes. "Here, then. Just take a fast goddamn look if you have to." He passed the binoculars over to Obstat and rubbed his face.

Obstat scanned with the glasses. Lang could see that he was getting Pop Tart filling on them. "Oh Jesus God I'm in love," Obstat whispered. "This is it. Mommy."

"I told you to cut that shit out about Lenore."

"Who's talking about Lenore? I'm talking about this totally unbelievable babe under a sun umbrella that Lenore and the little double-chinned guy just went by."

"Just went by?" Lang sat up. "Where're they going?"

"They just turned around, looks like. They're going back the way they came I guess." Obstat was still aimed at the beautiful woman, in a black swimsuit, under an umbrella.

"Turned around? The *fuck*. Give me those things."

Obstat looked up from the glasses, pissed off. "Hey," he said.

"Look here. If my ass gets dragged all the way out here and then gets made to row a stupid boat so you can try to read people's lips, and if you're going to get all hinkey about Lenore and not let me express feelings, you can at *least* let me scope a little bit."

"You little skull-head," Lang said. He yanked the binoculars out of Obstat's hands and scanned the black rim of the Desert. "Holy shit, they are goin' back," he said. Obstat munched his Pop Tart in a funk. "I don't like this at all," Lang was saying. He reached out and knocked the Pop Tart out of Obstat's hand into the water.

"Hey!" Obstat said.

"Row!" yelled Lang. People in the other boats looked over. Lang squatted back in the bow. "Turn this fucker around and row back the way we came." He looked through the binoculars again as Obstat muttered and picked up the heavy oars.

"And also start gettin' us in closer to shore,'" Lang said, pausing for just a moment to look back at what was undeniably a really unbelievable woman, in that swimsuit. "I want us a whole lot closer to shore."

/f/

11 September

"So where do you get off, Fieldbinder?" Slotnik said, crossing and uncrossing his legs on the love seat.

The living room smelled vaguely of burn. Fieldbinder sat in wet clothes, shivering, the black wires of his burnt hair protruding up in a fan from his head, his hands full of stiff black feathers.

"What can I say, Don?" he said.

"An excellent question, Monroe," said Slotnik, glancing over at Evelyn, in a new dry robe and nothing else, looking at her reflection in the dark living room window and trying on wigs. Slotnik turned back. *"Just what can you say, my friend, with your wet wrinkled clothes and smelly, kinky head? What can the universe say, when my supposedly good and respectable neighbors worship my children on the sly, and my supposedly good friend and colleague balls my wife, pokes and punctures the object*

of my every non-professional thought, tries to take my wife away, from me, to whom she rightfully belongs." He stared at Fieldbinder. "What is to say, Monroe?"

"Don, you've raised a number of interesting points," said Fieldbinder. He glanced up at the staircase and saw two sets of pajama-feet, the children's, as the Slotnik children stood at the top of the case and listened, and perhaps sucked their thumbs.

"Just where do you get off, is what I want to know," said Slotnik, crossing and uncrossing his legs, jangling a pair of open handcuffs. "Because, for your own information and files, you've gotten off for the last time. This is the end. This is it."

Fieldbinder grinned coolly, then wryly. "Is it," he said. He slowly felt at the feathers with his good hand.

"Yes," said Slotnik, returning Fieldbinder's smile with one equally wry. He went to Evelyn, at the window, and in a single motion calmly handcuffed her wrist to his wrist. Evelyn said nothing; she continued to put on wigs, making Slotnik's arm rise and fall with her own. Slotnik stared past his wife at Fieldbinder's tiny reflection in the dark window.

"Yes," he said again. "This is it. You've let yourself in for it, Monroe." He turned. "You've put your precious, prodigious self in connection with another. And now I'm taking the other back. Evelyn and I are now joined together, forever, in discipline and negation."

"Discipline?" Fieldbinder said, removing some mud and a twig from the crease of his slacks.

"She is now gone, the connection severed, and so you are done," said Slotnik, holding up his handcuffed wrist for effect. Evelyn's arm moved with his.

"I see," said Fieldbinder.

"Yes I'm sure you do," Slotnik said coolly. "The connection is severed, you are yourself punctured, you are done. You will bleed out of yourself and rise like a husk on a dry wind. There will be less and less of you. You will grow smaller and smaller in your stylish clothes, until you disappear altogether." Slotnik grinned wryly. "You will return to the night sky with your satanic bird, and every dawn and dusk the horizon will run with your juices."

"What an interestingly absurd theory, Don," Fieldbinder said coolly.

"I'm afraid he means it, Monroe," said Evelyn into the window. "Don has always been a man of his word." She turned and cocked her head, *modelling a blond wig. "What do you think of this one, before you have to go?"*

Fieldbinder moved to look at his watch, but it had already slipped off his wrist onto the carpet without a sound.

/g/

"What's this? Are we checking out today?"

". . . ."

"Is that what we're doing, Mr. Beadsman? Checking out?"

"Yes."

"Well I have a form for you to sign right here, and then I guess off you go into the blue."

". . . ."

"We usually don't release on Saturday you know Mr. Beadsman. I had to get this form out of a locked drawer you know."

"I apologize for any inconvenience."

"Oh I was just joking with you. That was just a joke. There's no inconvenience at all."

"May I please leave, then?"

"That's a good signature you've got there, Mr. Beadsman, isn't it? Now is somebody meeting you, or what?"

"No."

"Dr. Nelm told me to expect somebody to meet you, Mr. Beadsman. Are we being naughty?"

"I want to take a taxi to the airport."

"Are we going home, Mr. Beadsman? Are we going home to see our family?"

". . . ."

"Well all I can say is you just get your mother to give you something to eat. You just don't eat enough, is part of your problem, if you want my two cents' worth. You just eat, you hear?"

"Can you please call me a taxi?"

"And your father's been notified, Dr. Nelm told me."

"I'll notify everyone."

"Looks like a beautiful day out there. I heard it was going to rain, but I'll take sunshine bouncing off our lake any old day won't you?"

" . . . . "

"I wish *I* was going to the airport on such a beautiful day."

"I'm afraid the sun will hurt my eyes, I've been inside so long."

"Now don't you worry. You can just squint until you get used to it. Your old eyes will adjust to the outside lickety-split, mine always do."

" . . . . "

"This is just a bright town we live in Mr. Beadsman."

/h/

"So this goes on, really for longer than is necessary in order to get the narrative job done, with scene after scene of the wife coming in, tapping some *McTeague* onto the theoretical dentist's lip, the psychologist coming in and fondling the achingly lovely wife from behind, even as she taps the *McTeague* code, the wife finally unable to resist any longer and throwing herself into the arms of the psychologist, and their rutting like crazed weasels on the hospital room floor while the theoretical dentist lies helpless in his bed, drowning in numb blackness and despair, vividly imagining precisely the scene that is taking place on the floor below him.'"

"Although I bet it's at least ninety-eight point six out here right now, don't you think? I don't know about at night, but I think the Desert could maybe support Lenore during the day. But maybe I'm just grasping at straws. Do you think I'm just grasping?"

"But see, part of the theoretical dentist's despair stems from the fact that he really doesn't and can't blame his achingly lovely wife for what is happening. He knows all about his wife's being troubled. He knows that she needs something which he is now, through no fault of his own, unable to give her. So he doesn't and cannot blame her. But imagine his despair, Lenore. In his numb helpless black isolation he needs the emotional center of his life, the object of his complete adoration, his fiancée, more than ever; and yet he knows that it is precisely his state of helpless, inefficacious isolation—a state he is in through exactly zero fault of his own—that is of necessity driving the lovely woman he adores farther and farther away. So he forgives, Lenore. He forgives. But he burns every minute in a cold flame of unimaginable torment."

"What's going on, Rick?"

"He forgives her, Lenore. From the icy depths of his helpless isolation and fierce and complete love, he extends a theoretical hand of forgiveness, like so . . ."

"Ow!"

"Dear me, excuse us, please."

"Watch where you're waving your hands, buddy!"

"Terribly sorry."

"Freaking crowds. Let's get, Rick. We're just playing games. Lenore isn't around here."

"So on it goes. Finally the theoretical dentist's brother, who is an estate attorney in Philadelphia, is able to break away from his incredibly successful practice and personal life to come see the withered husk of the theoretical dentist. Since the brother had gone through the Scouts right alongside the dentist, for him Morse code communication to the dentist is no problem, though communications from the dentist are still cumbersome as hell. Nevertheless we're subjected to long and difficult coded conversations between the two in the hospital room, while the lovely wife, consumed with understandable self-loathing, and afraid that she would not be able to help making a pass at the devastatingly handsome estate-attorney brother, stays shacked up in the malevolent blond psychologist's apartment, rutting, and also watching gymnastics on television, the symbolism of which doesn't escape the reader, rest assured."

"OK Rick, that's it. Cut the story charade. We're having a talk."

"You bet your lovely bottom we are."

"So why can't we just have a talk without you pretending it's something else, Rick? I find this pretty disturbing."

"But see finally the wife can no longer stay away, she realizes that whatever physical connection she may crave because of her disastrously weak self-network, she and the dentist are connected in a much deeper and more profound and yes in some sense even more fulfilling and three-dimensional way, namely an *emotional* way, and so she rushes to the hospital, brushes aside nurses and orderlies, and bursts into the theoretical dentist's room, only to see to her horror the dentist's brother, leaning over the prone dentist, beginning to remove the dentist's upper lip with a Boy Scout knife."

"Oh, really, come on."

"As the dentist, it turns out, had *requested*. Which, given the context, the sensitive reader of course regards as food for thought. But and so the wife screams, and the previously brushed-aside nurses and orderlies rush in, and they restrain the estate-attorney brother, and he is carried off, and the achingly lovely woman positively falls on the dentist's mangled upper lip, trying to stop the bleeding and save the lip, lashing out at doctors who come near, tapping over and over into the gore that she loves the dentist, that she is sorry, please to forgive her. And through his pain the helpless dentist feels her tap, and his heart almost breaks, and though he knows it will do no good, because her pathetic neurosis will, he knows, soon drive the wife into outside connections again, he does forgive her, he does, and he moves his lip in his pathetically tiny way, to let her know he forgives her, but the heart-tweakingly tiny familiar movement of the lip is here of course obscured by the flow of blood from the attempted lip-removal, and so the wife just cannot see the movement, no matter how frantically the helpless dentist tries to move his lip, and so the wife, getting no visible results, finally reels from the dentist's room in despair and horror and guilt, and immediately goes shopping."

"Shopping?"

". . . ."

"Shopping?"

"Lenore, look out there. What is that flash, out on the water? Is that a sunlight-off-binoculars flash?"

". . . ."

"Good Lord it is. Lenore, what's going on?"

". . . ."

"It is. It's Lang, in a boat. They're rowing this way. They've been watching. Lenore, what is Lang shouting? Is that Lang, shouting?"

"Rick, I can explain . . ."

"No problem at all. Let me just . . . I have to hurry."

"What are those?"

"These are our connection, Lenore. I forgive you."

"Handcuffs? You're going to forgive me with handcuffs that say 'Bambi's Den of Discipline' on them?"

"The . . . achingly lovely woman returns that night to the dentist's hospital room with her copy of *McTeague*. She comes in the night to the numb dentist and taps to him. She taps the conclusion of *McTeague*. The book's climax. Have you ever experienced the climax of *McTeague*?"

"Rick, you just take it easy."

"The climax consists of McTeague, the dentist, handcuffed to the corpse of his malevolent foe, Marcus Schouler, in the middle of a desert."

"Desert? Handcuffs? Corpses? Oh shit. Andy! *Andy!*"

"Andy? No, *Schouler*."

"Rick . . ."

"And as she taps it, ever so gently, taking care not to hurt him any more than she has already, she looks at the dentist's motionless face and sees a single tear emerge from one partly sedated eye and course down his cheek until it is silently absorbed by a cotton bandage. She, too, weeps, with no sound. . . . And she produces a pair of handcuffs, which she had gone to enormous expense and embarrassment to buy . . . and . . . joins herself . . . to the wrist of the theoretical dentist, his inefficacious wrist . . ."

"What are you *doing*? Let me *go!*"

". . . with the deep oiled . . . *click* of the handcuffs."

"Jesus, Rick. This is it. You get these off right now. You get me out. I've told you I hate this torture and pain stuff, and you just don't care! You're a sick man!"

"Torture and pain? Lenore, I *forgive* you."

"Forgive what, for Christ's sake? Help! Andy! Neil!"

"*Lenore!*"

"God damn it, Rick, this is it. No talking, even. I wanted to talk, I said let's talk Rick, but no, so now forget it, I'm sorry but that's it."

"We are now joined, my center and reference! In negation and discipline! Our bodies are husks!"

"You just better have the key. God, Andy, see if he's got the key."

"What the fuck's going on here?"

"Can't you see? He's *locked* us together!"

"Look you little wiener, cough up the key to these things or your ass is grass."

"You are *fired*, Lang! You are *dismissed!*"

"Fuck being dismissed. You let this little lady go."

"Lenore, we will shrink into husks together. We will bleed in the sky. See it?"

"Wanger, is he crying? Is the little sucker crying?"

"Shut up, Neil."

"Rick, please don't. Let's just talk about it. Don't sit in the sand and cry. Everybody can see. Let's stand up."

"We'll be joined in the light of the sky, Lenore. See the light of the sky? The dawn and sunset will be fed from our veins. We'll be spread all over. We'll be everything. We'll be gigantic."

"How fucking pathetic."

"Shut up, Neil."

"Larger than life."

"Look here, R.V., let's just stand on up and talk this over, and unlock all this shit."

"She is handcuffed to a corpse, in the Desert. Don't you see the . . . irony?"

"Want me to just get a cop, here, Wanger?"

"If she weren't three-dimensional, she wouldn't be caught! Don't you see? A three-dimensional husk!"

"I think old R.V.'s just lost a few cards out of a certain deck, Lenore."

"Rick."

"That's where we'll be. We'll be prodigious enough to feed the whole sky! Don't you see? And whose fault is it, after all?"

"Aw, Rick, don't you see? Fault just doesn't enter into it at all."

"Exactly. Exactly. It's *no one's* fault. We all agree."

"Rick . . ."

"Lenore sugar doll I care about you. I do. I don't care who knows it. I care about you as a person. R.V. can put all the shit on you he wants. You're mine now. I don't care if the whole world knows it. Hey y'all! I care about this little lady right here!"

"We're in the sky. We can't hear you."

"Fuck off, R.V. Look, Lenore, I'm gonna go ahead and just break the chain on these things. OK? I think I can break 'em. I've broke shit like this before."

"Go ahead and try, Lang. You just go ahead and try it, and see what happens!"

"Is that OK, Lenore?"

". . . ."

"You ready?"

19 1990

The time last night when Lenore Beadsman cried in front of
Andrew Sealander Lang was the first time she had ever cried in
front of anybody else, at all.

Rick Vigorous has cried in front of lots of people.

Disorder asserted itself in the lobby of the Bombardini Building soon after Lenore Beadsman arrived, in a nearly unprecedented state of piss-off, to clear her personal items out of the Frequent and Vigorous/Bombardini Company switchboard cubicle.

Candy Mandible was at the board, filling in briefly for Mindy Metalman, who'd been installed as a temporary at the say-so of Rick Vigorous, and who was for starters supposed to work the day shift today, Saturday, but who had, this morning, finally been able to get hold of Dr. Martin Tissaw, the oral surgeon, Lenore's landlord, at home, in East Corinth, and had dashed over at lunchtime to see him, to talk about "birds, miracles, dreams and professionalism, not necessarily in that order," as she'd said to Candy when Candy came in to relieve her. Mindy's call had awakened Candy at Nick Allied's Shaker Heights home, where Candy had spent an unhappy night waiting for Allied, who was supposed to return from a product-evaluation trip with his stenographer around midnight, but never had, and hadn't even called.

The thing is that even before Lenore and Lang arrived, Candy Mandible was getting a hard time of it from any number of sources. There was, for example, Judith Prietht, who had weekends off because the Bombardini Company switchboard was down from Friday night to Monday morning, but who usually came on into the lobby on Saturday anyway, to knit shapeless sweaters and listen to her radio and watch the Erieview shadow move along the lobby walls, and who had today actually brought in her cat, which, when Judith saw that it was Candy at the console, she was for obvious reasons very anxious to introduce to her. And so Judith was hanging around the outside of the cubicle, hefting the cat, being bothersome and artificially nice, and dropping all sorts of heavy hints about blessings and autographs and partnership. Her new idea was to have the Reverend Hart Lee Sykes deliver a personal blessing to the cat, whose name was apparently Champ, and who was the single most obese cat Candy had ever seen, anywhere, but anyway who was supposed to receive the blessing, personally, while he placed a chubby paw on Judith's television screen. Judith told Candy that Reverend Sykes made time for a viewer-touching-the-screen moment in every installment of 'The Partners With God Club,' believing that theologically and economically important Sykes/viewer communications could be established this way.

There was also the matter of Clint Roxbee-Cox, who had kept calling Candy at Nick's place last night, and not saying anything, and who was now doing the same thing at the F and V board, although he must have had to call many times just to get through at all, because the Frequent and Vigorous switchboard situation was worse than ever. Mindy was too new to get really pissed off yet, but Candy had just about had it with the switchboard. Not only was she getting illegitimate calls for other places, with Fuss 'n' Feathers Pet Shop and Cleveland Towing both enjoying unprecedented volume, but now the board had taken to lighting up and ringing and beeping her console phones for what appeared to be no reason at all, with no one on the other end, at all, just static, which was distinguishable from an illegitimate but still human Roxbee-Cox call by the breathing that was a prominent feature of the latter. The phones simply would not shut up, and Candy couldn't shut down the console, because she didn't have a ratchet wrench. With great reluctance she tried calling to complain at Interactive Cable, and was informed that Console Service Technician Peter Abbott should at that very moment have been on his way over to the Bombardini Building, by way of Enrique's House of Cheese, to relate news of some importance to the appropriate Frequent and Vigorous personnel. Ms. Peahen had already been contacted, and they were trying to reach Mr. Vigorous.

"Super," Candy said.

Then there was the unlikely pair of Mr. Bloemker and Alvin Spaniard, whom Candy didn't know from a hole in the ground, and who had been lurking in the lobby for about half an hour, waiting to see Lenore. Mr. Bloemker claimed that they'd called the Tissaws' boarding house and spoken to a strangely familiar-sounding young woman who had said she knew for a positive fact that Lenore was on her way to the Bombardini Building. Candy had shrugged, at the console. She assumed the woman on the phone had been Mindy Metalman, but had no idea how Mindy was supposed to know where Lenore was. Anyway, the two men had looked at their watches and at each other, and said they'd wait, and their waiting had made for an unpleasant half hour, because Alvin Spaniard kept making what Candy thought might have been eyes at her, and Judith Prietht kept making what Candy knew from her long acquaintance with Judith definitely were eyes at Mr. Bloemker, and Mr. Bloemker was just being unnecessarily creepy—scratching violently at his beard, having bits of random sunlight reflect off his glasses, sometimes acting as if he were whispering to someone under his arm when there was clearly no one there, and asking Judith and Candy how they perceived their own sense of the history of the Midwest. Champ had hissed at him. Now Bloemker and Alvin Spaniard were walking slowly around the huge perimeter of the inside of the lobby, pointing at the floor in various places and speaking in low tones. Candy just could not wait for Mindy Metalman Lang to get back.

But now in through the revolving door came Lenore, and following her was Andy Lang, and out in front was the sound of Neil Obstat peeling out in Lang's Trans Am, he having been signalled on his Stonecipheco beeper the minute the three of them had gotten far enough north on 77 to be in beeper range. Obstat was supposed to come back for them as soon as he could.

Lenore didn't even seem to notice her brother-in-law and Mr. Bloemker when she came in. She didn't seem to notice anything. She was also walking funny, and her dress was dirty, and she had a smear of black dust on her face, plus a brightly sunburned nose, and on her wrist Candy could see what was pretty clearly a handcuff, trailing a short length of broken pretend-silver chain.

"Jesus Lenore," Candy said when Lenore got inside the cubicle. Judith and Champ were staring from the counter.

"Don't want to hear it Candy," Lenore said, without looking up.

She opened one of the white switchboard cabinets and began taking some of her books out and sorting them on the counter. Out came a little cloth bag with soap, toothbush, and toothpaste. Lenore wordlessly hunted for other items in the cabinet. She opened the next cabinet door and brought out a stack of old lottery tickets bound with a rubber band.

"Hey there Candy," Lang nodded tiredly from the switchboard counter, rubbing his face.

Candy folded her arms and looked at the handcuff hanging from Lenore's wrist. The handcuff kept clanking on the insides of the cabinets. The skin of Lenore's wrist was all red. On the handcuff itself Candy could see part of a pair of metal lips shaped in a kiss-design; on the lips was embossed "Bambi's Den Of."

" 'Bambi's Den Of?' " she said. She looked up at Lang. Lenore was sifting through some of her magazines.

"Hi there, Lenore,'" Judith Prietht was saying in a high, pretend-cat voice, holding Champ and moving the cat's paw up and down in a hello. She made a move to bring the cat back into the cubicle.

"Please stay out, Judith," Lenore said quietly.

"Ladies, let's not give Lenore any more grief than need be, she's had a bad enough day as it is," Lang said, leaning his elbows on the counter.

"A bad day?" Candy said.

"Don't want to talk about it."

"Bad grandmother-news?"

"Don't want to talk about it."

"Grandmothers and Desert bondage?"

"Hush, now, Candy," said Lang.

It wasn't clear how long Mr. Bloemker and Alvin Spaniard had been at the edge of the counter, next to the hissing Champ. Now Mr. Bloemker rubbed an eye and cleared his throat.

Lang looked over at him. "We help you, chief?"

Mr. Bloemker gave him a bland look. "We are here to speak to Ms. Beadsman," he said.

Lenore had meanwhile sat down, in Judith's Bombardini-switchboard chair, and closed her eyes. Now she looked up at Bloemker and Alvin, as if she didn't recognize them for a moment.

"Hi," she said.

"Well hello, Lenore," Alvin said. He was smiling the way someone smiles when he doesn't feel very well.

"Hi."

"We come on unprecedentedly urgent business, Ms. Beadsman," said Bloemker.

"Do you."

"Gentlemen, the little lady's had herself a rough morning," Lang said, moving over behind Bloemker and Alvin and putting a hand on each man's shoulder. "What say we all just give her some time to collect, here."

The phones had of course been ringing and beeping like crazy this whole time. Candy Mandible kept Accessing one trunk after another, and there would just be static, and tones.

"The phones have finally gone totally insane, Lenore," she said through clenched teeth.

Lenore was looking from Mr. Bloemker to her brother-in-law. "Do you guys even know each other?" she said slowly.

Alvin looked decidedly uncomfortable. He kept doing something to the collar of his shirt. Half of Mr. Bloemker's face was in the shadow.

Now a new head just barely appeared above the top of the switchboard counter, bouncing up and down a little, in the middle of everyone. Lang looked down in irritation. Lenore stood up to see.

"Dr. Jay?" she said.

"Greetings, Lenore," said Dr. Jay.

"Well hi," she said.

"Looking a little dishevelled today, aren't we?" Jay looked her over.

"Can we help you out with somethin', here, bud?" Lang said from between Bloemker and Alvin.

Lenore saw the top of Dr. Jay's head turn. "I'm a friend of Ms. Beadsman's, young sir," he said. "I'm here to see Ms. Beadsman if I may."

"What're you sniffin' like that for?" Lang said. "You smell somethin' out of the ordinary do you?"

Dr. Jay was hauling himself up over the top of the counter as far as he could. He looked down into the cubicle at Lenore, who was back in Judith's chair. "Lenore, I'm afraid I've just gotten off the phone with Norman Bombardini," he said. He tested the air of the cubicle. "I would be inclined to say that it might be better for you not to be in the Building right now. Norman apparently saw you arrive from some restaurant down the street. I'm afraid he's in a bit of a bad way, emotionally speaking, at the present time."

"Mr. Bombardini's in an emotional bad way?" said Judith.

"How do you even know Mr. Bombardini?" Lenore said. "You never told me you knew Mr. Bombardini."

Dr. Jay made as if to wipe his nose with a handkerchief. He left the hankie over his nose and mouth. "Ethics, et cetera," he said through the cloth. "Actually a longtime client and friend." Lang was giving Dr. Jay a very unfriendly look indeed. "He's unfortunately very upset," Dr. Jay continued, pushing himself even higher over the counter with his elbows so that his feet were off the lobby floor. He leaned toward Lenore with his hankie. "I'm afraid he's talking with some earnestness about . . . consuming people."

"Consuming?"

"All metaphorical, I'm firmly convinced. Surely you're in a position to see that this eating business masks membranous turmoils far too . . . tumultuous to go into here." Jay looked around. "Shall we perhaps—?"

"Eating?" Lang said.

"The crux here being that in his present state of emotional turmoil and physical . . . girth," Jay said, struggling now to keep himself above the counter, "it appears prudent to err on the side of—"

"Hold it a second," Lang said, his head cocked. "What in the hell's that sound supposed to be?" Everyone stopped and listened.

And there was a bit of a distant sound, like a train or thunder, that grew slightly and then was for a moment obscured by the shriek of some phones.

"God damn it," Candy Mandible said.

"Lenore, as a professional and a friend, I suggest that we quickly and quietly leave," Jay said, struggling. His elbows finally gave, and he fell back out of view. Lang looked down at him. Jay's voice came over the counter. "Other issues we need to countenance together,

Lenore. I've been doing some thinking. A discussion is imperative."

"I've decided we're finished, Dr. Jay," Lenore said from her chair. "Our relationship is over."

"I'll make it a free session."

"Relationship?" said Lang.

Mr. Bloemker cleared his throat again and stepped forward under Lang's hand. "Ms. Beadsman before you go anywhere with anyone I really must ask that we all speak, here, in the lobby, on a matter you and I had agreed I should bring before you, should any—"

"And I thought we said we weren't gonna be makin' stressful demands on the lady just now, Gus," Lang said, pulling Bloemker back to him. Bloemker looked over at Alvin Spaniard.

Candy was watching Wang-Dang Lang from the console, whenever she could look up. The noise of the phones was now constant. All the trunk lights were illuminating.

"Are you here with Mr. Bloemker, or what?" Lenore said, looking at Alvin Spaniard.

Alvin pushed his glasses up. He looked across Lang at Mr. Bloemker. The rumbling sound was getting louder.

Judith Prietht and Champ had turned around; Judith was looking into the shadow. "Hey Mr. V!" she called suddenly. "Whatcha doin' back there?" Everyone turned and looked. Rick Vigorous was back against the rear wall of the lobby, in the edge of the Erieview shadow, moving gradually with it. He was filthy with black dust, and melted partway into the dark. It was hard to see him. But Candy could see something gleaming on his wrist when his arm came into the light. It was another handcuff. Candy looked back down at Lenore. Lenore had one of her sneakers off and was holding it upside down, pouring black sand through the day's wreath of roses on top of the switchboard wastebasket.

"Fucking sand," she said. Her sock was incredibly dirty.

"Greetings, Rick!" Dr. Jay shouted.

"Can't believe you got the balls to be here right now, R.V.!" Lang called loudly across the empty lobby to Rick Vigorous. "And how the hell'd you even get here so quick?"

Candy began to have a really bad feeling, and she looked at Lenore, who was emptying out her other shoe.

"You better just git!" Lang was calling.

Rick Vigorous didn't say anything.

The rhythmic rumbling was now too loud even for the phones to cover. Candy thought she could feel the marble floor of the lobby vibrating slightly. The shadow was bigger than it should have been for one o'clock.

"What the hell *is* that?" said Lang. He looked down at Dr. Jay.

Now through the revolving door in big hurries came Neil Obstat, Jr., Sigurd Foamwhistle, and Stonecipher Beadsman III. Right behind them was Peter Abbott, and right behind him was Walinda Peahen. Peter's big toolbox somehow got jammed in the door, and Walinda yelled at him from her glass compartment until he got the box free and the door spit them both out.

Mr. Beadsman was looking at his watch as he came. "Lenore!" he called.

"Jesus Lenore it's your Dad, and that cable guy, Abbott," Candy said.

Lenore stayed where she was, in the Bombardini-switchboard chair, holding her sneakers. Mr. Bloemker and Alvin Spaniard headed over to Obstat and Foamwhistle and Mr. Beadsman, and the five stood in the middle of the lobby floor, conferring. Obstat was looking at a large piece of paper and pointing to a section of the floor in the back of the lobby, over near Rick Vigorous. Meanwhile Walinda had come straight to the cubicle, brushing aside Dr. Jay, who was hurrying back toward the revolving door.

"Girl all I can say is whatever happened it damn well better be important," Walinda said, coming inside. She stopped and looked around. "Where's that new girl that's supposed to be on?"

"I quit, Walinda," Lenore said.

"Quit?" Candy Mandible twisted around in her chair to look at them both. A phone rang.

"Yes." Lenore raised her voice to get it all the way to the back of the lobby over the rumbling. "I *quit!*"

"Quit?"

"Girl answer the *phone*," Walinda said, pinching at Candy's shoulder.

"There's nothing on the other end," Candy said quietly, staring at Lenore. "Just static and tones. Lenore, what do you mean quit?"

"Hi Peter!" called Judith Prietht, manipulating poor Champ's paw yet again. Peter was doing something over near the section of the lobby floor that Neil Obstat had pointed out.

"The matter Lenore, you and that bitty fella back there have a fight?" Walinda chuckled and reached for the Legitimate Call Log. "Too bad. You need any help gettin' your stuff together?"

"Hey Geraldine, why don't you just jump on back," Lang said to Walinda. "Little lady's had herself a rough day." Walinda slowly turned eyes to Wang-Dang Lang, and they stared at each other. Lang grinned.

"Lenore, sweetie, tell me what I can do," Candy was whispering into Lenore's ear, an arm around her shoulder. Phones jangled. The lobby shook faintly. Lenore closed her eyes and shook her head.

Now Peter Abbott appeared at the counter. He was smiling broadly. "Satis*fac*tion, ladies," he said, hefting his toolbox and patting it. "Satisfaction?"

Lang looked down at Peter's box and toolbelt. "Hey there good bud," he said. "You want to see what you can do about these crazy-ass phones?"

"Tex, that's the exact reason I'm here," Peter Abbott said. "To start clearin' up and explaining maybe the bizarrest phone-tunnel snafu in Cleveland history." He came around into the cubicle. "And to start to take steps to give you good folks some of the satisfaction you've been waitin' for, and also to remove this pesky old tunnel-test cable, down here." He produced a ratchet wrench with a flourish and with two quick turns shut the F and V console off. Now there was only the outside rumble. Peter turned to Walinda Peahen. "The tests are officially completed." He lowered himself under the counter, humming. Candy shot her chair back.

Lang leaned way over the counter into the cubicle. "*Lenore,*" he whispered, smiling and snapping his fingers. "Let's just git. What do you say? Car's out front. We can just come on back in a bit, R.V. and all these folks'll be gone. Let's git."

"So are you saying you're actually fixing our lines?" Candy was saying. "Is that what you're saying?" She kicked a little at Peter's jiggling boots. "And also maybe explaining a little bit? For Christ's sake now they ring and there's nobody there! What kind of phone rings when there's nobody there?"

"All I can say for openers is that Interactive Cable's own Ron

Sludgeman is a certifiable genius," said a muffled Peter Abbott. "This particular tunnel-test was certifiably ingenious. You just hang on up there."

"Lenore," Lang was whispering.

"Lenore, please come here immediately," Mr. Beadsman called from out in the lobby.

Lenore stayed slumped in the chair, looking at the open cabinets and her pile of books and other items on the counters, and at the handcuff. Candy Mandible looked out at Mr. Beadsman and his group. They all seemed to be gathered around Neil Obstat, Jr., in the corner of the lobby, while Obstat lay on his stomach and did something to that section of the floor Peter had been at. Rick Vigorous watched from nearby, along the back wall. Everything rumbled.

"What're they trying to do to the floor?" Candy asked, tapping Walinda on the shoulder.

Walinda looked out. "Hey fools!" she called. "Hey!"

"You tell everybody to just hang onto their hats about the tunnel," Peter Abbott was saying. He emerged with one end of the long test-cable and unhooked it from the side of the Frequent and Vigorous console. He held it up for everyone to admire as light slowly went out of it. "*Damned* smart, is all I can say," he said. "Put this particular console technician right back in his place, let me tell you that right now."

"Lenore!" Mr. Beadsman was calling, looking at his watch again.

"Lenore?" Lang was saying. "You all right?" Lenore was staring into space.

The very top of Dr. Jay's head reappeared at the counter. "*Really* have to advise in the very *strongest* possible terms that we leave," he said through his handkerchief, lifting himself up again. "Really strongly advise it, Lenore."

"What's up?" Candy said. "What's the noise?"

"I'm afraid it seems to be poor Norman," Dr. Jay said. "He is in considerable distress, and is . . . having at the rear wall of the whole Building with his . . . his stomach." He looked Candy up and down. "He is demanding, and here I use his words, 'admission to Ms. Beadsman's space.' "

"Space?" Candy said.

"Having at?" Lang said.

Jay turned his head to look up at Lang. "Battering, you might say."

Lenore looked up at them.

"Heat problems," Peter Abbott said. "Let me just say temperature-problems, for starters, and then let me apologize for not doing my job as good as I maybe should have on this one, I guess. I'm sorry." He rubbed his hands on his pants. "Like Mr. Sludgeman said to me he said Peter, if you got line trouble, and it's affecting targets over more than just one circuit, you start to look around for some kinda temperature problem, is what you do if you're smart."

Mr. Beadsman appeared overhead. "Lenore," he said. "I'll assume you were unable to hear me calling. Please come. We must talk. This is a family matter." He threw a bit of a sidelong look at Lang, who stared straight ahead and made as if to tip his hat. "A family matter," Mr. Beadsman said. "Please come out of there and over here with me immediately."

"You the chump be makin' that nasty food my child like to choke on one time?" Walinda Peahen put her hands on her hips and glared at Mr. Beadsman.

"My what a perfectly charming negress," Mr. Beadsman said.

"Boy, I gonna kill you for that."

"Lenore, please note that this is *professional* advice being given here," Dr. Jay said from under Mr. Beadsman's arm. "Really think it would be best to come back another time." He shifted on his elbows and looked at Walinda Peahen, who was giving Mr. Beadsman perhaps the world's biggest fish-eye. Mr. Beadsman was looking expectantly at Lenore.

"Just a second, please, Dad," Lenore said, looking at the shoes in her hand. "I'm in the process of quitting."

"Family emergency, Lenore."

"Sir, Miss Lenore and I were hopin' to be on a plane to Nugget Bluff, Texas, by suppertime," Lang said.

Candy stared at Lenore. "Nugget Bluff, Texas?"

Mr. Beadsman seemed not to hear. He was looking at Lenore's wrist. "And what may I ask is on my daughter's wrist?" he said.

"Chief!" Sigurd Foamwhistle was calling from the rear of the lobby.

"Well sir whyn't you just ask that little dung beetle right back there?" Lang said, pointing at Rick Vigorous, back in the shadow.

Mr. Beadsman turned. "Mr. Vigorous?" he said. There was a particularly loud rumble, and the marble floor shook a little. Mr. Beadsman looked over at his group. "Foamwhistle!" he yelled. "What's going on?"

"See," Peter Abbott was saying to the women in the cubicle, "the thing you got to remember is that the tunnels are incredibly temperature-sensitive. There's just few things in this world more temperature-sensitive than a phone tunnel." He bent and took a crowbar out of his toolbox.

"Lenore."

" 'Cause see you got to remember that all the calls in the lines are is just basically lines of heat," Peter said, hefting the crowbar. "They're just little lines of a kind of heat going back and forth, is all they really are." He ran a hand through his bright yellow hair. "So it's only logical that to get satisfactory service, the tunnels've got to be one temperature, and the lines another, and the calls in the lines another." Peter happened to look over the counter at the Stonecipheco group and Neil Obstat, on his stomach. "Hey buddy!" he yelled. "You wanna just get back from there? What're you trying to do?" He turned to Walinda. "They're right over where your tunnel is, ma'am," he said. "That guy's trying to get into your tunnel. Who is that guy?"

"Baby food chemist," Candy Mandible said.

"Hey boy you just get on out of here!" Walinda was yelling.

"Do not yell at my employee," said Mr. Beadsman.

"Why don't you just go and sit on somethin' sharp, chump?"

"Well if he gets in there like it looks like he's tryin' to, without some trained personnel on hand, he's gonna be sorry," Peter Abbott was saying.

"How come?" Candy asked.

"Lenore, your behavior is now becoming unacceptable," Mr. Beadsman said.

"I'm afraid I'm forced to agree," came Dr. Jay's muffled voice from behind the counter.

Lenore closed her eyes. The lobby thundered.

"Peter for Christ's sake how *come*," Candy Mandible said.

" 'Cause according to our data it's gonna be bitchin' hot," Peter said, turning to Candy and looking briefly down into Lenore's dress. " 'Cause what I've been trying to explain is that it looks like that's your whole trouble right there. Hot tunnel."

"Hot tunnel?"

"Well yeah," Peter Abbott said. "See there's supposed to be special temperature levels in each tunnel. Tunnel's supposed to be sixty, sixty-five degrees, tops." He looked around. "Otherwise, see, the heat of the tunnel infects the heat of your calls, and you get what we call call-bleeding into the circuit. Which actually it turns out is what you've been having, we think. Mr. Sludgeman told me he's suspected some kind of bleeding all along, really."

"Infection? Bleeding?"

"Just like a big old cranky nervous system, like I been tellin' you," Peter said. He was looking back at Neil Obstat, who along with Alvin Spaniard was trying to pry up a whole section of the lobby floor, which was now revealed not to be real marble at all. "Hey you drips!" Peter yelled. "There's gonna be trouble!"

Obstat looked up and over at the cubicle in alarm, but Mr. Beadsman motioned to him that it was all right. Mr. Bloemker was cleaning his glasses on his tie.

"So that's all it was?" Candy Mandible said shrilly. "Hot frigging tunnels? That's why our job's been biting the big kielbasa for two weeks? The lines are nerves and the nerves are too frigging hot?" She was really mad. "That's all it is? Heat? I don't believe it's just heat." She looked at Walinda Peahen.

Peter was still watching the Stonecipheco group. "But see the whole thing's exactly right for nerves, if they were nerves, is what's weird," he said. "Your test cable shows it, too." He looked critically at the length of dark cable on the counter.

"Shows *what?*"

The rhythm of the rumbling in the lobby walls and floor increased. The wreath of roses abruptly fell off the switchboard wastebasket. Cigarette ashes and part of Mr. Bombardini's latest note fell on Lenore's socks. She didn't see them.

"Lenore," said Mr. Beadsman, "I am now officially insisting."

Lenore's eyes stayed closed. She looked as if she was asleep. Mr. Beadsman looked at Dr. Jay. Andy Lang worked on a hangnail.

Peter Abbott was grinning and shaking his head at Candy and Walinda. "The upshot here is that your particular line tunnel looks like it's kind of decided it's a real freakin' human being or something," he said. "You want my opinion, this whole thing could get on television real easily." He looked around at everyone. They stared at him blankly. "You don't get it, do you?" Peter said. "Look. Your tunnel's like I said supposed to be around like sixty-some degrees. And instead our test cable shows it's a perfect ninety-eight point six. You believe that?"

"Boy what you talkin' about?" Walinda folded her arms.

Lenore opened her eyes.

"I'm *talking* about your subpar service is due to your lines are bleeding calls into each other because somehow your tunnel's ninety-eight point six goddamn degrees," Peter said. "That's what I'm talking about."

Mr. Beadsman looked at Lenore. Dr. Jay's head popped up. The lobby positively shook. Lenore was looking up at Wang-Dang Lang:

"Hey."

21 **1990**

/a/

PARTIAL TRANSCRIPT OF 'THE PARTNERS WITH GOD CLUB,' SATURDAY, 11 SEPTEMBER 1990, 8:00 P.M. EASTERN DAYLIGHT TIME. HOSTS: THE REVEREND HART LEE SYKES, AND HIS VERY WELL KNOWN COCKATIEL UGOLINO THE SIGNIFICANT, THROUGH WHOM THE LORD HAS BEEN HEARD PERSONALLY TO SPEAK ON SEVERAL TELEVISED OCCASIONS.

THE REVEREND HART LEE SYKES: Friends.

THE PARTNERSHIP SINGERS: *(Personally directed and accompanied on the xylophone by Mrs. Fanny May Sykes)* Friends . . .

REVEREND SYKES: Dear, dear friends.

UGOLINO THE SIGNIFICANT: God bless everything and everybody!

THE PARTNERSHIP SINGERS: Friends . . .

REVEREND SYKES: Friends, what is a partner?

UGOLINO THE SIGNIFICANT: Friends.

REVEREND SYKES: Friends, I stand before you tonight to say that a partner is a worker. That a partner is an individual who *recognizes* that individuals working *together* are stronger in the service of the Lord than individuals going their own *separate*, individual ways.

THE PARTNERSHIP SINGERS: Oh yes, a partner is a worker . . .

REVEREND SYKES: Friends, a partner takes what is *in* his hand, and casts it down into the *soil*, to *grow*. A partner sows, friends. A partner sows. And friends, who reaps?

THE PARTNERSHIP SINGERS: Oh yes, a partner is a worker who sows . . .

REVEREND SYKES: We the partners take the seed of *faith* which is in our hand and sow it in the *soil* of partnership, and now *who reaps?*

THE PARTNERSHIP SINGERS: Who reaps, oh, who reaps . . .?

UGOLINO THE SIGNIFICANT: Jesus reaped!

REVEREND SYKES: That's right friends we can see together tonight that the one who reaps is none other than *Jesus.*

UGOLINO THE SIGNIFICANT: That's right friends.

REVEREND SYKES: That's right: Jesus. And now friends we have *this* question, to introduce tonight's food-for-thought segment of our time together tonight. Friends, who is Jesus?

UGOLINO THE SIGNIFICANT: Who?

REVEREND SYKES: That's right friends *who* is Jesus?

UGOLINO THE SIGNIFICANT: Who?

REVEREND SYKES: *Who is he?*

UGOLINO THE SIGNIFICANT: I have to do what's right for me.

REVEREND SYKES: *Who?*

UGOLINO THE SIGNIFICANT: He is we! We are He!

THE PARTNERSHIP SINGERS: Oh, we are He and He is we . . .

REVEREND SYKES: That's right friends *we* are Jesus! In a theologically important sense we *are* Jesus!

UGOLINO THE SIGNIFICANT: How can this be?

REVEREND SYKES: Shall I tell you how this can be?

THE PARTNERSHIP SINGERS: Tell, oh tell us, how all this can be . . .

REVEREND SYKES: Friends I stand before you tonight to say that it is for no other reason than that we, like Jesus, are *partners with God.*

The Partnership Singers begin to hum a pleasing harmony.

UGOLINO THE SIGNIFICANT: Hart Lee, we are He.

REVEREND SYKES: You're so right, little miracle. We *are* Jesus. We are Jesus because Jesus is a *worker.* Like us. And a *partner.* Like us. Can we not see friends that in partnership, and now friends I mean here *true* partnership, *everything* comes together?

UGOLINO THE SIGNIFICANT: God bless everything! Make me come together! Like this!

REVEREND SYKES: So friends we come to see together once again tonight that the *answer* . . . is partnership.

UGOLINO THE SIGNIFICANT: I don't know what you mean by that word. Tell me what you mean by that word.

REVEREND SYKES: Friends what I mean is nothing less than a *miracle.*

THE PARTNERSHIP SINGERS: A miracle . . .

REVEREND SYKES: Friends, whether you choose to become a partner with God by just picking up your telephone and dialing us here at the Partnership Pledge Center at 1-800-PARTNER, and becoming a Lifetime And Beyond Partner with your contributing subscription of five hundred dollars or more, or whether you choose to dial us here at 1-800-PARTNER and become a Lifetime Partner With God for two hundred and fifty dollars, or a Star Partner for one hundred, or a Personal Friend Of Ugolino Partner for fifty, or yes friends even an equally important Prayer Partner for just twenty dollars, whatever you choose, *something* will happen. Friends, what will happen?

UGOLINO THE SIGNIFICANT: Friends, as subscribing members of the Reverend Hart Lee Sykes's Partners With God Club you can expect the entry of the Almighty Lord Jesus into your own personal life in twenty-four hours or less.

REVEREND SYKES: That's exactly right the *entry* of Jesus into *your* life. The *habitation* by Jesus of *your own* heart. The existence of the Lord Himself *inside each* of you, as He is inside all of us here at the Partnership Pledge Center studio. What a glorious and miraculous thing! Partnership!

THE PARTNERSHIP SINGERS: Miracle, glory, *partnership* . . .

UGOLINO THE SIGNIFICANT: Inside out!

REVEREND SYKES: What was that, now?

UGOLINO THE SIGNIFICANT: Let us not forget, friends, that all subscriptions are deductible from love.

REVEREND SYKES: Were you trying to say just now that the entry of Jesus into an individual's life will in some theological sense turn that individual inside out?

UGOLINO THE SIGNIFICANT: Pardon me?

THE PARTNERSHIP SINGERS: What, oh what, was he trying to say . . . ?

REVEREND SYKES: Friends, did the acknowledged tweeter of the Lord's own sound system mean that when Jesus dwells in us, we dwell in Jesus? Can this be what he meant?

UGOLINO THE SIGNIFICANT: I'm a pretty boy.

THE PARTNERSHIP SINGERS: Oh, is he not a pretty pretty boy . . . ?

REVEREND SYKES: But friends this would have the spiritual consequence that all our dreams and wishes and needs and goals and *desires* of our own lives also become *Jesus's* desires. And thus that in true partnership with God, the desires of each individual man, woman and child become the desires of Jesus, in Jesus's name.

UGOLINO THE SIGNIFICANT: Women have desires, buster. Don't think they don't have desires.

REVEREND SYKES: Of course women have desires, friends, everyone has desires in their lives, that's part of the *experience* of what it is to be human in God's world. We all have desires, friends. And now we can see that if all us partners work *together*, in the Lord's *soil*, our desires are automatically spiritually transformed into *Jesus's* desires, too.

UGOLINO THE SIGNIFICANT: Holy cow!

REVEREND SYKES: A *need* in *us* is a need in *Jesus*. And friends can't we see together that a need in Jesus is a need *automatically*, by theological *definition*, fulfilled and satisfied?

THE PARTNERSHIP SINGERS: We need to know, why this is so . . .

REVEREND SYKES: So that a need in a partner with God, a need that exists simultaneously in our Lord Jesus Christ, is a need instantly, completely, satisfied and met?

UGOLINO THE SIGNIFICANT: You fill me up. You satisfy me like no man did before. I can't deny it. God.

THE PARTNERSHIP SINGERS: Can't deny, that you satisfy . . .

REVEREND SYKES: Yes friends I stand before you on national prime-time *television* talking about the satis*faction* of your every *need*. The fulfillment of your every *wish*. Friends *hear* me! What I tell you tonight is that if you are a partner with God you are automatically *in Jesus*, we know that now. You *are* inside out! Your needs are now *Jesus's* needs, and thus you *will* not go wanting. You *will* not go wanting. *Why* is this so?

THE PARTNERSHIP SINGERS: Why . . .?

REVEREND SYKES: *Why is this*, I say *why is this so?*

UGOLINO THE SIGNIFICANT: Because Jesus shall not want!

REVEREND SYKES: Oh say it *again!*

UGOLINO THE SIGNIFICANT: Who's got the special-wecial book?

REVEREND SYKES: Oh say it *again!*

UGOLINO THE SIGNIFICANT: Jesus shall not want.

THE PARTNERSHIP SINGERS: Amen, Aman, Amen, Aman . . .

REVEREND SYKES: Amen, and Aman. For here friends is tonight's "Partners With God Club" food-for-thought spiritual message. It is that Jesus shall not want. *Jesus* shall *not* want! There it is.

UGOLINO THE SIGNIFICANT: Has the little turd learned his lines yet?

REVEREND SYKES: Friends let us all pause here and listen together and reflect on the implications of such a revelation. That's right . . .

THE PARTNERSHIP SINGERS: Hmmmmm . . .

REVEREND SYKES: . . . a *revelation*.

UGOLINO THE SIGNIFICANT: (*Accompanied by the pleasing harmonies of the Partnership Singers*)

Oh, when I'm feelin' down, down as I can be;

When there's a giant shadow, a-fallin' over me;

My spirit's still as strong as steel, my hope you cannot daunt;

For I stand firm in my belief . . . that Jesus shall not want!

/b/

"Do you want to hear what I think?" says Mindy Metalman Lang.

"I am one enormous ear," says Rick Vigorous.

"I think you're just tired, and tense, and understandably upset, and that's why you're not being fair, and making up these lies."

"And who may I ask has the temerity to allege that I am making up lies," says Rick Vigorous softly, looking up and away. His face is running with light.

What is going on is that tonight it is raining, between the moon and the window. It is raining awfully hard. Lines of rainwater run down the window, and the moon shines through the rain and the window and makes the rear wall of the dark bedroom run with reflections. Back against the wall leans Rick Vigorous as he sits up in bed, in his underpants. He looks like he's running with moonlit rain. So does the bed. The whole room, running with clear white. The colored chalk sketch of Rick and Veronica Vigorous in their Scarsdale yard, the one that's framed in dark wood and hanging above the bed, seems almost to glow. The television is on, over by the window, but its cold flicker is lost in the moon's million white trickles.

"Rick," Mindy says from the window.

"Don't look out," says Rick.

Mindy turns and waggles her finger. It runs down all the walls. "Rick."

"Do you know why I don't want you to look out?"

"Sweetie pumpkin," says Mindy, "I'm trying ever so hard to still be pleasant about this whole thing, but it's wrong of you not to tell. It's not right, and you know it."

"My God the window's drooling," Rick says. He points. His wrist hangs with light. "Doesn't it look as though the window is drooling? Salivating at the prospect of absolutely everything there is to impart?"

Mindy starts to turn back.

"But don't look out," Rick says.

"So start imparting," says Mindy.

"Haven't I already?"

"I want to know where my husband is," Mindy says softly, looking down into the television. "I don't care about your 'context,' and I'm more than a little upset and worried that you're sitting there with that thing on your wrist seriously trying to tell me that Lenore Beadsman died in your phone tunnel."

"You saw the lobby floor."

"But Andy and Lenore went to the airport *tonight*, I happen to know. I talked to Dr. Tissaw *tonight*."

"Context is essential," Rick says.

"But I don't care about context Rick," says Mindy. "If you want to know the truth I don't really care that much about Lenore. And I don't care about some book, which I have no idea what you're talking about, which first you say you wrote, then you say is the Bible, then you say is the dictionary, then you say is the Sears Catalogue, so what am I supposed to think? But anyway I don't care about that." Mindy crosses her arms over her bra. The moon is white jelly through the top of her hair. "Honestly," she says.

"But it's essential to the whole story," says Rick. He is playing with his stomach, over the band of his underpants.

"Or about alphabets of old people, or children singing like birds, or fat men chewing on buildings, or phone crews fishing in black air, or people eating each other's membranes—you can just stop whispering about all of it, because I don't care about it right now."

"What do you want," says Rick.

Mindy taps a foot on the floor. "I either want to watch the bird's show, here, which by the way don't think I've forgotten you practically promised to call, last night . . ."

"I forbid you to look at it directly."

". . . Or then I want to know where my husband and ditzy little Lenore are, so I can begin to take steps. What branch are they supposed to be at?"

"Lenore Beadsman and W.D.L. are finished," Rick says. He looks around him, his shadow on the flowing wall. "They're over."

"Rick sweetie I'm so trying to be nice but that's just a lie," says Mindy. She comes to stand at the bed. "Can't you tell what's a lie? I don't know what happened to you today, and how could I since you won't tell me, but you're in bad shape if you sincerely think people are done who are obviously not done, I've got to tell you. I've got to think you're either lying for fun, or you're maybe just not a well man. Daddy always said you weren't a hundred percent."

Rick looks up at Mindy.

"Honestly," Mindy says. She looks back at the television. "I can just watch the news, you know." Rick keeps looking at her. "I can just watch the news at eleven, if you want to be a little dung beetle about it," she says. "Why lie if I can just find out the truth in a couple hours?"

"I think you're confused," says Rick.

/c/

REVEREND SYKES: And so friends if we are to be in Jesus and so never want, never *ever* want, what must we do here tonight?

UGOLINO THE SIGNIFICANT: Use me. Satisfy me like never before.

REVEREND SYKES: Tonight we must attempt to see together that to be *satisfied* in a spiritual sense is to be *used.*

THE PARTNERSHIP SINGERS: Oh yes that's right, to be satisfied is to be used . . .

REVEREND SYKES: For we've seen together that to be satisfied is to be in Jesus, and to be in Jesus is to be a partner. And what is a partner?

UGOLINO THE SIGNIFICANT: Who cares *how* many partners I've had, Clinty?

REVEREND SYKES: Yes friends it makes no difference how many partners work together, *what is a partner?*

THE PARTNERSHIP SINGERS: Partner, oh what is a partner . . .?

REVEREND SYKES: Is not an individual who is a *partner* with God simply an individual who *recognizes*, and finds within his own soul the strength to perform, the *function* God has *assigned* to him? We must ask how can we be *useful* to God.

THE PARTNERSHIP SINGERS: Oh, how might I personally be used . . .?

UGOLINO THE SIGNIFICANT: Sunflower seed, please.

REVEREND SYKES: But friends can't we see that it's all just a glorious living circle of faith, because now to be useful to God is merely to be a *partner with* God!

THE PARTNERSHIP SINGERS: Oh, it's all a glorious circle . . .

REVEREND SYKES: And to be satisfied is to be used, to be used is to be a partner, to be a partner is to be a worker, to be a worker is to be *one of many*, locked and nourished, *together*, in the *soil* of faith.

UGOLINO THE SIGNIFICANT: Sounds pretty healthy!

REVEREND SYKES: Friends, tonight I want us to think together of this humble program as the soil of faith. I want us to think of ourselves . . . *joined* here tonight, *together*, in the electronic soil of *faith today*. I want us to feel used and satisfied by the Lord together tonight.

UGOLINO THE SIGNIFICANT: Miss Beaksman, hear the mandate!

REVEREND SYKES: So friends, laugh if you will, but tonight I have a game for us to play together. A profoundly and vitally important game for us to play together tonight. The stakes'll be as *high* as the stars in heaven, friends, I'll warn you now.

The Partnership Singers begin to hum a harmony even more pleasing than the pleasing harmonies previously hummed.

REVEREND SYKES: Friends, I want us all to get up and put our hand on our television screen. Those of you who might be unable to get up with us tonight, why you have a friend or loved one bring your television close to you. Friends I want you to come to me and place your hand on my hand, that I hold out to you tonight. Let us all place our hands *together* in the electronic soil.

UGOLINO THE SIGNIFICANT: Sow to reap a pretty boy!

REVEREND SYKES: So there is the game, friends, and now here are the stakes tonight.

THE PARTNERSHIP SINGERS: The *stakes* tonight . . . (*They return to the pleasing harmony.*)

REVEREND SYKES: *Every* player, every one of you who *feels* something, who feels what I can feel standing right here before you tonight, who can feel the individual imprisoned inside these secular shells of impotent pain and desire *flow* out of you, *flow* out into the soil, who feels the sort of union with all and with the Lord our Savior Jesus Christ that I feel *right now*, when you touch my hand, each one of you who *feels* what I know in my heart we shall *all* feel together tonight . . . each player who feels it will go straight to his telephone and call us here at the Partnership Pledge Center at 1-800-PARTNER, to become a partner with us and with God, tonight. So to feel what I feel tonight, friends, is to become a *partner*. No two ways about it. This game is a challenge, friends. Are you up to it? I stand here *challenging* you tonight.

UGOLINO THE SIGNIFICANT: Holy holy!

REVEREND SYKES: Use me, friends. Let us play the game together. I promise that no player will feel alone. You see my hand? Here it is. I hold it out for you to touch. Touch it. Lay your hands in the soil and touch me. Here I am for you. Friends I sense we are all ready tonight.

/d

"Well no I'm not angry, you silly," says Mindy, kneeling in front of the television. Cold light comes out from between her fingers, on the screen.

"I promise to tell," Rick says, looking down at himself.

"I know you'll tell," Mindy says softly into the television. White shimmers melt down her back. Drops of light stop and start. She reaches back with her free hand, tosses her hair out of the way, unhooks herself.

"What are you doing?"

Mindy rises and turns and slides out of everything, moving her hips.

"I said I'd tell," says Rick.

"I know you will," says Mindy. "I know you're upset, but I feel like I just know you will." She comes to the bed. Her body moves a million ways in the wet white light. Behind her Rick can see a flickering hand, dead and cold. It covers everything.

"I really will," he whispers.

Mindy touches his leg. Light comes out of his leg, between her fingers.

"Don't you worry about anything," she says. "I know you."

"You can trust me," R.V. says, watching her hand. "I'm a man of my